Stars of Darkover
Darkover® Anthology 14

Edited by
Deborah J. Ross
&
Elisabeth Waters

**The Marion Zimmer Bradley Literary Works Trust
PO Box 193473
San Francisco, CA 94119
www.mzbworks.com**

Copyright © 2014 by the Marion Zimmer Bradley Literary Works Trust
Cover art and design © 2014 by Dave Smeds
Source photography: Photowitch, Dreamstime
All rights reserved
Darkover® is a registered trademark of the Marion Zimmer Bradley Literary Works Trust

All characters and events in this book are fictitious. Any resemblance to persons living or dead is coincidental.

The scanning, uploading and distribution of this book via the Internet or any other means without the permission of the publisher is illegal, and punishable by law. Please purchase only authorized electronic editions, and do not participate in or encourage the electronic piracy of copyrighted materials. Your support of the author's rights is appreciated.

ISBN: 1-938185-25-0
ISBN-13: 978-1-938185-25-0

DEDICATION

To Marion, in gratitude.

CONTENTS

Introduction by Deborah J. Ross	1
All The Branching Paths by Janni Lee Simner	3
The Cold Blue Light by Judith Tarr	24
Kira Ann by Steven Harper	45
Threads by Elisabeth Waters & Ann Sharp	65
Wedding Embroidery by Shariann Lewitt	71
The Ridenow Nightmare by Robin Wayne Bailey	90
Catalyst by Gabrielle Harbowy	101
The Fountain's Choice by Rachel Manija Brown	117
House of Fifteen Widows by Kari Sperring	140
Zandru's Gift by Vera Nazarian	157
Late Rising Fire by Leslie Fish	173
Evanda's Mirror by Diana L. Paxson	195
At the Crossroads by Barb Caffrey	216
Second Contact by Rosemary Edghill & Rebecca Fox	232
A Few Words for My Successor by Debra Doyle & James D. Macdonald	256

Introduction
by Deborah J. Ross

For readers and aspiring writers of my generation, as well as the generations that followed, Marion Zimmer Bradley's Darkover represented the best of science fiction/fantasy: the world we wanted to run away to, the place we wanted to write adventures in, and the people we wanted to know and to be. In the early years when copyright infringement was not an issue, Marion was immensely generous with her "sandbox," welcoming fans to create their own stories in her wonderful world. From the magazines and newsletters put out through the Friends of Darkover to the series of professional-level anthologies edited by Marion and published by DAW Books, Darkover has nourished the imaginations of readers and writers alike.

I cannot claim to have sold my first professional short story to a Darkover anthology. "Midwife" in *Free Amazons of Darkover* was my second sale (the first being to the first volume of *Sword & Sorceress*, another of Marion's anthology series). Even before those sales, I had the honor of receiving Marion's kind words of encouragement on stories I submitted to *Starstone*, the Friends of Darkover fiction magazine. Over the decades that followed, Marion became not only my teacher and mentor but my friend and co-writer. Or maybe I became hers, the relationship was so mutual. Collaborating with her on a series of Darkover novels, and then continuing the series under the supervision of her Literary Works Trust, presented an extraordinary opportunity to carry forward her vision of this world and its people.

I have gone on to create my own world and characters, as well as editing a number of anthologies. Marion influenced my editing as well as my writing style, and I hope I have been as supportive to the many writers who over the years have entrusted me with their stories as she was to me. In a fannish corner of my heart, I always hoped that someday I might get the chance to edit a Darkover anthology. This anthology, the first of a renewed annual series, pays tribute to Marion's legacy, both in the world of the Bloody

Sun and in the community of superb writers who began their careers with her.

I did not restrict the lineup to authors whose first sales had been to Marion's anthologies and her fantasy magazine. In the marvelous way that we are all connected, every contributor has benefitted, either directly or through the tradition of "paying it forward," from Marion's commitment to young writers. As she wrote, "One generation plants the trees, the next eats the fruit."

We follow in the footsteps of those who have gone before us, forging the trail and planting the Yellow Forest. An anthology of short fiction by different writers offers a landscape of the secret places, minor but fascinating characters, and hidden histories that novels can suggest but not explore. Editing such an anthology is an unfolding wonder as themes, histories, races human and nonhuman, Gifts, and Domains are woven together in a dance, sometimes echoing and complementing one another, other times offering sharp contrasts, but always engaging and exciting.

I invite you to come with me on a journey of time and space and heart, whether you are a traveler new to the world of Cottman IV, popularly known as Darkover, or whether you have a treasure trove of dog-eared paperbacks from the 1960s, when Lew Alton, Regis Hastur, and many other beloved characters first saw print. Here you will find strangers and friends, and even stranger beings and happenings, for Marion never shrank from tackling difficult issues with courage and sensitivity, and we who walk in her footsteps can do no less. I hope these tales of wonder and despair, of love and betrayal and hope, will delight and challenge you as much as they did me.

All The Branching Paths
by Janni Lee Simner

Many of us began our love affair with Darkover with *The Sword of Aldones* (1962). This was not the first published Darkover novel—*The Planet Savers* had come out in 1958 in *Amazing*—but in many ways it was the origin of all the adventures that followed, for Marion had conceived the story when she was only fifteen. The front matter to *The Sword of Aldones* introduces one of the most memorable and complex characters in the series:
Lew Alton was returning to Darkover...a Darkovan on his father's side and a Terran on his mother's....
And his mother was not just any Terran, but the daughter of Wade Montray and Mariel Aldaran, and the sister of Larry Montray, who as a teenager met and befriended Kennard Alton. In the skillful hands of Janni Lee Simner, the story of Kennard and Elaine comes alive.
Janni Lee Simner is one of the many writers who sold her first short story to Marion Zimmer Bradley—for the anthology *Leroni of Darkover* more than two decades ago. She's gone on to publish more than three dozen short stories and right novels, including the Icelandic-saga-based *Thief Eyes* and the post-apocalyptic *Bones of Faerie* trilogy.

He wouldn't meet her eyes.

That was the first thing Elaine noticed, when he walked in three weeks late for the autumn term, his gray Terra Academy uniform stiff with first-day creases. She forced herself to look up with the rest of the class, though the Terran habit of meeting gazes still didn't come easily to her.

She took in a shock of red hair, proud gray eyes—and then he looked down. Not as if he was embarrassed for himself, with all those eyes on him. As if he was embarrassed for *them*.

Not that her Terran classmates seemed to notice. "Off-worlder," one of them whispered, as the boy stalked to his assigned seat. By lunchtime, the whispers had become more specific. "Darkover."

In the cafeteria, Elaine focused on her lit tablet while her friends debated why he was here. She deflected the occasional glance they cast her way by furrowing her brow and swiping a finger across her screen. Better to let them think she was engrossed in her studies than to have to explain that no, she didn't know every last motive of a Darkovan boy she'd never met, because she'd been raised on Terra and was no less Terran than them. Never mind that the boy must have come in on the same big ship as Dad—most of her friends didn't know her father had spent the past year off-world, either.

From across the room, uneasy laughter drew Elaine's attention away from the star map on her screen. She looked up and saw the new boy staring at the cafeteria food dispenser with cold disdain, as if he were better than any machine made of plastic and steel. A line had formed behind him, but he didn't seem to care.

"Just turn the knob," one of the waiting students said.

"Didn't they teach you anything on that Class D backwater?" another sniggered.

The boy stiffened and reached toward his belt. For his knife, Elaine realized, though of course he didn't have one here.

More laughter. The boy's arm fell, and he turned slowly around. The glint in his eyes made the cafeteria's gleaming metal floor and walls appear warm by comparison. "I'm sorry, but I am still learning your language." The temperature-controlled room seemed to drop ten degrees at his words. "Would you care to repeat that?" Elaine knew then—*knew*—that he wasn't going to avenge these insults with a few cutting words.

She was on her feet, not sure when she'd gotten there. She had full Empire citizenship, but if this Darkovan boy didn't, fighting at school would get him thrown off-world so fast it'd make his head spin, and he'd never even understand why.

She raced across the room, putting herself between him and the line behind him. "Here! Let me help!" She turned the dispenser's knob and pushed buttons at random. A tray shot out, and several vacuum-sealed cubes of food clunked onto it, loud in the suddenly-silent cafeteria. "It's really quite simple, once you get the hang of it."

The boy's fists had been raised. He lowered them as Elaine dropped her eyes. It was a lowland custom for men and women to never look directly at one other, but her mountain-bred mother had insisted on it when they came to Terra, saying that Terrans were unpredictable and could not be trusted.

"Thank you, Lady." The ice hadn't left the boy's voice. Elaine remembered, too late, that no Darkovan boy would appreciate having his honor defended by a girl.

This wasn't Darkover. He could adapt, just like she had. *"Z'par servu,"* she said, not without irony.

At her perfect *casta* the boy started and looked up, like one of the deer on the reserve where her mother worked. Elaine lifted his tray and offered it to him, her own gaze still cast modestly down. She wanted to get out of there, to snatch up her tablet and flee the cafeteria before her friends could ask her, with words and with glances, just how Darkovan she really was.

Elaine shoved the tray toward him. Her hand brushed his, and she felt a short, sharp shock, like lightning bridging the space from land to sky. She jerked away, nearly dropping the tray, only the boy caught it in time.

She fled back to her table thinking, *What in any world was that?*

The boy was truly Darkover-bred. He didn't even try to follow her.

~oOo~

By the time school was out, Elaine wanted nothing more than to go home and shed her itchy school clothes. But Dad had asked her over for dinner, which meant staying Terran a while longer yet. She caught a pod from school to his new apartment complex, wondering whether once she was there he would answer the questions he'd avoided by phone. Like why he'd transferred away from his civil service job on Darkover as unexpectedly as he'd accepted it, and why he'd left her brother Larry behind when he did.

Outside Dad's apartment a camera took her retina scan while the gleaming metal door cast her reflection back at her, dark Terran hair and Terran eyes so like Dad's. It was Larry who'd inherited Mom's Darkovan features. That was pretty much the only Darkovan thing about him. That he got to go return to the world of their birth while Elaine remained grounded on Terra was obscene.

The door chimed as it slid open. In a few years Elaine would be an adult, and then she'd find her own way off-world. She stepped into the apartment's small entryway. In the gray-carpeted, gray-walled living room beyond, a boy looked up from his school tablet. The Darkovan boy from school.

"You?" Elaine didn't know which of them was more startled.

His ears turned bright red as he dropped his gaze, stumbled to his feet, and fled the room. If meeting a woman's eyes was improper, talking to her with none of her kinsmen present was grounds for a blood feud. At least that was what Mom said. Elaine had left Darkover before she could speak, and she had no memories of any Darkovans who weren't blood kin.

She walked over to the Darkovan boy's tablet. He had a Level 1 reading lesson up, the sort of thing most kids mastered in grade school. Elaine felt a twinge of sympathy as she scanned the basic exercises. Mom, who spoke Terran Standard passably enough, still sometimes needed Elaine's help with written passages. On Darkover, she'd had scribes to read for her.

"Hey, kid."

Elaine whirled at her father's voice, and he grabbed her into a bear hug. Elaine hugged him back, inhaling the faint metallic scent that had clung to him even when he did his translation work in spaceports here on Terra. Elaine's own comfort with the written word had come from Dad, during the handful of years he and Mom were together.

"Hey, Dad. Been a while." Since the divorce, she'd only seen him a few times a year, mostly around holidays. She'd been surprised how much she missed him once he was gone.

He held the hug longer than he would have before he'd left. Maybe he'd missed her, too. "Crazy year," he said when he pulled away. He glanced down the hall and called, "You can come back in, Ken!" More quietly he told Elaine, "I should have known better than to leave him alone here, but this is an education for me, too."

"What'd you do, Dad? Trade my brother in for a newer, more Darkovan model?"

"Something like that," Dad said, which wasn't the answer Elaine was looking for.

The boy returned to the room and moved politely to Dad's side, looking uncomfortable in his gray Academy uniform. A copper chain disappeared beneath his tunic. Mom had one just like it, attached to a silk pouch whose contents she'd refused to show Elaine as surely as she'd refused to explain why she wouldn't go back to Darkover, not even for a visit, not even when she missed it so much.

"Okay, time to do this right." Dad switched from Terran Standard to *casta*, which Elaine had never heard him speak. "Kennard-Gwynn Lanart-Alton, allow me to introduce my daughter, Elaine Montray-Aldaran."

"*S'dia shaya.*" The rote *casta* phrase felt strange on Elaine's tongue, standing in Dad's cramped Terran apartment as she was. *Casta* was for Mom and for home, Terran Standard for Dad and school and all the rest of the wide world.

"The honor is mine, Yllana." Kennard spoke the Darkovan version of her name, which no one but Mom ever used. That was more than strange, and it set off a sharp electric jolt beneath her skin, familiar and unsettling at once. As if they'd met before, or else would meet again. Except that made no sense.

"There." Dad kept talking in *casta*. He'd gotten better at it while he was away. "Now you two can talk without poor Ken here worrying I'm going to challenge him to a duel." He laughed. "Though given my poor fencing skills, I really don't see what he's worried about!"

Kennard looked relieved, and that told Elaine, more than anything else, that all Mom's talk of unforgiveable insults and duels to the death was more than just talk, after all. "Lerrys did not tell me he had a sister." Kennard used the Darkovan version of her brother's name, too. "Let alone one who spoke as if she were one of us."

"That's my brother for you," Elaine said. "Not much of a talker." When Mom and Dad had split up, they'd split the kids with them—Elaine going to Mom, Larry going to Dad—and Larry had found the whole business so uncomfortable he never visited Mom and barely spoke to Elaine outside of her visits to Dad, even though they still went to school together.

Had gone to school together. "Dad, where *is* Larry? Is he in some sort of trouble? What's going on?"

"Lerrys is well," Kennard said.

"What's going on," Dad told her, "is that Larry's accepted his Darkovan heritage. Your mother was right. I had no right to keep that heritage from either of you."

"So Larry went native? Skinning his own bears, living off the land, that sort of thing?" Elaine couldn't even picture him speaking *casta* or wearing Darkovan clothes.

"We do not know bears on Darkover." Kennard stumbled over the Terran word for the animal.

"Not even in the mountains?" Elaine asked wryly.

Kennard smiled. "More likely to meet a banshee in the Hellers, and I'm told they make bad eating." He had a cute smile, kind of shy and entirely different from the sharp pride she'd seen at school.

"I'm afraid banshee isn't on offer locally," Dad said. "You'll have to settle for some ordinary Terran hamburgers. Should be out of the food dispenser in five, but I'd better go check on them. They say you can't burn anything with the newer models, but this wouldn't be the first time I proved them wrong."

Kennard sighed as Dad disappeared into the kitchen, and his hand went to the chain around his neck, the one Darkovan thing he wore.

"Let me guess," Elaine said. "Terrans using machines to do things they're perfectly capable of doing for themselves?" It was one Mom's biggest complaints about Terran life.

Kennard's shoulders slumped, making him look suddenly young. "How can you stand it?"

"It's easier for me. I just..." Elaine had never put this into words before. "I switch, depending on where I am." *On who I am.* "Most of the time, I don't think about it. It just happens, the way—the way the food dispenser switches from hot to cold drinks and back again."

Kennard laughed, as if that were the most ridiculous image ever. "You are more than some mere Terran machine, Lady."

That was sweet and awkward and embarrassing all at once. "So you see, when I'm at Dad's, overcooked burgers are just normal, and I wouldn't know what to do with anything else. But when I'm at home—well, my mom doesn't rely on machines. *Especially* not for cooking." Even an ancient microwave was too modern for Mom, who'd only reluctantly accepted electric burners in place of open flames. "You should come over for dinner sometime."

Kennard's face lit up—she caught a glimpse at the edges of her sight—but he kept his voice carefully neutral. "If your mother were to extend an invitation, I would be honored to accept."

Of course. An unmarried girl inviting an unmarried boy into her home wasn't proper either, even if they intended to nothing more scandalous than go over their astrophysics homework together. It had all seemed so romantic back when Mom had explained it to her, perhaps because Elaine had never known a boy she actually wanted to invite over. Without thinking about it, she'd always understood that her Terran friends, boys and girls both, were for school. Bringing them home to Mom would have felt as wrong as, well, speaking *casta* in her father's apartment.

Dad came out with the burgers, sparing Elaine from having to put any of that into words. Over a properly tasteless Dad-cooked meal he explained everything to her: how Larry and Kennard had met by chance on the streets of Darkover, become friends, and had adventures together—the sort of adventures that involved kidnapping and bandits and yes, even banshees. Surviving all that had left Larry as mad to learn about Darkover as it had left Kennard mad to learn about Terra, so they'd arranged an exchange program. "To help build a bridge between our worlds," Dad said.

"So now your father is my foster father." Kennard politely took another bite of the bland, processed meat. "And your brother is my foster brother. And you—" He stopped abruptly, and his ears turned nearly as red as his hair.

If Elaine was his foster sister, meeting her eyes or accepting her dinner invitations or talking to her without a chaperone wouldn't be a problem. With a word, she could erase the awkwardness between them. They'd be kin.

But never more than kin. Elaine's burger grew cold in front of her. She fought the urge to look at Kennard, to see if his thoughts echoed hers. It wasn't as if you could ever really know another person's thoughts, anyway.

"I'll talk to my mother about dinner," she said instead.

~oOo~

A proper first invitation needed not only to come from the head of Elaine's household, but to be delivered to the head of Kennard's. That meant Mom had to talk to Dad, something they both did as little of as possible.

The resulting argument was all about Mom giving Dad hell for taking Larry off-world and leaving him there. Elaine heard *you never consulted me* and *he's my son, too* and *Terran custody laws be damned* and *if only you knew what I saw*. She had no idea what that last even meant.

But at the end of Dad's yelling and Mom's bitter, hissed accusations, Mom issued an invitation, Dad passed it on to Kennard, and Kennard accepted it.

He showed up a week later at their house near the city's edge, far enough from the city center to have real grass out front. Mom worked even further away, with horses and hawks and other animals at a reserve dedicated to keeping dying Terran species alive.

Kennard halted at the edge of the property, staring at that patch of green as if it could slake some deep thirst. He wore leggings and a tunic almost the same shade of green, and his long cloak, embroidered with an eagle atop a rocky cliff, set off his bright hair and fair skin. He didn't look uncomfortable in those clothes. He looked—Elaine's skin grew hot as she thought about how he looked, and she forced her gaze to her feet. It was all she could do to stand there and let her mother cross the lawn to greet him alone.

Mom's bright scarlet cloak bore the same double eagles as Elaine's own. She gave Kennard a formal bow as she spoke in *casta*. "Kennard-Gwynn Lanart-Alton. Your mother and I met once, when we were young." That was news to Elaine. "Be welcome in my home."

"My thanks, *domna*." Kennard returned the bow, while behind them the sun grew red as it touched the horizon. Watching in her full scarlet skirt and gold-laced black blouse, Elaine inhaled the evening air and let herself believe, just for a moment, that she was a Darkovan woman standing on the world of her birth, like she and Mom used to pretend at sunset, when Elaine was small.

She opened the door to let them inside, and though he didn't look at her, Kennard's small smile echoed Elaine's own. She followed in time to see Kennard take in the first floor of their home, with the floor-to-ceiling windows that let in the setting sun, the airy and translucent screens that took the place of walls. Mom said no civilized person should live huddled in the dark, no matter what world they lived on.

The chandelier that hung over the dining room table had real candles in place of bulbs, and they cast soft orange light. More candles flickered in the sconces Mom had installed around the room. If Elaine switched from Terran to Darkovan and back again without thinking, that didn't change the fact that coming home to this, after the harsh yellow lights of school, was as restful as shedding her itchy Terran clothes.

Kennard drank in the Darkovan furnishings with stark hunger before turning to Elaine's mom with another bow. "*Domna*, I bring you a gift." He drew a small package from his cloak and handed it to her. Elaine caught a whiff of something that smelled a little like chocolate and a little like coffee and a lot like neither one.

"*Jaco!*" Mom said, and formality gave way to a warm smile. "Do you know I've never found a Terran drink that even came close? Coffee is a poor substitute. You are doubly welcome here, young man."

"I like coffee," Elaine said.

Mom didn't seem to hear. "I imported seeds once, at great expense," she told Kennard. "They came up well enough, but the taste was entirely wrong."

Kennard nodded soberly. "Some things can only grow properly on their home soil."

What would I be like? Elaine wondered. *If I were grown on my home soil?*

You would be splendid, Kennard said. Elaine looked at him, startled, but he still spoke to her mother. He hadn't—couldn't have—spoken aloud.

Because she hadn't spoken aloud, either.

~oOo~

Over a dinner of roast rabbit, which Mom and Kennard agreed tasted almost like Darkovan rabbit-horn, Elaine and Kennard talked about school and their classes. Elaine was focusing on mathematics and celestial dynamics. She hoped one day to serve as an astronavigator on one of the big ships, and so to see other words—including Darkover, but not only Darkover—for herself. With Kennard sitting there, Mom spared Elaine her disapproving speech about how if you traveled among all the stars, you could never belong to any one of them.

Kennard was focusing on learning to read well enough to master other subjects. Elaine offered to help him after school.

"Consider our home your own." Mom seconded the invitation, making it one he could accept. She liked him, Elaine realized, as she'd never liked any of the Academy students she'd met at school events.

"You lend me grace." Kennard bowed his head.

As Elaine looked between him and Mom, she felt dizzy, balanced between the worlds of her Terran father and her Darkovan mother. The air blurred, and for an instant she saw herself stepping off one of the big ships whose courses she hoped to chart, onto a world whose noon sun was red as a Terran sunset. *Darkover.*

"*Domna*, have you had your daughter tested for *laran*?" The image faded as Kennard spoke.

"What's *laran*?" Elaine asked.

Elaine's mother snorted, a rather un-Darkovan sound. "How would I do that here?"

"Of course." Kennard's ears flushed. "I know it is none of my concern, but by your leave..." He drew the chain from beneath his tunic, cradling the silk bag that hung from it. "I'm no Tower technician, but I'd be happy to perform some basic tests."

"If I wanted that done, I'd have done it myself. I'll kindly ask you not to speak of it again." Mom forced a smile as her hand brushed the silk bag that hung from her own neck. "Now, let's try that *jaco*, shall we?" Mom's skirts swirled around her as she swept from the room.

"What was that about?" Elaine asked.

Kennard's hands fidgeted in his lap. "I'll not defy your mother in her own home. Please don't ask me to."

You're too damn honorable, Elaine thought.

"Without honor, what's left?" Kennard muttered, as if to himself. Elaine must have spoken aloud without realizing it, both now and earlier.

Without honor you'd be just another Terran boy, she thought, and found she no more wanted that than he did.

~oOo~

They didn't need to talk about *laran*, whatever that was, to have things enough to talk about.

In the weeks that followed, after school at her mother's house, Elaine explained the vagaries of Terran verb conjugations and Terran social customs to Kennard, while Kennard spoke about his Darkovan life to Elaine. Years of retelling had worn her mother's stories down to smooth familiarity, and Elaine found herself as hungry for Kennard's new tales as he was for airy rooms and home-cooked meals.

Kennard talked about helping his father raise horses in the hills of his family estate, about serving in the city guard, about fighting on the fire lines beside Elaine's brother—hard work, grueling work, *real* work. He talked about living in a place where people didn't spend their teens hunched over tablets, but learned adult work out in the adult world.

If she were a Darkovan astrogator, Elaine thought once, she'd already be on a big ship, learning alongside those already doing that work. Except there were no Darkovan astrogators. *Not yet.* Why shouldn't she be the first? Again Elaine saw herself stepping off a big ship and onto a world with a deep red sun, only this time she could tell it was like no big ship she'd ever seen, its lines sleeker and more graceful than any Terran-made craft.

Kennard smiled, as if whatever she saw, he saw it, too. His hand moved towards hers, not quite touching. Elaine had the strangest feeling then, a feeling she'd never had with any Terran friend.

Like they didn't really need to speak. Like they could move beyond words, if she could figure out how.

No one could move beyond words. Weeks gave way to months, and it was through words that she and Kennard became friends, at her mother's house and at her father's, too. She saw more of Dad now and thought of him less as a stranger and more as, well, her father.

What would it take to become more than friends? Words had little power when put up against Darkovan customs that seemed designed to set walls between them, customs that prevented the slightest casual touch or held gaze and that wouldn't even let Kennard talk to her at school, because she had no kinsmen there. Elaine couldn't shake the feeling that there was a missing piece that could breach those walls, some piece she didn't understand.

Yet she and Kennard *were* friends, and she treasured that as its own true thing.

She reminded herself that one day, surely, he would leave again. But as the years passed, Kennard showed no more sign of leaving Terra than Elaine's brother showed of leaving Darkover and coming home.

~oOo~

She was in her final year at the Academy when everything changed.

She was sitting in her Multispace Group Theory class—a class she and Kennard didn't share, since he was more interested in balancing household accounts than in higher mathematics—when out of nowhere, red-hot pain seared her side.

Elaine screamed, barely aware she was doing it, as that pain burned through muscles and shot into her stomach. Images flashed before her. *Swords ringing. Steel piercing cloth and skin. Her brother, falling to the ground. Blood, far too much blood.*

"Ms. Montray, are you all right?"

She clung to her teacher's voice like the lifeline it was, forcing herself past those horrid visions to focus on the woman in Terra Academy grays who stood beside her desk. There was no blood. There was only a class full of Terran students, staring at her.

Filthy Terranan. *Don't need a spaceship to send you back to the stars.* The voice rang through Elaine's head, loud as the clashing of swords.

Except there was no voice in her head. There couldn't be. "I'm okay." Elaine's side burned, but she forced the words out. "I just...don't feel very well. I can get myself to the medic's office."

She fled the room, but not for the medic. If she showed up in his office with no visible injuries, he'd want a psych evaluation, and emotional stability was one of the things the astrogation schools she'd applied to looked for. Better to let everyone think she'd just ditched class. It'd be her first offense in all her years at the Academy, and she could serve detention for it later.

She ran out the door and down one of the city's long alleyways, clutching her side, though there was no good reason, because she hadn't been hurt. Yet she did hurt. She hurt so much. She fell gasping to her knees, while around her the city's high-rises caught the yellow afternoon sun.

"Yllana!" Kennard knelt before her, steadying hands on her shoulders. Kennard, who never spoke to her at school or when they were alone, Kennard who never, ever touched her. Pain fled as he lifted her chin and looked right into her eyes, and Elaine found she could breathe again.

It's my fault, Kennard said, his own eyes anguished. *I should have had better control, only I never imagined the connection between me and my foster brother could travel so far. Zandru's Hells, what's happened to him? He was in so much pain.*

No. Kennard didn't say any of that. He *thought* it. Staring straight at him, his hands trembling against her face, there was no denying it. "Kennard, what's going on?"

"I'm sorry." He spoke aloud now, his lips moving like they were supposed to. "I've grown so accustomed to living among head-blind Terrans that I stopped worrying about what I might be broadcasting. He's so far away, Yllana. I cannot protect him this time."

"Protect who?" But Elaine already knew. She'd seen her brother fall. "Larry's half a galaxy away. Did he send you a message? Is that what you...broadcast?" Text or video, it didn't matter. Messages took weeks to travel among the stars.

"He reached out to me, in his need and in his pain," Kennard whispered. "And I'm helpless to do a damned thing about it!" Elaine heard—heard and *felt*—the anguish in his voice.

That was impossible. "Are we both going mad?"

An untrained telepath is a danger to herself and all those around her, Kennard thought, clear as speaking. *I have to tell her.*

"Telepath." Elaine should have been surprised, but she wasn't. "That's what you are."

"Not only me." He let his hands fall, and it was all Elaine could do not to reach for him again. "*Laran.*" He spoke the half-forgotten word from her mother's house years ago. "That's what the Gift is called. Most of our people have it. Living among head-blind Terrans as you are, your own Gift lay mostly dormant until I woke it, much like your brother's did. Your mother will be very angry. I am sorry."

"I'm not." Now that she'd met his gaze, she never wanted to look away again. She didn't know why her mother had kept this knowledge from her, but if *laran* was the reason for this new thing she felt between her and Kennard, so much closer than touch, she wasn't sorry at all. *No more distance. No more loneliness.* Had she known she was alone before now?

"Without a starstone, your powers will be limited." Kennard drew the silk pouch from beneath his shirt. "But I'll teach you the basics. How to control and block your thoughts, if nothing else, so that you don't broadcast in turn."

I don't want to hide my thoughts from you. This new closeness left no room, no desire for secrets.

Kennard laughed, and the sound echoed somewhere deep inside her. *Trust me, Yllana, no telepath wants their thoughts laid bare* all *the time.* Aloud he said, "We need to tell your father about Larry."

They didn't hold hands as they caught a pod to Dad's apartment. They didn't need to.

Lord of Light, I've been alone too long, Kennard thought.

You're not alone anymore, Elaine thought.

She didn't know which of them thought, *Now neither of us need ever be alone again.*

~oOo~

Kennard didn't know much, only that Larry had fallen to another man's sword and been sorely wounded. Their contact had broken before he could learn whether Elaine's brother had survived those wounds. There was no way to find out but to wait for either Larry or Kennard's father to send a message—a message that would tell them whether Larry's attempt to build a bridge between worlds had killed him instead.

So Elaine waited. There was nothing else she could do.

Kennard taught her enough control to hide her *laran* from her mother, who would surely banish him from her house if she knew. He still wouldn't talk to her at school, but it no longer mattered. Elaine felt his presence, every moment of every day, and she knew that he felt hers. She'd had no idea how alone she really was, trapped within the silence of her own thoughts, until they were silent no more.

Close as she and Kennard now were, she knew the moment the message came. As she woke that morning she heard him from across the city. *He's okay! Yllana, he's okay!*

The breath whooshed out of her. *Tell me!*

Come to your Dad's and I'll show you.

That was the second time she skipped class, catching a pod straight to her father's apartment. Her hands shook as she swiped through Larry's letter on Dad's tablet. Some minor noble had challenged her brother to a duel at the Midsummer Festival Ball, saying a Terran had no right to wear Alton colors and claim kinship to Kennard's family. Larry had had no choice, he said: he could have accepted the challenge like a Darkovan man, or crawled back to the Trade City like a Terran child. So he accepted the duel and killed his challenger, but not before being critically wounded himself. It had taken three trained telepaths to heal him. "So it all turned out all right in the end," Larry said, as if killing a man and nearly dying himself were no big deal.

They weren't a big deal on Darkover. Mom's stories had taught her that, and Kennard's, too. But a stranger dead, and her brother nearly so, for a few harsh words? Sitting in her father's Terran apartment, wearing her Terran school uniform, something within her protested the thought. *This is more than honor should demand.*

She almost didn't hear when Dad said, "Ken, you'd better show her the other message."

What other message? Elaine thought.

Kennard turned away from her. He was hiding something, Elaine realized. Ice trickled down her spine. She hadn't known a telepath could hide anything.

She rubbed at her itchy uniform sleeves. "What is it?"

Dad quietly left the room. Kennard reached for his own tablet, then shook his head. *I've always taken responsibility for my own actions. I'll not stop now, nor retreat like a child behind words on a Terran screen when this is mine to tell.* "What happened to Lerrys was not an isolated incident," he said slowly. "Anti-Terran sentiment is rising on Darkover. My family is at the heart of it, because my brother and foster sister... that's a long story, for another time." He crossed the room to stare out the apartment's small window, where a high-rise identical to theirs blocked the sky. "The Comyn need reasonable voices on the Council right now." Kennard drew a breath. "Lord Hastur and my father are calling me home."

"So I'll go with you." How could he doubt it? Yet it was her own doubt Elaine felt at the words. Two days ago, she'd been accepted by her first choice astronavigation school. Was she ready to give that up? To her Darkovan self, charting star courses was a way to back to the world of her birth, but to her Terran self, it was something more. There were so many worlds. As a Darkovan she longed for one of them, but as a Terran she wanted them all.

Kennard's next words made clear it didn't matter what she

wanted. "Lord Hastur has also arranged...an honorable *di catenas* marriage for me, to a well-respected woman from a family known to have strong *laran*."

For a heartbeat Elaine didn't understand. It was that absurd. "I have *laran*." And no one had arranged a marriage for Elaine's mom. She'd chosen Dad herself. *Arranged marriages are as barbaric as...as blood feuds!* she thought.

Did choosing keep your parents together? Kennard wondered. No sharing of thoughts could bridge this new distance between them. "I love you." He'd never said it aloud before. "I will always love you. I would marry you with full Comyn honors if I could, but that choice is not mine to make. This is about more than either of us. It's about Darkover's future."

The future of a world that tried to murder my brother and that would tear my beloved away from me. She'd never said she loved him aloud, either. She didn't say it now. "Maybe that's not a world worth saving."

"You don't mean that!" he cried. She felt his shock, sharp and cold as if she'd slapped him.

I no longer know what I believe. Why was it easier to think that truth than to speak it?

Yllana! His thoughts held the anguish his voice did not. *I do not want to leave you!*

"But you're doing it anyway."

"Yes." *Because my father, my lord, and my world ask it of me.*

"Then there's nothing left to discuss." She would not beg. She would not plead. She would not cry in front of him. "When you see my brother, give him my regards."

She left her father's home with her head held high and her pride—Terran pride or Darkovan pride, it mattered not—still intact.

That, and the silence of her own thoughts, were all she had left.

~oOo~

The moment Elaine walked in the door, her mother knew. Elaine's control was shot, her every nerve laid bare. Of course Mom knew. Elaine felt it as surely as she felt her mother's mind touch hers for the very first time.

She wanted to apologize for Kennard's waking her *laran*. She wanted to never apologize for anything Kennard did again. She wanted to flee behind the screen to her room and never come out.

Oh, chiya. No electric jolt at hearing her mother's thoughts. They felt familiar as her mother's presence, as comforting as the arms Mom wrapped around her. Mom held Elaine, as she hadn't since she was small, and Elaine felt as well as heard Mom's soothing words as she cried herself out. Why had she assumed her mother wouldn't understand?

Later, over the last of the hoarded *jaco*, Mom removed a faceted blue jewel from the pouch around her neck. "I'm sorry, Yllana. I never should have hidden your *laran* from you, but I feared if it woke you'd share not only my surface thoughts, but my nightmares as well."

"What nightmares?" Elaine asked, but even as she did, she knew. She *saw*.

A spaceport, a city, all of Darkover aflame. A woman, sheathed in fire, reaching burning fingers toward Mom, and Elaine, and Elaine's children, and her children's children, reaching through time itself to reduce a world to ash. Flames flickered around Elaine, moving closer, ever closer....

The vision ended as abruptly as it came, leaving Elaine staring at Mom, and Mom staring at her, and the *jaco* cooling between them.

I've lived alone with it this so long, Mom thought. *Laran or no laran, I'll not burden my daughter with it now.*

"How...when did that happen?" Elaine took a gulp of lukewarm *jaco*. Her throat felt dry, as if the flames had sucked the moisture away. A fire like that should have destroyed Darkover whole. There should be no world left for Kennard to return to. *Not that I care what he returns to.*

You don't need him, chiya. Mom sipped the tepid liquid. "The Altons like to say that in their family time slips out of place from time to time, revealing glimpses of the future. The Aldaran family Gift—our Gift—is not concerned with mere glimpses. We see the future whole. The strongest of us see it with all its branching paths. I'm not that strong, yet I am the strongest of my generation. The visions began when I was still a child, terrors of fire and power consuming my world and everything I held dear, down to the very air and soil. I do not know when it will happen, but I think it will be within my lifetime."

Mom turned the blue gem—a starstone, Kennard had called it— in her hand. "I was willing enough to die with my world. I am no coward. But the visions grew stronger once you and Lerrys were born, and I found what I could face for myself, I could not face for my children. So I suggested your father put in for a transfer off-world. I told him I wanted to see the Empire our marriage had made me a citizen of, and being head-blind, he did not hear the lie.

It was the first lie I told him, but it wasn't the last. It's not an easy thing, loving someone who cannot share one's thoughts." *Of course you fell in love with the first man who could share yours.*

There was more to it than that! Elaine thought. Wasn't there?

Mom carefully returned the starstone to its silk pouch. "By the time your father and I grew apart, we were safely on Terra, and I had no more visions, only memories of them that haunt my dreams to this day. That mattered less to me than knowing my children were safe—until my son returned to Darkover as the foster son of a lowland lord, and my daughter began to talk about flying Terran spacecraft among the stars. Fly wherever else you wish, but you must not go back. You must not let that fire find you. I would call Lerrys home too, if I could."

Elaine drew her arms around herself. She needed no apocalyptic visions to tell her future after today.

"I'm not going back to Darkover," she whispered. *Not now. Not ever.*

~oOo~

She left for astronavigation school the same week Kennard left for Darkover, trading her Terra Academy grays for an astrogator's blues.

Within a few years, she was apprenticed to a professional astrogator on a big ship, doing in her twenties what Darkovans did in their teens, and not more than once a day did she think about Kennard living a proper Darkovan life with his proper Darkovan wife.

If no Terran could penetrate the silence of her thoughts, well, in the emptiness of space that silence seemed less lonely and more right. Space was supposed to be silent, after all, silent and dark and filled with a beauty all its own. Astrogators had little time for relationships anyway, shuttling from world to world as they were.

The ports and trade cities of those worlds were not nearly as peaceful as the stars, being filled with minds closed to her own, so Elaine spent less time exploring them than she'd once imagined she would. It was just as well she was rarely planet-side for more than a day. Her leaves on Terra were almost as short, though she always visited both her parents before launching into space once more.

It was on one of those visits she found a red-haired stranger sitting in Dad's living room, in the chair she had—almost—stopped thinking of as belonging to Kennard. The man stood when he saw her. "Hullo, Elaine."

Elaine frowned before she caught his thought. *It's been so long. Who can blame her for not recognizing me?*

Larry? It'd been a decade since he'd left for Darkover. She'd assumed he was no more coming back than Kennard was.

"Yeah, Lainey, it's me." Larry limped toward her. For a moment they were strangers still, only then Elaine grabbed him into a hug, and somehow they were all right with each other after that. *My little sister is no longer head-blind.*

Maybe it was hearing his thoughts that closed the years-long gap between them. *No longer little, either*, she thought.

Larry laughed quietly. Everything about him was quieter than she remembered, for all that he'd never talked much.

"Kennard sends his best," Larry said in Terran Standard. His thoughts had been in *casta*.

Does he? Even to Elaine, the thought felt bitter. "And is his wife well?"

Her brother fell silent, and Elaine saw something haunted in his gray eyes. *What happened?*

"Go easy on Kennard, Elaine. He's been through a lot these past few years. We all have."

She caught a quick succession of images: *A Tower rising out of a flat plain. A golden-haired woman, fleeing with a small band of Darkovans and Terrans. People rioting in the streets. A broken door, a child's sobs, and a room bathed in blood.*

"We failed." Larry's voice tightened. "All we hoped to build—me and Kennard, Andres and Jeff, Magda and Dan and all the rest—it's gone, and for what? An old folk belief, a scrap of superstition. We tried to save Darkover. We learned it cannot be saved. In a generation or a little more, Darkover as we know it will be gone, replaced by one more Empire world. You're well away from it." As he spoke, Elaine knew he didn't believe that, knew he wanted to go back more than anything.

She couldn't help it. The old longing came back, the one that had made her listen so intently to Kennard's stories, the one she'd set aside when he returned to Darkover without her. *What is it like, the world of my birth? What have I lost, growing up away from it?*

What am I missing?

~ooo~

In the end, it wasn't any decision of Elaine's that brought her back to Darkover the first time, but the quirks of galactic geography.

Introductory texts claimed Cottman IV was between the upper and lower spiral arms of the galaxy—a simplification that made astrocartographers bang their heads—but it *was* in a convenient position for fuel stops on several different standard cargo circuits.

Six months into her first stint as a full member of an astrogation crew, Elaine found herself on one of those circuits.

She told herself it was just another world. She told herself there was no more reason to get off the ship here for her short leave than there was anywhere else.

She got off anyway. Of course she did.

She had a moment to step outside and take in the red sun rising over the distant mountains, another moment to wonder whether she should feel some connection to those mountains—and then the vision slammed into her.

Heat.

Flames.

Pain.

She was burning, burning, burning, fiery fingers caressing her skin. She tried to run, but the fire raged within as well as without. She tried to scream, but the flames burned her voice away.

A woman draped in fire rose before her. Asphalt and spaceport and world all bubbled and melted away, unable to withstand such power. Elaine's skin bubbled and melted too, as flames seared her thoughts and melted her very soul....

A barrier slammed into place between her and those flames. She fell gasping to her knees, breathing the cool metallic spaceport air. If this was what her mother saw, no wonder she left Darkover and never came back.

Yllana? Even after so long, Elaine knew the touch of Kennard's thoughts. Knew, too, that the barrier was his, and that, just then, it might well have saved her sanity.

She didn't respond. What would she say? She focused on finding the small travel bag she'd dropped, and Kennard withdrew at her mental silence. She got trembling to her feet, looked around to make sure none of her crewmates had seen, and headed for the first spaceport bar she could find. She didn't know how Darkovans dealt with visions of death and destruction, but any Terran knew there was no answer but a good stiff drink.

The Darkovan server took in her Terran clothes and eyes and dismissed her as another spaceport employee before taking her order in Terran Standard. Elaine answered in Terran Standard, too. Her *cahuenga* had never been as good as her *casta* anyway.

As she drank, her shaking eased. She stared out the bar's grimy windows, watching the sun clear the mountains. It didn't feel like home. She didn't know what it felt like.

She wasn't surprised when Kennard slid into the seat beside her. She didn't look at him, but it didn't matter. She felt his presence, as familiar as if he'd left only yesterday. He squirmed, uncomfortable beneath the bright Terran lights, surrounded by head-blind Terran minds. *I have missed you, Yllana.*

Damn him, anyway. She tightened her hold on her glass. "So how's your wife?"

The sharp pain that followed that question surprised her. *Gone,* Kennard thought. *So many gone. Lewis and Cleindori. Cassilde and Arnad. The little ones, too. And now Caitlin, least beloved of them all, but the Lord of Light himself knows I tried to be a good husband to her.*

Elaine couldn't help it. She turned to him. His shoulders were hunched, his hair touched with the first hints of gray. He looked so much older and sadder than she remembered. "I am sorry for your loss." The ritual Terran Standard phrase sounded stiff on her tongue.

So much loss, he thought. *So much time. I'll not marry to please them again, though the world itself depend on it.* He lifted his head then, and though he did not meet her eyes, his question was clear enough.

Elaine set down her drink. Did he really think they could just return to who they were on Terra, before Kennard left to serve his world and Elaine found hers among the stars?

"You were right, Yllana." His voice was a hoarse whisper. "I should never have let them make this decision for me." *I serve my world so many ways. But not in this one, not ever again.* "If you will have me, I swear I will marry you in full view of your gods and mine, Council approval be damned and just let those gods *try* to stop me."

She wanted to tell him he was too late. She wanted to say something bitter and cutting about his asking this, of all things, with no kinsman present, about his asking at all after so much time.

She'd never been able to lie to him, with *laran* or without it. She didn't now. "I don't know, Kennard. I just don't know."

He bowed his head. "I cannot blame you for that."

Elaine thought of her mother's vision—her vision—of fire consuming this world. She thought of Larry, telling her Darkover could not be saved. *What does it matter what we decide, if the world itself is doomed to fall?*

Even should the world fall, Kennard thought. *I would have you by my side.*

She looked straight at him then, and as she did, a gentler vision slid over her thoughts.

A spaceship nestled among snow-capped mountains, like no big ship she knew: sleek and copper-bright, no bulky Terran engines weighing it down. The ship lifted off without smoke or flame, graceful as a bird, and somehow Elaine knew it was the same laran *that Kennard had woken, the* laran *her mother had feared to wake, that lifted that bird into the sky.*

Knew, too, that she was the one who charted the course that Darkovan craft followed as it wove among the stars, meeting as equals the Terrans who'd once claimed those stars as their own.

She could tell Kennard saw it, too. As the vision faded she kept looking into his gray eyes, and it seemed in them she saw no single inevitable vision, but all the branching paths: flames and flight; Kennard by her side and not by her side; two boys riding together through the hills, one with his eyes, one with hers. She heard Kennard's joyful, startled thought. *Our sons.*

But that was only one future. Elaine knew then that there was no single future, but only a universe filled with possibilities, and that no *laran* and no visions could chart her course now.

Only she could do that. "I need some time," she told Kennard. "To think." To sort through those branching paths. In the silence of space she'd have that time, until her circuit took her this way again.

"Then you shall have it," Kennard said. "I will wait as long as I must."

Even forever? Elaine thought.

If that's what it takes, yes. His ears grew red as he looked back at her.

Elaine laughed, feeling the same lightness she felt when she rose into the stars. "Listen, I have thirty standard hours until liftoff." *Time enough to start over.* "Care to show a Terran girl the sights?"

You'll never be just a Terran girl to me. He stood, breaking her immodest gaze, and swept his arm out in front of him.

"My lady," he said, "it would be an honor."

The Cold Blue Light
by Judith Tarr

Like readers, characters come to Darkover for a variety of reasons. Each person and each reason is a story, and each creates ripples in the complex tapestry of the planet of the Bloody Sun. Some come for escape, others for adventure or romance or trade...and some for even stranger, more wonderful reasons. Like the magnificent horses of the Alton Domain.

Judith Tarr is the author of over forty novels and numerous short stories, including World Fantasy Award nominee *Lord of the Two Lands* and the space opera, *Forgotten Suns*. She writes that she has been a Darkover fan since a college friend tempted, er, corrupted, er, encouraged her to read *The Heritage of Hastur*. She devoured it, then every one of the others as she could find them. The world of the Bloody Sun remains one of her favorite alien worlds, and she is honored and delighted to be allowed to play in it.

The horses, her heroine reflects, *were worth the journey....*

Spend enough time on any world, and you can get used to anything. Even a sun the color of blood, and snow at high summer in what passes for temperate latitudes, and people who...

But that's getting ahead of myself.

This story begins on a different world altogether, under a yellow sun, with a single moon hanging over a palace that had been old when the first rocket dared the sky. It was a brisk day in early winter, and the horses were fresh for the morning exercises. Even the veterans snorted and danced, and the young ones, just beginning their life's work in our ancient school, ranged from energetic to downright obstreperous.

There was always an audience in the galleries, either smaller or larger depending on the weather and the season. That day I remembered because the Director was entertaining dignitaries: not particularly rare or remarkable, except for one young person with an outworld accent, who came down to the stables afterward and asked penetrating questions about the horses.

That wasn't unheard of, either, though I happened to be handiest for fetching out horses, and he wouldn't look at me at all. He was rude, I thought, but I'd met enough outworlders to know that one world's rudeness is another's good manners.

I'd never heard of his world. Darkover—odd, evocative name. He was a fine specimen, big and broad-shouldered, with the reddest hair I'd seen outside of the Scottish Highlands.

"We breed for blacks," he said, "but we have our share of greys, as well. Is it true your silvers don't keep their dark points? They grey out as they age?"

"Yours don't?" I asked.

He still wouldn't look at me, except sideways, but he answered politely enough. "Some do. But a few of our lines are born black, and the body goes silver but the points stay as they were."

"A mutation, maybe," I said. "We preserve the old lines here—genetics that go back more than three thousand years."

"I can see that," he said in clear admiration, running his hand down the neck of my lovely, if headstrong, Galatea. Galatea, who despite his feminine call-name was quite the studly personage, arched against the touch and pawed imperiously.

The outworlder laughed. "Yes, indeed! Apologies; I am keeping you from your breakfast."

"So you are," I said, but with a spark of humor.

As I led Galatea back into his stall, where the manger waited, overflowing with good mountain hay, I heard the outworlder say to the Director, "Someday, sir, you must come to my world and see my horses. There's much that we could learn from you, both of riding and of breeding."

"That would be a fine thing," the Director said, diplomatic as always, but I could tell he was tempted. He used to love to travel, before duty and the needs of the school bound him here in Old Vienna.

~oOo~

The visitors went away; the school stayed where it was. I pursued my studies in the riding hall in the mornings, and in the university and at the stud farm in the evenings and the holidays.

Then one morning, twenty years after the young man from Darkover admired my stallion, the Director found me in the stable, taking down the name of Galatea from the stall and not trying to fight the tears.

The Director is a horseman. He said nothing of the four younger stallions in my charge, or the fifth doing his duty in the mountains with the mares. Nor did he utter platitudes about a quick end as opposed to a slow decline, or how we still, after all these millennia, could do nothing of any use when a horse fell prey to his damned primitive digestive system.

No one had ever been able to change that without changing the species itself—and we preserved the old lines. With all that meant, for good or bad.

He said nothing about any of that. He said, "I have a task for you, if you'll take it. A mission. A sabbatical, if you like."

I glared through the tears. "I'm not *that* traumatized. I don't need to be put on psych leave."

"Of course you don't," he said, "but we've received a rather unusual invitation, and the Federation has had one of its intermittent attacks of indulgence. It asks—no, requires us to accept. It's even offered a bribe: five years' worth of support for the school."

My eyes went wide. The school has a very long history of struggling to survive—and those struggles have at times come close to death-throes. We were nowhere near that desperate just then, but five years of operating expenses were a considerable incentive.

"What do we have to do for that?" I asked. "Move all the horses to Ceti IV?"

"I should hope not," he said with a hint of starch in his tone. "We've been asked by a planetary dignitary to send one of our riders to his own estate to evaluate his horses, advise on his breeding program, and instruct his trainers in our methods."

"Just one rider? Not half a dozen? And horses with them?"

"Just one," he said. "It's at the back of beyond—a proscribed world, no less."

"For how long?"

"An Earthyear," he said. "Plus transport time."

I released the breath I hadn't realized I was holding. I'd been expecting him to tell me I'd be sent out for the rest of my life. For what the Federation was paying, it might actually be worth it.

A year—that was just enough to make it an adventure. I'd earned my academic degrees long ago; I'd gone on tour with the school and taken vacations on an assortment of worlds. But never on a restricted world, let alone a proscribed one.

"No weapons that leave the hand," the Director said when I asked. "Swords and knives, that's all. No tech beyond the medieval. No aircraft or paved roads. No computers; no web connections. Not even a cellular communicator."

That gave me pause. "What are they, New Amish?"

"I don't think they're that technologically advanced," he said. "But they have horses, and they want to learn from us. The Federation is willing to pay for it. I can send Harald—put that passion for mock-Old-Medieval reenactment to use—but he doesn't have your knowledge of genetics or your years of work at the stud farm. He's a rider, not a breeder."

"Yes, I am a mutant," I said. "I have the genes for training *and* breeding. A combination not usually seen in nature."

That wasn't all I had in my genes, but the rest wasn't relevant, I thought then.

I turned Galatea's nameplate in my fingers. For an instant I felt him close behind me and felt the warmth of his breath on my neck.

"I'll go," I said.

~oOo~

The Director should probably have sent Harald after all. Cottman IV is one of *those* worlds: males in charge, females suitably repressed and perpetually pregnant, and no skin tone darker than light Mediterranean.

By the time I rode up to the grand estate in its ring of mountain-sized hills, I'd been stared at, muttered over, and even spat at, and the guards who rode with me had a bet going as to whether and how much the brown of my skin would wash off with a good scrubbing. All that kept me from turning around and heading straight back to the spaceport was the mare I was riding and the prospect of more like her in these fields that rolled away under the blood-red sun.

The lord of the manor wasn't waiting for me. The man who met me at the gate was dark and wiry, with a look I knew well: poised and quiet, as one learned to be around horses.

"*Mestra* Tahawy," he said, not mangling my name too badly. His accent there was certainly better than mine in his language. "Lord Alton sends his sincerest regrets. He was called away unexpectedly, and will greet you properly on his return. Meanwhile, I'll be your host here, and your guide about the estate." He bowed. "Angus MacAran, *z'par servu*."

This man, I noticed, didn't stare as hard as most. He'd been forewarned, maybe. I nodded as we learned to do at the school, where riders outranked everyone but their horses and the only reverence we offered was to the ancient portrait above the royal gallery in the Riding Hall.

"You'll want to meet the horses first, I'm sure," he said. "Though if you'd rather I showed you to your rooms—"

"Horses, of course," I said, though my hands and feet were numb with cold and the sky looked ready to drop a spit of snow. This man knew. Horses first, always. Everything else came after.

~oOo~

The horses were worth the journey. The men who cared for them—all men, of course, on this world—were horsemen by any reckoning, but most of what they did was strictly on the utilitarian side. They used horses. They weren't, for the most part, inclined to see them as we did: as partners; as fellow sentients.

Riding for them meant transportation. Riding as art, focused through years of close study, was almost as alien to them as I was.

My genetic studies had to wait until I was back in the Terran Zone. All I could do here was pull and store hair samples, study bloodlines and stud lists, and set one earnest young person to work copying, by hand, such of the studbooks as I might find relevant. No copying machines here, no mechanical reproduction equipment of any kind.

But the horses—oh, those horses. Blacks mostly as I'd been told, but greys and bays, too, and the rarer, distinctive silvers. I saw the ancient Iberian in them, and the alterations of time and use and alien feed and care and sunlight.

Nothing in any world could compare to our dancing white beauties, but these came close. They were more tolerant of human blindness and unthinking force, but they had their own way of training those who handled them. They were subtle about it, with a kind of wry humor that made me swallow laughter, the first time I watched an arrogant twit of a boy try to teach a mare a set of movements that she had long since learned for herself.

Animals are often more intelligent than we realize. Our species is all up in its head, framing the world in its own invented words. It's a rare human who pays attention well enough, or long enough, to understand what the less verbally or technologically minded sentients are saying.

These horsemen had a gift—strong, some of them, Angus MacAran most of all. But it was oddly constrained. They would command the horses, but it didn't seem to occur to them that communication could go both ways. That horses were more than simple-minded animals without much by way of higher intelligence.

They were tools to be used. Beautiful ones, finely honed and, as far as their handlers knew how, exquisitely trained. They were valuable and highly prized, like the swords that males of status wore, but not granted much more emotional autonomy than that.

"Horses have neither memory nor imagination," MacAran told me in all seriousness as we stood by the rail during a training session.

Training on this cold and frequently storm-ridden world took place, sensibly enough, in a covered arena surrounded by horse stalls: a courtyard with quite decent sand footing and the benefit of heat from the bodies of the horses in the stalls. They were starting young stock this tenday, colts and fillies brought in from the pastures to be evaluated and marked either for breeding or for sale.

The young ones had been within walls for long enough to have lost some of their nervousness after a lifetime in open pastures, but they were still inclined to shy and snort and ignore the monkeys on their backs. One had just shed her rider and tossed a kick at his head on the way past, which occasioned MacAran's remark.

"You believe that?" I asked. "That they have no memory?"

"They're animals," he said. "Prey for anything that can stalk them, out there. Creatures of flight, without much by way of common sense—except what we can teach them."

I'd been keeping my mouth shut and my judgments strictly to myself. I was a guest here, after all, and every word and move was watched and noted. But the boy who had been thrown had picked himself up and got hold of the reins and hauled on them so hard that the mare reared in protest.

The young idiot reached for the stick that he had dropped in his fall and swung it whistling across the mare's sensitive nose.

I was over the rail and on the horse and the boy before anyone could have seen me move. When the dust stopped flying, the boy was flattened to the wall and the whip lay in the sand a dozen meters away, and I had the mare in hand, calming her with touch and voice and the stillness of my body.

She was not in a mood to listen or to believe that a human could have anything to say to her, but there was nothing especially complicated about her. She was young, raw, and justifiably angry. The person underneath, the mind and heart, was still unspoiled; still able, and eventually willing, to learn.

I was focused on the horse, but I heard the whispers behind and around me, echoing faintly in the stone vaulting of the court. My command of the language was good enough, I had thought, but this word was new to me: *leronis*.

Whatever that was, it struck them with a kind of awe. That, I was used to, and had been trained to let pass. What I did was art and long practice, and three millennia of teaching, passed down from master to student, generation after generation.

"A horse has memory," I said as this one bent her head, licking the salt from my palm: claiming me and deigning to accept the knowledge I brought. "She dreams; she feels. She's a living being, as we are—not the same, no, but neither is she our inferior. For us, for my school, these are our companions and often our masters. And always, our partners in the dance."

With that word I broke down a barrier. They understood dancing here. It was one of their arts, like swordplay and breeding fine horses.

"Show us," Angus MacAran said. "Teach us your dance of horse and rider."

I could have said there was no time; if a student comes in young and unspoiled by wrong teaching, in ten years maybe, or fifteen, he begins to be a rider. I had less than a year, and these were horsemen who already knew what they thought they knew.

The young mare blew softly into my hand. For her I said, "I can try."

~oOo~

The grey stone halls of Armida are full of ghosts. I've learned to shut them out—otherwise I'd never sleep. They flock around anyone who can hear or see them, begging for help or simply wanting to be noticed.

These offworld ghosts were downright importunate. The things they said...

"All the telepaths in the world," said one irascible old lady, "and not a medium in the lot."

She was remarkably coherent for a spirit. She could form words as clearly as if she spoke them in life, though it cost her—and me— a great deal of energy.

Even wrapped in quilts and blankets and furs and with a fire roaring on the hearth, I was cold to the bone. The air was full of whispers and faint flutterings.

"Mechanics," the old lady said in my ear. "Skeptics. Blind and deaf to anything outside their own heads. And they call themselves sorcerers."

The dead speak to be understood, and mostly we understand

them in our native language. But the word that floated beneath was one I'd heard before: *leroni*.

I said it aloud. "*Leroni*. What are they? They can't really be—"

"Ask them," the voice said. It was fading, the room warming as the spirits receded.

Spirits had their humor. I thawed slowly, now they'd let me be. Eventually I managed to fall asleep, and dream of the dance in the Winter Hall, with Galatea warm and alive and strong as we went through the paces of the stately Quadrille.

~oOo~

Our school lives by a paradox. Our horses are not ours; they're State Treasures. But we belong to them, and they to us. We're assigned to them when they come in fresh from the pastures, not quite four years old, ready to claim their inheritance. We stay with them for twenty years and more, their health and the school's Director willing.

They are our art, and we are theirs. We live for each other; for the training, and the dance.

Every one is special, unique; wonderful. But some more so. Some are our hearts, and when they die...

My heart was dead. I was a trainer of horses and a teacher of riding and a sometime geneticist; that was all I had any need to be, on this world or any other. I thought I was content with that.

Especially since, because of what I was, I still kept some remnant of Galatea. The spirit, the presence. Whatever one might like to call it. He was with me wherever I went.

The local spirits found him as fascinating as they seemed to find me. They followed both of us into the stables and gathered like a panel of judges as we trained, and had so much to say that I could hardly hear myself think.

They were growing stronger. My defenses were just sufficient for Terran ghosts. These taxed me more with every day that passed.

No human here seemed to sense them. The horses did, oh yes, and at times it was more than they could cope with. And then their trainers ate arena dirt and cursed the flightiness of the species.

It came to a head as such things do, in the midst of one of this world's fierce and sudden summer storms: thunder, lightning, sleet, snow, and torrents of rain. The stone-vaulted roof of the arena held it off easily as it had for years out of count, but the wail of the wind and the clatter of sleet and hail robbed the young horses of what sense they had.

Thunder fed spirits. I saw a row of faces in the gallery, some as solid as in life, but none of them had drawn breath in at least a century.

After the third rider flew off and landed awkwardly—but only bruised, nothing broken—I sent them all out with their snorting, rearing, tail-flagging charges. MacAran stayed, because he was stubborn and because the middle-aged mare he was training for a lady was disinclined to be an idiot, even for an army of ghosts.

She would do. I'd just brought out the young mare of that first day, whose name was Aili. She vividly remembered her inauspicious beginning but had made up her mind to trust me. I set her an exercise just within her capacity, one that absorbed her mind and made the wild weather and the crowding spirits matter less to her than the careful precision of step and step and step.

It was hard. Her back was tense; her ears twitched. I persuaded her gently to relax, breathing with her, making a world that held nothing in it but the two of us and the movements we performed together.

Very simple ones still, circles and changes of hand. Her young balance and skill had all they could do to carry both herself and me.

I felt the change in her as a gradual thing. Her back became more supple, but at the same time her gaits seemed a little less certain. At first I thought she was responding to my training, but there was something not quite right about it.

A young or untrained horse has a certain feel to him: not quite sure of himself, sometimes stopping, sometimes rushing ahead, as he learns to carry a rider in motion and at rest. This was…different. Not just in the way she moved, but in the quality of it. It was as if—

It was not Galatea. Even in a strange and female body, my lost stallion would have called to me with blessed familiarity. This had not been a horse before, I thought. Its awkwardness was completely different from what I'd felt a few moments before.

"Out," I said to the ghost that possessed this lovely young horse. "Out of this body. Now!"

I was so angry that I forgot there was any other human in the arena, and spoke aloud, snapping out the words.

Aili jibbed, throwing her head from side to side. She was fighting the spirit, too, with such utter lack of fear that I went from admiring her to actively loving her.

I gritted my teeth while my body did what it had to in order to stay on that rearing, plunging back. "Whatever you want of me," I said to the ghost, "tell me. But get out of this body first."

I had a sinking feeling that the spirit was refusing to obey because it couldn't—that it had been trying to jump into me and had trapped itself inside the mare. I would appreciate the irony later, when I wasn't trying to ride a whirlwind.

It took all the skill and guile and sheer ferocity I had to ride through the explosion, calm the dual entities and bring us all to a quivering, snorting, sweat-streaming halt. I would have stroked Aili's neck to calm and thank her, but I didn't dare move except to vault off her back.

I kept a grip on the reins, expecting her to erupt again once my weight was gone, but she stood frozen. Her eyes rolled white; her breath came fast and hard.

This was not good. She could throw herself into shock or lose her mind completely and never get it back.

I began to breathe deep and slow, calming myself down to my center. I was distantly aware of the arena around me, the older mare and her rider gone still, the flock of ghosts in the vaulting. My focus narrowed to the mare in front of me and the battle inside her.

"Out," I said. "Be gone. Leave!"

I could feel the spirit battering against its bonds. A horse's mind has depths and heights that most humans would never believe, let alone comprehend. It's as alien as anything you might find out among the stars. For a human consciousness to be caught in it, even decades after death, must be a peculiar horror.

I was not about to invite the ghost into my own mind. I have empathy enough, but I'm not insane. Whoever it was—he, I thought; it had that flavor about it—was well and truly dead, and should have the grace to remain that way.

"*Out!*"

Aili bucked and plunged. The reins tore out of my hands; I stood with stinging fingers and aching throat, while she circled the arena, around and around.

I followed her with the edges of my vision. My focus was on the wavering, shadowy thing in front of me, hardly more than a shimmer in the damp, chill air.

"Whatever you want," I said, "whatever you need, ask. But no more stealing."

The ghost drew himself up. In life he'd been one of the redheaded Darkovans, with a cast of feature that I'd learned to notice.

Aristocrat, I thought, as this world measured such things. Even depleted by his battle, he had strength enough to show himself to me in almost solid form. Not long, still, and not enough to speak—or maybe he chose not to. Ghosts can be capricious.

Well, and so can I, and I have the weight of flesh behind me. I swept my hand through him, dissipating him like mist.

Aili wound down slowly. She was a wise one even in a galloping fit: her reins were unbroken, though she'd trailed them in the dirt. After some little time she let me catch them as she cantered past, though I had to run with her down half the long side of the arena before she stopped.

She stood wringing wet, with sides heaving, but her head was still up, and she snorted at the ghosts in the vaulting. "Those won't hurt you," I said. "Or touch you, either. I promise."

She rolled a skeptical eye at me. I walked forward, and she followed; that habit had formed already.

On my third circuit of the arena, as she began to cool down perceptibly, MacAran stepped in front of me. "That," he said, "was impossible."

He looked angry. That often happens when the world and the world view clash. I met his anger blandly, as I would with one of the horses, and said, "Shall I apologize? Or may I cool down this horse first?"

He stepped aside. He still had his own mare in hand, with her air of lofty calm. I felt her spread it like a cloak over the young one. Aili sighed and at last, if stiffly, lowered her neck.

"There are no ghosts," he said, stalking along beside me. "When we die, we go to the Overworld, and then...somewhere. No one knows where. We don't walk without our bodies. Not once those bodies are gone."

"You're very sure of that." I shouldn't have said it; it's never wise to get into religious arguments, on any world. But I couldn't help myself.

"I *know*—" He broke off. "This must be a *Terranan* thing. Something you brought with you. Some—*thing*—that has nothing to do with us. Or our world."

"It is possible," I said as neutrally as I could manage. I had brought a gift with me that seemed to be unknown here, or so deeply denied that no one would recognize it. The ghosts' frustration was rather extreme, as was their strength, once they managed to manifest.

I'd learned, with difficulty, not to miss the Terran databases or the ease and speed of access that I would have had even in that distant outpost which was our spaceport, but just then I craved them with an addict's ferocity. I wanted to know what was really going on here. I *needed* to know.

Even if I could have run the searches, this being a proscribed world would have meant an impenetrable wall of *Access Denied*. I heaved a sigh as deep as any long-suffering horse's, and kept my mouth shut, and focused on Aili. She was a little shocky still; I didn't want her colicking after all she'd been through.

~oOo~

I stayed with Aili that night, wrapped in blankets and bedded in straw. The stable hands clearly thought I was insane, but that's a condition common to horse people; they shrugged and left me to it.

MacAran stayed for a while, which let me catch a little sleep. He left after evening stable rounds. Aili was a little low but otherwise normal; my gut told me she'd taken no lasting harm.

Still, I stayed. I didn't trust the ghosts of this place to let her be, now she'd been ridden. One of them would try to succeed where the first had failed. Spirits' hunger for the warmth of flesh was strong, and she was open in ways she hadn't been before this long day began.

"It is your fault, you know," the ghost of the old woman said. She seemed to be standing outside the stall, with her feet braced sturdily on the floor. The lamplight shone through her.

"You want me out of here," I said. "Off this world."

"Oh, no," she said. "We need you. That's irony, you know. Or you will know. Tell MacAran you want to meet his sister."

"Why?"

She was already beginning to fade. I couldn't shout at her—I'd wake the mare, who had fallen into a doze. I hissed instead. "I hate coy, damn you. Tell me what you want me to do."

"Her name is Mhari," the ghost said. "Tell her the truth."

"Will she believe me?"

Of course there was no answer. The ghost was gone. One last word she left with me—a name. "Valery."

~oOo~

Angus MacAran's sister found me before I could go hunting for her. She rode into Armida in the calm after the storm, accompanied by a pair of women armed with swords, and a small, wide-eyed, tongue-tied girl with hair so red and skin so white they glowed in the fitful blood-red sunlight.

Mhari was older than I, taller than her brother by a head, and as strikingly redheaded as the child with her. They might be mother and daughter, but my breeder's eye said no, not quite. Related, yes, in the convoluted way of rare breeds of any species.

I wasn't introduced to the child, which might be significant or might not. I'd learned already that this culture was complicated. Mhari dismounted briskly, strode up to me, and said, "Well, then. You're not what I expected."

"Nor are you," I said. "I thought women were seldom seen and never heard, here."

She laughed, a deep, infectious sound that startled me even more than the rest of her. "Not hardly! You've been mewed up here the whole time, haven't you? Don't you miss the company of women?"

I'd thought she was going to ask if I missed my fellow Terrans. I had to stop and shift, and find an answer that would make some sort of sense. All I could manage was, "One learns to cope."

"That is true," she said. She had managed to draw me in and turn me without touching, leading me into a part of the great house that I hadn't entered yet.

The little girl followed us silently. The swordswomen were gone, and the men as well, even MacAran.

My quarters were serviceable and, I'd thought, rather elegant, but now I saw that I must have been housed in servants' accommodations. The suite of rooms in which Mhari settled all of us had a considerably more palatial air, though there was a sense of age and long use about them.

Here were servants in the plural rather than the taciturn if efficient elderly woman who had been looking after what needs I had. They fed us a minor feast in the warmest room I'd been in since I left the spaceport, and left us to enjoy it at our leisure.

Mhari had a noble appetite and no shame about it, either. I was fairly hollow around the middle myself; I matched her plate for plate and bowl for bowl, until there was nothing left but crumbs and a bottle of fairly acceptable wine.

"You can grow grapes here?" I asked.

"There are relatively warm areas," she said, "and varieties of grapes that have adapted, as have the humans and their horses."

And their ghosts, I thought.

There were none in evidence here, but I knew better than to think that meant anything. I sipped my wine and basked in the warmth of the fire, and did my best not to fall asleep.

"Tell me," Mhari said, "*Mestra* Tahawy, how it is that a woman becomes a master of horse."

"Noura," I said. "My name is Noura."

"Noura," Mhari said. "Were you born to the art?"

"Not really," I said. "My aunt by marriage was a rider in the school, and I was horse-mad as girls often are on Terra. I begged, she submitted my application, I passed. I groomed horses and oiled saddles for years, and learned to ride in among the rest of it."

"Very well, my brother says."

"Your brother is kind."

She snorted. "My brother is a man, and men have to bestow their approval in order to feel manly. He admits you have skills he never thought possible, and gifts that he didn't know could exist."

Her brow arched at that. Even across the gulf of cultures, I caught a whiff of meaning. "What, that I believe horses are sentient, and he's of the dumb-animal philosophy?"

"That," she said, "and more. Our family has the Gift of mastering animals."

The way she said it, she wasn't speaking strictly metaphorically. She meant something specific. "There's more to what I do than mastery," I said.

She bent her head.

"I'm to tell you," I said, or the wine said, or the ghost running the chill of her presence down my spine, "that I speak not only to horses but to the dead. They gave me a name for you. Valery."

Her face went stark white. She swayed, but caught herself on the table's edge.

I drained the last of the wine. It had already gone to my head; now it sat leaden in my stomach. I set the cup down carefully and folded my hands and waited.

Patience is a horseman's skill. It took Mhari a long count of heartbeats to find her composure again. Her voice when she spoke was barely steady. "Who gave you that name?"

"She never has introduced herself," I said, "except to give me the impression that she lived a very long time ago, and is extremely frustrated with what she calls the head-blindness of the living on this world."

Mhari choked. She was laughing, I realized, though it had a distinct edge of pain—or maybe panic. "She said that? Head-blind?"

"Is that not a word?" I asked.

"Oh, it is a word," she answered. "It's the irony that cuts."

I went back to waiting again.

Finally Mhari said, "Oh, you're good. You won't ask, will you?"

"What should I ask?"

She drew a pendant from beneath her bodice: a pouch of what looked like silk, on a silken ribbon. She handled it with care, as if it would break, or perhaps explode.

I continued to wait. I could feel the ghosts now, crowding close; they drained the room of warmth and reduced the fire to a low flicker.

Mhari seemed oblivious. She tipped the bag's contents into her palm: a faceted blue jewel, flickering deep within. "Do you know what this is?"

I shook my head. The ghosts knew, but they were refusing to tell. Mhari would have to do that. It was her task, they gave me to understand. Her responsibility.

"This," she said, "is why our world is proscribed. It's our greatest asset, and our greatest secret—though there are those who would make it known everywhere that humans go. I have doubts as to the wisdom of such a course, myself, but I'm no great power in this world."

The ghosts had their own opinions of that—and not all agreed. The old lady had to shout them down so that I could hear what Mhari went on to tell me: briefly, as such things went, and rather clinically, as if reciting from a book.

Laran and *leroni*. Magic, if you will. Psychic powers. Sorcery and sorceresses—female stronger than male, for the most part, and greater in worldly power, too.

She opened a whole world to me that evening in front of the dying fire, a whole new way of understanding this place to which I had been sent. The depth of her trust startled me at first, until she made it clear how little I could hide from her—thoughts, memories, reactions.

And ghosts. Through me she could hear them, and sense them, too; they weren't manifesting for anyone's sight tonight.

"Mechanics," I said. "That's what she called you. Technicians. What do you suppose that makes me?"

"An artist," Mhari said. "You're not the usual run of *Terranan*, are you?"

I had to think about that. After a while I said, "I'm quite usual, in many places. Better at horses than most, maybe, but in the rest, I'm nothing exceptional. But you wouldn't see that, would you? Soldiers, diplomats, traders—that's what comes out here. Male, mostly, because of what's understood of your culture. They're a very small fraction of what we are."

"I see that," she said as slowly as I had—thinking, too, and processing. We both had a great deal to ponder.

We might have gone away to do it, but the ghosts had no patience. A gust of icy wind killed the fire. In the darkness a thin small voice said, "Light. I need light."

A blue glow swelled in the room. Mhari had unveiled her matrix.

I saw the little girl's face in that eerie light, blank and pale, with shadowed eyes. Her mouth opened in a shriek that came near to splitting my skull.

One word, over and over. *"No! No! No! No!"*

Darkness fell again. Silence was slower. Little by little my eyes adapted to the faint glow of embers.

My ears were ringing, but I heard Mhari say, "Valery?"

There was no answer. My hands, groping, found a candle on the table; I inched toward the hearth.

I deliberately kept my eyes on the embers and not on the crowded blackness of the room. All the ghosts were there, more than I could count, or wanted to. Centuries' worth.

The candle sprouted a flame that grew tall and still, nothing like any natural flame I'd ever known, but it shed enough light to drive back the ghosts.

All but the one that had possessed Mhari's young companion. She sat bolt upright beside the table, and the candlelight turned her face into a death mask.

Those were not her small pointed features, to my eyes, though they had a similar cast. This was or had been male, and he was older than the child he inhabited, though not very old.

Mhari couldn't see him. She was staring at me, as if she'd forgotten the child existed. "Tell me about Valery," I said, not taking my eyes from him.

"Valery." The breath she drew in had the catch of a sob. "He was one of us in the Tower at Dalereuth. Technician in the circle. Talented, a little wild, and arrogant, but young ones often are. He'd heard a little too much about forbidden towers and altered traditions.

"One night when he was on the relays, doing maintenance only, and alone but for the monitor, he tried something that he must have been planning for some time. I don't know if I can explain it. It had to do with enhancing the power in the screens, making them more efficient, but also with taking the Keeper's place—channeling forces that needed far more skill and strength than he had.

"He was dead before we could get to him, and the monitor near death; she died a few days after, but her mind was gone long before her body let go. The damage to the screens was considerable; and the circle...it was as if we'd lost a part of ourselves. Some of us never recovered; they left the Tower and didn't come back. I was too stubborn to do that, but it was a good long while before I was myself again."

She spoke clearly, dispassionately, distilling that terrible night and its aftermath into a few bald words. Even I could feel the pain behind them. The grief, the guilt.

"If he died in a Tower," I said, "what's he doing here? Ghosts stay where their unfinished business is. Or where they were happy, or miserable. Or they attach to things, or people—but he was here before you came. Is there someone else here who mattered to him? Or something that was his?"

"Or someone who can see him?"

That startled me. I hadn't had time to understand what it meant, the things she was and could do. She was a magician in the very old sense: a master of technical magic. Psionics. Matrix technology, which I would have to think long and hard about, ask many more questions, before it all made sense.

Of course she could make connections that managed to elude me. She was trained to do just that.

"*Ya Allah*," I said in the language of my childhood. "If that's true, every wandering spirit on Darkover is going to find its way here—drawn to me like a beacon in the dark." I had a desperate urge to leave then, ride out no matter the hour, and bolt for the spaceport—hoping and praying to outrun the ghosts.

Sanity prevailed. Or what passed for it in the state I was in. I had a commitment here. Obligations. And who could be sure that if my fears were real, the ghosts wouldn't follow wherever I tried to go?

I had to stay. Valery was lodged deep in the little girl's body and mind, doing what damage I could only imagine.

She sat perfectly still, hands folded her in lap. Whatever battle she was fighting, she showed no sign of it.

"Valery," I said. "Valery, come out."

Neither he nor the child moved. I glanced over my shoulder at Mhari. "I'm sorry," I said, "but what is her name?"

"Callie," Mhari answered. "Callista."

"Callista," I said, pitching my voice to be heard through the veils of consciousness. "Callista, help me. Tell him to leave. We want to help him if we can, but not if he keeps stealing bodies."

"I need life," Valery said through Callista. "I need to be warm. It's cold. So cold."

I'd heard of such things but never seen it. The spirits I'd spoken to might have business to finish or messages to send, but outside of stories I'd never seen any that wanted to be alive again.

"Something's not right," I said.

Mhari snorted. "Is there anything right about this?"

I shook my head. It might be rude, but I needed space to think. "We hear of spirits who ride the living to feed their own or a sorcerer's power. Genuine possession—taking a body to live in it— is the province of things that have never lived. This is a human spirit, but what he wants doesn't fit. I'd say it's another aspect of your world's unusual nature and talents, but the rest of the dead here are as ordinary as the dead can be."

A blast of cold pierced through me. "*Ordinary?*" The old lady sniffed loudly, though she'd had no breath for several hundred years. "I resent that."

"Normal, then," I said. "As you should be."

"We are that," she said, mollified. "By the numbers, as you people like to say, death is considerably more normal a state than life."

"Is it life he craves?" I asked. "Or warmth? Blood? The ancient dead fed on that, I'm told, though they got out of the habit after the Christians bent the world in their direction."

"We certainly don't crave blood," the old lady said, "and as for warmth, we can feed on that whenever there's a fire. Or any other energy that might happen past—sunlight, even. That boy over there—he's odd."

"How?"

She didn't answer.

Of course not. That would have made things simpler.

Mhari was staring at me with an expression I could all too easily read. She was trying not to think that I'd lost my mind. Talking to myself; hearing voices.

Callista hadn't moved at all, or spoken. I could still see that other face laid over hers.

"Mhari," I said. "Take out your matrix again."

She didn't argue, for which I breathed a blessing. The cold blue light swelled in the room. It was stronger than before: brighter, steadier.

I could feel Mhari's startlement, a tightening in my own stomach. My body tingled; I hovered just on the edge of an urge to sneeze. I wanted to laugh at that, but I didn't dare.

Callista had been still before, but now she was frozen, absolutely motionless, inside and out. Valery's terror had gone beyond voice or speech. He was completely lost—drowned in light.

"Cold," I said, or thought, or breathed. "So cold. Trapped in the blue. Lost—bound—can't—"

I felt him inside me. He'd leaped out of the child. Her skin was tight and cramped. Mine was better.

I had a moment's vision of the world as he saw it: networks of energies contained in crystal lattices, structures so intricate and so precise that the scientist in me joined the artist to stand in awe. They were beautiful, and they were terrible. They were traps to snare a soul.

The gathering of ghosts at Armida had drawn him. He saw them as clusters of energy, constellations of light both large and small. He couldn't touch or merge with them, but he could follow them toward the warmth of the living.

And there I was, able to see and hear him, with living things all around me, both animal and human. He could force his way into them, but they weren't enough. He wanted—he needed—

My heart was slowing. My body was cooling as he drained it of warmth. He was desperate, but not to feed. To be free.

"Mhari," I said. My voice sounded faint and far away. "Mhari, can you, will you—"

She didn't understand. How could she? I barely did myself.

Soft presence wrapped around me. A memory of warm breath, strong neck, mane falling like water.

Galatea.

Mount, he willed me. *Ride.*

I saw him in the Winter Hall, in a slant of sunlight through the crystals of a chandelier. He was saddled and bridled in white and gold. The scarlet of the saddlecloth was as bright as blood.

That broad back was home, that lift and coil of effortless power, that swift response to rein and weight and leg. I took the reins in my left hand; in the right was the birch sapling that was all the whip we had ever carried, in all the years of our schooling, held upright like a sword.

We rode the pattern cast in light on the floor, lines of blue and gold that recalled the facets of a jewel. There were others with us, riding on either side: Mhari, and an older woman of impressive girth and upright carriage. The horse that Mhari rode looked remarkably like the mare Angus had been training for her, and the old lady was riding the young one who had won my heart.

Galatea snorted gently—even in death he was a gentleman of parts—but his steps never faltered and his balance didn't waver. Forward in passage; collect; canter; pirouette; canter; collect, collect, collect; piaffe—gathering strength, sinking deep on his haunches.

And then up, with a pure and exhilarating surge of power, a leap into the light, and a kick so fierce it flung me straight up out of the saddle—and broke the bonds of energy that had trapped the young man's spirit.

I came down as I had a thousand times, back to the solidity of Galatea's saddle, finding my own balance again, coming to earth and sudden, singing stillness.

Valery was gone. I ran my hand down Galatea's neck, committing the sweep of it to memory—as if I hadn't done that already, year after year, since that first day when I settled gently on his young and untried back.

He blew out softly, as horses do when they're content. More than one spirit had released itself tonight.

I dismounted slowly. I let the tears come; there was no shame in them.

He laid his head in my arms, resting against my chest and holding for a long moment. As my own breath sighed out of me, he melted away, dissipating into the last of the light.

~oOo~

"Do you think anyone will ever believe us?"

Mhari had come down to the riding hall in the morning, ostensibly to inspect the mare her brother was training for her. But I knew, and Aili knew, that there was more to it.

Aili stood relaxed under me while MacAran put the older mare through her paces. Mhari leaned on the rail as she spoke and stroked the sleek silver neck—idly, it seemed, but I could feel the lines of energy shifting, smoothing rough edges, strengthening weaknesses, bringing the whole into balance.

Not many on Earth would believe what we had done—and no one on Darkover. Their arts of the mind had taken a completely different direction.

"Would you be offended if I observed that Darkovans and Terrans are more alike than they might imagine?" I asked.

Mhari narrowed her eyes at me. "I might. Or I might ask what you mean by that."

"Mechanics," I said. "Focused on their technologies. Blind to the worlds beyond, and so very sure that those worlds don't exist."

Mhari sniffed, sounding remarkably like the most outspoken of Armida's ghosts. "I am offended, rather—but it's true. He really is gone, isn't he?"

"Yes." I smoothed the dark mane on Aili's pale neck. Mhari

meant Valery, of course. I meant someone else, too. Someone I'd never forget, but whom I'd begun, finally, to let go.

"When you've been here a while longer," Mhari said, "and your students of both species are ready to work on their own, you should come to Dalereuth. See a little more of our world; visit me. Show us some of your art with horses."

"And with something else?"

"Maybe," she said.

And maybe I'd be pursued by hordes of spirits, all clamoring for me to hear them, see them, help them.

It might have been exhaustion after the night before, or Aili's deepening calm under Mhari's hand, but I found I wasn't afraid. Rather the opposite, in fact.

I took a deep breath, all the way down, and let it go in a long sigh, and smiled. "I'd like that," I said.

Kira Ann
by Steven Harper

Not every traveler comes to Darkover in joy; some travel for reasons that are far darker and deadlier. No world is immune from crime, from hatred and exploitation, and therefore there will always be a need for those whose mission it is to prevent harm and bring wrong-doers to justice. But on Darkover, neither is a simple matter, as Steven Harper's hard-boiled cop discovers.

Steven Harper is the pen name for Steven Piziks, a name no one can reliably spell or pronounce. Marion Zimmer Bradley bought his very first short story for *Sword and Sorceress IX* way back in 1990, and his keyboard has been clattering ever since. He's written some twenty novels over the years, including *The Silent Empire* series and *The Clockwork Empire* steampunk series. Steven also teaches English in southeast Michigan. When not writing, he plays the folk harp, dabbles in oral storytelling, and spends more time online than is probably good for him. Visit his web page at www.stevenpiziks.com.

Alone, David North pulled the stupid cloak tighter around his body and slunk through the darkening streets of—what the hell was this city called? Bender? Thunder? Thendara. The name made him think of his ex-girlfriend. Her name was Brenda, though she'd been a damn sight warmer than this godforsaken shithole of a city. The wind slid under his cloak like a cold fish that wanted to get cozy, and a thin sleet pissed all over him. Snow crunched beneath his boots. This was supposed to be spring? Right now, North wanted nothing more than to wrap himself around a space heater, a cup of hot decaf, and a warm lady, and not necessarily in that order. Throw in a rare steak, and he'd ascend a golden staircase to heaven.

With an inward sigh, he crunched past cold buildings of stone, wood, and even thatch. To a cop's eye, Thendara looked like something out of a bad fairy tale—lots of winding streets, hidden alleys, and overhung second stories that cast purple shadows on the people hurrying through the street below. The place was practically designed to give crooks, cons, and pissant pickpockets easy places to hide. The cloaks that the natives wore disguised body shapes, and the hoods hid faces and hair. You could slice someone in half with one of those swords and vanish into the crowd, and no one would be able to identify you later, no they wouldn't. On the other hand, the cloaks also hid the identity of a Terran cop who was as out of place as a parrot in a fish tank.

A small tremble grumbled through the ground under North's boots. Did Thendara get earthquakes? North had no idea, and frankly he didn't give a flip. He wouldn't be here long enough for it to matter. He checked his retina display. Twenty yards, then left. A pair of women passed him, baskets under their arms, their cloaks half open against what they probably thought was a fine spring breeze. Beyond the city, the last bit of red sun slid toward a distant horizon. The cold gnawed through North's bones, and he wondered how anyone survived winter on Cottman IV, where winter clamped down seven or eight months out of its long year. This section of Thendara was given over to a litter of inns and taverns, and most of them hung lanterns and torches over the front doors, but the yellow light only lengthened the shadows and made them stronger.

A laughing, raucous crowd of people in the ubiquitous cloaks and old-fashioned dresses, breeches, and tunics milled about, wandering in and out of the taverns in a gelatinous street party, enjoying the Cottman spring. But for the strange clothing, they looked like any other humans—tall, short, thin, heavy, young, aging. Except all of them were white, with fair hair and pale complexions. No one got a suntan under the weak Cottman sun. In this case, North lucked out. His ash-blond hair and blue eyes blended right in. He hadn't quite reached forty, so he didn't even stand out as particularly young or old. North could slip into nearly any crowd, but stay apart from it.

Apart. That seemed to be his lot, alone even in a group or a relationship. Brenda had said he was untouchable, so she had left him for some guy with more touchable qualities. North didn't blame her. She hadn't been the first to do this, and she wouldn't be the last. It was part of the noise that made up North's life.

A clump of food-sellers washed through the crowd. Two men waved seed cakes for sale. One teenaged girl with a tray around her neck did a brisk business with some kind of dried meat. A woman stood next to an enormous keg, hawking ale to passers-by.

She called out to North, but he moved on as if he hadn't heard her. North didn't touch the stuff. No alcohol, definitely no drugs. Just the thought of sending a foreign substance through his veins gave him cold shudders.

His cop eye automatically flicked over the crowd, taking in the view. These two men had already drunk too much of the barrel woman's ale and would end the night with a shiner each. That gal with the four-acre chest was selling more than just the flowers in her basket. The kid over there was sidling too close to the passers-by for North's comfort, and was probably—there! His hand ghosted under a woman's cloak and he flicked down an alley with a pouch in his fist. The lady continued on her way, completely oblivious. Outraged, North automatically started after the boy, then checked himself. He had no official status here, wasn't even supposed to be away from the Terran port. This time, the bad guys would have to win.

At his display's instruction, North turned down a side street, stepped in something that squished, and found an empty courtyard ringed by tall, shabby houses that wore their thatching like witches' hats. A blue light burned in one window. North raised his hand to knock, and another little earth grumble made the bottoms of his boots itch. Inside the house, something glassy smashed on the floor, but he heard no outcry. He rapped on the battered door, then slid his hand back under his cloak. The stock of his blaster slid under his palm, slick and comforting. A flick of his thumb could set it to deliver anything from a tooth-jarring jerk to a speedy meeting with the almighty. His hand was steady when he set it to speedy.

The door opened. On the other side was a thin young man with a hook nose and shaggy hair the color of a half-ripe strawberry. A pus-filled boil the size of a small walnut bulged on his left cheek. The sight of the punk tightened North's hand on the blaster and he half-yanked it out of the holster.

Six days ago, North's nephew Jake had celebrated his fourteenth birthday by convulsing his way into an early death due to a bloodstream packed with killya, or Kira Ann, or mindblow, or whatever the hell kids called this latest designer drug. Five days ago, North had beaten the snot out of a simpering smear of slime in a back alley and gotten a description (strawberry hair, walnut boil) and the name of a backwater planet: *Darkover*. Four days ago, North's captain had refused him permission to follow the trail of suppliers because Darkover—Cottman IV—was in a politically sensitive zone. Three days ago, North had contacted an old buddy of his still in the service and finagled a limited visa. Two days ago, North had taken a leave of absence and boarded a ship. Yesterday, he had arrived on Darkover, where he'd been assigned some cheeky lady as some kind of liaison and told to wait for a visa. But he didn't want to wait—every hour he delayed meant Kira Ann dug her claws in deeper, addicted more and more people. He had to stop it at the source. Now.

He'd ditched the liaison lady, snuck into the city for look-around, and lucked out almost right away by nearly running over a chick high on mindblow near the spaceport in Thendara and getting her to give him the address of her dealer. Now North was facing the same trickle of piss who had sold Jake a needle full of death, and North's blaster was cranked to almighty.

"He said you'd come. You better get in here," Boil Boy said without preamble. He vanished into the dark house and left the door standing open.

It wasn't the reaction North had been expecting. He blinked once or twice while his brain fought to catch up. His cop instincts told him not to go in there without backup, especially if the guy he was trying to catch was expecting him, but the memory of Jake's thin body arching on the hospital bed while his sister wept in anguish shoved him forward like a giant hand. North stormed toward the house.

A grip on his elbow brought him up short. North spun, his hand already on the blaster under his cloak. The grip was connected to a woman his own age. Her auburn hair was pulled back with a butterfly clip, and her dark blue cloak fell neatly over an athletic figure. Loret Ridenow-Castamir, the liaison lady. Apparently his ditching skills weren't what they used to be.

"What in Zandru's hells are you doing here?" she demanded.

"Read my mind, Loret," North shot back. "You Cotties are supposed to be good at that."

Loret slapped him. It was a good slap, thick and meaty. The burst of pain rocked his head back. "I know how you *Terranan* use that word. Don't use it again."

"Yeah, sure." North put a hand to his stinging cheek. "Look, I work alone, okay? Always alone."

She ignored this statement and repeated, "What the hells are you doing here? You don't have permission to leave the port without your liaison. You don't have permission to wander about Thendara in Darkovan clothing. And you definitely don't have permission to enter the house of a Comyn lo—"

"I don't give a red shit," North hissed at her. "You...Darkovans may not care that Kira Ann has killed at least forty people on my own world, and god knows how many on your own world, but I do care, and I'm going to end it."

"And how will you do that? Do you know whose property this is?"

"Does it matter?" Normally North would have been frantic to run after Boil Boy, but the kid had actually invited North in and, in contradiction to the generally accepted relationship between cop and perp, hadn't seemed in any hurry to rush off.

Loret snapped a gesture at the half-open door as if it were a snake. "Ferrick Alton, my second cousin on my mother's side, owns this house. He is Comyn, just as I am *comynara*. You can't barge in there and make unfounded accusations. I was working on getting—"

"Can he use that *laran* stuff you Darkovans put so much stock in?" North interrupted.

Loret hesitated, and her hand stole to the pendant on the silver chain around her neck. North had done his research. Inside the pendant was a blue starstone, a matrix which focused mental power—*laran*—and made it stronger, like an amplifier strengthened a guitar. A Darkovan telepath with a matrix could literally bring the house down. But without one? May as well give a rock concert with an unplugged guitar.

"That's what I thought," North finished. "Tell me if I'm wrong. Your cousin Ferrick's *laran* is as small as his balls. He's pissed off at being limp-dicked, has been for decades, but now he's found a way to get it up by building an empire around a new street poison."

"Crude, but accurate," Loret agreed.

"Meanwhile, the Comyn Crankheads—"

"Comyn Council."

"—can't decide what to do about this guy because he's nobility and your laws are squeamish about arresting someone whose shit comes out wrapped in plastic."

"It's not that simple." Spring sleet was freezing into a shimmery shield on Loret's cloak, and North might have found the effect attractive if he weren't so pissed off. "His brewing houses make him wealthy. He has powerful friends on the Council, and a large part of the army owes allegiance to him. Besides, Thendara does not get earthquakes; the Council is more worried about these little tremors that keep cropping up. Lord Regis has called a meeting of the Council to investigate. They're meeting tonight, in fact, and once they've looked into the earthquake problem, they may or may not talk about Ferrick."

"Which makes me, a free agent, the perfect person to deal with him." North turned for the door again, and again Loret took his arm.

"You can't go in there!" Her face hardened. "We will do things the right way. It will be done perfectly or not at all."

"His lackey said I should come in," North said. "An invitation from a Comyn lord to visit his home is the same thing as a visa from the spaceport. Those the rules, yeah? Perfect rules?"

Loret folded her lips in the blue light, but didn't stop North from crossing the threshold.

The first floor of the house was nothing more than a single large room that stank of chemical sweat, a stench North knew all too well, oh how he knew it. Addiction and overdose dogged the North family like a pair of Dobermans chasing a squirrel. An overdose had taken North's grandfather long before North's birth. Alcohol poisoning had drowned his grandmother before he finished kindergarten. North's dad turned up in a river, his veins filled with coke. North's sister, the one who had wept over her son's grinning corpse, had gone through rehab so often, she knew the cafeteria workers' birthdays. A big dose of fear had kept North clean and sober his entire life, and a bigger dose of obvious psychology had pushed him to become a narcotics cop who worked without a partner. Partners, like family, slowed you down and eventually left you. Best to work alone.

Stone floor. Rotting rushes. Rickety furniture. Dirty windows. Smoky fireplace. Tiny fire. More than a dozen people sprawled on little rugs or on the floor. Some rocked with their hands wrapped around their knees. Most stared blankly at the ceiling. A few more looked wildly about the room at strange visions only they could see. But every one of them was smiling. Teeth glistened in the dim firelight, and saliva dripped down a dozen chins. A chill skittered over North's skin, and he swallowed acid. These people had sucked seriously weird molecules into their bloodstreams, and those molecules had glommed on to their brain cells like billions of tiny leeches, changing their thoughts, making them into someone— some*thing*—else.

"Not even caffeine, man, not even caffeine," he muttered to himself.

"It's one piece," giggled a woman who couldn't have been more than nineteen. "A great circle. It loops over and over."

Small vials of glass and ceramic littered the floor in the familiar pile of the addict house. Kira Ann, the bitch kitty who purred in your lap while she unsheathed her fishhook claws. Hatred and distaste fought like a pair of black dogs in North's stomach. In the last several days, North had become more of an expert on the shit than most doctors. The drug had shown up on Terra barely a month ago, but its white scythe had sliced through the underground culture in what seemed like a few hours. Users drank it or put it in nasal spray, then lay back and let the good times steamroll over them. Reports talked about a feeling of connectedness, oneness, bliss, and other Zen crap.

But when you came out of it, the sense of disconnect, of being utterly alone in your own skull, crashed through you in granite blocks, and you wanted more, and more, and more again, until you weren't just drinking or huffing—you were jabbing and poking, sending a sweet line straight to your brain. It was the bliss that had killed Jake, and the twisted smile on his dead lips would hover in North's dreams for the rest of his life.

"One of a oneness," laughed a man. "Bliss. Love. I'm pure love. It'll happen again and again and again."

The drug's official name was psychotropazol. Its source was the pollen of a particular flower found only on Cottman IV. According to North's literature, the natives called the flower *kireseth,* and they were aware of its effects. They even made the pollen into a drink or medicine they called *kirian,* and they used it to help sick telepaths, or something. Kira Ann, though, was something else, *kirian* that had been slapped around in a lab until it was mad enough to punch your clock and strong enough to make you beg for more. But no one made it on Terra. *Kireseth* pollen was too delicate to transport very far. Someone was making the junk on Darkover and smuggling it to Terra.

Loret cautiously followed North into the room, shut the door behind her, and snapped the sleet off her cloak. Boil Boy was waiting with his arms crossed near a staircase against the far wall. What the hell was going on? He seemed to know who North was and why he had come, and he didn't seem afraid in the slightest.

"The river flows in a circle," another addict burbled happily. "It's all one piece. Everything happens over and over again, all at the same time. One direction. One time."

Loret staggered and wrapped her hand around her matrix locket. "What happened to these people?" she asked. "Their minds are...open. Their channels are functioning. But they have no *laran.*"

"Let's ask him." North picked his way across the room toward Boil Boy, who simply trotted up the stairs. He was the carrot and

North was the donkey, but North couldn't stop himself now. Loret, looking unhappy and puzzled, followed.

The stairs creaked, and North kept his hand on his blaster. In a world of swords and knives, the blaster equalized everything.

Upstairs, he and Loret found a second floor open much like the first, except it was colder. No addicts up here, but several tables piled with laboratory equipment and little gas burners were scattered everywhere. Soft blue lights burned, and the sharp smell of cooking chemicals permeated the air. Incongruously, one table was taken up by several pots of small yellow flowers. *Kireseth* flowers, no doubt, and North knew a drug lab when he saw one. Handy. Make the stuff up here, sell it down there. His skin crawled with maggots. North wondered where the security guys were. Addicts weren't known for their ability to follow rules. Loret, meanwhile, drew in a sharp breath.

"What is this?" she gasped in outrage. "It's against all rules! Such...*Terranan* technology is strictly—"

"—forbidden, *domna?*" From the shadow in the corner emerged a whipcord man perhaps a few years older than North. His red hair was combed back, and his blue eyes reminded North of a fish staring up from ice water. He wore no matrix around his neck. "Not at all. Beakers and bottles and such are perfectly allowed, as any alchemist will tell you. Thendara Tower bottles gas for its own experiments with—"

"You bought these from the Terran port, Ferrick," Loret snapped. "That makes them illegal."

"Prove they are Terran," Ferrick replied smoothly. "Glass is glass. And before you cry havoc about my little drug, Detective North, I will remind you that Kira Ann, as you like to call it, is perfectly legal, both here and on Terra. I don't even have to smuggle the stuff. I can send my nephew Alaric over there with a sackful. His father was Terran, you see, and he can move freely between both worlds. Pity about your own nephew, Mr. North—he was a good customer for those two weeks."

He was trying to piss North off, and it was working. The words dripped acid into his brain, and he wanted to see the bastard's head vanish in a little red cloud.

Loret flicked a glance at North. "What does he mean it's legal?"

North made himself scan the room for Boil Boy—Alaric. There he was, hunkering over a pair of beakers like a scientist's assistant in a vid from the *real* old days. Ferrick's nephew was alive, while North's was dead. Justice bent over backward, didn't it? No matter how hard you worked to balance the scales, the blindfolded bitch herself always tipped them back the other way. Alaric sipped from one beaker, sighed, and poured the clear yellow liquid into a separate vial. Kira Ann. North tightened his hand on his weapon. Two flicks of his trigger finger and both of them would be dead as crows in a combine. Jake's grinning face cried out for him to do it, to make it fair.

"The drug is so new, the law hasn't kept up," North told her. "Legislation is working its way through the government on Terra. Your Comyn Council seems hesitant to ban the stuff here because Ferrick here is connected, just like I said before."

Ferrick smiled, alive and painless, nothing at all like Jake's death grimace. "Yes. Young Lord Regis is too cowardly to take the reins and actually rule. Getting new laws through the Comyn Council is difficult without his cooperation, and he's away so often. By the time Regis decides to act, my position will be consolidated, in more ways than you know." His eyes glittered. "The one who serves the brew will stand at the top of the table instead of the bottom."

Loret shook her head impatiently. "This can't go on, Ferrick. *Mestre* North may have no authority here, but I do. You'll come with me until Lord Regis has a chance to sort out what you're doing and decide what to do."

"No."

"No?" Loret raised delicate auburn brows. "Kinsman, you have no choice. If you won't come quietly, I will march you down to Comyn Castle. This will see to that." She held out her pendant on the end of its loop of chain.

That thin smile danced on Ferrick's lips. "You haven't been paying attention, cousin."

Loret flew backward and slammed against the wall. She hung there like a cartoon character stuck in glue. Her hair came out of its clip and splayed in all directions. Her dress and cloak flapped with unnatural ripples. Contortions crossed her face, but she didn't scream. Alaric watched with a rapt look on his face.

North was already moving. His blaster leaped into his hand, and he dove behind a table. The blaster was cranked to sucks-to-be-you. "Freeze!" he barked at Ferrick. "Let her down!"

"Speaking of illegal," Ferrick said mildly. "You've violated the Compact, *Terranan*. No projectile weapons allowed on Darkover. You should be more ready to uphold our laws than worried we've broken yours."

He strolled toward North's table. North should have warned him a second time, should have given him a second chance. But the enraged family guy inside him overrode the narcotics cop, and he fired a deadly, disintegrating barrage at Ferrick's head.

Or tried to. His finger refused to move. It had become a wooden stick. North felt like he had turned into a department store manikin. He struggled to move. Panic flopped around his stomach like a beached salmon and a line of icy sweat cracked out along his hairline.

"You...don't have the *laran*...for this," Loret gasped from the wall. "You don't even have...a matrix."

"You always were the slowest chervine in the herd, cousin." Ferrick cocked his head, and North's body snapped him upright like a toy soldier on a string. Alaric giggled. "Let's see how much *laran* I have."

North's hand, the one with the blaster in it, cranked around until it was pointed at Loret. North fought it every inch of the way. His teeth clenched and tension hummed in every nerve, but his muscles ignored him. His eyes met Loret's, and he could read the fear there. It mirrored his own.

"You see what comes of underestimation, *Terranan?*" Ferrick said to him. "You thought that a bunch of backwater Darkovans who rely on knives and swords would be no match for your ultra-advanced Terran weaponry, that you could just walk in here and kill me. Yes, I know you had no real intention of arresting me. I can see it in your mind, along with everything else about you. So I'll show you why the Comyn Council created the Compact against projectile weapons."

North's finger squeezed the trigger. A red beam of energy cracked through the air and struck Loret's left hand. It vanished in a cloud of smoke and blood. Now Loret did scream. It was a high, thin sound. North tried to scream with her, but his voice wouldn't cooperate, and the only sound he made was alone inside his own head. In those long, horrible seconds, he tried to tell himself he hadn't pulled the trigger, it wasn't his fault. But if he hadn't ignored the Compact in the first place, Ferrick wouldn't have had a blaster to control. The sweet smell of charred meat hung on the air.

"Imagine, *Terannan,* that I controlled a dozen, or a hundred, or a thousand blasters. Oh, the damage one person can do. That's why the Compact exists." Ferrick sighed. "But I'm not trying to overthrow the Compact. The humble brewer, the one no one notices, the man who enters at the servant's door, is thinking much larger, and you arrived at the perfect time. Alaric."

Loret's scream faded to a whimper. No blood dripped from the wound. Behind her wrist, the wall was charred black but for a hand-shaped white patch that hung there like a kid glove surrounded by ashes. Alaric scampered over to North with his little glass vial of piss-yellow fluid. North, still kneeling and immobilized, looked down as the boy grabbed North's lower lip with his fingers. He carefully pulled it out like a bureau drawer. Growing horror mounted, and North struggled to move, but his body wouldn't obey. He trembled all over and managed a tiny whimper as Alaric carefully emptied the contents of the vial into North's mouth. The tasteless fluid trickled a warm tentacle across his tongue and down his throat.

"I've changed the formula just a bit. This newer version should be much more addictive," Ferrick said. "Especially when one's family runs toward addiction. I'm sure you'll enjoy it."

The house turned inside-out with the sound of a rainbow imploding. North's mind rushed outward in a cherry bomb blast that left a purple symphony coating of sugar on the inside of his skull. He touched a dozen, a hundred, a thousand minds that sang like stars, and they caressed him with warm, supple hands that left him panting and ecstatic and horrified. Even Alaric was there, and for a moment, North *was* Alaric, a cast-off *nedestro* child, beaten and abused and looking for a way to escape the daily pain of his life until Ferrick came along with his glass vials and yellow flowers to take the pain away. A great toroid of water rushed in an endless circle, filled with endless minds going about their business, and those minds didn't understand that they were part of a greater pattern, a pattern that repeated itself endlessly, like a quilt that was a patch of a greater quilt that was itself a patch of an even greater quilt. And through it all, North felt...Ferrick. Ferrick's mind was everywhere, governing it all, pulling, teasing, yanking the pattern into taffy strands. Power sloshed through it, rushed along channels, out of every mind North felt, including his own, and the power rushed to Ferrick, feeding him a greasy orgy of power. All the minds joined to feed him that power, and it became the vomiting rush. He was losing himself, losing his strength, his mind, his very identity. North struggled against it, hating it, but the power burst out of him in an ecstatic stream. He cast back his head and let it go and go and go even as tears streamed down his face. It felt fantastic.

"One," he groaned. "It's all one piece."

North! Loret's voice in his head cut through the dreadful bliss with a glass knife. *North! You have to listen to me!*

The bliss melted like a candle in a bonfire. The sensation was wearing thin now, oh thank god it was wearing thin, becoming pale as water. North became aware of the hard floor digging into his joints. When had he collapsed? His mouth was raisin dry, and his eyeballs were tiny suns in his head. But now hunger roared through him. He *needed* the caresses, the awful, sweet feeling of oneness.

"No," he croaked.

"I'm so glad it worked," Ferrick said. North's blaster hovered above the man's open palm. North felt a flicker, like fireflies spinning inside him, and that felt wonderful, too. Not as good as the first rush of bliss, but wonderful nonetheless. A bit of power pulsed through him, and through all the other minds he had sensed before. Ferrick pulled the power into himself. With a popping sound, the blaster crumpled into a tight metal ball. Ferrick let it fall. It dropped toward the floor, tumbling end over end with aching slowness.

The awful need prowled North's insides like a hungry cheetah. Now that the bliss of oneness had faded, his original feeling of being alone came rushing back at him, but this time it brought an aching void. No one cared about him. He had no children, no wife, not even a casual girlfriend. Not even a partner on the force. He was stranded beneath a weak, foreign sun on a frigid, deadly world. Never had he felt more friendless, more alone.

The ruined blaster crashed to the floor.

Loret had slid to the floor and was now slumped against the wall, cradling her destroyed wrist. Her mental voice touched North again, though it did nothing to dispel the hunger or the loneliness. She was all but a stranger to him, an alien woman from an alien culture.

Ferrick has become a tenérezu, she said. *He's created a Tower matrix made of people instead of crystal. Kireseth pollen opens the mind and clears psychic channels among people who have* laran, *but this altered form of it opens the minds of people who have no* laran *at all, and it lets Ferrick use their* laran *channels for himself. Just like a Keeper in a Tower uses the channels of the telepaths in her circle.*

Even her thoughts were alien. Only one word in three made sense. God, he wanted another hit of unity bliss. North dragged himself to his knees. Holy mother of Christ, he was an addict. The long line of North addicts strung out behind him, and he had joined at the head. His stomach flipped over. Vomit spewed over the floor, but it didn't stop the screaming hunger inside him. That spreading warmth, that feeling of—

North! Loret said again. *We have to stop him! Ferrick isn't a properly trained Keeper. That kind of power in angry, untrained hands could level Thendara or punch a hole through the planet. Those quakes—*

"You know I can read your thoughts now, don't you?" Ferrick said pleasantly. "And you're absolutely correct, Loret. The number of users in this city alone is growing every day. Each one who joins my matrix gives me a little more power, and a little more, and a little more. No one will push this humble brewer aside again."

He strode over to Loret and tapped the locket on the chain around her neck. Loret arched her back and screamed. He spat at her feet, and she slumped panting against the wall. North couldn't think why she hadn't gone into shock.

"Keep your thoughts to yourself, cousin," he said in that maddeningly pleasant voice. "My human matrix arcs across Neskaya and Armida and Valeron and three cities on Terra. Soon I'll make inroads to Arilinn and Carthon."

"It's all one piece," North whispered against his will.

"It will be," Ferrick replied. He took up another vial of the yellow liquid and poured a measure of it into a series of brown ale bottles on one of the work tables. Alaric followed behind with corks that he pounded into place with a wooden mallet. Then Alaric piled the bottles into a large basket. The clinking was happy, even innocent.

"My own special brew," Ferrick said. "The Comyn Council are too sharp to accept a drink from any bottle I provide now, but these will arrive in the kitchen before the Council meeting, and a small mental command to the serving staff will ensure my recipe reaches their cups for the traditional toast to Regis. So kind of him to call them here for a meeting this week so they can all drink at once, and so ironic they'll do so while discussing me."

"Ferrick, you can't do this." Loret's cripsy wrist was still cradled in her lap. "Those earthquakes we've had—they're a side-effect of what you're doing. You're not trained as a Keeper. You'll kill these people, and the power you're taking from them is rippling through the very stones."

North watched the brown bottles with the kind of desire with which a starving rat watched the motherload of Swiss cheese. He wanted more, and he loathed the fact that he wanted more. He knew it was the drug talking, that the shit was bad for him. He told himself it was nothing, that *he* was in control of his own body, not this drug. It didn't lessen the need one bit. His skin itched and tongue was going dry. The dose of Kira Ann hadn't worn off yet, and the rest of him felt warm and floaty, even as he wanted more of the stuff and hated wanting more. Was this how all addicts felt, or was it just him? All his career, all his *life*, he had been pissed at his family for choosing drink or drugs over everything else. He despised them when they blubbered that they would do better, that they would stop using next time because they knew how awful it was and they really hated being screwed. He hated them for being weak. But after that first rush of Kira Ann, he would have given his right foot for another.

"The quakes have nothing to do with me," Ferrick said. "They're a purely natural phenomenon."

"I won't let you do this," Loret said from the floor.

"What do you intend, cousin? To run and tell them? I won't stop you."

That was when North's half-baked mind realized that Loret's left ankle lay at a bad angle. It must have broken when Ferrick flung her against the wall.

"I'm glad I don't need to kill you." Ferrick knelt before her and kissed her cheek. "We swam in the lakes and hunted rabbit-horns together when we were children. And you're a good enough healer that your injuries won't kill you or even send you into shock. Once the toast to Regis is over, I'll send someone for you. By then, the Council will do anything to keep me producing my new *kirian*, and I'll be Keeper to the largest matrix in history. The Sharra matrix will fade in comparison."

"And you'll tear the planet in half," Loret whispered.

"I can control it," Ferrick snapped. "I'm no weakling! Do you understand? *I'm not weak!*" North heard a tiny echo of the word *father* after that final sentence. Ferrick took a breath and calmed himself. "Not weak. Come along, Alaric."

Alaric followed Ferrick down the stairs with the basket of bottles, pausing only long enough to give North a two-fingered salute from the nose. The drug made North's legs wobbly, or he would have gone after them, and in his own head he had to be honest—he didn't know whether he wanted more to catch them or take those bottles for himself.

"North," Loret said from her wall. "North, we need to stop him. He doesn't know what he's doing."

"Hell he doesn't," North slurred. "Son a bitch, I want more of that. Do you think he left any?" And he hated himself for even saying the words. He was a cop, damnit. He forced himself to get some control and lever himself upright. "You stay here. I'll run for help."

He did two steps. The boards under his feet turned to rubber and he found himself back on the floor. It felt nice to lie there and stare up at the ceiling, letting the remnants of good feeling course through him. He could feel the other minds around him, though not as sharply as before. They were all connected to Ferrick's mind, heavy and sharp as a Claymore sword, which moved steadily away from him with the little speck, that Alaric, sputtering close behind. It was the strangest feeling. Small sparks of energy pulsed from his body into Ferrick's, like tiny orgasms. It felt nice, and he loathed his own enjoyment.

"You'll run for help?" Loret repeated. She was only a yard away, but her voice came from a great distance. "You can't even stand."

North fought against the need, the desire. It had ripped up his family, but it wouldn't tear him. The drug was a chemical, a string of molecules, and it had no real power. He told himself he was unique, untouchable, *alone*. Alone among his family, he had resisted the siren song of drugs and alcohol, and that gave him strength to rise above their weakness. But the more he thought about Kira Ann, the more it beckoned to him, sinuous and sly, and it dragged him back to the desire.

The house rumbled again, harder this time. One of the tables tipped over, sending glassware and crockery smashing to the floor.

David North! Loret's mental voice slapped him like a nun's ruler, gave him a small jolt. *We can stop him! But you have to help me.*

"How?" His voice sounded silky and dry at the same time. The bottles were moving farther and farther away, and he sensed Ferrick's killer shark eagerness. The bastard who had created the drug that killed Jake was swimming free in dark waters, and not only had North failed to kill him, North had become the very thing he hated most in the process. The bliss faded further, and the gnawing hunger grew. From below came uneasy murmurs like little ghosts. The other addicts were getting restless, too.

I'm a Ridenow. I can communicate and empathize, and I know something of being a Keeper. Now that the drug has shoved your channels open, I might be able to merge us, if you'll let me. She stretched out her good hand. *Concentrate. I can reach through you to Ferrick, and together we can steal his control of this dread matrix.*

North automatically grabbed her hand. It was cold and sweaty. At her touch, her presence in him fireworked into full bloom. She was beside him, in him, *through* him. The layers of his soul peeled away like clothing from a virgin sacrifice, and at the same time,

Loret's own layers peeled back. Thoughts and memories flooded over him. He was Loret as a child, tottering in her first steps in a sunny room and glad that Mama was pleased, then disappointed when Mama corrected her. He was Loret as a girl, trying to perfect her swim stroke in a chilly lake with her cousins Ferrick and Valo, and noticing a strange flutter in her stomach and loins when she saw Valo's lithe form cut through the water. He was Loret as a teenager, sitting before Mama with the *ryll*, and wincing when Mama cracked her wrist with a stick at each imperfection in the song. He was Loret as a young woman, concentrating over her cool blue matrix and worrying that she'd never perfect what little healing she had. He was Loret as an adult, storming through the darkening streets of Thendara, desperate to catch up with the foolish *Terranan* who had slipped away from the space port, unescorted and without a visa, knowing the mistake was on her head for letting him out of her sight. He was Loret now, in pain and terrified that the fate of her entire world was in the hands of this foreigner who knew little and cared less for her beloved Darkover.

But Loret was also North. She stood with him at his grandmother's tiny funeral after her overdose when he was looking up at his father's stony face with a child's incomprehension. She was there when his mother collapsed from drink for the last time, and North frantically shouted for help. She walked with him when he graduated the academy, earned his badge, and got promoted to detective. She watched while young Jake squirmed and grinned himself to death on his hospital bed while North's sister stole slugs from the bottle in her pocket. The shame of what she saw spread through him, and it was like standing naked in front of a crowd of Lorets, with his slight paunch and his wrinkled genitals and the hair on his back on full display.

"Stop it!" North pulled his hand away and tried to block her out. "Leave me alone!"

We need to pull fully together, North. Let me in. I can't do it without your cooperation.

But the disgrace was too great. He curled into a ball, covered himself, and he couldn't tell if it were his mind or his body or both that did the curling. Ferrick was approaching Comyn Castle now, Alaric still carrying his brown, clinking payload. Through the matrix, North felt Ferrick's every step crunch across the crust of sleet on the street while his once-private shame oozed from every pore and paralyzed him.

We don't have time to wait, David. Loret's mental voice was soft, insistent. *I already know your shame, and don't judge you for it it. There is no shame in coming from a family of addicts.*

"That's—" He stopped himself, tried to halt the thought before it formed, but it was too late.

That's not what you're ashamed of, Loret finished.

Ferrick and Alaric reached the sprawling stone labyrinth that was Comyn Castle and went round to an entrance for delivering supplies. Ferrick hung back while Alaric pounded on the door.

North stayed wrapped around himself, keeping Loret out. It was the last shred of himself he had left. Meanwhile, the new hunger nipped at him, tugged at him, demanded of him. Fear of what Loret would see kept North's mind as tight as a fist. He would find a way, a different way. There had to be one. He would fight this problem—

Alone? Loret finished for him. *David, you don't have to be alone. I came here for you. Let me help.*

No.

A small pause. Footsteps came from behind the castle door. *Jake wouldn't want Ferrick to get away,* Loret said. *Jake wouldn't want you to be alone.*

He had never mentioned Jake to her. He tried to be resentful of the way she had read his mind.

Jake loved you. Loret's mental voice was quietly relentless. *He wanted you to be proud of him.*

His will cracked. He couldn't stay like this. A small sound escaped his throat, and he grabbed Loret's hand. Once again, she was beside him, inside him. The final layer peeled away, and she stood inside his final shame, that his entire family had traveled the addict's road, and he hadn't done enough to prevent it. His grandparents, his mother, his father—all filled graves because North hadn't tried hard enough.

Loret watched while North answered his own front door to see his nephew Jake on the doorstep. She listened while Jake, weaving, slurring, and high as a cloud, begged North for money. Again. She felt both his anger and his sorrow as he firmly closed the door in Jake's face. The next day, Jake, the boy he loved like a son, was dead.

A hot tear trailed down North's cheek. He welcomed the gnawing hunger for Kira Ann now. If he had let Jake in, given him money or a place to sleep just one more time, he would still be alive. North deserved every piece of pain and every acre of loneliness. North lay on the unforgiving floor and waited for Loret to draw away in horror so he could die.

But Loret remained, tall and strong. *Everyone has their private pain, and there is no shame. I know your pain, just as you know mine. It has killed neither of us.*

And he realized that in her mind, there *was* no disgrace. He felt everything she did, and she felt not one iota of guilt, not one shred of shame. Cautiously, he brought his head up, daring to hope. At Comyn Castle, a servant opened the door.

I'm still here, Loret said, and her voice was warm as cinnamon. *I won't leave you. Join with me now.*

Someone else had learned of his secret, and didn't hate him. The shame dropped away like castoff chains, and, for the first time in his life, North felt light, even free. A bit of happiness sparked in him. Not a lot, but enough to pull North and Loret together and merge their minds. They joined like drops of water, became a single thought, a single being. The rush was greater than anything Kira Ann had shown him.

Together, North and Loret reached outward. Even without the drug, North felt every mind in the living matrix, and he gathered them to him like a spider pulling threads. Loret gave the matrix a sharp jerk. Every mind snapped to attention, including Ferrick.

The castle door opened a crack and a servant peered out. "Yes?"

How dare you? Dog snarls filled Ferrick's mental voice.

Like this. And through the matrix, Loret smashed Ferrick's mind. Only barely did Ferrick manage to shield himself and strike back. Then the battle began. Blow and counterblow, so fast that even North, bound with Loret as he was, could barely follow. They tugged the matrix back and forth between them, and addicts on two planets clapped their hands to their heads and howled their pain. The ground bucked hard like a horse, and screams erupted all over Thendara. The servant in the doorway cowered. But Ferrick was forced to give a little ground, then a little more. Loret grimly pressed forward, and Ferrick turned a flicker of attention on North.

Help me, he said hoarsely. *Let go of the matrix and I'll brew you all the new* kirian *you want.*

A thousand addicts on a pair of planets shouted the word *kirian* at the same moment Ferrick thought it, and need for Kira Ann exploded through North again. His head throbbed and every cell in his body cried for more. He was weak. He was alone. He was—

I'm here, Loret said.

And she was, and the addiction became something he could handle.

Bastard! North cried, and this time *he* pulled on the matrix as well. He pulled *hard*. Ferrick screamed, and the addicts in the matrix shuddered with delight as their power rippled in a new direction. Ferrick's mind flashed in agony red as the sun, and his mind popped out of the matrix. North found both Loret and himself in full charge of more than a hundred minds that fed them power. The ground trembled again, but Loret reached down with a mental hand, and it instantly stilled. North snapped out with a new move of his own, and every bottle in Alaric's basket shattered with a *pop*. Shards sliced his arm, and North felt Alaric's distant pain and fear as his own. The ale—and the drug with it—poured through the basket's weave. The trembling servant slammed the door. Through Alaric's eyes, North caught a fleeting image of Ferrick sprawled on the cold street, semi-conscious.

Back in the squalid house, Loret's body rose from the ground and floated in mid-air. Air whirled about her, swirling her cloak and skirts. The matrix around her neck glowed a blinding blue, and North threw up a hand against the light. Through their bond, he felt the nova burst of her exultation.

So this is real power, she thought, and thrust out her broken ankle. With a wet movement, the bones pulled together and healed. *I see it now.*

A drunkenness splashed through her—through him. She devoured power from the living matrix now, and the people in it worshiped her in rapt delight. North felt every loving thought. She was beauty and love and kindness and delight. Even his hunger for the drug faded.

The ankle was easy enough. Even perfect. Loret held up her charred wrist. Before North's eyes, a baby hand pushed out of it like a pink tulip. It pulsed and grew until her hand was whole again.

Also perfect. With this power, we can change the world for the better, North. Like Zandru and Sharra, we can reforge both our worlds. We will perfect them both.

He realized she was talking to him. Her thoughts came to him, a world cleansed of all evil, of all bad thoughts, of all poor intent. No addiction, no crime, no hatred. No one would be allowed to be unhappy or frightened or angry. A smile on every face from sunup to sundown. Always perfect. The image chilled him. North got to his feet and stood before her.

"No," he said aloud.

You can't be serious. The pain your own family underwent—

"Was tragic. And it might have been their choice, or it might have been their nature. I don't know. But no one person should have the power to change everything. That's the wisdom of the Compact. I see it now." He came forward and took her newly-healed hand in his. The skin was perfectly smooth. "Let go of the matrix, Loret. Please. You have to let it go."

She hesitated. He felt her anger toward him, and he feared for his life. Power built within her and he steeled himself for more pain. But then, with a rush of relief, he saw that she was angry that he was right. With a wrench, she released the power into the matrix itself. It burst into a countless starlight pieces and vanished.

Loret dropped to the ground. Her feet touched the rough boards, and North's hunger snarled back to life. Sweat popped out on his forehead and he staggered under the brunt of it.

"David!" Loret cried, reading his distress in his expression. "I'm so sorry! I could have healed you while I had the matrix. Everything was so overwhelming, I didn't think—"

"It's all right," he said through gritted teeth. "I'll get through it somehow. It's not like…I can backslide. There's no new *kirian* left."

She put an arm around him to help keep him upright. "It's the same for those other poor souls from the matrix. Once Ferrick is arrested, I'll speak to Lord Regis about setting up healing houses to help them through it. We can help you, too. If you want it."

And then he felt it. A tiny thread of their original bond that remained between them, strong and delicate as spidersilk spun of starlight. He could snap it. He could let it hang between them. It was his decision.

If you want it.

"I want it," North said, and meant it with every goddam fiber. "God, I want it. I won't go through this alone."

Together, they headed down the stairs.

Threads
by Elisabeth Waters & Ann Sharp

One of the delights of editing an anthology is discovering how stories flow one from the other, sometimes sharing a common theme, time, or characters, from very different creative perspectives. Sometimes two stories will complement each other in this way, but a third will resonate in a completely different direction. To begin one of these sequences, we journey now to the Dry Towns for a light-hearted tale of courtship strategy and the resourcefulness of young women.

Elisabeth Waters sold her first short story in 1980 to Marion Zimmer Bradley for *The Keeper's Price*, the first of the Darkover anthologies. She went on to sell dozens of short stories to a variety of anthologies. Her first novel, a fantasy called *Changing Fate*, was awarded the 1989 Gryphon Award. She is now working on a sequel to it, in addition to her short-story writing and anthology editing. She has also worked as a supernumerary with the San Francisco Opera, where she appeared in *La Gioconda, Manon Lescaut, Madama Butterfly, Khovanschina, Das Rheingold, Werther,* and *Idomeneo.*

Ann Sharp, who edited *The Darkover Newsletter* for ten years, is known for her articles on writing. After the *DNL* was no longer published, she continued to write these articles for *Marion Zimmer Bradley's Fantasy Magazine*. She is also interested in genealogy and is active in the Daughters of the American Revolution, Daughters of Founders and Patriots, the National Society of New England Women, and the Colonial Dames of the 17th Century. She and Marion Zimmer Bradley are distantly related, being ninth cousins.

"Sare, I have had an offer for you," her father said. Sare looked up with interest, until he continued, "—from Varlach." The expression on her face promptly turned to horror. Between them she and her mother had persuaded her father to turn down suitors from half the families in town—all of them more interested in Sare's dowry and the political and business connections with her father than in Sare herself. She was pretty enough, but not a beauty. But Varlach had money and connections of his own, although apparently not enough to suit him.

"I don't want to marry Varlach," she protested. "He has six wives already."

"Five," her mother corrected, looking up from the sewing in her lap. "Another one died in childbirth last week and the babe with her. His senior wife told me that he didn't particularly care—the babe was only a female." She frowned. "He really should stop marrying such small girls; the babies he fathers are too large for the type of girl he fancies to give birth to safely." She looked pointedly from her narrow-hipped daughter to her husband.

He sighed. "I'm not in favor of the match, but Sare has been putting off marriage for so long that it's getting difficult to refuse a reasonable offer. Varlach may have a dozen wives, but he can well afford to support them."

"Especially since seven of them are dead now," his wife said.

"That many?" He looked worried. "Sare, is there any man that you *would* be willing to marry? There are other offers, but he's the most difficult of them to refuse without offending."

"Well," Sare temporized, "it's hard to find a man who can equal my father. Do you realize that Mother and I are the only women in Daillon who can stretch our arms wide enough to hug you?" She reached out to the side with both arms, demonstrating that she could extend them fully without being stopped by the chain that ran from wrist to wrist, passing through a loop on her belt. "If I married Varlach, I'd be reduced to using one arm—my other hand would be stuck at my waist."

"I can see the value of not offending him," her mother agreed, "but I don't really want him as part of our family."

"What about calling a Suitor's Challenge?" Sare suggested. "If there are multiple offers, then there will be other families to help enforce the decision—at least until the final trial."

"And by then there will be precedent and a loss of *kihar* to anyone who objects," her mother added. "You could start with simple, crowd-pleasing contests to narrow the field: footraces and such. Once it's down to the last candidates, then hold the Three Final Trials."

Her husband looked at her fondly. "I suspect you can probably plan the entire event better than I can."

"I'm certain my sewing circle will be happy to assist me," she said demurely, but Sare saw the smile they exchanged.

That's why I want Erald. That's what I want in my marriage.

~oOo~

The traditional Three Final Trials tested skills useful to support a man and his family. The First Trial sent the contestants into the Dry Lands with instructions to return with provender, demonstrating the ability to survive themselves and to feed others.

Late that afternoon Sare and her mother sat behind her father as the contestants returned and he recorded the haul. Sare's part in this trial was to cook for the men in town from the ingredients provided.

A number of young men had made no provision to drink, guaranteeing a short and unpleasant survival time. An interesting collection of plant leaves, stems, roots, buds, and flowers told her the stillroom would be well stocked with the inedible choices. She spotted what looked like an entire colony of smoked insects and a plant whose nuts would cause double vision for at least the next two days. *Could I feed some of them to Varlach? I'm pretty sure he was the one who brought them. No, better not. Either he doesn't know what they are—or he does and is counting on my being ignorant enough to take out some of his competitors.*

There were also leaves which, if added to a common dish, would have the diners itching all the way from the mouth to the stomach. Varlach's pickings also included a sand-snake, an unidentifiable plant with oozing milky sap, and two endangered species of mushroom.

Erald had returned with a small critter, tubers, and—*where did he find it?*—spine-puff bloom stems, and a generous pail of juice from the spine-puff's barrel.

Sare cooked an ample meal from the ingredients provided, and everyone enjoyed Erald's desert rodent, broiled on skewers in alternate chunks of fresh meat, browned fat, slices of parboiled tuber and green hot-berry, accompanied by slices of baked spine-puff stems and hard-cooked sandbird egg slices, with spine-puff juice and desert tea to drink. Varlach seemed happy to eat what his rival had provided. *Of course, he doesn't know that Erald is the one I want to marry. He probably thinks I'm thrilled beyond words by his offer and that father is just using the Trials to get more influence in the city.*

Even the fact that Erald was chosen as winner of the First Trial by popular acclaim didn't seem to disturb Varlach. *He has something planned for tomorrow. I'm sure of it.*

~oOo~

The Second Trial, which Sare was not expected to watch, tested fighting skills. Sare had planned to watch through the lattice-work covering the windows on the upper floors. Her mother, inexplicably, had decided that Sare should be progressing on her sewing and made certain that she did, using the patch design of her half-finished coverlet to illustrate the progress of a contest where contestants were steadily eliminated. Only after her stint was completed and she had threaded all the sturdiest needles, normally used for leather, onto a hank of heavy thread, could Sare slip away to where she could overlook her father in a crowd of other men. At first it seemed just a confusing mass, but then she could tell that the men were in several groups. She saw Varlach, Erald, and several others, each apparently surrounded by friends or backers. She noticed with interest that one of Erald's backers was the brother of Varlach's late sixth wife. Sare didn't understand the rules, but she did observe that Varlach, wider and heavier than most of the others, probably should not have assumed that age and experience would necessarily prevail. Continuing on to treachery did not improve matters for him, and only confirmed what Sare had expected. *He did know what that plant was, and he expected fewer men to be able to fight today.*

Voices bellowed, "Foul!" loudly enough that she could hear them. Her father and two of her uncles joined Varlach's group, listened to excited talk, and then conferred. Then three of the men—Erald, Varlach, and a third she couldn't recognize from her vantage point—were led to a side table and presented with drinks. Everyone else followed and conversation clearly became general.

When her father came in for supper, Sare asked about the results of the Second Trial. His lips tightened, and he said only, "I hope young Erald wins tomorrow."

"So does Sare," her mother remarked.

Her father raised his eyebrows. "I approve your taste, Daughter, but could you not have told me you favored him *earlier*? Last year, perhaps?"

~oOo~

The Third Trial demonstrated the ability of the suitor to provide shelter for his bride. It also demonstrated the antiquity of the Trials, for the requirement was tent-making. Each of the three remaining candidates was given several pieces of leather to be sewn into a tent. As the pieces—and the finished tent—were the same size, the Trial was judged on speed and workmanship. Sare sat on a leather cushion in the middle of the group, all of them surrounded by what seemed like the entire population of Daillon.

This is it. At least there are plenty of witnesses, so Varlach will have trouble cheating. She pulled the first needle from the hank of thread she had prepared yesterday, picked up the spool from which all of the thread used in this Trial would come, looked up at Varlach, fluttered her eyelashes, and asked "Would you like a long piece of thread, or a short one?"

As she had expected—and rather counted on—he asked for a piece of thread the length of her arm, adding that she would see soon enough something else that was long. Under cover of a lot of ribald comments from the men around him, she turned to the next contestant. He smiled and murmured quietly, "About half that length."

She gave it to him and turned to Erald, who leaned in so she could hear him through the jokes and said softly, "Minx! Give me the best length for this job. I'm not stupid enough to think the length of thread I use says anything about my virility. Besides, I've watched my mother sew. Just keep a new needle threaded and ready when I need it."

Sare handed him a needle with the shortest thread of the three and prepared a second one the same length, sticking it into her cushion where he could reach it easily. As she prepared additional threads for the other two men, she looked around her. The men were still joking about items of various lengths, but every woman in the crowd was either watching the contestants—some with looks of horrified fascination—or staring firmly at the ground with a carefully expressionless face.

Erald was on his fifth thread, quickly stitching neat seams along the leather, and Sare was about to hand a second thread to the man she was now fairly certain had never been one of *her* suitors. She was looking around the crowd again—*anywhere but at Varlach!*—when she noticed a girl watching the third man while speaking into the ear of a man who was obviously her father. She handed over the thread and said softly, "It's not *my* father you're trying to impress, is it?"

He shook his head. "No, it's not. But I'm not the one you want to impress him."

"No. I'll make your next thread a little shorter if you like; it's easier to sew with a shorter thread."

"Thank you." He cast a glance at Erald's quick movements and bent over his work again.

He's doing nice work, and he listens. I hope she gets him—or he gets her.

Varlach growled, and Sare looked over to see if he was ready for another long piece of thread. Her eyes widened, and she hastily lowered her gaze to her lap. Not only had his thread knotted, as she—and every other woman in town—could have told him would happen, but he had caught the end of his sleeve in one of the knots.

Someone in the crowd, perhaps one of the brothers of Varlach's late wife, remarked that some long tools were obviously not as useful as their wielders believed. That was greeted with chuckles from the men that turned to full-blown laughter as Varlach stubbornly carried on a losing battle with his thread.

"Don't *you* laugh," Sare's mother whispered grimly as she came to give her another spool of thread. "You still have to live in the same town with him."

"Yes, Mother. I'll leave him with what *kihar* remains to him."

~oOo~

Sare didn't laugh. Erald finished his tent, and it was inspected. After he was proclaimed the winner and her father placed her hand in his, she did permit herself a smile.

It wasn't until she and her parents were safely indoors, having supper with Erald, that she finally broke. "I asked him how long he wanted the thread to be," she protested, "and I gave him exactly what he asked for!"

The whole table broke into gales of laughter. "You certainly did," her father said, "and plenty of people heard your question and his answer. I believe that Varlach will be taking a trading caravan out very soon."

"So his senior wife tells me," Sare's mother said. "He was going to wait, but now that he's not getting married right away...."

"I wish him a long and prosperous journey," Sare said sincerely.

Wedding Embroidery
by Shariann Lewitt

From the Dry Towns, the needlework theme leads us to the Ridenow Domain in its formative years. The earliest Ridenow had intermarried with Dry Towners, which is why so many of them were fair-haired, and then with the noble family of Serrais. The Ridenow Gift was empathy, particularly with animals.

Shariann Lewitt writes that reading Marion Zimmer Bradley's work when she was a girl was part of what inspired to her become a science fiction writer. Today she has published seventeen books and over forty short stories under five different names. When not writing she teaches at MIT, studies flamenco dance, and is accounted reasonably accomplished at embroidery.

Mhari had known Jhokan since they had discovered a rabbit-horn warren with a litter of babies just a tenday old, tiny and soft. She had found them and calmed their mother so she could hold the soft newborns that fit into her eight-year-old hands when the silver-haired nomad boy came up behind her. He was going to scare them and then the mother rabbit-horn wouldn't let her hold the babies anymore! Only he had been as intent on petting the babies as she, and as good at communicating his harmless intent to the small parents.

"Can all of you speak to them?" she had asked him, for his tribe were famous for their horses and their horse training.

"No, but a few of us can. Can you?"

She shrugged. But she and Jhokan, from utterly different worlds, established their own private understanding. He, after all, was Ridenow, of that nomad tribe that roamed the waste between the Dry Towns. She was Lady Mhari Serrais, eldest daughter of *Dom* Felix Serrais, and if no brother were born the heiress of all Serrais. Well, her husband would of course rule and she would be the greatest matrimonial prize among all the Comyn, or so her parents had repeatedly told her, and she informed Jhokan of that fact proudly.

"And if you have a brother, what then? I have a sister, Tsena, and she is still a baby," he said.

Mhari had shrugged. Her fate, so far as she knew, would not change. The *leron'yn* at Hali would consult the genetic records and decide on her husband, and everyone would hope that she would escape the Serrais curse and bear sons with *laran*.

Jhokan's people came every year in late spring to trade horses. Sometimes they brought other goods from the Dry Towns as well, spider silks or strange spices and sometimes the fine needles and narrow scissors she used in her embroidery work as well. Mostly, though, they were the people of the horse, nomads who roamed the great desert between the Dry Towns and sometimes wandered into the more fertile regions of Serrais and Armida to vary the breeding stock of their herd. Much as the *leron'yn* of Hali were custodians of the great Comyn breeding books, the Ridenow kept track of the bloodlines of their herds going back a hundred generations.

Dom Felix Serrais and his daughters looked forward to the Ridenow encampments, the brightly striped tents blossoming in the winter pasture, the music, and of course they always raced horses. When she was eleven, Mhari found herself thinking of the Ridenow boy who had a magical gift with animals and looking forward especially to seeing him. Together they rode horses and sought out the nests of birds and warrens of small animals.

One day a large fledging hawk perched on a branch nearby, a spider spine stuck in its foot. Clearly the bird was in pain and Mhari reached out with her mind to calm it as she approached. But she felt Jhokan, already surrounding the hawk in a blanket of goodwill and caring that was very unlike her own. He was not using telepathy to touch those not human, but something in his emotions reached them. The hawk permitted him to pull out the spine and then flew off.

~oOo~

When she was twelve, her mother died from milk fever after Eloni's birth in the middle of a winter storm. Mhari became the Lady of Serrais with three younger sisters, one an infant and Rafaela only a toddler. She had cried constantly and been afraid and felt terribly alone, for although her father tried to comfort her, he was wrapped deep in his own grief. And besides, her father knew nothing of consulting with the cook on the menu for the day and ordering the rotation of the laundry so that there were always clean linens and shirts. She had been trained to be a good girl, raised to be a proper *comynara*, to care for her estate and her people as well as show proper deference and obey those above her.

With grim determination she tackled preserving and drying food, making soap, ordering the cellars, keeping the medicinal herbs, and tending the barn fowl and the kitchen garden. At night she cried into her pillow until she fell asleep from exhaustion. Her one pleasure was embroidery, the beauty she could create with glorious color and her own skill. She had art in her fingers, and as fantastical flower gardens grew on the necklines and hems of her gowns, on her father's cuffs, on ribbons for her sisters, she could hear her mother's voice praising her fine stitches and exquisite shading.

That spring when the Ridenow arrived, Jhokan came to her with a special gift. Somehow he had known of her despair, or perhaps it was simply something from his heart, but he had trained a horse for her. The gelding, Dewdrop, had a mane nearly as silver as Jhokan's long wild hair, and a gentle personality. He seemed to choose Mhari immediately, followed her, wrapped his head around her body and pressed her close to him. She reached out and knew his feelings, and felt wrapped in warmth and care.

"When you are sad, crying into the mane of a horse who loves you is good medicine," Jhokan said as he handed over Dewdrop's bridle. "But it is best to ride."

"Shall I ride upon you, Dewdrop?" Mhari asked carefully. The gelding did not answer in words, but the snort and stomp that came in reply made Mhari giggle all the same. *Silly human, how else are we to go? You cannot carry me!* Then Dewdrop pawed the ground, impatient. Clearly he had answered the stupid question and still she stood there while he was ready to be off.

Jhokan boosted Mhari onto the gelding's back. He had no proper saddle, only a heavy blanket across his back and the bridle, but Mhari had ridden since she could walk and was as comfortable bareback as barefoot. Dewdrop knew the precise moment she had her balance and he took off.

They needed no signals of leg muscle and posture to communicate between them. They had one mind, one body, one sense between them. Together they flew across the pasture, down the old trail, over the fence. Dewdrop knew the land intimately from Mhari's mind, knew where every rock and unsound hollow lay. For the first time since her mother's death Mhari felt truly alive and whole again. Dewdrop felt like a missing piece of her soul restored.

When finally they returned to the encampment with the striped tents it was late in the day. The great Bloody Sun was low in the sky and the Ridenow camp smelled of roasting meat and *jaco* and the flat fry bread the women baked on hot stones.

"He is too wonderful," she had said to Jhokan. "I cannot afford to pay you, not even a fraction of his worth."

Jhokan had frowned then and turned away. "You insult me. I said he was a gift. There is no talk of payment between us. He is yours, and it seems of his own desire as well. If you ever speak of payment between us, I will never speak to you again."

~oOo~

When she was thirteen her *laran* came upon her with her womanhood. She could hear the thoughts of the rabbit-horns and barn-fowl and even Dewdrop so clearly that sometimes it overwhelmed her. Often she was dizzy and and her head hurt. *Domna* Carla, the house *leronis*, tested her and said that she needed to go to Arilinn. Then she gave her some drops of unpleasant tasting medicine and the headache stopped and she was fine, and her father and six men and Dewdrop took her to Arilinn Tower where she trained for a season.

She loved Arilinn. She loved the fact that she did not have to worry about the menu, the sheets wearing out, or whether the leg of beef in the cold house had truly gone bad and had to be sacrificed or if some part of it could be salvaged. No one called her from the middle of a task that took serious concentration to calm down the nursery maid who was angry at the laundress for some perceived disparity in a serving of cake or an afternoon at the market. Here was quiet and discipline. Here she was valued not for her name or her face or the fact she was eldest, but for the *laran* she possessed and effort she put forth to train it.

Here her dark red hair was only hair, darker than many in the Tower but remarkable only because it was so very straight and thick and down to her hips. Here she was remarkable because of how quickly she mastered what her Keeper insisted was a great Gift. Within four tendays she had completed the most basic training, for she absorbed the lessons like the desert soaked in the rain. Within eight, she had mastered the rudiments for monitor training and had begun to study as if she wished to qualify as a full monitor.

"You know you cannot stay, Mhari," Valentine Aillard, Third Under-Keeper of Arilinn, told her. "Your genes and your heritage are too important and since your father has not sired any sons and has no brothers, you will have to marry. We have strict instructions from Hali."

Mhari had nodded. She had always known her duty to her caste, to her clan, to her land. Arilinn was just a short respite in a life that she knew was bound to be full of small children, servants' squabbles, and storage closets.

"I still wish to learn. To monitor is to learn some healing, and that shall be useful in my position."

The Under-Keeper smiled. "You are wise as well as talented. I am truly sorry that this is not a different conversation. I should like to be trying to convince you to stay."

That, at least, had made her smile. But there was no need to answer, no need to think what her answer might have been. When she returned to Serrais, Mhari found that she had missed it far more than she had realized. Every tree was dear to her. She had to inspect the berry brambles she had planted to see if they had been stunted in the winter frost and check the apples in the cellar and the nut-flour barrels and ride among the herds. Dewdrop had to inspect the creek and the place where the fence had fallen and the very large patch of clover hidden behind the greenhouse. Much as her time at Arilinn had been a respite, Mhari was truly glad to be home.

Late in the spring before her fifteenth birthday, during the time the Ridenow were camped in the winter pasture, an aircar with the silver fir tree on blue of the Hasturs arrived. Mhari had seen aircars before, of course, at least three or four times at Arilinn and maybe as many times before when her mother had been alive. Her mother had been a Hastur and her family had used one to come to visit, and had sent one down to bring her to visit them. Mhari even remembered riding in one and looking down below at a herd of *chervines* running on the plains.

Her uncle, Lewis-Gabriel Hastur, got out of the teardrop-shaped car and, in his fine court velvet tunic, came up on the porch where Mhari stood with her father and made a courtier's bow. Behind him came a *laranzu* in a loose gray robe (who was not the *laranzu* who piloted the aircar. That *laranzu* went around the back to the kitchen entrance as if he were a servant and not a highly trained *laran* worker in his own right, which bothered Mhari).

She said, "Welcome to Serrais, *vai dom*, you lend us grace," to the man who looked far too old to be her mother's eldest brother. Indeed, she thought, with his white hair and the deep craggy lines on his face he could well be her grandfather. It seemed strange to her that he came to visit now when he had never come when her mother had been alive. Still, Mhari curtsied and went to the kitchen to fetch refreshment for such a distinguished guest, and to change the dinner menu at the last minute, which would create havoc in the household, but could not be helped.

She was delayed by the fuss as Neri, the cook, tried to work out a meal that would be fancy enough for a Hastur from Hali. Finally Mhari had had enough. "We will have plain beef and boiled vegetables as we planned. There is plenty. For dessert we can have stewed apples. I don't care what is fancy enough for Hali, he's my mother's brother so he's family and he can eat Serrais fare."

Thinking she had ended things well enough, she stomped back into the Great Hall only to see her father white-faced and her uncle leaving, trailing both *laranzu'in* behind him.

"They're not staying to dinner?" was all she could think to ask.

Dom Felix was still as stone and said nothing until the aircar lifted from the front yard. "No. I doubt we shall ever see them again. Mhari, you know that the genetics program at Hali commands Comyn marriages. None of us choose freely. Family and politics play a role, but in the end Hali has the final word. We all serve the genetic requirements of our caste, and whatever we must do to insure stronger, better, more stable *laran* for the next generation we will do. I have never questioned this. It is what makes us Comyn. But." He raised his fist, and then sank down into a chair. "Child, your uncle and that *laranzu* on a leash of his suggested that *he* be your husband."

Mhari felt sick and cold and like the world was about to end. She felt the way she had when the midwife had come in and explained that her mother had milk fever and was dying and Mhari had tried to make bargains with the goddesses, first with gentle Evanda and then with dark Avarra, knowing full well that there was no hope.

"I told him no. I told him that was impossible. He is older than I am and this is his sister's daughter. He told me that closer relatives had been mated before and we all know that is true. But damn that man to Zandru's coldest hell, he wants Serrais to add to his own holdings. He's buried two wives and six children and I don't care what they say at Hali Tower, they're in his pocket anyway."

Mhari had, for the first time since her mother's death, held on close to her father. Telepath-empaths together, she could feel his rage and astonishment along with his deep understanding of Lewis-Gabriel's pathology. She felt safe knowing that her father had refused this very powerful, important man. She had never imagined that anyone would ever think of giving her to someone so old and so closely related. The notion was vile.

"At least Nira won't have to worry about stewed fruit being a good enough dessert for a Hastur," she said.

~oOo~

That had been over a year ago.

In that fall, Jhokan and the eight survivors of a poisoning in Shainsa had come to Serrais. The Ridenow had been declared outlaw in the Dry Towns and had been hunted down. Finally Jhokan had come begging to *Dom* Felix, asking for work for the few who survived. Even stranger, Jhokan asked if he could tell his story under a truthspell.

"I know you to be honorable, Jhokan, and your father was always before you and your tribe as far back as any of my family can remember," *Dom* Felix said. "If you say a thing is true, I will believe it."

Jhokan shook his head and Mhari noticed that his long hair was matted and not so shining silver. He still wore the silly vest she had embroidered for him, but he look haggard and grim and far older than the years she knew him to have lived.

"My tale is strange and the Ridenow have been declared outlaw in Shainsa by the high lords. I accuse them of murder and stealth to steal our horses, and I wish to prove to you that what I say is truth, so far as I know."

Dom Felix nodded and summoned *Domna* Carla, who cast the truthspell. Mhari had seen it cast only a very few times before. The household *leronis* held up her starstone and it lit with a steady pale blue light. "Only truth will be spoken here while this light shines," she said, and the light spread to each of their faces, illuminating the room beyond the few candles. Jhokan knelt formally before them and spoke, and the blue light never wavered from his face.

"We came to Shainsa, where one of their great lords agreed to buy twenty of our best horses. We had agreed on a price, and when we arrived some of us, those of us who were not of the highest status, were told to stay with the horses and mind them while the rest of the tribe feasted and celebrated the great races that were to be held in a month's time. We did not trust these city lords, and my father said that they might slip something into the horses' feed so they appeared unwell tomorrow and insist on a lower price. It is not unknown in Shainsa. So some of us stayed out at the camp, and we did not eat the foods that they sent because we had our own and the food they sent smelled strange.

"Tsena, my sister, tried some spiced meat. Later she complained of a stomachache. I tried to feel my parents. You know I can feel people's feelings and sometimes hear their thoughts if they are dear to me, but this time I felt nothing at all, and I was afraid and said to pack up the camp and saddle the horses and prepare to ride.

"A slave came among us, a nomad by his speech but not Ridenow, and he said that all our tribe had been poisoned and they would come to take our horses and goods soon and we must leave. I touched his mind and he spoke only truth, so I offered him a place among us, but he was afraid and did not join us.

"We mounted and rode. We rode through the heat of the day, through the dry places until we found water. We nearly died, and then we learned at the oasis that we were outlaw and the men fought us away from the well. The lord of Shainsa said that we cheated him, but you see before you, you know, *Dom* Felix, we have never cheated. We asked a fair price for fine horses, trained without whip or spur or harsh words, horses who know only they wish to run and bring joy to those who ride them. The Shainsa lord did not wish to pay the worth of the horses, and Tsena died."

"You are the finest horse trainers I have ever known," the Lord of Serrais finally said. "I would be proud to have you work with our stock. We will need you to assist moving the cattle now, though. If you can bring them down from the summer pasture into winter quarters, we can leave some of the men who usually ride to work on repairs to the trail house and the cattle sheds before the storms come."

Jhokan and the remaining Ridenow lived in the hayloft over the stables and took their meals in the kitchen. Mhari found ways to spend as much time with Jhokan as she could, and he with her. They rode together in the soft winter snowdrifts under the ghostly pale light of Momallor and watched violet Liriel rise. She taught Jhokan the dances of her people so that he would enjoy the Midwinter Festival with them, and embroidered bands of golden flowers in green leaves, the Serrais colors, for cuffs and a matching collar for a Festival shirt. Jhokan taught her songs of the nomads, which she learned well, and to crack a whip, which resulted in broken crockery and much laughter.

Their relationship deepened as their rapport became easy and natural. They shared the healing knowledge of their people, what Mhari had learned as a monitor at Arilinn and from the healer at

Serrais. Jhokan taught her what he had learned of the craft of his people, for with his own gifts he had apprenticed as a healer himself before the murders in Shainsa. She learned from him of different herbs that came only from high in the Hellers or from the Dry Towns, and of healing horses and cattle, for to the nomads their animals were part of their families.

At Midwinter Festival, after *Dom* Felix and the other older people left the dancing so the younger people could enjoy themselves, Jhokan took Mhari's hand and led her to a dark corner between her father's office and the kitchen and they kissed, not at all for the first time. Then Mhari led Jhokan up to her chamber, for it was Midwinter and the knowledge of what had grown between them shimmered more brilliantly than all four moons. The knowledge that it was hopeless, too, wove through their love, but it was just the start of winter and the deep snows. Soon everyone would be snowed in until spring, and anything could happen. They would have, at least, until then.

Still, Jhokan and Mhari were careful and discreet during the depths of winter. Both of them knew that come the spring she would be treated as a prize mare of the very finest bloodline.

~oOo~

"A messenger has arrived from the road. Your bridegroom will arrive presently for the betrothal and for us to set and plan the wedding."

Mhari Serrais looked at her father and put down her embroidery. *Dom* Felix Serrais looked pained, aged, as if he had to admit something he wished he could spare her. They both knew this day had to come, but something about his expression made her stomach knot although he was smiling. They bred good horses and better cattle at Serrais, and she wondered if the mares and cows felt like she did, bartered flesh bred for her genetics and the possibilities of her progeny. Probably not. Mares had more authority in the herd than a *comynara* in her own household.

"Do you know who it is?" she asked finally.

"Donal Castimar-MacNair."

Mhari's perfect oval face, already pale, went dead white. "A *nedestro*? They would give me, the first born heiress of Serrais, to a bastard?"

"The *leronis* at Hali who wrote to me said there were special indications," *Dom* Felix said. "She said he carries the full Alton Gift, and that moderating it with the Serrais empathy was necessary in future generations. In the end she said she was under orders and so were we."

Mhari looked away from her father, blinking back her tears. The Great Hall was washed with crimson sunlight that warmed the stone under foot, and in this spring weather there was no need for a fire. Fine tapestries adorned the walls, softening the stone, and a thick Ardcarran carpet lay across the table. Copper and gold plate and goblets sat in the sideboard, silver candlesticks with expensive wax candles in the middle of the table waiting for dark to be lit. Anyone with half an eye could see the wealth here, the richly-carved blackwood chairs, the six generations of swords bracketed the great fireplace, which was so large that even her mother's grandfather, Damon Hastur, called "the Tall" because he stood over six and a half feet without his boots, could stand inside without ducking his head. All this to go a *nedestro* with nothing of his own, not even a name to bring her.

Dom Felix smacked his hand onto the wood of the table so quickly that two men at arms and one serving girl appeared at the doorways. "This is Lewis-Gabriel's doing. This is his revenge, Alton Gift be damned to Zandru's coldest hell."

Mhari lowered her eyes to her embroidery and she began to ply the pale green thread through the pattern of the leaf on the gray band that grew into a bower under her skilled hands. She said nothing, but set stitches quickly, a series of tight chain stitches to make a stem and then a series of knots to depict pollen. She neatly cut each of the knots at the base with a pair of elegant silver-washed iron scissors that hung from her belt along with the other tools she needed close to hand. Immensely valuable, as were her needles, they showed not only her wealth but her mastery of needlework, for Mhari was acclaimed one of the finest needlewomen in the region and in any gathering of women. The scissors had been a gift from Jhokan, costly metal brought from the Dry Towns, and she caressed them as she thought about her coming marriage to the hateful Castimar cast-off. Though what should she expect, when her father had refused her uncle's offer?

She had always done the right thing and played by the rules. She would stay and lower her eyes, dress prettily and consult with Nira the cook on appropriate dishes for each meal while her undeserving bridegroom was here. She would embroider more flowers on bands of fabric to edge the neck and cuffs of a new gown for herself or perhaps a tunic for her new husband. She would embroider cushions to replace those that had become worn on the seats of the Great Hall in Serrais, the once brilliant green and gold now faded and indistinct. She would embroider forever, so that her hands should be busy so that she would never have to look up from her work. That way no one would see the resentment in her face.

"Mhari, I will not give you unwilling. If he is anything but a decent man, to be a good husband to you, I will refuse. That is within my rights as your father and as Lord of Serrais. If that means war with Hastur, so be it."

"Do not worry so, Father. Perhaps he is not so bad. Perhaps you will be able to teach him and it will all be much better in the end than we expect. Please, Father, go spend the time you had planned with *Domna* Carla. We don't know when they will arrive, and you will feel better for her tending." She smiled at him softly, for she understood how things stood between them. And truly, for the last few years since he had taken a bad fall from a horse, *Domna* Carla had spent many of their hours together easing her father's aching shoulder as well as his aching heart.

She touched the back of her father's wrist and took her embroidery out to the porch as she often did that time of day, the better to catch the light before dinner. She knew that *Dom* Felix could read her despair as easily as she could sense his anger, but there was nothing to be said. Perhaps this MacNair was not as bad as she could imagine, perhaps the fact that he was *nedestro* and an insult was enough to assuage her uncle's pride.

The whole system made her sick. She jerked her long needle into the tightly woven fabric and the delicately colored finely spun floss snarled. She breathed deeply and cut the tangled threads, then pulled them through the back and knotted off the end before threading another color. Perhaps she would be happier with the yellow.

The very pale yellow that made her think of the bright yellow Jhokan had wanted embroidered on the vest she had made him before she left for Arilinn. How she had laughed. Bright yellow and orange and pink on the brilliant blue fabric. It had hurt her eyes, but she had done it, in thick yarn so the figures went quickly. Still, he had been impressed and had strutted around like a barnfowl with new plumage.

She cast out in search of Dewdrop and Jhokan, and the small minds she had always known flying overhead and scurrying through the pastures. As she searched for Jhokan she sensed another consciousness, one that drifted through the bright warmth of her living world like a faintly bad odor. Men. Not the men she wanted. She brushed their minds as she reached for Dewdrop and recoiled from greed and arrogance, conquest and *laran*. The shock brought her out of rapport and back into her own body, sitting on the porch with her embroidery in her lap like any proper *damisela*. On the road ahead she saw the dust cloud of riders and shivered. Her promised husband and his entourage must have been the minds she had touched.

The party came through the gate and Mhari rose. That must be Donal in the lead, and in truth he was good to look upon. His light red hair curled around his neck and shoulders, his bright blue eyes showed intelligence, he appeared well formed in body and rode beautifully. Perhaps he would love her and her father and all would truly be well.

She curtsied.

He dismounted and threw his gloves at her. "Go, girl, and bring your mistress and master. Tell them that Donal Castimar has arrived to wed."

Mhari froze in sheer incredulity. She had never been treated with such arrogant disregard, nor would she nor her father treat any person, servant or commoner though they might be, with such discourtesy. It was one thing that he had no family. But no manners?

"Are you deaf, girl? Best get going before I have you whipped for disobedience."

Jhokan, she screamed out, searching for him telepathically through the rapport they shared. *Jhokan, where are you?* She touched his mind, saw that he was repairing fences from winter damage out in the low pasture far from the house. He'd turned out the horses who'd wandered in search of clover.

She reached, searched desperately. Clover. Dewdrop. And then she touched Dewdrop, not so very far from Jhokan if he ran his fastest...

I am very fast, Dewdrop assured her.

Bring Jhokan to me! Danger! She had to break the rapport before MacNair realized what was going on.

"Let the girl gape for a minute, Donal," one of his attendants said. "She hasn't seen a man under her father's age. They don't breed any at Serrais, hear to tell. So you go get your mistress now, girl and there'll be plenty of young men come around the likes of you."

"I am Mhari Serrais. I will call for the stable boys to take your mounts." With that, she turned and went inside without inviting them in, without any of the proper polite welcomes and courtesies that she had recited all of her life. They were a pack of ruffians, barely better than cattle thieves, and she wondered how she was going to be rid of them.

Not that they needed any welcome. They tramped right in, lounged on the chairs, including her father's favorite, and called for food and drink to be brought before she could properly go to the kitchen and call for a boy to run out to the stables to see to the horses and instruct Nira to send only serving men with food, as she would risk none of the maids around these hooligans. When she returned with a tray of sliced nut-bread, cheese, a bowl of apples and a jug of water, she saw the men fondling the copperware and eyeing the swords.

"Well, my promised wife has finally returned," Donal announced. Then he glanced at the tray. "That's all you have for us after our ride? Water? Bah, bring us wine, woman, and ale, and meat."

"Our cook is preparing a proper repast, but you have taken our kitchen unaware," Mhari replied.

Donal scowled. "When I am master here, you will have to do better. I will require decent food and drink available when I arrive. And no on has removed my boots."

"I will get the boot boy, though the boot jack is just inside the front door and my father the Lord of Serrais and I myself find it more convenient than calling a servant away from more pressing duties."

He smiled with nothing of warmth or kindness and reached out to her shoulder and pressed down. "No, girl, you. I want you to remove my boots."

"I am *comynara* and Lady of Serrais. I am no man's boot boy," Mhari replied.

He did not know how to treat a lady, a *comynara*, or a Tower-trained telepath. Only marginally trained as a telepath himself, he was more interested in forcing others to his will than listening to them. He pressed down on her shoulder and, resist as she would, she felt her knees buckle beneath her. "That is how it should be and how it will be when this is all mine," he said.

And much sooner than you think. His thought filled her head so clearly she wondered if he had spoken aloud, but the threat in them lay embedded in emotion that she knew was purely projected and not voiced.

"Now remove my boots."

As she did so, Mhari felt his pleasure in exerting his dominance, his anger at the Comyn and especially his father for treating his kitchen-maid mother as the incidental pleasure she had been to him. Donal's mother had felt he had done well enough by them with casual gifts of money and a nice cottage, along with some education for the boy, and Donal hated and resented her for that as well. It was hard to say which of them he had hated more. Her well-developed empath's sense teased apart the various strands of resentment and jealousy and realized that she represented his opportunity to avenge himself on his parents, on all the Comyn, and to become wealthy in the process.

He gave away too much too easily. Something changed inside of Mhari, and instead of being afraid she felt calm and in control. She had to do her duty and her duty was clear. She had not only been raised to be a proper *comynara* and a good girl, she had chosen to follow this path, to serve her caste and her family.

Jhokan, Mhari thought, would have grabbed one of the swords from the wall and removed his head. Mhari knelt and removed his boots.

Above all, she must not ask her father to save her from this monster. Much as she knew he would go into battle for her without thought, she was certain that underneath Donal's cruelty he was baiting her, both of them, to just that end.

He has the full Alton Gift. Which meant he could force rapport, but there was another, darker side to that family's particular power. When angered they could kill with *laran*. He didn't want to wait to inherit. Donal didn't want to spend years learning to manage the estate, to be son-in-law and second to Lord Serrais when he could be Lord Castamir-Serrais himself. He planned to provoke *Dom* Felix, she was certain, and unleash the Alton Gift on him, the sooner the better. Uncle Lewis-Gabriel had laid his trap well.

And who was she, little Mhari, who curtsied prettily, ran a neat household for her father, and was known above all for her exceptional embroidery? Which, among noblewomen of Darkover, was no mean accomplishment, but no one thought of Mhari Serrais as anything more than her father's prize breeding stock. Even her powerful *laran* was useful only to be combined with another strain and passed to a son.

Jhokan would have to come. Meanwhile, she would have to keep her promised husband from infuriating her father. Which would be nearly impossible.

She was going to have to do something, Mhari thought, but she had never been trained to fight. Still, her *laran* was strong and she was trained. Donal, she thought coldly, had two disadvantages. He not only did not have her training, but he did not take her as anything more than a kitchen maid and rather less than his horse.

She had placed Donal's boots aside and came to rise, but Donal pushed her down and rested his foot on her shoulder. "Stay there and get used to it," he said, smirking. Mhari stared at the rushes and prayed that her father did not come downstairs until she could rise.

She kept her eyes on Donal's feet. His big toe had worn a hole through his stocking and it was dirty. These stockings would never see the wash. She could feel him gathering power to him, feeding his anger as he eyed the things that were her father's, that would be hers, that belonged to Serrais. He wanted to hate as he built his resentment against a man he had never seen.

Wait, she sent the thought above to her father, but she could already sense him moving downstairs. *Not yet,* she begged him, but he would not be stayed.

I will protect my own daughter or be damned to all of Zandru's nine hells.

She knew that her father could feel what the *nedestro* wanted. He was trying to build his own emotional energy to unleash that full Alton Gift, not to force rapport but to kill. To kill her father, to take Serrais even though it would be his by right of marriage in the course of time.

Where were Dewdrop and Jhokan? *Hurry,* she pushed the thought hard at them, and she could feel them riding, flying towards the house as fast as any horse had ever run. She linked lightly to Jhokan and the two entered rapport as if he had been trained in Arilinn as well and they had been working together in a Tower for years. Jhokan understood Donal's power and his intent, and the anger rising in him. Through Mhari, he could sense *Dom* Felix pulling on his boots, buckling on his sword.

And Mhari felt a burst of impossible speed as Jhokan approached the door and flew up the front steps, two other Ridenow riders in the dust behind him.

Donal removed his foot from her shoulder and leaned forward. She could feel the satisfaction in him as he sensed Dom Felix descending the stairs. Though he had no training as a telepath and little interest in anyone else, Mhari recognized that Donal was a warrior and used his *laran* when it benefitted his goals. Fortunately he had not yet acquired the subtlety to understand why he might want to develop more abilities. She could read the excitement growing in him along with the anger he stoked as he concentrated on trying to read *Dom* Felix.

Without proper training, Donal Castimar-MacNair could not pay attention to two telepaths at the same time, Mhari realized. All his concentration was on *Dom* Felix. He had no sense of Jhokan's approach, of Mhari's rapport with him or with Dewdrop. Blind and crippled, Mhari thought, and she quivered with a taste of hope.

If only her father moved more slowly. She wanted to scream at him telepathically, but MacNair would hear and besides, her father would never listen. Each step echoed as her father moved down toward the Great Hall and the death she knew MacNair had planned.

He had done this before—and enjoyed it. She could see it shimmering in his mind as he gathered up the emotional energy to unleash at her father, the memory of previous kills. More than one, she realized, and the names tumbled out of his mind. He didn't even realize that she knew, that she saw the images he broadcast so clearly that any telepath would have to shield strongly to block them out. Kiril Ardais. Damon Storn. Camilla Leynier and her infant son.

Mhari saw their faces as their names floated at the edge of Donal's consciousness. Felix Serrais was destined to join them and he could taste the victory, seeing that strong face added to the rest in death. She could see another face too, shadowed in the background, and a soft voice that promised more. Money, power, violence, and above all revenge, all the things that Donal MacNair wanted, and from a Comyn so high MacNair believed him. A Hastur.

Lewis-Gabriel Hastur.

Her father descended three more steps. Both she and MacNair were riveted to his approach.

Donal pushed her roughly so she had little choice but to move under his hand. "No, stay on your knees, girl. I want your father to see you on your knees at my side."

With that push Mhari quivered between the strands of emotion that held her taut. She could see it all as if she had stepped outside of herself and sat upon the thick beams high above the Great Hall. Time appeared frozen and she had intense insight into the emotions fueling events that were to come. She saw that Donal MacNair grinned and fed his fury as her father came down the stairs. She knew without question that as soon as her father reached the large landing three steps above the main floor Donal would unleash the full power of his killing *laran*. Lewis-Gabriel Hastur had known what he was and had planned this instant.

No, this was not simply an insult, she realized in that perfect crystal of frozen time. This had been intended as an assassination from the beginning. She would be married to MacNair, but there were other Serrais daughters with *laran* as great as her own that her uncle could claim with their new guardian's blessing.

Outside she could feel Jhokan approach as her father came down the stairs. Donal MacNair gathered his power, concentrating on his hatred of his father, of the Comyn, of all his grievances building to the blinding killing fury he needed. He hadn't quite touched the central core of that anger yet when Jhokan burst through the front door.

Lightly in rapport with him, Mhari understood suddenly that Jhokan planned to divert MacNair's killing rage to himself. He could not marry her but he could save her father.

For a split second MacNair hesitated, caught unaware by the shock of this huge, raging silver-haired barbarian before he realigned his killing fury, but that moment was all Mhari needed.

Mhari could see her father's boots on the stairs, feel Donal's *laran* coil, see Jhokan running across the Great Room with his curved blade before him. Before any of the men could move more than a step Mhari raised her arm with the long sharp embroidery scissors in her hand and, before he could release the killer bolt of power, she hammered them deep in Donal MacNair's ear.

Mhari heard his thoughts as clearly as if he had shouted them in those last moments. This could not be happening. When Lewis-Gabriel had planned this with him, he had tasted his own destiny. He had been born to become Lord of Serrais. So this was not, could not be happening. There was no man in the room who could touch him. She knew that his last emotion was sheer incredulity, and then his consciousness faded and went dark.

She withdrew from all but the most cursory rapport, as a monitor observing as blood flooded his brain. His breathing grew weak and finally she felt his heartbeat first slow, and then cease altogether. She almost saw him slip out of his body and into the Overworld, and then she knew she had best return entirely to her own body and to the chaos in the Great Hall.

She felt as if she had been wrapped in Donal's death for an eternity, but only a second, or at most two, had passed. When she was fully anchored in her own flesh again, the time returned to normal and events speeded around her.

Donal MacNair fell dead.

The men who had accompanied him stared at his body, lying in a heap in front of the carved blackwood chair. Mhari sensed their bewilderment as they tried to understand what had happened. She willed herself to invisibility, crouching behind the mass of chair.

In that moment when the men were frozen in their confusion,

Dom Felix and Jhokan fell upon the troop who had accompanied MacNair and made short work of them. Several of the men did rouse themselves in time to put up some fight, but being head-blind they were taken unaware. Two of the other Ridenow riders had followed closely behind Jhokan, and with four armed men ready and angry the few who did survive the Great Hall ran.

Jhokan went to give chase but *Dom* Felix called him off. "Let them go. They will spread the story and it will grow, and it will become quite strange and outsized."

Mhari still stared at her scissors stuck deep in Donal's head.

"You are one good girl, Mhari Serrais. One fine, brave, dutiful *comynara*," her father said, holding her fiercely.

"What do we do now?" she asked.

Her father, his leather gauntlet covered in blood, took her hand and pressed it into Jhokan's. "When Hali Tower gave you as a pawn to Lewis-Gabriel's plot to assassinate me, they cancelled any duty I had to them. Our duty is here, to our own. Jhokan has more than proven himself, and anyone should know better than to part two telepaths who have already pledged themselves. We shall ready the Great Hall for a wedding this tenday."

"But it cannot be," Jhokan said softly.

"It must be the will of the gods," Neri said soundly, as if that answered everything.

"But what will happen when they find out what we have done? What I have done? People will ask questions when Donal MacNair disappears." Mhari asked.

Her father shrugged. "Nobody will ever think that you have killed a man and so we will tell the truth. We say that no one was here except his men and Mhari, and that we think he died of a brain hemorrhage. *Domna* Carla can even confirm that this is true, since it is. No one can question how he happened to get that brain hemorrhage since only his own men and Mhari were present. Then we let the Comyn make up their own stories. They will anyway. We are the only ones who know what really happened here today, and who would believe that a good girl like Mhari could do anything to a man like Donal MacNair? Lewis-Gabriel Hastur isn't about to stand up in the Comyn Council and announce that his plan to assassinate me and claim Serrais went wrong, and that this delicate flower of a lady was able to thwart an experienced murderer with the full Alton Gift. And if he does..." Here Dom Felix beamed at his eldest daughter. "I will present them with Mhari, my excellent, obedient daughter. Everyone on the Council knows she is a paragon of housewifely arts, and is one of the finest needlewomen on Darkover. And I will say under truthspell that MacNair died while he was alone with his own men and my gentle, dutiful daughter. Come, we must start preparations for the wedding."

"This is true, then? Mhari shall be my wife?" Jhokan asked. Even the headblind could feel the hope and fear mixed from him and Mhari both.

Dom Felix took his hand, still dirty and bloody from battle, and Mhari's, stained with MacNair's blood as well, and joined them together. "Jhokan, you shall be my son and my daughter's husband, and Lord of Serrais after me. And if the gods will, you and Mhari shall have sons, and all the Lords of Serrais after you shall carry the name Ridenow, and that shall be the name of our family forever. Serrais and Ridenow are now one and the same and can never be separated."

The joy that Mhari and Jhokan felt spread through the Great Hall and glowed so brilliantly that even those who had not the least spark of *laran* could see the nimbus of power and emotion emanate from them.

Then Mhari looked around the Great Hall and grimaced.

"Are you not happy?" Jhokan asked.

"Oh yes I am! But now we will have to wash all the floors."

The Ridenow Nightmare
by Robin Wayne Bailey

The Ages of Chaos, when *laran* Gifts were developed and all too often exploited, hold a special fascination for writers and readers alike. Perhaps this is because of the juxtaposition of immense psychic power, political ruthlessness, and deeply human stories.

Robin Wayne Bailey is the author of numerous novels, including the *Dragonkin* trilogy and the *Frost* series, as well as *Shadowdance* and the Fritz Leiber–inspired *Swords Against The Shadowland*. His short fiction has appeared in many magazines and anthologies with numerous appearances in Marion Zimmer Bradley's *Sword and Sorceress* series and Deborah J. Ross's *Lace and Blade* volumes. His novelette "The Children's Crusade" was a 2008 Nebula Award nominee. Some of his stories have been collected in two volumes available from Yard Dog Press. He is a former president of the Science Fiction and Fantasy Writers of America and co-founder of the Science Fiction Hall of Fame, now located in Seattle, Washington. He lives in Kansas City, Missouri.

We have never been respected. Among the Seven Domains and the Comyn, the Ridenow are too often ridiculed and denigrated. They dismiss us as the descendants of bandits, barely civilized uplanders. Yet, like the other Great Families, we possess *laran*, however strong or weak they think we are, so they do not ignore us.

So it was that when, a few short months ago, the Hastur lords called a Grand Council meeting in Thendara, I left my wife and family behind and made the journey by aircar through dark dust storms across the central peaks of the Kilghard Mountains to the City of Trade. *The City of Sin and Vice* we Ridenow call it, and it was there that I fell into that sin and vice and was swallowed.

On the first evening of the council, as the Darkovan sun slipped below the distant mountains, I spied the Lady Karin Ardais. She stood apart from her husband and all the gathered Family members and leaned on a parapet gazing into the fading light. The chilly wind stirred her chestnut hair and rippled the folds of her dress and thin cloak. Her hair and soft throat glowed in the rays of final daylight. She radiated loneliness and boredom that bordered on despair.

Laran is weak or non-existent in Ridenow men, yet I felt these things from Karin Ardais with an intensity that made them feel like my own. Even before she turned and let me see her perfect face, I wanted to hold her and be with her. Our gazes met only for a moment, and then I hurried from the reception hall, embarrassed by the strength of my physical reaction.

Throughout the night and the next day, she filled my thoughts. The business matters before the Council seemed petty and uninteresting. I listened without hearing, spoke little, and contributed nothing. In my mind's eye, she still stood waiting for me on that parapet, cloaked in a perpetual twilight, her too-brief glance seeking mine. Feigning some excuse, I left the council meeting early and sought my personal quarters.

Instead, lost in a swirl of troubling emotions, I turned from my intended course, left Comyn Castle, and wandered alone through the city, avoiding the crowds, until I found myself on the docks and then on the grassy bank of the river. I tried to think of my wife as I stared into the water, of my own prestige and reputation, of the danger I courted. She was Karin Ardais, wife of Dyarlis Ardais who headed the Ardais Family.

Among the Comyn, wars had been fought for the deed I considered on that river bank. With an angry growl, I ripped up a handful of grass and cast the blades into the water. The current took them and swept them away. I felt caught up in a similar current and wondered if there was any way to resist it—or if I wanted to resist it.

In the setting sun, the water turned blood red. I took it as an omen, a sign from the god Zandru. My skin felt hot and cold at the same time, as if a sickness had come over me. I clenched my fists and swallowed, and in that moment I resolved to leave Thendara, to make what excuses I could to the Council, and go home at once to my lands and my wife while I still had the strength.

Determination quickened my stride. I walked back along gloomy streets as lights began to burn in the windows of shops and houses. Then I heard music and laughter, and sounds of many voices. When I turned a corner into Lender's Street, a kaleidoscope of color and lanterns greeted me. I found myself in a carnival atmosphere of dancers and acrobats and celebrants, although what they were celebrating I couldn't guess. It was the madness of decadent Thendara that they needed no good reason.

I pushed through the throngs, resisting the drinks that were offered me, avoiding the eyes of the men and women who offered themselves for unspeakable services, my senses burning from the smoke of dizzying herbs. I told myself over and over that I was a Ridenow and above such vices, that I could not be tempted.

Yet I felt the excitement, the passion, the heat of every heart around me. The joy and pain of the crowds overwhelmed my carefully maintained defenses, and my façade began to crumble. I stumbled. A young man caught me by the arm, and with that touch came a flood of emotion: confusion, anger, and disgust. He started to push me away, but a young woman by his side stopped him. She stood before me, a shape aswirl in auras of compassion and pity, and she held out a hand.

"Are you all right?" she asked in a sweet voice.

I recoiled. "Don't touch me!" I shouted as I clambered to my feet. "I—I am a Ridenow! I am...!" Before I could stop myself I blurted my deepest secret. "I am an empath! Get away!"

I ran, turning into empty streets as soon as I found them, avoiding the voices and the stares, fleeing the chaos of emotions, struggling to find my own sense of self again. When I found an alley away from the noise, I cowered down in the darkness against a rain barrel and sorted through my mind in methodical fashion to identify my own thoughts and feelings and to push out those of others. It was hard sometimes to know what was truly mine.

This was my darkest secret. That I possessed *laran* in some small measure was well-known, but from my earliest youth I had guarded the knowledge of my true strength. For that reason I lived apart in the isolation of the uplands, keeping mostly to my own properties and avoiding extended contact with other Comyn. I had never had any desire to be hauled off to some Tower to be examined and tested or to be pressed into service for some convoluted Darkovan purpose. My life was my own.

And if my secret gave me some edge in business dealings, so much the better.

In the shadows of the alley, my pulse calmed, and I erected my personal barriers one at a time, brick by brick as it were, like a wall to keep out the waves of emotion that surrounded me. I knew who I was again, where my personal world began and ended, what was real to me and what were the echoes of other hearts and minds.

Sure of myself once again, I made my way quietly back to

Comyn Castle. Most of the Council members had long since retired for the night, but a servant greeted me at the door. "*Dom* Viktor," he said, acknowledging me with a bow. "We are relieved by your return."

"As am I," I admitted with a forced smile. "I have sampled enough of Thendara's pleasures. It's my intention to leave at morning's first light. Please prepare my vehicle for my homeward journey."

The servant regarded me with surprise as he straightened, and I smiled again inwardly as I easily blocked his emotion. I made my way alone through the ancient, lantern-lit halls to my assigned chambers, completely sure of myself and of my decision to depart.

Yet, as I quietly opened my door, stepped inside and closed it again, I saw my own doom. Framed in moonlight, draped in a diaphanous gown of saffron-colored nothingness, Karin Ardais waited for me on my balcony. She turned to face me, her pale exposed breasts blazing with heat, her beating heart a quicksand of need.

I crossed the room without thinking. Her arms encircled me, and her lips lifted to mine. So easily did she ensnare me. Let there be shame or disgrace if we were caught. Let there be war among the families. Nothing mattered in that moment but the possession of her and the fulfillment of our hungers.

"Viktor." She breathed my name once into my ear, and it sounded like *victory*. I took her there in the moonlight on the balcony as we both fought not to scream. Then she rode me on the bed until the first signs of approaching dawn. For a few precious moments, we held each other, and I imagined I could hear the lapping of the river.

"Tomorrow night again," she whispered as she slipped from bed and dressed. That was all, no other words. The door opened and closed, and Karin Ardais departed.

My mind echoed with thoughts of her as I rose. It was almost first light and with a sudden new determination that bordered on manic anger, I dressed and flung my few belongings into my bag, thinking that I could still escape Thendara.

Yet her promise haunted my every step and motion. *Tomorrow night again.*

I tossed my half-packed bag into a corner and sat down on the bed with my head in my hands. The sheets and pillows bore her perfume. The mattress still bore the imprints of our bodies. Numb, I watched the sky brighten with all the unlikely shades of morning, and when a servant knocked on my door with breakfast, I ate without tasting anything.

I did not go home. I sat through the day's council meetings saying little, speaking only when necessary, avoiding the eyes of the boisterous Dyarlis Ardais, who never seemed to stop talking and who was, of course, his own favorite subject. He was a man easy to dislike, but I hid that emotion behind my barriers just as I blocked the emotions of the rest. Still, in a moment of fatigue, I felt a small quake from the man. It shivered across the room and touched me: Dyarlis Ardais harbored an intense fear of inadequacy and of being thought a fool.

Without giving myself away, I reinforced my barriers. I wanted no part of Ardais or any of the Comyn in my head. All I wanted was for the day to end and night to fall and Karin Ardais in my arms again. Still, I pushed the thought aside and tried to focus on the business of the council. With so many telepaths in the chamber, I had to be careful.

I took my evening meal alone, apart from the others. For a time afterward, I paced my balcony, taking in the spires and architectural marvels of Thendara, drinking the beauty of Darkover's star-speckled sky as night fell, the promising brush stroke of moonlight from Idriel, just rising above the line of the roof. Somehow, my mind far from my once-beloved uplands, I felt as if I belonged here now, as if Thendara had claimed me and I had surrendered.

My door opened and closed with the barest draft of a breeze. Karin Ardais did not even bother to knock. The moon and stars disappeared, and she was all there was. I went to her in a rush and buried my face in her shoulder, in her soft hair and hypnotic scent. I understood her loneliness better now, and I wanted—no, needed—to soothe her, to satisfy her even if it meant that she would drown me.

For three more nights, Karin Ardais came to me. By day, I avoided the Council meetings, fearing that my barriers would slip, that I would give us away with a careless thought. I sent a message that I was ill, which wasn't far from the truth, for I began to look like a man half-dead.

At the end of our last night, with the Council's business concluded and dawn approaching, Karin Ardais sat astride me, taking her pleasure. "I am leaving Dyarlis," she declared as she rocked gently. "I will go home with you instead, Viktor Ridenow, and be your wife."

In five nights, it was the longest sentence she had spoken, and her declaration shocked me. My hands slid from her breasts down to her hips, and I held her still. "I already have a wife," I answered. A sudden clarity stabbed like a spear of ice through my brain. I lifted Karin Ardais off me and rolled her gently onto the bed. I got up, the stone floor cool against my feet.

"What you said," I continued, struggling inwardly to remain calm, "what you want cannot be." My own words tore at my heart. Only a moment before, Karin Ardais had seemed like my entire world, my reality. Yet I had another world, too, and responsibilities. I looked at her and shivered, and the force of her emotions shattered all my barriers. I felt her surprise, her hurt and fear. Then I felt her rage.

"My wife is pregnant," I tried to explain. "I will be a father soon. That outweighs everything."

"Of course it does," she answered in a cold voice as she got up and dressed. I clenched my fists against the power of her sullen anger and squeezed my eyes shut. I heard the door, and when I opened my eyes again, Karin Ardais was gone.

I didn't try to sleep. Instead, I left before any of the Council members had awakened. Speaking to no one, not even the servants, I found my aircar and left Thendara behind, my mind focused on what lay ahead, my emotions locked behind walls upon walls.

My wife was waiting to greet me when I landed. In a soft white dress, her long red hair stirring lightly in the wind, her belly rounded with our child, she looked more beautiful to me than I had ever seen her. Yet she was not Karin Ardais. Nevertheless, I forced a smile, embraced her, and kissed her cheek.

"I missed you, Valeria," I lied. It was a mistake. Valeria's empathic abilities were as strong as my own, and perhaps stronger, for she had been trained at an early age in their uses at Neskaya Tower. I noted the change that came over her face and felt her doubt. Yet she rose on tiptoe and kissed me back.

"What transpired at the Council meeting?" she inquired as she took my hand and led me toward our home. It wasn't like Valeria to make small talk, and she seldom inquired into business matters.

"Inconsequential twaddle," I answered as I shouldered my traveling bag and walked at her side. "Some territorial disputes among the families in the north, an appointment at Corandalis Tower, some proposals regarding water rights. The Hastur lords must dip their hands into everything, you know. It makes them feel important."

I put my free arm around her shoulder and glanced sideways at her. I loved her, despite all that had transpired in the City of Sins, and perhaps she sensed that, for she became more at ease. I tickled her ear. "But I've had a week of that. Tell me, instead, how our child fares!"

Valeria put a hand upon her belly as we entered our home, and a warm smile lit up her face. "She kicks a little but seems content."

"She?"

Valeria nodded as her smile broadened. "I can read that much, Viktor," she answered. "You've planted a daughter in my womb. I hope you are not disappointed."

Taking Valeria by the shoulders, I turned her and stared into the sparkling blue of her eyes. "Of course I'm not disappointed! We must think of a name!" I drew my wife close, pressed her head upon my shoulder and kissed the top of her head. Another thought occurred to me. "Will she have *laran*?" I asked. "Can you read that yet?"

Valeria slipped out of my arms and stretched like a cat. "It's far too early to know," she said. "Now, Viktor Ridenow, you have been gone a week and come home with no gift for me. How do you intend to make up for that?"

I grinned, sensing her meaning. She was as desirable in her own way as Karin Ardais, and with our child in her body, even more beautiful. "I've traveled all day," I answered as I tilted her chin up. "Let me bathe, and then I'll think of something."

She squeezed my hand. "Luckily for you, I've thought of everything," she answered with a soft laugh. "Your bath is warm and waiting. I'll soap you myself."

I liked the sound of her laugh and the promise conveyed in the touch of her hand on mine. It felt good to be home.

In the days that followed, Thendara dissolved in my mind like a dream. The events and details, so vivid at first, slipped away little by little until I barely remembered them at all. I busied myself with household matters, tended to my lands and to the affairs of the Ridenow Domain, and contented myself with these. Valeria, with one of our servants, made a nursery of the room next to our bed chamber. I listened to her in secret sometimes as she hummed and sang, and I watched her happy moments when she didn't know I was looking.

Yet Valeria was an empath. She read my moods in my quiet moments when my guard slipped and knew that something was wrong, that I had changed somehow. Then she would come to me, sit on my lap and put her head on my shoulder and become very still. Those moments became precious to me. I would touch her belly, feel our child inside, and all would become right again.

"Christina." I whispered the name into Valeria's ear at such a moment on such an afternoon when I held her.

Valeria shivered, then chuckled as she nuzzled my ear. "Tell Christina to stop kicking me," she whispered back, and we laughed together. I might have carried her to the bedroom and made love to her again. We both were ready for it. Yet, before I could act upon the impulse, our servant interrupted us.

"An aircar is landing," she reported with unseemly excitement, forgetting her station. "I saw it from the nursery window as I was sewing curtains!"

Unannounced visits were considered rude among the Ridenow. Valeria gave me a questioning look as she got up, smoothed her dress, and prepared to assume the role of a Ridenow noblewoman. I shrugged, unable to answer her unspoken query.

Then the hairs on the back of my neck prickled. The servant, whose name was Therese, hurried to the door and opened it before I could stop her. Already halfway across the yard and accompanied by two guardsmen, came Karin Ardais.

I knew her at once, despite her black traveling garments and fine, swirling cloak and the dust mask that concealed the lower half of her face. My eyes met hers, and I despaired. All my mental barriers shattered in one unguarded instant.

Close at my side, Valeria gazed at Karin Ardais and then at me. Then she turned cold as ice.

"I'll send her away," I promised.

Valeria shook her head without bothering to conceal her bitterness and hurt. "Comyn courtesy requires us to receive her, but when she's gone, choose another room for your sleeping quarters." She beckoned to Therese and headed toward the kitchen. "I'll make some tea."

With a hand gesture, Karin Ardais ordered her guards to remain in the yard. I watched her from the door, bracing myself for a confrontation, trying to read her, but her passions danced around her like a scalding chaos of fire, beautiful and mesmerizing, but too hot to touch.

"What do you want?" I said, impolitely blunt, when she stood on the threshold of my home. Even then, as she so casually destroyed my life with her mere presence, I felt something for her. My heart began to race as she stood so close; my skin tingled from every remembered touch of her body, and all the dust of the Plains of Valeron could not conceal her perfume from my senses.

Karin Ardais lowered her mask. "I've left Dyarlis, as I said I would," she whispered. "I'm on my way to the Sea of Dalereuth and the Bay of Dreams where I will live out my life, but my course took me over your lands."

"You took a roundabout course, then," I answered.

She inclined her head only slightly. "I wanted to see you one more time, Viktor Ridenow, and meet your lovely wife. If you will allow it, I have gifts for her and for your unborn child." She threw back one side of her cloak to reveal a hand-woven baby blanket draped over her right arm. "I promise not to stay long, and hopefully we can part as friends, at least."

Every instinct cried out to send her away, yet I stepped aside in silent invite, allowing her entrance. She looked around the hallway with casual interest, then spied the parlor and walked into it as if she knew the house well. I followed her, and in the center of the room, she turned and faced me. She was as beautiful as when I first saw her, but I wanted only to strangle her as she made a show of refolding the pale blue baby blanket. "I'll put this here, if you like," she said, setting it upon the seat of a chair.

"You should have brought a pink one." Valeria came into the room bearing a tray with tea cups and a steaming pot. She looked clean and regal, having taken time to sweep up her hair and apply some minimum of paint.

"Really?" Karin Ardais and Valeria Ridenow regarded one another as enemies in a stand-off. Then Karin Ardais looked to me. "I would have borne you sons."

The tea cups rattled on the tray. Therese, coming behind Valeria, quickly took it from Valeria's hands. "Then you should have borne them for your own husband," Valeria answered. She came to my side and locked my hand in hers with a possessive strength that surprised me.

"But I brought you gifts," Karin Ardais said as she gestured to the blanket.

My senses began to swirl. Such powerful emotions filled the room that I felt like I was falling. Karin and Valeria were both wide open to me suddenly, and Therese as well, and all of it so intense and raw that I could block none of it.

"The blanket is only one gift," Karin Ardais continued. "Here is the other."

Valeria screamed. Therese dropped the tray. "Get away from me!" Valeria shouted. "Viktor, she's insane! She's a catalyst!" Valeria screamed a second time, but the sound was different, a note of pure terror. She clutched her stomach.

Then, another scream came, different from all the rest, a high-pitched, primal shriek that echoed Valeria's terror. It reverberated, not through the room, but through every mind of every adult in the room and across the Ridenow countryside.

Christina!

"What have you done?" Reeling from the psychic assault of my unborn child, I crossed the room and locked my hands around Karin Ardais's throat. I knew exactly what she had done. The Ardais were catalyst telepaths with the ability to awaken latent *laran*. She had just used that power on my daughter.

But the surprise was on Karin Ardais, for Christina was the child of not one but two of the most powerful Ridenow empaths on all of Darkover, and I felt her infantile rage. With the full extent of her *laran* abilities suddenly awakened in the womb, her sense of comfort and security within her mother's body destroyed, she lashed out in a crippling display of nearly limitless telepathic potential.

Christina screamed again. Valeria crumpled to the floor, bleeding from her nose. Karin Ardais stared in shock, all the color draining from her face. Therese curled up in a catatonic ball. Through the window, I watched the two Ardais guardsmen do the same. I had never felt such power. I doubted that anyone on all of Darkover ever had.

Unable to stand, I sank to all fours and opened my mind to Christina. I had to calm my daughter down; it was the only way to save her and to save my wife. *I love you! It's all right! We're here!*

None of it seemed to soothe Christina. I crawled to Valeria, gathered her in my arms, and rocked her. Her eyes were rolled up in her head, but her lips moved slightly, making a tiny sound, a hum, and I remembered listening to her hum and sing as she worked.

I remembered all those songs and echoed them to Christina. Then some small, weary part of Valeria's mind joined us as well, and we consoled our daughter together like mother and father, like a family.

The days that followed were not easy ones. Karin Ardais escaped but was found, a suicide, on the shores of the Sea of Dalereuth. She had tried to murder Valeria and Christina; no mother or child had ever survived an in-vitro awakening. Perhaps she thought that I would then be free.

The day after Christina's awakening, a committee of Comyn arrived on our doorstep, demanding that Valeria be taken to Hali for study. Neither Valeria nor Christina wanted to go, and when Christina became agitated, the committee leader's legs suddenly shattered. *Telekinetics*! They whispered in urgent tones before they all rushed back to their aircars. They have left us alone since, but we feel their psychic eyes upon us.

Christina will be born soon, and I dread what may occur on the painful journey from the womb into the new world. Of one thing I am fairly certain, though. All of Darkover will sense it. I don't know what Christina is. Nobody knows her limits. Perhaps she is something entirely new to Darkover. Time will tell.

But this I know. I am her father, and I will protect her.

We Ridenow have never been respected. Among the Seven Domains and the Comyn, we are too often ridiculed and denigrated. They dismiss us as the descendants of bandits, barely civilized uplanders. Yet, like the other Great Families, we possess the *laran,* however strong or weak they think we are, so they do not ignore us.

No, they do not ignore us.

Catalyst
by Gabrielle Harbowy

Marion Zimmer Bradley introduced the consequences of awakening *laran* in the unborn in *Stormqueen*. In that novel, as in the previous story, this is portrayed as hazardous to the baby and even more so to the mother and those around her. In this next tale, also set in the Ages of Chaos, Gabrielle Harbowy approaches the concept from a different angle. Robin Wayne Bailey's catalyst telepath was ruthless and vindictive, unlike the protagonist here, who reflects, *"There was an art to speaking with the unborn."*

Gabrielle Harbowy is an editor for such SF/F publishers as Pyr, Circlet, and Dragon Moon Press, as well as co-editor of the award-nominated *When the Hero Comes Home* anthology series with Ed Greenwood. Her short fiction has been a finalist for the Parsec award, and her next story is forthcoming in *Carbide Tipped Pens* from Tor Books. Her shared world story "Inheritance," for Pathfinder Tales, is free to read at Paizo.com. She is currently working on her first novel.

The women clustered tightly around Dorian's sister, cooing praise and admiring her new *catenas*—the wedding bracelet that had just been fastened about her wrist. After so many months of Tower training in relative isolation, it almost hurt to look at the flurry of women, bright in their silks and satins like a bouquet of wildflowers. Dorian knew he shouldn't stare, anyway, but he couldn't quite make himself look away.

"Serra looks happy," a voice said at his shoulder. He turned, finding he had to dip his head to meet Larisa's eyes. When he'd left for the Tower, he'd been eye to eye with his distant cousin. Now he was a full head taller. "As do you, Dorian Ardais," she added with a shy smile.

His palms were suddenly wet, and his mouth dry. "You're looking happy, as well," he managed to stammer out. Looking down to meet her eyes meant looking down the length of her body. He'd dreamed about those eyes, that body, for years. Except...

"And...and *round!*"

He winced as soon as he said it, grateful for once that Larisa had no *laran* and could not compound his guilt with her hurt emotions.

But she merely laughed. "Indeed, I am both," she agreed, and even as relief washed over him, his heart sank. Beautiful, brilliant Larisa had wed in his absence, and no one had told him?

"Don't look so shocked!" she said, eyes bright with mischief. "Don't you know it's the natural order of things?"

"The natural order in which I live is a bit different," he reminded her. It came out more harshly than he meant it to; again he winced, and again she took no offense.

Quite the contrary: "Oh, Dorian—I'm so sorry! I don't mean to flaunt at you. I'd forgotten the celibacy requirements of Tower work."

As had he, until just then. But his smile was as charitable as hers. "No, no, cousin. I didn't mean it like that. Just that..." *Just that, if only things could be different, that I might be your child's proud father and not a gawkish fool saying all the wrong words.* "Just that I'm surprised! Happy for you, and surprised!"

Though Larisa had no *laran*, Dorian could sense the golden spark of the life growing within her. It was unusual for *laran* to be present in a child and not the parent, but not unheard of. There was much that was not yet known about the telepathic gifts. A center at Hali was dedicated to the study of *laran* and its assorted abilities, along with a breeding program whose purpose was to come to a scientific understanding of the genetics of the phenomenon. They were trying to breed for the talent...which was the main reason Dorian had always known he had no chance with Larisa. He would be bred with a woman with *laran*, likely with more than one, once he left Tower service. He had always known it would be so. If she had married a man with *laran*, he thought with a hollow ache, after that path had been closed to him...

"Where have you drifted off to, kinsman?" Larisa was looking up at him with patient amusement. For a moment, he considered answering truthfully, but only for a moment.

"I'm not used to such noise and festivity. I think I should like some air. Will you join me for a walk?"

It would have been unseemly for the two of them to slip off alone together, but that they were kin. Plenty of others had also abandoned the ballroom for the gardens. Just enough moisture hung in the air to make silvery halos around the lanterns. It was slightly cool, but there was no breeze to stir ice into the air. Dorian breathed deeply.

"You haven't asked after my husband," Larisa said. There was an edge under her playful scorn that suggested it wasn't *entirely* in jest.

"And you've not asked after my life at the Tower," he returned, more smoothly than he felt. He could see it wasn't enough to soothe her, and added, "Besides, I can't think of a way to ask whose child you carry without sounding unspeakably rude." *Or jealous*, he added silently.

She pursed her lips. "For that, I should make you guess."

Dorian made a study of her, silent until he could see her twitch with impatience. "Is it someone I know?" he asked.

She seemed surprised at his willingness to play the game of questions. Perhaps she knew he was holding off the inevitable. "No," she answered.

Dorian threw his hands skyward with an exaggerated sigh. "Then how am I meant to guess, my lady? You've won this game already."

Her quiet laugh pleased him. "His name is Lewis Alarin, third son of Lord MacAran's sister."

"And why isn't he with you tonight?"

"His father is ill and he's journeyed home, leaving me in your sister's care."

"Because you're too far progressed to travel?" he asked, slowing his pace. She strolled along by his side, not seeming to notice the protectiveness that the reminder of her pregnancy had spurred in him. Perhaps she was used to it.

She nodded. "Quite so. But it's just as well. I wouldn't have wanted to miss Serra's wedding, or a chance to see you again." She blushed, but he told himself it was his hopeful imagination and refused to let himself acknowledge the flutter that stirred within him. "How long will you stay?"

"Just a tenday," he answered. "I must get back."

Larisa frowned. "Then you won't be here when the baby comes. The midwife says I've only a month or so to go." Her hands smoothed absently over her belly.

Dorian guided Larisa to a nearby bench and removed his formal cloak, spreading it over the seat to keep the stone's chill from her. She sat with a grateful smile, and he sat beside her.

"I am sorry," he said quietly, and brushed her swollen belly with his fingertips. "Larisa, I do dearly wish I could stay until the birth, and know your child." He quested outward as he said the words, guided by feelings rather than thoughts. And there was that glowing spark, just a tiny point of golden light. He caressed it with his *laran*, as if to convey those same sentiments to the unborn babe.

And the spark flared to brightness.

~oOo~

If it had been Dorian's imagination alone, he would have apologized to his kinswoman and withdrawn. But it was not. Every *laran*-bearer in the gardens and the ballroom felt the bloom of awareness from the unborn mind—a rush of wordless wonder and curiosity. Dorian could feel the surprise and confusion from all of them, solid but everchanging like the buzz of bees.

"Are you all right, cousin?" he asked Larisa, while silently providing her child a calm, soothing presence under which to shelter from all the minds suddenly seeking its own. He was not a monitor at the Tower, practiced at easing the discomforts of the technicians so that they could work their *laran* uninterrupted, but he understood how a monitor's work was done.

"He...he kicked, I think," Larisa said weakly. She looked no worse for it. "Did you feel him?"

She has no laran, he thought. *She does not know.*

"He did more than that, I think," Dorian answered lightly, not wishing to worry her. Before he had a chance to explain, Magda, the house *leronis*, arrived at Larisa's side, flushed and quite out of breath. She looked from Dorian to his kinswoman.

"What did you do?" she demanded.

He was still trying to determine that, himself. "I...I think I awakened him."

Magda shook her head—not quickly in disbelief, but slowly. In wonder. She was a tiny, wizened woman—the same who had tutored Dorian in his own youth. "Tower monitors can examine the unborn and detect whether they are healthy, or if they have *laran*, but they cannot activate it. Such a thing has never been seen before."

Her gaze turned blank and distant, and Dorian knew she was conversing with someone not immediately present.

"*Domna* Larisa," she said then, "are you well?"

Larisa's hands still rested protectively, though lightly, over her belly. "I...well, yes. He kicked, but that is all." Dorian could not feel her confusion, but apparently it bled through to the babe, for the unborn boy's projecting thoughts turned to worry and doubt. Had he done something wrong?

Magda and Dorian exchanged a sharp glance. Then he could feel Magda soothing the child wordlessly, with feelings and images. Dorian was glad of her presence; he would not have done the same with nearly the skill. He supposed it might be a mothering instinct.

It freed his attention for Larisa, and he smiled gently. "Congratulations, my dearest cousin. Your child has *laran*."

It was more a cause for surprise than celebration, and by the next day the news of Larisa's fortune had already paled under the news of Dorian's newfound ability. Dorian performed like a trained falcon under the gaze of Lord and Lady Ardais, and Magda, the *leronis*, using his keen sense to coax latent *laran* to life in several kinsmen and women who had not been thought to have it. In Larisa, as Dorian already suspected, there was none.

"You must go to Hali," Magda said to Dorian. "Your *laran* is quite a significant and unique talent, and it must be studied."

Dorian thought of the friends he'd left behind at Corandolis Tower—his circle, to whom he had expected to return. Magda read his unshielded concerns. "We will contact Corandolis on the relays and inform them of this change, just as we shall contact Hali to expect your arrival."

It was not enough, but it was all he could expect for the moment. Corandolis was a large enough Tower to be able to replace him permanently with another matrix technician.

Dorian bowed his head to Magda. "I will prepare at once."

~oOo~

Dorian had grown up hearing the phrase "sent off to Hali," but though he had communicated with Hali through the relays, he had never been there himself. He forced himself to focus on the pleasant anticipation of being able to put faces to the minds he had spoken with in the relays, rather than the anxious uncertainty of not knowing what might be in store for him.

The Tower rose narrow and tall, made of some pale, translucent stone. Despite all Dorian had been taught of crystal matrices and energons and science, the sight of the ethereal Tower half-embraced by morning fog and limned by dawn's red glow made his breath catch somewhere deep in him. For just a moment, magic was the driving force in the world. It tugged at Dorian's heart and brought his eyes to tears.

Then a cloud occluded the rising sun, casting the world and the Tower in gray, and rationality returned. There being nothing for it, he shrugged his disappointment off his shoulders, lifted his chin, and went forward to meet his fate.

The tests, at first, were not so bad. Dorian was deeply examined twice, by two different monitors. This was not as uncomfortable as he had anticipated—he had expected it to feel like another mind was rifling through his, upturning his library of thoughts and sifting his blood to peer beneath and within. It was his own uncertainty that had given him that fear, however. He had worked with monitors at Corandolis Tower and knew their touch to be subtle. A monitor sat outside the matrix circle and kept watch over the linked minds, soothing discomforts and removing distractions. As a result, Dorian experienced these examinations as merely the comfort of not being alone, with a drowsy sort of contentment. When he surfaced each time, he was aware only that some measure of time had passed.

They brought to him a number of teens whose *laran* had not yet surfaced, and watched from without and within as he coaxed their fledgling talents to life.

"This talent of yours has never before been documented," said Carys, the *leronis* who seemed to be in charge of studying the phenomenon that was Dorian. "We have named your talent catalyst telepathy, since you are able to draw forth the latent *laran* in others."

This Dorian had already realized, but the choice of title for his talent was an intriguing one. Catalyst made him think of chemical reactions, and it therefore seemed to imply science rather than sorcery. Deliberately so, Dorian guessed.

His was certainly a valuable talent for the breeding program to have at its disposal. The *leroni* studied him to determine with which bloodlines he should mate, but they intended to put him to work, as well.

"Until now, we have had to rely on monitoring germ plasm to detect *laran* potential in the unborn, but potential is not ability. Now, with you, we can *activate* that potential. We must experiment to see how early an unborn you can affect. Imagine knowing immediately if a particular sought-after gene has manifested. Just think how much we can refine and learn, with you to help us!"

~oOo~

There was an art to speaking with the unborn. Even their emotional vocabulary was limited. Comfort and discomfort, they understood. Safe and not-safe. Though they hadn't the frame of reference to articulate what forms not-safe might take, they knew when all was not as it should be.

Dorian gradually learned how to project comfort and safety into the awakening minds he touched, and how to teach the mothers and fathers the limited but powerful language of unborn emotions.

All children were special in the breeding program, but once Dorian had proven his competence, he was brought to an unborn who was *important*.

"*Domna* Francesca." He greeted the young mother-to-be with a formal bow. Francesca was wispy and slight, barely more than a spectre with a belly not yet swollen. Dorian could see, now, why this girl's family had a history of losing women to childbirth. All the more reason why this heir needed to be the successful culmination of the breeding program's efforts. Francesca herself was the result of careful planning, and if she could bear only one, it must have the traits the breeders desired.

Dorian had not yet awakened so new an unborn, but he had learned in his month at Hali that women with *laran* could detect the sex of their growing children quite early. If a babe were advanced enough in its growth to have the necessary organs, then it should also be advanced enough to have a mind—the most necessary organ of all.

Dorian had been privately skeptical that something so new might have consciousness, but now as he quested with his *laran*, he found it—that same golden spark he had felt in Larisa, and in all the expectant mothers since.

He reached for it, coaxing and caressing with messages of safety. When the spark flared, he implored young Francesca to do the same.

"There, now, my lady," he said. "Just as we practiced..."

She was too stunned to respond at first, but then instinct took over and she soothed the tiny child within her. Dorian withdrew from their minds, and then he and Carys withdrew from the room.

"Well done, indeed," Carys said once the door to her study was closed behind them. "The child was gently catalyzed, and is everything we hoped he would be."

Dorian could not entirely share her elation. Instead, he gave voice to what he had been wondering since his introduction to Francesca. "Forgive me, but...what if the child had not met your standards?"

Carys gave him a questioning look. "Why, we would have terminated him and tried again, of course."

Dorian spread his hands on the desk, focusing on his fingertips and shielding his thoughts. "So, you would use me to kill innocents?"

It had not been explicitly laid out this way to Dorian, but some part of him had suspected that the utility of his talents was in making a child's ability known early enough that it could potentially be removed without damage to the mother, who could then be prepared for another try.

Carys stared at him, then suddenly laughed. "Oh, you are such an innocent yourself. Sometimes I forget! Dear Dorian, that is nothing women have not been doing themselves for ages."

It was Dorian's turn to stare. "I—"

"Really, now. What better way to provide your lord with sons than to quash his daughters unhatched? Come, I won't get into this debate with you, child. Today you have validated years of our work for us. You should be celebrating, not considering the gloomy side of morality."

Dorian's head spun nonetheless. "I hesitate to think about what the removal of an unborn with active *laran* would be like."

"If the child had *laran*, removal would probably not be necessary," Carys countered.

"Probably" was small comfort.

"Here," the *leronis* continued. "I was going to tell you later, but you seem to need some cheering. A mate has been chosen for you, to try to breed your gift true. A kinswoman, and a kind and lovely one." She winked, as though this was somehow good news. "She's of sturdy stock and should be able to bear you many children."

Dorian thought only of Larisa and the children they might have had. He knew that whoever this lovely noblewoman was, she would be bearing children for Hali, not for him.

"I will do my duty," he said, because it seemed a response was expected.

Carys smiled, a genuinely pleased smile that lit her face and gave hint to the beauty she must have been in her own youth. "To your rooms, then. I'll send her along presently to...make your acquaintance."

~oOo~

Dorian paced his bedchamber. He'd never done anything like this before—not any kind of tryst with any kind of woman, sanctioned by his elders or no; not meeting someone explicitly for the purpose of putting a child in her; not anything more than a tongue-tied attempt to be charming to Larisa, where there'd been absolutely nothing at stake and nothing that could have come of it anyway, and he'd still felt like an inarticulate fool.

How was one supposed to dress for this sort of encounter? He changed into his formal suede suit. Then into his nightclothes. Then considered stripping completely and crawling under the sheets. Then back to the formal suit again. When she finally made her presence felt—a light and questioning touch of her mind, gentler than any knock on any door—he was just slipping on his indoor boots. Before he'd even seen her, they had the rapport of shared nervousness binding them. And then his sweaty palm was upon the door latch and he caught a glimpse of soft gray gown and a cascade of dark curls, and the brightest eyes he'd ever seen.

"*D-domna*," he greeted her, stepping back and opening the door wider.

Her smile was shy but sincere, eyes wide to take in the sight of him. He wondered if she found him handsome, or just refreshingly non-horrid.

He wondered too loudly, apparently, for the gentle touch of her mind brushed his through their tentative rapport. "Quite handsome," she answered quietly, and smiled.

"Quite beautiful," he answered, in the same hush. They brushed fingertips, the customary greeting of telepaths, and then her palms slid across his. His fingertips rested at her wrist, and he felt her pulse, fluttering as wildly as his own was.

"Please, you must call me Alanna," she said. "It's the least of the intimacies we're to share." She looked about his age, perhaps a year or two older. Taller than Larisa—they could nearly look eye to eye. He imagined how it would be to dance with a girl his same height, and she smiled. "I should like that."

He drew her hands up and kissed them, one and then the other, and then both together.

"Have you ever...?" he asked. She hesitated, then shyly nodded her head, as if she expected his disappointment. Dorian gave her a lopsided smile. "Good. So at least one of us will know what we're doing."

~oOo~

The next afternoon, when Dorian finally wandered out of his room, Carys was waiting for him in the common room where they took their meals. "So," she said, taking in his relaxed stance and dreamy gaze, but she said no more.

He sat; stretched. "So," he answered. "So, in spite of my cynicism about being flagrantly taken advantage of as a stud pony, I can't seem to stop smiling."

Carys chuckled, and brushed her fingertips near the back of his hand in a gesture that carried with it no contact, but a maternal warmth all the same. "I must be the bearer of unfortunate news," she said, while holding him in the cushion of that warmth.

Suddenly, Dorian felt quite sober.

"We've had a relay from your parents. The child you awakened...it was lost at birth."

Dorian was half out of his seat before his mind realized he had moved. "Larisa..."

"The mother is fine. Your house *leronis* suggested it was her lack of *laran* that spared her; apparently, the babe took quite a fright at the sudden changes that herald the birthing process, and could not be soothed."

"May I have leave to go to her?" he asked, though mentally he was already working through the logistics and packing his few belongings. "I'm the one who gave it awareness. This is my fault."

Carys canted her head like a curious hawk. "And how would your Alanna take your sudden absence?"

Dorian landed firmly in his chair, wishing it were sturdy enough to keep the world from spinning madly around him. "I...Oh." For a moment, concern for Larisa had blotted out even the momentous occasion of his first time. And second. And third...

"It is important that Alanna's feelings be considered," he agreed, speaking slowly. Then, inspiration struck. "Perhaps she could come with me."

Now Carys's expression was something else altogether. It was as if he had suggested the rain might try rising instead of falling, for a change. "I understand your feelings for your kinswoman, but I assure you, she is well attended. It is for her husband to rush home to her side, not for you. Go back to your rooms, Dorian. I will have a meal sent to you. You will feel more yourself once you've regained some energy."

Dorian felt full of energy—it was zinging along his nerves, prodding his muscles and pushing him to act, to do something, to go to Larisa. But, no...perhaps Carys was right. It would appear most unseemly if he rushed to her side like a concerned lover. And he would not be able to hide his feelings for her if he saw her despair.

Anger and fear and frustration had burned brightly in him, but now they were burning themselves out like the guttering last moments of a candlewick. As he ascended the stairs, he could feel it all draining out of him. By the time he reached his room, there was nothing left but the momentum to fall into bed.

Alanna herself came up to bring him a tray from the kitchens, with hearty stew and dense black honey bread for two. Watching her lift spoon to mouth, he mirrored the action without thought. Then appetite flared in him and he outpaced her, until only the last droplets remained to be soaked up with his bread.

Alanna sat and ate with him silently. When he was done, he watched her finish the meal. There was such grace in her movements, such beauty in her gentle face. Looking at her reminded him of the passions of the previous night, and he felt a pang of guilt for having been so ready to leave her behind without a thought. It occurred to him that she could already be carrying his child.

For now, keeping his own emotions tightly contained was more important than extending his *laran* to find out.

"Thank you," he said finally.

"For?" Alanna asked.

"The meal. And the company. And the silence."

She rose from the table and came around behind him, her fingers brushing the air above his shoulders. "You can't take it onto yourself. Children die in the birthing all the time. There's not an expectant mother in the world who doesn't know that."

It was scant comfort, after Carys had told him that the babe's *laran* had indeed been a factor, but he could see that Alanna was trying to soothe him. For the sake of their continuing relationship, he chose not to argue. But something else nagged at his mind...

"How widespread is the news of my kinswoman?" he asked.

Alanna leaned around to look at him with a pointed gaze and an arched eyebrow. "In a building full of telepaths, you ask how far news has spread?"

He gave her a rueful grin, then reached back for her hands and covered them, on his shoulders. "There is that. I only thought that they might have kept it secret for worry that it might panic any expecting mothers here at Hali."

Alanna gave his shoulders a squeeze. "You can relax on that account. We women are made of stronger stuff than you credit us."

~oOo~

Women were, but barely sentient fledgling telepaths were not. In the dark hours before dawn, not long after sleep had finally found Dorian and given him respite from his churning thoughts, a searing scream of pain tore through his mind and jolted him awake, panicked and confused.

Instantly, he recognized the feel of the mind—it was that very new unborn child he had awakened a few days before. The one with the weight of prominent genetics resting upon its yet-unformed shoulders.

Alanna awoke beside him, her ashen pallor mirroring his own anguish, water already filling her eyes. "Oh," she whispered, and reached for him. Dorian clung to her, both of them drowning in the babe's pain and Dorian's own despair. He knew he could not reach mother and child in time to be of any help; he could only feel the scene unfold from afar.

Now he felt the touch of the mother's mind wrap around the child's—awakened and bleary, trying to find her bearings and remember how to be a calming presence as she'd been taught.

But the unborn life within her, having been successfully bred for powerful *laran*, was stronger than she. Her spark went out first. Then, moments later, the little life followed. Dorian clung to Alanna, too aggrieved for tears. Once, he felt the questing brush of Carys's mind. When he confirmed that he was all right, she withdrew and let him be.

~ooo~

Sleep eluded Dorian and Alanna both. For a while, she shut her eyes and tried to find slumber, and he contented himself with emptying his mind of anything but the way the thin sheet clung to her soft curves. When his thoughts woke her, they found many ways to drown their sorrows—none of them restful.

Giving up on sleep altogether, they stood together on his balcony, leaning on each other and watching the red sun peek over the horizon. "What do you suppose this means for you?" she asked aloud. His mind had been churning around that question and others like it all night, but being asked to give voice to his thoughts helped him to distill the essence of them.

"I hope it means I'm of no use to their breeding program. If catalyzing has such a risk of killing the very high-talent subjects they meant it to identify, then it can't be risked. How many generations before they can breed another Francesca?" He allowed bitterness to leak into his voice; he could have contained it, but knew he was safe with Alanna and chose not to.

"I should like," she said after a long and pensive silence, "to seek out Carys and see if they've managed to isolate a cause. There's no use stirring this pot over the fire til it burns. If there are answers to be known, we should seek them."

Dorian found himself smiling. He kissed Alanna gently, and let her lead him back into the room to dress.

Carys was waiting for them. Her eyes were sunken and red, and it seemed she had not slept either. She refused to discuss the matter until they were all seated with cups of *jaco*.

While Dorian knew that going through the ritual of proper courtesies was crucial at times when the world was in disorder, he finally could wait no longer. "Please tell me...about *domna* Francesca—was the news of Larisa's loss in any way at fault?" he asked. Steam rose gently from his untouched cup, and he searched it for patterns and answers.

"No, *Dom* Dorian," Carys said at once. "You mustn't think such a thing."

"But if she thought of it, or dreamed it, and the babe felt worry or fear from her..."

Carys touched the back of his hand lightly. "No. I swear it." She looked away, toward a safe spot between Dorian and Alanna. "In truth, the reason is both better, and worse."

Dorian exchanged a glance with Alanna. Under the table, she rested her hand on his thigh for comfort.

Carys took a slow breath, as if bracing herself for the words that followed. "It was threshold sickness, Dorian. It came upon the babe quite suddenly, and there was no way to reach it, to soothe it." She lifted a hand to forestall his protest. "Usually, threshold sickness comes on at adolescence, it is true...but usually *laran* comes on at adolescence, too. It seems it is linked more with the onset of *laran* than with a person's stage of growth."

There was silence for a few moments while the three of them each considered that. Dorian finally remembered his cup and took a careful sip. "Then," he said slowly, "is that what happened to Larisa's child, as well? Only because she had no *laran*, her child didn't kill her in its panic?"

Carys nodded. "We believe so. It is also possible that the prospect of birth frightened the child, and without the mother's ability to soothe it through telepathy, it may have brought an episode of threshold sickness upon itself through its anxiety and fear."

"It's a lot to digest, but the solution seems clear," Alanna said. "Dorian cannot use his catalyst telepathy on the unborn. The risks are too great."

"Indeed," Carys answered. "We have been debating this all night. If this talent kills those whose value it detects, it is a certain danger to our telepaths and our breeding program."

Dorian let out a breath of relief he had not realized he'd been holding. His cup was steadier this time when he lifted it to his lips.

"However," Carys added, "we do still have much to study about the catalyst talent and how it works, so you will not be returning to Coriandolis Tower in the immediate future."

Alanna's touch tightened on Dorian's leg, and he covered it with his fingers and gave her hand a fond return squeeze. "I think I can accept that decision." They shared a brief smile. Her eyes glowed with such happiness and potential as to melt his heart.

"I have arranged for you to have some time at the relays, Dorian," Carys said, "to speak to your family and your circle, and inform them yourself."

It was a generous gesture, and he bowed his head in sincere gratitude. "Thank you. I will go at once."

~ooo~

Dorian did not see Alanna for the rest of the day, and when evening came, she did not come to his room. He extended his *laran*, but couldn't find her. Confused, he set out in search of her, but found a maid in Alanna's room, stripping the linens from the bed. The wardrobe was open and bare.

Feet racing down the stone hallway, Dorian came to Carys's rooms and made to pound on the door, but it was already cracked ajar so he merely pushed his way inside. The older woman sat alone in front of the fire, ignoring the needlework in her lap. "Congratulations, Dorian," she said without turning. "You're to be a father!"

It was not what he'd expected to hear, certainly, and it stopped his feet in their tracks. "I...what? Please, where is Alanna?"

"Already gone, dear boy. She took a carriage back to her family this morning, right after we all broke fast. Sit with me."

He focused on putting one foot in front of the other; at least, the act of walking still made sense. Finding himself in front of the second chair and at a loss for else to do, he sat. "But..."

Carys's eyes held sympathy, but her voice was steady. "It wouldn't do to have you ruin your own son. I saw it in her this morning, but I couldn't tell you, lest you use your catalyst talent accidentally. We've sent her away from you for her own safety. You want her and the baby to be healthy, don't you? You do seem to have gotten quite attached to her in a very short time. But then, there have been tragedies, and we telepaths are more prone to form deep emotional connections when we're intimate."

Dorian's mind had already skipped forward, fitting together scattered shards of thought, too numb to feel their painful edges. "So...letting me use the relay..."

It wasn't sympathy in her eyes. It was pity. "Was calculated, yes. I'm very sorry, but I'm sure you understand that it has to be this way. You've proven your power isn't safe to use on the unborn—and especially not on your own issue. Imagine him reaching out and catalyzing the entire women's wing, without realizing that he's doing so. Why, we'd lose all the children, and probably many of the mothers, too."

Dorian rubbed at his eyes, trying to contain the burn of angry tears. "But you *made* me use my power that way. It wasn't my choice, and now you punish me for it?"

She reached out to him, but he flinched away. "I did make you," she agreed softly. "We did. You are correct that it was *our* mistake, not yours. We did not realize how dangerous the catalyst power could be. It is not your fault and the consequences are not your punishment, they are for your safety. You already have three innocent deaths on your hands. You are a kind boy; I know you don't want to wear the blood of your own child, as well. Better that Alanna takes him away, and you remain and learn how to harness your talent, and perhaps even how to ease the catalyzed through threshold sickness, in time. Your talent could hold the cure, Dorian. Would you deny all your people that possibility?"

He regained control of his breathing, counted to ten, and then met Carys's gaze. "I won't participate in your experiments any longer. My blood and seed may be your toys, but my mind is not. I will depart for home in the morning, and use my talent not upon command, but where and when *I* deem it safe. I will contact Alanna only by letter until my son is born, out of concern for her safety. After that, you will allow me my judgment and not restrict my movement or actions. Whether or not you have the boy to study will be Alanna's choice. I will train him, if she wishes it."

Dorian stood, inclined his head in less of a bow than Carys's station deserved, and left the room without another word.

~oOo~

The moment Dorian slid off his horse, Larisa flew into his arms. He held her tightly, breathing in the lilac scent of her hair. "I am so very sorry, my dearest kinswoman," he murmured. His heart felt as if it were filled with lead, its cold melancholy replacing the anger that had fueled his journey.

She pulled back just far enough to seek his gaze. "Hali has aged you, cousin," she said. "You left here a boy, but now you speak as a man."

She was still beautiful, even as pale as she was from her ordeal.

"Come. Let's get you inside before Magda runs out here to scold me." He shifted so that his arm was around her shoulders and led her indoors. "Most important, how is your health?" he asked.

Her lips drew tight. "The birthing did too much damage. The healers say I will likely not be able to bear again. On hearing this, Lewis left me. It—I understand. I do. He needs a woman who can give him an heir."

Dorian turned to her and brushed her cheek gently with his thumb as if brushing away a tear, though Larisa had not shed any. The gesture contained all his love for her, more safely than any attempt at words might. It softened her, and suddenly her exhaustion was plain upon her face and body, her regal pretense shed.

"If only I could wed someone like you, Dorian," she sighed, stepping up into the circle of his arms again. Her cheek rested on his chest and, heart overflowing, he lifted a hand to stroke her hair. "But I know you must be given to someone with *laran*."

"At Hali, I catalyzed *laran* in others, but Hali was a catalyst for me as well. I am done with them. I am no longer anyone else's to give," he said, schooling his voice to remain even. "And nor are you."

She was silent a moment too long. He felt himself about to apologize for his boldness, but then she spoke.

"No," she said slowly. She seemed conflicted, but with a growing resolve and awareness, testing the idea as she spoke it. "I am no longer anyone else's to give." She looked up at him. "But I would share myself with you, if it would please you to blend your fate with mine."

The careful choice of her words struck him most deeply. Not giving herself to him, but blending and sharing. It seemed the most precious way to live—not as property or tool of another, or as a vehicle toward sons, or power. But to own one's self, and to joyfully share. He thought briefly of Alanna, who would always have a place in his life, but with whom Hali would never let him have such a union.

He would tell her of his time at Hali, but now was not the time to think of it. If he was meant to be a catalyst, let it be a catalyst of happiness and autonomy.

"*Domna* Larisa," he said, and paused to kiss her forehead, "there is nothing I have ever wanted more."

The Fountain's Choice
by Rachel Manija Brown

Another of the inventions (both in the literary and genetic sense) of *Stormqueen* was the *riyachiyas*, human-animal hybrids created by *laran*, often matrix-spelled for various purposes. The next two stories explore the nature of of freedom and compassion, and the age-old question of what it truly means to be human.

Rachel Manija Brown's post-apocalyptic YA novel *Stranger*, co-written with Sherwood Smith, is forthcoming from Viking in late 2014. She is the author of the memoir "*All the Fishes Come Home to Roost*: an American Misfit in India," and also writes short stories, graphic novels, poetry, television, and plays. She is currently a graduate student at Antioch University, Los Angeles, in the MA program in clinical psychology, with a specialization in trauma.

The sun lowered over the hills like a hot coal settling into a bed of ash. I pulled my coat closer around my chest, then slung my bag of rabbit-horns over my shoulder. I had to hurry home before I got caught out in the cold and dark.

I didn't move. Instead, I closed my eyes and let my other senses spread out like a spider web. Snow brushed feather-light against my cheeks. A few flakes clung and melted, dripping down like icy tears. A drop of mingled snow and sweat slipped salty into my mouth. A chilly breeze caressed my hair and rustled the leafy canopy overhead. I inhaled the faint mineral odor of the stony ground, the rich earthen scent of the crushed moss beneath my feet, and the coppery tang of the rabbit-horns' blood.

My own scent, the warmth of my body, and the sound of my breathing were part of the intricate world of the forest. *I* was part of it. The forest was the only place where I ever felt like I belonged. I wished I had been born a *chieri*, so it could have been my home.

I opened my eyes and forced myself to stride away from the comfort of the trees. I was much too old to waste time longing for impossible things.

As I neared the gates of Riach Great House, a tremendous roar filled the air. I stared upward at the silvery aircar that hurtled across the sky. Only one man in these parts had aircars or *laran* operators skilled enough to control them: Lord Elhalyn, whom my father had gone to visit a week ago. Lord Elhalyn must have offered his favored vassal the dangerous courtesy of a ride home.

My shoulders tensed. I had not expected my father to be back so soon. And he would be displeased if I was not present to greet him upon his return. I clutched the bag and ran, arriving panting and sweaty in the courtyard. My older brother Amador and a number of servants were already waiting there.

Amador smiled at me. "Good hunting, Val?"

I nodded, holding up my bag. "We'll have roast rabbit-horn tonight."

The aircar smoothly touched down. It was enclosed, with clear windows in front, through which I saw the red-haired *laranzu* controlling the car. But the windows in the back, where I assumed my father sat, were tinted dark. I had no *laran* to gift me with premonitions, but an eerie sensation went through me at the sight of those black windows. They seemed like bottomless pits into which I might tumble and fall to my death....

Dom Nestor stepped out of the aircar, letting the door swing shut behind him.

He glanced at my bag of rabbit-horns. "I am pleased to see that you are still good for *something*."

I gritted my teeth, unwilling to show girlish hurt in front of my father.

Dom Nestor raised a graying eyebrow. "Does a compliment sting so? I have never had any complaints about your hunting. You set a high standard."

He clapped Amador on the back. "One *you* don't live up to. I have not forgotten how we had to send a search party after you when you and that precious hound of yours ran off on a *chervine* hunt!"

"When I was eight," Amador muttered.

But though our father might tease Amador, it hardly mattered that his woodcraft was not quite as good as mine. A lord need never hunt for himself to be supplied with fresh meat.

Dom Nestor opened the door of the aircar and beckoned within. "Come on out. We're home."

To my surprise, a girl stepped daintily out. I stared. I could not help it. She was clad in nothing but gauzy pink draperies, with golden slippers on her high-arched feet, but she did not seem to feel the cold. Black hair tumbled over her bare shoulders, almost shocking against her milk-white skin. Her eyes were a blue so deep as to be almost violet, and her lips were red as cherries.

She was graceful and lovely, but something about her seemed strange. More than strange: *wrong*.

I surreptitiously counted her fingers, thinking that she might have six on each hand, but she had only five. It was her proportions that were odd: her legs too long, her waist and hips too slim, her fingers too delicate.

Dom Nestor snapped his fingers at his waiting servants. "Take the luggage to my room."

They hurried to do his bidding. Once they had gone, *Dom* Nestor gave a nod to the *laranzu*. The turbines began to roar, and the aircar took off. Normally I would have watched, fascinated. But there was something much more fascinating standing before me.

Once the noise of the aircar had faded into the distance, the girl turned to Amador and me. "It is my pleasure to serve you, *vai dom'yn*."

Her voice was sweet and clear as a glass bell. I glanced at Amador. He, usually so self-possessed, stood dumb, as if entranced.

Dom Nestor put a possessive hand on her shoulder. "Isn't she enchanting? Lord Elhalyn gave her to me."

"Gave her to you?" I echoed foolishly.

The girl bowed her head in submission, sending locks of midnight hair tumbling across her heart-shaped face. "I am honored to belong to *Dom* Nestor and the house of Riach."

"Oh!" I exclaimed. "She's a *riyachiya*."

I had never seen one before, but I had heard of them: genetically altered half-human playthings, matrix-spelled to attract and arouse.

My father nodded. "She was made from the seed of Lord Elhalyn and his most skilled *leronis*, Kiara. Usually they have eyes like animals, but not this pretty thing. She's one of a kind."

An experiment, I thought. I felt ill.

Lord Elhalyn had gifted our household with experiments before. Kiara loved to manipulate genes to create clever new creatures. Some of them had been charming, like the *chervine* with hooves like silver and antlers like gold, or the tree that bore apples in winter, pears in fall, cherries in spring, and peaches in summer.

Others had been less so. Ten years ago, when I had been six and

Amador had been eight, our father had come home with a hound pup whose fur changed color to blend in with her surroundings. He had given her to Amador, brusquely saying that I needed no assistance on the hunt. I had been jealous, and Amador had been thrilled. He named her Shadow, as she trotted at his heels everywhere he went. But she grew very quickly, reaching adulthood in a matter of weeks. Within six months, she was dead of old age.

An experiment, Dom Nestor had said, shrugging.

The *riyachiya's* beauty suddenly seemed overripe, almost repulsive. *Wrong.* I took a step backward.

My father's sharp gaze raked over me. "She does not charm you?"

"She's very beautiful, Father," I said hastily.

Dom Nestor laughed. "I didn't think she would. She's only spelled to charm men—and boys, too, of course."

The *riyachiya* tilted her head, examining me more closely. "My apologies, *vai domna.*"

I wished the polished stone of the courtyard would split open and swallow me up. I forced myself to sound unconcerned. *"Vai dom* was correct. *Dom* Nestor meant that I am an *emmasca.*"

"Not a *true* boy," my father explained. I wished he would stop talking—even a *riyachiya* had to know what an *emmasca* was!—but he went on. "A sterile throwback—we Riachs have some *chieri* blood in our line. But male. More or less."

"My apologies, *vai dom.*" The *riyachiya* did not seem embarrassed, but spoke as if she was truly pleased to have been corrected.

Amador managed to tear his gaze from her, though it seemed to take an effort. "Lord Elhalyn must be pleased with you, Father. She is a precious gift."

Dom Nestor gave him a long, measuring look. "She is. A gift for *me.*"

"Yes, of course." My brother's shoulders tensed.

My father beckoned us all inside, where servants took my rabbit-horns and his heavy great coat. None commented, of course, but I caught the men staring at the *riyachiya. Dom* Nestor noticed that as well, and his hand tightened on her arm, his strong fingers sinking into her flesh. Her skin looked so delicate that I wondered if he would bruise her, but she did not flinch.

"Get the men out," *Dom* Nestor commanded. "Women servants only. I'll have no men casting their lustful gaze over my property!"

In the Great Hall, the female servants brought in wine, but he dismissed them before they could pour it. The *riyachiya* poured the wine, her exquisite grace making that simple task look like a dance. Then she knelt at my father's feet.

It had been three years since our mother had died. I had expected *Dom* Nestor to eventually marry again, or take a *barragana* consort. I would have known how to behave with a wife or a consort. I wished that I knew what he wanted me to do now: ignore the *riyachiya*, or praise her beauty, or something else entirely. I wondered if she had a name, and if it would be more awkward if I asked now, or waited for him to reveal it.

Dom Nestor took a sip of wine, leaving one hand free to tangle in his plaything's hair. "Valerio! I have a task for you."

"What do you wish of me, Father?" I asked, startled. It was rare for him to set me any special task. Amador was the one he was training to inherit Riach Great House and all the responsibilities that went with it.

"My business with Lord Elhalyn is not finished. I must be off again tomorrow morning. I will be gone for a month or more, and I cannot bring this delicate flower with me. And that is why I need you, Valerio." He smiled down at the *riyachiya*, who tipped up her face to gaze at him adoringly. "It is a rare task which an *emmasca* can perform better than a man. You will guard her and allow no one to touch her. Understand me? *No one.*"

Amador spoke before I could. "I would never lay hands on any possession of yours."

"I do not know if you are lying or a fool," our father snapped. "Do you not recall that she is matrix-spelled to enchant? Whatever your intentions, she is irresistible to any true man. She will be locked in my chambers, and Valerio will guard her. I am confident that he can keep her safe from the likes of you."

Amador flushed a dull red. It was true that I could defeat Amador at swordplay or barehanded fighting, but I could find no pleasure in my father's praise when it came at my brother's expense.

"I will guard her with my life," I vowed.

Servants came in with roast rabbit-horn, which the *riyachiya* skillfully carved and served. At *Dom* Nestor's command, she took some for herself as well, and knelt at his feet to eat it. I would have been awkward trying to manage a plate and cutlery while kneeling, but the *riyachiya* made it look both easy and sensual.

As I watched her, a longing swelled within me, strong as pain. I wanted to do *something* to her. I wanted it desperately.

Could this be the desire I had never before felt—that I had

always believed I would never feel?

My mind was in such turmoil, I could not enjoy my food. Should I warn *Dom* Nestor that the spells laid on the *riyachiya* might be tempting even me? But what if, by guarding her, I could finally gain my father's respect?

I felt a wild surge of hope at the idea, then a stab of fear. Once before, I had thought that I would gain a skill that would make my father value me, but it had turned into almost as much of a disappointment as my birth.

I had suffered badly from threshold sickness when I had turned thirteen, not long after my mother had died. *Dom* Nestor had no *laran* himself, but he knew much about it, for my mother's *laran* had been powerful. He summoned a *leronis* to tend to me. But despite her best efforts, I became lost in hallucinations and distorted perceptions, uncertain what was reality and what was only in my mind.

Once I woke up with every muscle and bone in my body aching, too weak even to swallow the *kirian* that the *leronis* tried to drip into my mouth. I heard her whisper to my father that I'd been having convulsions and was likely to die.

My father sat beside me and took my hand in his. I could not recall him ever being so tender with me.

"Be strong, Valerio," he murmured. "The worse the sickness, the greater the power. *Emmasca* or not, you will be a true son of mine—a son I can be proud of. So live."

He took the cup and tipped the liquor into my mouth. I made an enormous effort and swallowed it.

"Good boy. I knew you had strength in you." He stroked my hair, and I relaxed at the touch of his strong hands. "I look forward to seeing what form your *laran* takes. Perhaps you will inherit your mother's gift and force men to do your bidding with the power of your mind alone."

But though I recovered, I never developed any *laran* at all. The *leronis* insisted that she could sense my power. But no matter how hard I tried, I could not read minds or command others or do any of the tasks the increasingly frustrated woman had set for me. *Dom* Nestor finally sent her away in disgust.

I threw myself into physical pursuits, using the deceptive strength of my long, fragile-looking limbs to my advantage. But no matter how well I rode or fought or hunted, my father never again looked at me with the pride I'd seen when I'd swallowed a single mouthful of liquor.

A scrape of wood against stone startled me out of my memories.

Dom Nestor pushed his chair back and stood up. The *riyachiya* immediately followed, her gauzy draperies fluttering around her shapely body.

"I wish I had more than one night to enjoy her," he said. "Well, I'll have my fill when I return. I depart at dawn, and then she'll be your charge, Valerio."

"Yes, Father."

Dom Nestor and the *riyachiya* went out. When the door closed behind them, Amador and I looked at each other, and then at our plates of untouched food.

Amador nudged me. "Eat, Valerio. I promise not to attack you to get to the *riyachiya*."

"I know that you will not." My own voice sounded stiff in my ears.

"Though I expect my own bride won't be half so pretty," he added wryly.

"What did you feel when you looked at her?" I asked.

My brother took a sip of wine. "Like I was burning up inside. Like I was dying of thirst, and she was a fountain of clear, cool water."

I drank as well, to cover my confusion. I too had felt something like that.

"Sometimes I envy you," Amador said, to my surprise.

"What? Why?"

"Desire is very distracting. I imagine that life would feel more peaceful without it."

"It doesn't," I said.

He drank again. "No, I suppose not. How could anyone be at peace when Father is here?"

"He's only trying to make us stronger," I said. "It's for our own good."

My brother walked out without another word. I sat alone at the great table, a lord of nothing.

~oOo~

Another aircar came for my father at dawn. Before he left, he gave me the key to his chambers, where he had locked the *riyachiya* inside.

The key was heavy and unfamiliar in my hand. Few other rooms in Riach Great House had locks. I had a servant fetch a breakfast tray, and then I unlocked the door and brought the tray inside.

The *riyachiya* lounged on the bed, wearing a thin, clinging robe. I could see every curve of her body beneath it. I hastily looked away.

"Good morning, *vai dom*." The *riyachiya* made even such a simple phrase sound like a seduction.

"Here's your breakfast." I set it on the bedside table. "I'm to guard you while Father is away."

I heard a creak as the *riyachiya* got up from the bed, then the soft padding of her bare feet across the floor. She came closer and closer, until I could feel the heat of her body. Then she knelt before me.

"Touch me," she whispered.

"What are you doing?" I exclaimed. "Get up! You're my father's..." *Pet? Consort? Slave?* "You belong to *Dom* Nestor."

"I belong to the house of Riach," she murmured. "Command me, *vai dom*."

I could see straight down her low-cut robe. A sweet scent rose up from the tangled locks of her black hair. If I moved my right hand by so much as an inch, I would touch it. I could imagine how smooth and soft it would feel.

I stood trembling, trying to force myself to either push her away or back away myself. I could not. I wanted to touch her more than I had wanted anything in my entire life.

So this was lust. Despite all the descriptions I'd heard, I hadn't realized how overwhelming it was.

What if only a matrix-spelled creature could make me feel this way? What if this was my one chance to experience what a true man felt?

You cannot betray your father, I told myself.

But it was just as Amador had said. I was burning up inside. I was dying of thirst, and she was a clear, cool fountain.

"What do you wish of me?" the *riyachiya* murmured.

She moistened her cherry-red lips with tiny flick of her pink tongue-tip. I could not help imagining those lips pressed to mine, or that tongue licking my body, so wet and hot....

"I long for anything you would do to me," she whispered. "Throw me to the floor. Beat me. Force me to—"

The heat burning through my body turned to icy horror—not only at her words, but at the *riyachiya* herself. Everything about her was *wrong*. Just being near her made me feel sick and dizzy. I staggered backward until my back banged into the opposite wall.

Her exquisite face tilted up, innocent puzzlement in her deep blue eyes. "Do you wish me to crawl?"

I wanted to tell her *no*. I wanted to run from the room. But it was as if my feet were nailed to the floor and the floor was tilting.

"I will crawl," she said, in a voice that was not innocent at all. "I will do anything. I am desperate for your touch."

The *riyachiya* got down on her hands and knees and began to crawl toward me.

My vision blurred. Light flashed before my eyes, then coalesced around the *riyachiya*. She shone and flickered, lit from within. I could see inside her body, but instead of bones and blood, I saw light. A web of glowing sapphire strands was knotted around sparkling currents of clear bright light, damming them, trapping them, chaining them...

I had to be hallucinating. I had seen similar visions when I'd had threshold sickness, but I couldn't be having another attack now. I'd recovered from it years ago.

The *riyachiya* laid her head on my feet. The locks of her midnight hair were as soft as I'd imagined. Her sweet voice rang in my ears, but I couldn't make out the words, only the pleading tone.

The ropes of blue light were tied so tightly around her limbs that they cut off her circulation. Strands wrapped in a garrote around her throat, choking her.

Instinctively, I reached out to help her. There was a light in me, too. I shaped it into a crystal knife with a keener blade than any metal could hold. I knew, though I did not know how I knew, that cutting any of the clear currents would harm her. Carefully, one by one, I began to slice through the blue strands that bound her.

When I finally cut through the last one, the freed clear light within her blazed up like a thousand stars. I heard a cry, not in my ears but in my mind. It was high and clear as the *riyachiya's* voice, but too raw with triumph to be sweet. Then I fell into a darkness like a moonless night.

~ooo~

I awoke sprawled on a cold hard floor. I had a splitting headache, and even the pale dawn light from the window hurt my eyes.

The *riyachiya* was crouched over me, staring intently into my face. I realized that only a moment or so had passed since...

...since whatever had happened. Since I had hallucinated and then fainted, I supposed.

"I feel different," she said.

If I had not seen her speaking, I would not have recognized her voice. She looked different, too: still beautiful, but no longer irresistible; still strangely proportioned, but only unusual, not repellent. The sense of *wrongness* that had clung to her was gone.

Pain twisted my belly. I was ravenously hungry. Maybe if I ate something, I would feel better. But I felt too dizzy to even sit up, let alone make it across the room to the table.

"Could you bring me the breakfast tray?" I asked.

She didn't move. Instead, a quizzical expression passed over her face. "You gave me an order, but I'm still sitting here. I don't *have* to obey you."

The pain knifing through my head made it difficult to think. "Well—would you please bring it anyway? I'm very hungry, and I don't think I can stand."

Immediately, I realized what a fool I was to say that. I was supposed to be guarding her, and I'd just revealed that I couldn't stop her from simply walking out the door.

To my relief, that idea did not seem to occur to her. She nodded briskly. "Yes, I remember how hungry Kiara became when she laid her spells on me. Lord Elhalyn always had food waiting if she was going to make great use of *laran*."

It was bizarre to hear her speaking so straightforwardly, without a hint of seductiveness. It was as if my horse had turned around and advised me that her saddle was cinched too tight. Her tone was so distracting that it took me a moment to take in her words.

"I have no *laran*," I said.

"Indeed you do, *vai dom*," the *riyachiya* replied. "You used it to break the spells that Kiara laid on me. And now you are as hungry and tired from breaking them as she was from creating them. More so, for I never saw *her* faint. But then, it took her many sessions to cast her spells on me. You removed them all at once. That must have taken more of an effort."

I shook my head, and immediately regretted it. Red-hot nails of pain dug in behind my eyes. "Not only that. It was my first time. I didn't know I could use *laran*."

It was still hard to comprehend, and harder when I felt so ill and shaky. I managed to haul myself up to a sitting position, but even that much exertion made the room swim around me.

A slim arm wrapped around me and pulled me to my feet. I could barely stand, but the *riyachiya* let me lean on her. She led me to the bed, then pushed me on to it. I sprawled on top of the covers, panting and dizzy, then realized that I could reach the breakfast tray from where I lay. My hunger took precedence over all else. I devoured a bowl of porridge, several rabbit-horn fritters, and a dish of stewed fruit, and drank a cup of tea. I felt better and more clear-headed when I was done, though I could have eaten three times that amount of food.

The *riyachiya* stood by the bed, eyeing me. "I have still not obeyed your order. You told me to bring the tray to you. I brought you to the tray. And only because I wanted to help you. I was not compelled."

She sounded half-pleased, half-bewildered.

"Was that what the spells were for?" I asked. "I thought they were to make you alluring."

She cocked her head, her huge blue eyes narrowing. "That as well. But I was an experiment, from Lord Elhalyn's own seed. Like his daughter, he said, with more natural will than the other *riyachiyas*. So Kiara also spelled me so that all I could desire was to obey and to please."

The *riyachiya* shivered.

"Are you cold?" I asked. "Father has coats in his closet."

She shook her head. "I was genetically altered to withstand cold, so I could wear flimsy clothing without getting ugly goose-bumps. I shivered because..."

Her voice trailed off. I too was silent, with too many thoughts flying through my mind to give voice to any one.

I *did* have *laran*! It was powerful, too, if I could break spells that Lord Elhalyn's most skilled *leronis* had laid. My gift must be specifically to break spells. That would explain why it had never manifested before—I had never previously encountered a person with spells laid on them. Nor had I even heard of that particular gift before. My father would be impressed, even though I had discovered my talent by breaking the spells on his *riyachiya*.

I snuck a glance at the *riyachiya*, wondering what would become of her. Would *Dom* Nestor return her to Lord Elhalyn and Kiara to have the spells re-done? My stomach twisted again, but not from hunger. Now that I had seen what the *riyachiya* was like without the spells on her, the thought of having them replaced was horrifying. She seemed like a different person without them—a real person, not a toy.

"Do you have a name?" I asked.

"Silla, *vai dom*." She frowned down at the tray. "You have eaten all of my breakfast. I was not altered to withstand hunger."

"I'll get another tray for you."

Cautiously, I swung my legs over the bed. I was exhausted and still ravenous, but I could stand. I left the chamber, making sure to lock it behind me, and headed for the kitchen.

I should have been rejoicing over my new-found gift, but my

thoughts kept circling back to Silla and her spells. Maybe *Dom* Nestor would choose to keep her as she was. She was still beautiful. And she would be less trouble if she was no longer irresistible to every man and boy who saw her. Surely he would see that.

In the kitchen, I explained that I had not eaten and was very hungry, and that *riyachiyas* had surprisingly large appetites. I returned to my father's chambers with a very lavish breakfast for two.

Silla stood at the window, gazing out at the distant forest. I joined her, chewing on a sweet roll.

"I would like to walk in the forest." Her blue gaze turned on me, startlingly direct. "I could not have had that thought before. A walk in the forest would please only me."

She went to the breakfast tray and pondered over it as if she had a very important decision to make. Finally, she declared, "*I want the rabbit-horn hash!*"

She scooped up a generous helping and began to happily devour it. I sat down across from her, trying to squelch the guilt welling up within me. It made no sense. I had broken the spells on her, not cast them.

"How old were you when the spells were put on you?" I asked.

Silla shrugged. "I don't remember ever being able to want things for myself. I suppose Kiara began when I was very young. I heard her saying the process took years to complete."

I lowered my gaze and stuffed another roll in my mouth, not even tasting it. A small hand laid itself over mine. I jumped, then met Silla's earnest gaze.

"Thank you, *vai dom*," she said. "I'm sorry if I frightened or disturbed you earlier. I sensed that there was something you could do for me, though I did not know what it was. It was the first time I had ever wanted something for myself. I asked for your help in the only way that I could."

A wad of bread stuck in my throat. I washed it down with a gulp of tea. "I understand. And I'm glad you did it. I always wanted *laran*, and now I know that I have it. My father will be pleased with me."

"Will he?"

"Yes, of course. I was a great disappointment to him. Now maybe he can be proud of me." I nearly bit my tongue, but the words were already out of my mouth. Silla's bluntness, as if she had never learned hold back what was in her heart, made me feel compelled to match her honesty.

"What was disappointing about you?"

I sighed. "As he told you, I'm an *emmasca*. That means that I'm sterile."

"So am I. Kiara altered me so in the womb."

"But I was supposed to have children, to carry on the family name and genes. You—" I couldn't say, *No one wants to sire children on a half-human sex toy.* "You were designed to be the way you are. I'm—I'm a genetic mistake."

Silla looked concerned. "Will you die soon?"

"What? No! *Emmascas* live longer than normal people, not shorter."

"Are you in pain?" Silla bent her head and peered intently at my hands.

"What are you doing?"

"Examining your joints. One of Lord Elhalyn's sons had a genetic malady. If he cut himself, he never stopped bleeding. His joints swelled, and he was in constant pain. He died when he was twelve."

"I don't have a disease," I said impatiently. "I'm just not what Father wanted. He wanted a true son, who could give him grandchildren, not a—a—"

The words caught in my throat.

"I'll come back with your lunch." I fled the chamber.

I locked the door, told a servant to come wake me at mid-day, and went to my chamber and slept as if I was some hibernating creature.

I dragged myself out of bed at the servant's knock and brought another tray to Silla. She was again standing at the window, seemingly deep in thought.

"I don't like being locked up," she said. "I want to walk in the forest. Would you take me on a walk, *vai dom*?"

"I..." I couldn't find any reason to deny her. My father had said to guard her, not to never let her leave his chambers. "If you wish."

She bounded to the door, her thin dress fluttering.

"You can't walk in the snow in slippers."

Silla looked at me as if I was a fool. "I told you that I was altered to endure cold."

"Were you altered to be immune to frostbite?"

"I don't know," she admitted.

"Then wear boots." I checked the clothing she had placed in his closet, but none of it was suitable for the outdoors. And she could never walk in my father's shoes. "I'll loan you some of mine."

I locked her in again and went to fetch some clothing of my

own. By the time I returned with it, she had eaten everything but the sticky pastry, which sat there rejected in the middle of a plate, with a single bite taken from it.

"I didn't like it, so I chose not to eat it," she informed me.

"You don't have to eat it if you don't want to." My curiosity got the best of me. "Did the spells force you to eat whatever you were given? Could you even taste it?"

"Do you choose to take each breath? Does one feel better than another?"

"No. And no."

"It was like that." She glanced doubtfully at me. "You said you were not a true boy. Are you a true girl?"

I wished she would stop going on about my gender. Maybe if I explained it clearly to her, her curiosity would be satisfied and she'd drop the subject. "I'm neither. Or both. I was raised as a boy because my father wanted a boy, and a sterile girl would have been even more useless than a sterile boy."

Silla looked hurt. "Am I useless?"

"No. Like I said before, you're what you're supposed to be."

She did not look satisfied with my response, but shrugged and reached for the clothing I'd brought. "If you're a girl as well as a boy, is it proper for me to undress in front of you?"

"No!" I shoved the clothing into her arms and nearly ran out the door.

I gave her a long time to dress before I opened the door a crack. To my relief, she was fully clothed. With her long legs, she had only had to roll up my breeches a little bit. My shirt fell baggy over her chest and the tunic hung over her hips, concealing her odd proportions. She looked like a pretty girl in boy's clothes, not like a *riyachiya* dressed like a human.

I hurried her outside, past the staring servants, out the gates, and into the woods. Once we were alone beneath the trees, I slowed down. Silla touched the rough bark of the trees, she sniffed at the leaves of bushes, she even took off her gloves and rubbed her hands over the snow. She paid such delighted attention to every detail that I felt as if I too was experiencing the forest for the first time.

Her ignorance of ordinary experience, which had been so frustrating in Riach Great House, became a source of easy conversation. I told her the name of every tree, which bushes had toxic leaves, and explained how to track and snare rabbit-horns.

The fifth time she scooped up a handful of snow, I did too.

"Watch this, Silla." I molded the snow into a ball and threw it to her. "Catch!"

Her delicate hands darted out to catch the ball. When it burst apart in her hands, she gave a cry of surprise, then laughed.

She made a snowball of her own and threw it to me. "Catch, *vai dom*!"

We tossed snowballs back and forth, laughing and playing like a pair of children, until the shadows lengthened into dusk. I glanced at the setting sun, and my heart sank with it. I had to take her back and lock her up, as if she was a hunting hawk that I had to return to its cage.

"Come on, Silla," I said. "Time to go home."

She did not move. "I do not have to obey."

I wished she hadn't said that.

"Don't you want to have dinner?" I asked.

"I do. But..." She frowned. "I don't want to be locked up."

"It's for your own protection."

"Protection from what?"

"From men."

"I am not protected from men," she said simply. "I belong to *Dom* Nestor."

I felt as if one of the icicles hanging from the trees had pierced me to the heart. Hoping I had misunderstood her, I asked, "Is it so terrible for you, to belong to my father?"

"I don't like it." To my relief, she spoke in the same tones she had used to tell me she didn't like the sticky pastry, rather than as if she was describing some torture.

The icicle twisted in my chest when it occurred to me that if I asked her how she would feel about being tortured, she would probably say, in those same calm, forthright tones, "I don't think I'd like that."

I wished I had never broken the spells on her. Before I had, she'd been content to obey. Now she was unhappy, and I was doubly to blame: I'd made her aware of being trapped, and until Father returned, I was personally responsible for keeping her that way.

Guilt and frustration boiled up in me, making my words came out more harshly than I intended. "It doesn't matter what you want. You can choose what you eat, but you can't choose not to be what you are."

"*You* can choose," she replied.

"No, I can't!" I yelled. "Don't you think I'd choose to be a true man, if I could?"

Silla seemed taken aback. "I meant that you can choose what

you do with me. You could let me go."

What she requested was so impossible that she might as well have told me that I could choose to grow wings and fly. "I can't."

"Please," she begged. "*Dom* Nestor will send me back to Kiara, to have the spells restored. I won't be able to choose any more. I won't be able to *want* any more. Please let me go!"

"Father might keep you as you are. You could ask him to."

"But he could choose not to," she said. "And then it would be too late. Please!"

She dropped to her knees. With her long limbs, wearing my clothes, it was as if I was standing over a younger, smaller, desperate version of myself. As if I were Father, about to speak the words that would doom me.

"I can't," I repeated miserably. "I swore a vow to my father. He would never forgive me. Anyway, there's nowhere for you to go. You couldn't survive a day alone in the woods."

"I could!" she insisted. "You taught me what to eat, and how to snare rabbit-horns."

"Silla, it's not that easy. You can't learn how to do something like that just by hearing about it—you have to practice."

"I could practice!"

I pulled her up. When I let go of her, she stood motionless as a *chervine* frozen under the shadow of a banshee.

"I'll ask Father not to send you back," I offered. "And you can promise to obey him, even without the spells."

She did not reply. I had to take her elbow and march her back to Riach Great House. She walked stiffly, like a living doll. I brought her a tray of food, but she did not touch it.

"I'll ask him for you," I promised her again.

But if a fountain could choose to flow or dry up as it pleased, what good would it be to a thirsty man?

I toyed with the idea of granting her wish. But even if I could bring myself to betray my father, she'd only die in the wilderness. I thought of her delicate fingers blackened with frostbite, and I couldn't bring myself to let her flee into the cold.

"Eat your dinner," I said.

"I choose not to," she replied.

I locked her in and returned to my room. It took me a very long time to fall asleep. I dreamed of cold clear water, and woke up shivering.

When I unlocked the door of Father's chambers, she was gone.

I couldn't believe it. There was no way out but the door, to which only I had the key, and the window, which was too small to squeeze through and overlooked a forty-foot drop. But the window was open.

An ordinary girl of Silla's size would have gotten stuck in the frame. But Silla's unnaturally slim hips, never meant to bear children, just might have wriggled through. And while I could never have gotten a grip on the tiny cracks in the stone wall, Silla's fingers and toes had been genetically altered to be slim and delicate...

I bolted out and shook Amador awake. "Silla's escaped!"

"Who?"

"The *riyachiya*. She climbed out the window. It's my fault!"

Amador blinked at me in amazement. "How could she— No, wait, Val. This can't be your fault. Someone must have stolen her. A *riyachiya* wouldn't have run off on her own."

I had been about to tell him everything. But now I couldn't bear to explain why it *was* my fault, and see his sympathetic expression turn to disappointment. "She said she wanted to take a walk in the woods."

He looked out his own window. Snow was falling. "She must be lost. You'd better hurry and find her. Take as many men as you want."

I shook my head. "She's my responsibility. I'll go alone."

Amador frowned. "Is that safe, Val? You don't know how far she might have gotten."

"I know. I might be gone for a few days. But you know how well I know the woods. Amador, I have to do this myself. I vowed to guard her with my life!"

"Then go, *bredu*." My brother clasped my hand. "Whatever Father thinks, I'll be proud of you."

I packed quickly but carefully, warmed by Amador's trust in me, however misplaced it might be. Then I set out into the forest.

I wished I knew exactly when Silla had made her escape. If she had squeezed out the window as soon as I had left her alone, she'd had more than enough time to freeze to death. I consoled myself with the thought that at least she couldn't have gotten very far; lost people tended to wander around in circles.

The falling snow hid all tracks. But, guessing that she'd have started by going somewhere familiar, I retraced the walk I'd taken her on. When I reached the point where I'd turned around and taken her back home, I found a freshly-snapped twig, suggesting that someone had ventured further. I pressed on, sure I would find her soon.

But it was mid-day before I found another trace of her—a black hair, easy to spot in the snow. And then nothing until I spotted a single thread snagged on a thorny bush. But by then I was a day's journey from Riach Great House and was forced to camp for the night.

I lay by my flickering camp fire and told myself not to give up. I had vowed to guard Silla with my life. I couldn't break my vow just because it was difficult, or because I felt sorry for Silla. She had been made to obey and to please, just as Amador had been born male and I, *emmasca*. None of us got to choose our destinies. But I could at least choose to keep my vow.

The next morning I set out again, working my way deeper and deeper into the wilderness, expecting at any moment to find her starved and frozen body. But by the fourth day, I was forced to admit that however naïve she might seem, she had a knack for survival. She might even pass all the way through the wilderness, and then vanish forever into someone else's kingdom. *Riyachiyas* were rare; few people would have ever seen one before. If Silla dressed like an ordinary woman, no one would think her anything but a lanky girl.

I had gotten so used to spotting Silla's trail by the tiniest of signs that it shocked me when I found the first footprint in the snow. I knew it was her: I recognized the tread of my own boots. Another footprint was within sight as well.

I followed the trail, wondering what had made her so careless. It was a hilly area where she could have easily stepped from stone to stone. But I did not have to wonder for long. The prints made an uneven line, as if she was staggering. Then I came to a churned-up shape in the snow where she had fallen. There were tiny handprints in the snow where she had picked herself up and gone on, only to fall again twenty paces later. I looked for blood, but there was none.

She's freezing to death, I thought. But why would it have taken so long?

I began to run, clutching the straps of my pack so it wouldn't smack painfully into my spine. I barely spared a glance for the marks where she had fallen again, and again, and again... How could she be so badly affected by the cold, but still manage to keep going? People who froze to death were done for once they fell, unless someone found them quickly. They got up once or twice, at most. Not five...six...seven times!

The trail ended at a small, dark cave. I hastily lit a torch.

"Silla!" I shouted.

There was no reply. Bending so I wouldn't hit my head, I

ducked inside, holding the torch before me.

Silla was curled up in a corner, bundled up in the clothes I had given her and Father's warmest great coat. I couldn't see if she was breathing. I jammed the torch into a crack in the wall and turned her over.

She blinked slowly up at me, her eyes unfocused. I had never felt more relieved in my life.

Silla clutched at my arms. Her grip was surprisingly strong. "I'm falling."

"You're not falling. You're just dizzy."

"I'm falling," she insisted. Then she moaned in pain.

"Where does it hurt?"

"My head."

There were no signs of frostbite on her nose or ears, or anywhere on her face. I took off my gloves and touched her cheek. Her skin was warm—even warmer than mine, since I'd been out in the cold.

I lit a fire, then pulled off her gloves and boots. Her fingers and toes were warm too, with no discolored patches. I sat back on my heels, wishing I knew more about medicine. Could she have eaten something poisonous?

"What are you feeling?" I asked.

Her gaze slid past me—*through* me. She spoke as if she was in a dream. "Everything's appearing and disappearing. The ground keeps going soft. Anything I touch changes."

When I'd had threshold sickness, all my sensory perceptions had become distorted, and my head had ached as if it would shatter into fragments. But *riyachiyas* couldn't have *laran*.

"I can see the light in you," Silla whispered.

She raised a trembling hand and ran a finger along my body. I remembered how I'd felt when I'd broken the spells on her, and looked within myself with that inward eye. She was tracing one of the currents of energy that flowed within me.

Silla had been made from Lord Elhalyn's seed. She was an experiment, with human eyes and a will of her own. The spells on her that suppressed her ability to think for herself must have been suppressing her *laran* as well.

"You have threshold sickness," I said. "Silla, you have *laran!*"

"Humans have *laran*," she replied.

"You're obviously human enough."

"Human and not," she mumbled. "Girl and boy..."

She was drifting into delirium. I tried to remember how my threshold sickness had been treated. The *leronis* had given me *kirian.* I didn't have any of that. She'd also done something to me with *laran.*

I concentrated until I could see within Silla's body. My currents of energy flowed freely, but hers were blocked, pooling up and turning back on themselves. I extended my energy into her, gently opening her channels until they began to flow again.

Her eyes opened wide, and she struggled to sit up. "You're fixing me!"

"I'm trying. Lie still."

"You're fixing me so you can take me back!" She tried to pull away from me.

"I have to, Silla. You're sick. You could die."

Her eyes focused on me, sharp and bright as stars. "I don't want to go back, *vai dom.* Don't fix me. I choose to die."

I heard the thoughts beneath the words, like an echo. But deeper than that, I felt her emotions. She truly would rather die than return and be trapped again within a net of sapphire light.

But I had known that already. I had known it when I had seen the marks where she had fallen, and gotten up, and fallen, and gotten up. I had known it when she had told me that she chose not to eat. I had known it when she had said, *I am not protected from men. I belong to* Dom *Nestor.*

I, too, belonged to *Dom* Nestor.

Unless I chose not to.

I opened my mind to her, so she could hear the truth beneath my words. "I won't bring you back. As soon as you're better, I'll let you go."

Silla relaxed, laying her cheek down on my thigh. "Thank you, *vai dom.*"

"Val," I said, stroking her hair. "Thank you, Val."

~ooo~

I tended to her for days, doing everything that I could remember the *leronis* doing for me. To my relief, she was not as badly affected as I had been. As soon as I thought it was safe to move her, I carried her to another cave farther into the forest, then went back and covered up all traces of our presence.

I wondered uneasily how long I dared stay with her. I had warned Amador that I might be gone for days, but eventually he was bound to send out a search party. But I hated to leave her alone. She was still weak, and she was a woman alone, with no family or friends or experience of the world. What would happen to her once I left? She would be easy prey for any man with evil intent.

I was so caught up in worrying about what Father would do when I returned alone, and worrying about getting discovered by searchers, and worrying about what would happen to Silla, that I forgot to wonder about her *laran*. But Silla did not forget about it. One morning she sat staring intently at me, then suddenly held out her hands, palms up.

"Play the slap game with me," she said.

By then I was used to her whimsies.

"I'm very fast," I warned her.

"I know," she said. "Put out your hands, Val."

Obediently, I laid my hands over hers. She flipped hers over, trying to slap mine. She was quick, but I was quicker. I jerked them out of the way.

I replaced my hands, then flipped them to slap hers. She yanked her hands away, and I missed.

I never missed when Amador and I used to play. I tried again. And missed again.

Silla laughed. "You look so puzzled, Val. Do you want to know how I'm doing it?"

"You're faster than me."

She shook her head. "It's my *laran* gift. I can see a few heartbeats into the future. Lord Elhalyn could see what *might* happen. I can see what *will*."

"A few heartbeats away."

"Yes." She shrugged. "I suppose it's not very useful."

My thoughts raced. If I stayed with her a while longer, I could teach her skills that could protect her for the rest of her life.

"How strong do you feel?" I asked. "I want to teach you how to fight."

She sprang to her feet. "I want that, too."

~oOo~

She was a quick study, but it takes time to learn to fight, even if you can see your opponent's next move. Every day, I told myself that I had stayed as long as I could, and now I had to leave her. And every day, I told myself that one more day of training would make all the difference.

One morning we fought in a snowy glen, Silla dancing and ducking away from my every blow, then darting her knife under my guard.

"Enough!" I held up my hand for a break. "You've worn me out."

She stopped, laughing. "I like to fight. Could I fight for a living, when you go?"

"Women don't do that," I began, then remembered something I'd heard Father mention. "Maybe you could. There's a group called—"

"Val!" Silla cried, pointing at nothing.

A few heartbeats later, Amador stepped into the glen.

I felt as if I was being ripped in two. Then, biting my lip, I moved to stand protectively beside Silla.

"I'm breaking my vow." The words tasted bitter as poison in my mouth. "I don't want to fight you, but I won't let you take her back."

My brother looked bewildered. "Why would I fight you? I don't care about the *riyachiya*. I came for you, *bredu*. I was afraid that you were hurt."

"Oh." Relief and embarrassment washed over me in equal parts. "But how did you find me?"

"I tracked you. I'm not as good at it as you are, but I'm not as bad as Father likes to imply, either." Amador eyed Silla. "What happened to her? She's different. She's not...um..."

"*She* can speak for herself," said Silla. "Val has *laran* and took the spells off me, so I ran away. Val tracked me down and then decided to let me go. I have *laran,* too. That's why Val is teaching me to fight."

After a long silence, Amador began to laugh. "Could I get a little more detail?"

We all sat down, and I told him the whole story. At the end of it, Amador put his hand on my shoulder. "I wish you'd told me earlier. I wouldn't have blamed you. Val, you have *laran*! I'm proud of you!"

But with that *laran*, I sensed the bitter undercurrent beneath his love and pride. "That's not all you feel." Then I bit my lip. "I'm sorry. I didn't mean to pry into your mind. Sometimes I read things without meaning to."

His chuckle had no humor in it. "You don't need telepathy to know I'm jealous of you."

"Jealous?" I echoed, baffled. "Why would you be jealous?"

Amador's eyebrows rose. "Because *you're* the son Father wanted! It drives him mad that you can't inherit or give him an heir, and he's stuck with me instead. Val, how can you not know that? Why did you think he was always so horrible to us?"

"I thought *you* were the son he wanted, and *I* was the disappointment," I confessed. "But he'll never be satisfied with either of us, will he? Even if I brought Silla back, it wouldn't matter."

"No," said Amador. "It wouldn't."

Silla broke in. "Don't go back, either of you. You can choose not to. Come with me instead!"

Amador chuckled, this time with more warmth. "I'm not giving up Riach Great House. But *Dom* Nestor can't live forever. And I promise you, Val, when I inherit, I will do things differently."

"I know you will, *bredu*," I said. "You'll do things better."

I took my brother's hands in mine. I felt as Silla must when she saw the future: everything suddenly laid our bright and clear, where a few heartbeats before there had only been a vast unknown. "I'm going with Silla. Tell Father you never found us. By the time you get back, we'll be out of his reach."

"But where will you go?" His hands clutched mine tight. "What will you do? An *emmasca*, and a *riyachiya*— what sort of life can you have?"

"We could join the Sisterhood of the Sword." I turned to Silla. "They're the people I was about to tell you about, a group of fighting women."

"I'd like that," Silla said immediately.

Amador looked at me as if I was out of my mind. "You're a man."

"I'm a woman *and* a man," I said. "I've already lived as a man. Now I'd like to try living as a woman. Who knows? Maybe I'll like it better."

"Maybe you will." Amador released my hands. "I hope we meet again some day."

"We will," I promised. "And that vow, I mean to keep."

Silla ran to the edge of the glen, then turned and beckoned to me.

"You can go back to your brother later, Val," she said. "Now, you're going to come with me. I see it!"

I did.

House of Fifteen Widows
by Kari Sperring

One of the trickiest challenges in writing nonhuman characters is portraying them as both alien and emotionally accessible to the reader. In "The Fountain's Choice," we saw a *riyachiya* through the eyes of another character. Here, British author Kari Sperring switches viewpoints to give us human characters, with all their strengths and vices, as seen by a *riyachiya* narrator. Immie's simplicity and nonjudgmental loyalty illuminate the altogether human dilemmas of her world.

Kari Sperring grew up dreaming of joining the musketeers and saving France, only to discover that the company had been disbanded in 1776. Disappointed, she became a historian instead and as Kari Maund has written and published five books and many articles on Celtic and Viking history and co-authored a book on the history and real people behind her favorite novel, *The Three Musketeers* (with Phil Nanson). She's been writing as long as she can remember and completed her first novel at the age of eight (twelve pages long and about ponies). She's been a barmaid, a tax officer, a P.A. and a university lecturer, and has found that her fascinations, professional or hobby-level, feed and expand into her fiction. *Living With Ghosts*, her first novel, evolved from her love of France and its history, ghosts, mysteries, Celtic culture, strange magic, sharks, and sword-fights: *The Grass King's Concubine* has even found a creative role for book-keeping. She lives in Cambridge, England, with her partner Phil (who helps design the sword-fights) and three very determined cats, who guarantee that everything she writes will have been thoroughly sat upon. She's currently at work on her third and fourth novels at once, because she needs more complications in her life. She can be found at www.karisperring.com, on Facebook (Kari Sperring), Twitter (@karisperring) and on Live Journal as la_marquise_de_. She says she's been reading and loving the Darkover series since she was thirteen and is delighted and honored to be allowed to write in this wonderful world.

My house has fifteen widows. They are Chrysa, Elena, Janet, Kathia, Laurenna, Lilias, Mikhela, Mirella, Moira, Patryce, Priscilla, Robina, Tessa, Valli, and me. Not all of us were once married, but Lady Laurenna says we are all widows because of *Dom* Justin, even me, and that all of us are sisters, even though Priscilla is old and half-blind and Lilias has not come to her woman-time. Even me and Valli, though no one is allowed to marry us because we are not really people, not like the others. Lady Laurenna is Lord of our house, because we have no menfolk anymore and because she is *leronis*, even though *Domna* Priscilla is the oldest and a proper lady because of being married to *Dom* Martin who was *Dom* Justin's grandfather and Patryce is the strongest and Mikhela has *laran*, too, although she was not Tower-trained and so does Lady Mirella, but she does not talk since the bad days happened and I made *Dom* Justin die.

I did not mean to make him die, only to make him stop hurting my Lady and her sisters, but I did it wrong and he died. Patryce said *Good riddance* but Lady Laurenna said it is like a proper person to care and that anyway she helped me kill him and she knew what she was doing, so it's all right and not really my fault, because although Lord Justin was my lord, and hers too and lord of all the other women, none of us really liked him, and especially not Lady Mirella who was his wife *di catenas*.

I hope I have spelled that right. Mikhela taught me to read and write and she is very clever like her sister Lady Mirella, but I am not very good at writing yet, and I need a lot of practice. That is why I am writing this, and Lady Robina is helping me because she says it's better than sewing and she says I have spelled it right. But I would rather do the sewing because I do not make mistakes at that and no one is upset with me, not even Tessa who does not like me. Lady Robina says sewing is stupid but I think we all need clothes to wear and Lilias and Lady Robina are still growing. And Lady Robina says if I think that, I can do the sewing and she will write this story, but she does not know all of it and I do. And Mikhela says that Lady Robina should be grateful she has sewing to do now she is a woman, because if *Dom* Justin was still alive she would have much less pleasant things to do, because *Dom* Justin would have made her get married to Lord Carsten or Lord Bruno or another of his hateful friends.

When Mikhela says that, Lady Robina gets angry and throws her sewing to the floor and runs out and slams the door and I make more spelling mistakes. But Mikhela says that does not matter because what is important is my story and she will help me write it.

Lady Laurenna told me to write this down, because it needs to be told and she thinks if I write it I won't have my nightmares anymore.

My name is Immie, and I am a *riyachiya*. This is my story.

~oOo~

From the moment he could walk, *Dom* Justin Rossell knew he was born for greater things than the lordship of Forest Lodge. His grandfather, *Dom* Martin, might be satisfied with a few miles of dense woodland, rights over a minor river, and such income as could be derived from nuts and timber and hunting, but Justin wanted more. His father, *Dom* Martin's son Marcus, was little better than Martin, as far as Justin could tell, but he had one virtue in his son's eyes. He had married a *nedestro* daughter of the Moray-Aillard line and gotten Justin on her before his early death in a border skirmish. *Domna* Kathia, raised in a great lordship, wanted more than Forest Lodge for her son and, once he was old enough, arranged for him to be fostered in the castle of her brother, *Dom* Ranald-Istvan, the current Lord Moray-Aillard, alongside that lord's own children. From the age of seven, Justin slept in a well-appointed tower room, wore fine-woven fabrics, and ate of the best the Aillard lands could offer. Gentle *Dom* Martin shook his head over his grandson's love of finery, but could deny neither him nor Kathia anything. Each quarter, he laid aside more and more of his income for his grandson's use and when threshold sickness came upon Justin when he was twelve, *Dom* Ranald-Istvan's own *leronis* watched over him. The Rossell line had little in the way of *laran*—Marcus Rossell would never have gained Kathia had he not saved the lord in battle and had Kathia not been marked out by a strange light streak in her red-brown hair which set better marital prizes worrying over genetic disorders. But Marcus had just enough of the family Gift—a sense for incoming danger—to please his lord, and blended with the potential coded in Kathia's genes, to give life to a son with powerful *laran*. When Justin was fourteen, the *leronis* declared she could teach him no more, and he was sent, again with his mother's help, to study at El Haliene Tower, where another of her kin was a matrix worker. Aged eighteen, trained in war with mind and blade, Justin joined *Dom* Ranald-Istvan's fighting band as warrior and *laranzu*. The *leronis* who had nursed him through his threshold sickness was old and her powers weakening. Before he was twenty, Justin had replaced her in *Dom* Ranald-Istvan's council.

The next year, the old *leronis* died. At Justin's suggestion, *Dom* Ranald-Istvan sent to El Haliene Tower for her replacement. "One *leronis* to care for your household and teach your family, and me to arm you for battle." But El Haliene did not sent one *leronis* but two; Laurenna as teacher and healer and Carsten to assist Justin in the making of *laran* weapons. It was ten days' long ride to El Haliene Tower and the old *leronis* had not had the skills or strength to make aircars to ease the journey, while Justin, engaged as he was with the lord's wars, did not have the time. With Carsten and Laurenna, and the others who soon joined them, *Dom* Ranald-Istvan had his own Tower.

His own, or Justin's. But Justin was loyal and all his efforts were bent to the lord's service, until *Dom* Ranald-Istvan's armouries were piled high and his armies ready. All through the summer of that year, the lord's warriors ravaged the borders of the Valeron and the Isoldir and the di Asturias, burning homesteads and crops, seizing women and livestock and lands. In every skirmish, every battle, Justin rode in the van, his red hair uncovered and his sword bloodied in his hand. No enemy could lay a hand on him; his *laran* warned him of every attack. "He is blessed by Evanda," the common soldiers said and gaped as he passed. But, "Zandru has his hand on him," muttered the sergeant who looked after his tents, and the orderly who cooked for him and the women who warmed his bed. But *Dom* Ranald-Istvan loved him, and when, late in that same year, old *Dom* Marius died, *Dom* Ranald-Istvan bestowed Forest Lodge on Justin and with it new lands taken from the Isoldir, and a fine sword and a breeding pair of good horses on top.

When Justin was twenty-four, *Dom* Ranald-Istvan at last turned his armies north, against Ridenow of Ferrach Fada, who had been his family's main rival through four generations. The late Lord Moray-Aillard—who was Justin's grandfather via Kathia, as well as *Dom* Ranald-Istvan's—had died in battle against *Dom* Pier Ridenow of Ferrach Fada. *Dom* Pier's father had in turn been killed fighting against Ranald-Istvan's grandfather and so back through the years. *Dom* Ranald-Istvan had nursed his need for revenge down fifteen bitter years. Now, with Justin's *laran* weapons and gifts, he was ready to strike. The army marched as the last snow cleared, and before summer was out *Dom* Pier and his sons lay dead on the battlefield, his castle burned, and his womenfolk were in *Dom* Ranald-Istvan's hands: his wife Elena, his legitimate daughter Mirella and his *nedestra* daughters Mikhela and Moira, and all the other women of the household, many of them high-born, and many gifted to greater or lesser extent with the Ridenow *laran*. Justin's sword had cut down *Dom* Pier himself, while his *bredu* Lord Bruno slew *Dom* Pier's eldest son; the bonedust and clingfire he brewed had eaten away at *Dom* Pier's armies and devastated his villages.

At the victory feast, Justin sat at the lord's left hand, lower only than the lord's son, Lord Alan, while *Dom* Ranald-Istvan divided the spoils in land and wealth and women and *cralmac* servants. The lord showered him with gifts: new pastures to add to his woodlands, horses and weapons, ornaments for his mother and sister, fine furnishings and tapestries. But all through the feast, Justin had eyes only for the beautiful Mirella, standing in chains at the end of the hall, with her mother and sisters and waiting women. One by one, *Dom* Ranald-Istvan assigned the women to this vassal and that. Elena he granted to his own wife, *Domna* Annilda, to wait on her or scrub for her as she chose. He gave Moira and Mikhela to Alan, who at eighteen was ready to beget sons. One by one, the women were led away until only Mirella remained and, alone of all the lords and captains, only Justin had been granted no paramour. His face remained calm and his body relaxed, but under his skin, his pulse raced and his heart pounded.

Mirella stood alone, still dressed in the garments in which she had been captured, now torn and dirtied from the long journey. Her ornaments were gone, to adorn the wrists and fingers and throats of more fortunate women. Her hair was matted, pulled back from her face and tied with a rag torn from the hem of her dress. She did not weep or shake or beg, only stood as she was with the chains about her arms and stared back at *Dom* Ranald-Istvan, chin high and eyes fierce. Some of the women wept as they were led away, others cursed and spat and fought, but Mirella kept silent.

"You are very proud, *mestra*," *Dom* Ranald-Istvan said. She made him no answer. "Your father is dead. Your brothers are dead. Your home lies in ruins. Your nearest kinsman is many leagues away and is doubtless already calculating the advantages he can garner from your father's fall. My *leronis* Laurenna has bound your *laran*. No one will help you. No one will save you. You have no at all reason for your pride."

"My honor remains," Mirella said, and her voice was rich and low.

"Honor?" Dom Ranald-Istvan shook his head. "Honor is easily tarnished. And the honor of women..."

"My lord," Mirella said, "as long as I remain true to myself, I keep my honor, whether that is in my father's hall or your scullery. My condition does not matter."

"Proud," said *Dom* Ranald-Istvan, "and brave with it."

"As you say, my lord."

"You have the Ridenow Gift, do you not?"

"I do, my lord."

"Will you use it in my service? There is room in my tower for another *leronis*."

"You flatter me, my lord. I am neither strongly Gifted nor Tower trained."

"And you do not wish to serve me." But *Dom* Ranald-Istvan was not angry. "Your father had strong *laran*." He gestured towards the clutch of servants bred in *Dom* Pier's laboratories, and now corralled at the back of the hall. "Will you not share his secrets with me?"

"I will not, my lord, for I do not know them."

There was a moment of stillness throughout the hall. On the dais, Justin held his breath. Then *Dom* Ranald-Istvan laughed. To the guard who accompanied Mirella, he said, "Release her," and then, when the chains were unlocked, he held out a hand and said to her, "Come here."

Mirella took time to rub her wrists and stretch her shoulders before she obeyed. Like some queen out of story, she walked the length of the hall, head high, and stood without curtseying before the lord. He studied her without speaking for some time. Then he smiled. "Brave and proud. You are mine, *mestra,* from this day." He turned to *Domna* Annilda, "She needs a bath and new clothing. Send some of your women to see to it." Annilda flushed and nodded. At his side, Justin let out his breath in a soft hiss.

Women came and led Mirella from the hall. At last, *Dom* Ranald-Istvan turned to Justin. "I have another gift for you, too, straight from *Dom* Pier's own bedchamber. A gift more unusual and more pleasant than any other. And more biddable, too, I'll warrant, than any of his women. I'd thought to keep them for myself, but... You have earned them, and more." And he gestured to the guards who watched the collection of created servants, and two of them led forth my sister Valli and me.

I am Immie. We are *riyachiyas*.

~oOo~

"What I want to know," says Lilias, "is why they just stood there and let those men give them away. *I* wouldn't let that happen. I'd bite them and kick them till they let go of me, and then I'd run away." She stops to think about that, and adds, "or I'd hit them with an axe, like Patryce."

"You couldn't pick up an axe," says Lady Robina. "You couldn't even pick up Janet's kitchen chopper. You're not big enough."

"If I was Immie or *Domna* Mirella I would be," Lilias says, sticking out her tongue. "I'd chop and chop until I was free and they couldn't stop me."

"They could if they had swords," says Robina, "and bonedust and clingfire and bows and..."

"And you two have neither, and these shirts won't mend themselves," says Patryce, throwing a look at Mikhela, who sits by the window. "Or perhaps you'd rather help Janet in the kitchen or Chrysa looking after *Domna* Priscilla? They can always use help."

"I like helping Janet," says Lilias, and drops her sewing on the floor.

Robina turns back to her work and sets more stitches. But after a while, she looks at me, and says, "Why didn't you run away, Immie?"

I don't really understand her question. I belonged to *Dom* Pier, then *Dom* Ranald-Istvan, then Lord Justin. They were not dogs that tried to bite me; why would I run away? I think about it, then I say, "They didn't tell me to, my lady."

Robina giggles. Mikhela turns round and says, "It wasn't that easy, *chiya*. *Dom* Ranald-Istvan had soldiers who watched us and *laranzu'in*, and his castle had high walls and locked doors and we didn't have the keys."

"You could have run away when they were bringing you there," Robina says, and Mikhela sighs. Robina did not see the fall of *Dom* Pier's castle. She was not there later, either, when Lord Justin rebelled, though afterwards....

But I have not got to that part of that story. Lady Laurenna says it's important that I tell it in the right order.

Lilias sneaks a glance at me and I pretend to be busy with my writing. She says, "My brother hit Immie. He hit Valli, too, and burned her face. I would have run away if he did that to me. I would have hit him back."

Human women are afraid to be hit. I have seen that. When Lord Justin struck Lady Mirella, at first she held her head up and hit him back. But he did not stop hitting her. And after a while she didn't fight him anymore or shout at him. She just cried. Valli and

I are not afraid if a man hits us. We like it. It pleased *Dom* Pier that we should and so he built us that way. I look up from my writing, and I say, "Valli and I didn't mind."

"But you should," Lilias says. "I don't like it when Mommy scolds me, or Chrysa or Patryce. I cry. Justin was a bad person. He shouted at me. He hit Mirella. He nearly hit me when I said I didn't want to marry Lord Bruno." Her lip wobbled. "He hit Mirella and now she won't talk to anyone."

Mikhela rises and takes the child in her arms. "She'll get better, *chiya*."

I don't know if that is true. Lady Laurenna looks anxious when she talks about Lady Mirella. Domna Elena sometimes cries. Valli cries, too. Lady Mirella was kind to us. When her father beat us, back in his castle, she sent her tiring woman with salves for bruises and smiled at us when she passed us by. *Domna* Elena pretended she did not see us, though once when *Dom* Pier was not there, she spat at us. Later on, when we belonged to Justin, and he beat us—he hit harder than *Dom* Pier ever did—Lady Mirella sometimes came to us herself. When Valli dropped his wine cup and Justin pushed her face into the fire, Lady Mirella brought us salves for the burn. Justin was angry, but he had to pretend, because then she was still *Dom* Ranald-Istvan's.

I don't think she liked Justin, not even then.

~oOo~

Mirella was lying about the extent of her *laran*. That was clear to Justin from her first days in *Dom* Ranald-Istvan's stronghold. To the *Dom* and his household, she was all grace and politeness, but under it, she hated them all. Justin was sure of that; in her place, he would have, and she was only a woman, and thus weaker and more prone to wasting her energies in emotion. Had she been his, he'd have broken her of it soon enough, but the *Dom* was softhearted and indulged her. She was his war-prize and the daughter of his enemy, whose bones lay bleaching under the red sun, but he treated her like a favoured pet. Within a month, she had the run of the castle, though Justin, as *laranzu* and adviser, counselled him otherwise. He watched her with eyes that were hot and greedy. Laurenna also had Ridenow blood, though several generations back.

"You're much of an age, and a stranger here, too. Get close to her, find out what she's hiding. She could yet be a danger to our lord," Justin said, and set Laurenna to watch her. He instructed Bruno to try and flirt with her, persuaded Carsten to engage her in conversation about her father's experiments. And over and over, he sought to rouse the suspicions of the *Dom*.

Perhaps he told himself, at first, that he did this for the safety of the domain. Perhaps he even believed it for a while. But he had wanted Mirella and been refused, he had seen others honoured over him (or so he thought) and in his heart, his resentment festered.

He had served *Dom* Ranald-Istvan loyally since he was old enough to fight, and his lord—his *kinsman*—had betrayed him. His skills had brewed the clingfire and created the strategy that brought down Ferrach Fada; his sword had cut down *Dom* Pier. He was *Dom* Ranald-Istvan's nephew, albeit by a *nedestra* sister. He had twice the talent and intelligence of *Dom* Ranald-Istvan's heir, Lord Alan, who preferred the *rryl* to the sword, and the company of his two new concubines to the hunt, and whose *laran* was negligible. Justin watched Mirella and he watched the *Dom* and his ambition grew.

He had been raised to be a lord, after all. Why should he not be lord over a greater domain than just Forest Lodge? As summer turned to fall and fall to winter, and the lord dismissed the bulk of his army for the duration, Justin drew his friends and allies close and together they planned.

"I should not have listened," Lady Laurenna says sometimes, her brow furrowed. But Justin was her colleague and her Tower mentor and, with her Ridenow blood, thin though it was, she was not well-liked by many of *Dom* Ranald-Istvan's people. In the tower, Justin and his fellow *laranzu'in* worked over new weapons, and spoke to the *Dom* of his plans.

The first signs of the fever appeared in early winter. It seemed at first to be nothing of consequence: a stable-boy came down with it and recovered, then a girl from the laundry, and the son of the steward. The first death was Cloris, Lady Annilda's sewing woman, who was old and infirm already. Two days later, a groom died. Then two of the kitchen staff and the valet who served Lord Alan. Within a week, half the castle was sick and all the *laranzu'in* were kept busy brewing nostrums, whether they were healer-skilled or not. After the seventh death, servants and soldiers began to disappear, slipping away by night. Lord Carsten came down with the sickness and hovered for two days between life and death. *Dom* Ranald-Istvan raged and issued commands, but with the guards reduced by illness and the winter, they were hard to fulfil. And by then, the *Dom* himself had begun to shiver. *Domna* Annilda lay sick in her bed, as did Lord Alan and one of his two concubines. Mirella herself was observed to cough and grow pale, though she refused to take to her bed, insisting instead on helping to nurse the sick. *Domna* Annilda died on the tenth day. At the end of the second week, Lord Alan died and little Lilias was taken delirious to her bed. *Dom* Ranald-Istvan—a shaking, sweating ghost of himself—sent for Justin and the steward.

When the *Dom* died, two days later, Justin was proclaimed his successor. A week later, the sickness burned itself out. The master-at-arms was the last to die, another aging man. "Everyone who might threaten or question Justin," said Mikhela, much, much later. "The *Dom* and his family, apart from Lilias. The steward. The senior captains. And just enough of the servants that it didn't seem too obvious."

"Yes," said Laurenna. And then, "He should have killed me, too. But he didn't realise, not then, and neither did I." She would not say, not then, not ever, how exactly Justin had done it, though I know it was to do with the sickness.

For two months before the sickness came, Lord Justin made me drink a bitter potion every night. But I never got sick. Neither did Valli. We are *riyachiyas*, we are not made like humans. He made his groom take it, too, and he was the second man who died. Once I saw Lord Carsten drink it, and two days later he took sick, but Justin dosed him with another potion, the same one he gave to Lilias and Mirella and those he liked or wanted. He had a different medicine for everyone else. Sometimes, he gave the potions to me to carry or to feed to his patients, and I could smell that they were different.

Everything was different, then. Lord Justin sent to Forest Lodge for his mother and sister to come and live at the castle. He made *Domna* Elena serve them. He gave Mikhela and Moira to Lord Bruno. He promised Lilias to Lord Bruno, too, as soon as she was old enough, and she screamed and cried and tried to bite him. Moira cried, too. She had grown to like Lord Alan. Justin made Carsten his *laranzu* and Keeper of the Tower, and promised him Robina in marriage when she came of age.

Mirella he kept for himself, locking the copper bracelets about her wrists in the great hall before all that remained of the household.

~oOo~

Perhaps Justin—*Dom* Justin now—tried to be a good lord. I don't know how lords are meant to be with other men or with people outside their household. He pleased us, Valli and me, well enough, though sometimes he made the human women who served him cry. He made Mirella cry, often and often. We cried, too, but only when he wished us to. He did not make the men who served him cry, but as days became weeks and weeks became months, more and more of them frowned when he gave them orders. *Dom* Ranald-Istvan had eight men who sat on his council, as well as his *laranzu*, and sewing room gossip claimed *Domna* Annilda had influence over him too. Justin listened to no one but himself, not even Carsten or Bruno. Sated with women and hunting, Bruno did not care, but Carsten grew silent and spent ever more hours in the Tower at his studies.

I do not know who first suggested to Justin that Carsten plotted against him. Perhaps no one needed to. Perhaps the suspicion grew all by itself. If one *laranzu* might overthrow his lord, why not another? I do not know who suggested to him that Carsten had an eye to Mirella. From the day he took over the domain, Justin had put an end to her freedom of the castle, restricting her to the solar and the sewing room and her own quarters. "It is not appropriate for a woman of the Comyn to be befriending servants and wandering about where any petty guardsman might see her." At first, he permitted her to continue with the work she did among the sick and elderly, though he deprived her of Patryce, who had been her tiring woman since she came to the castle, and set Laurenna to watch her. To watch and to report on each and every use Mirella made of her *laran*. He instructed Valli to wait on her, to draw her bath and help her dress and sleep in her chamber on nights when he was elsewhere.

I was lonely without Valli, and Lord Justin only came to me now when Mirella had her courses or she made him angry. When she made him angry, he beat me until my blood ran, and forbade her to tend me. "Immie is not a person, she's a thing. You don't waste your energy healing the furniture."

"You mend your armour if it is damaged. You take care of your weapons," Mirella said.

"Weapons can be replaced," Justin said. "And I will not have you spending time with servants and animals."

The truth was, he was jealous of everything and everyone she spent time with. He burnt any book he found her reading. When she showed affection towards one of his hounds, he slit the animal's throat in front of her.

"The animal is innocent," Mirella said. "Why punish it, in place of me?"

That was the first time he struck her in the presence of others.

In private... Valli whispered to me of beatings and blows.

It seems to be the way of men, to hit those they love, though Chrysa, whose husband had been *Dom* Ranald-Istvan's steward, says her man was kind, and Moira swears Lord Alan never raised a hand to her or Mikhela. Even Patryce, who does not like men at all, says some of them are kind.

I was wrong when I said I do not know who first told *Dom* Justin that Mirella had an eye to Lord Carsten and him to her. It was Lady Laurenna.

~oOo~

"You were jealous," *Domna* Kathia says. "You wanted my son for yourself. You wanted to be the only significant *leronis* in his household. You wanted to have power for yourself."

"Power?" Laurenna says. "Who does not want that? You do. You had it at Forest Gate. You had it at the castle. Your son made you first lady of his household. You had it over Elena. Yes, I wanted power—power over my own life. But I did not want your son."

Kathia laughs, and her voice is harsh. "You expected him to marry you when you came from El Haliene, and he never gave you a look. As if he'd wed a girl who knew her mother's name but not her father's, other than he was some soldier of the Ridenow. I saw how you were with him, in the days of *Dom* Ranald-Istvan. With him and with Carsten, too."

Laurenna shakes her head. "Tower ways are not those of the domains. I do not deny that he and I were lovers, betimes. But there needs to be no more than brief desire for that. I would not wish your son as husband on any woman." Her eye falls on me. "Or any near-woman, either."

Domna Kathia spits. She does not like me or Valli, any better than she likes Laurenna, or Mikhela or Patryce. I sometimes think she does not like any of us, apart from Robina.

She has to like Robina. Robina is her daughter. When we came here, when we fled the castle, it was Robina who made the steward let us in. We could not trust Kathia, then. Patryce says we should have killed her, but Laurenna would not let her. "There has been enough killing," she said, "and Justin was her son."

"Then leave her for the high lord's soldiers, when they come. For *Dom* Ranald-Istvan's cousins."

"Justin was her son," Laurenna repeated. "Justin slew *Dom* Ranald-Istvan. Do you think his kin will let her live?"

Laurenna saved *Domna* Kathia's life, but *Domna* Kathia is not grateful. "Nor should she be," Laurenna says. "We keep her captive in her own home. That is no cause for gratitude."

~ooo~

"Carsten is a better teacher than me," Laurenna said. "I'm impatient, you know that. And Mirella is old to begin Tower training."

"You have Ridenow blood," said Lord Justin. "You understand that gift. And she has far stronger *laran* than she admits. I can feel it." He took another gulp of wine from his copper cup. "She's mine. She ought to be of use to me. Instead... Sometimes I feel danger around her. Danger from her."

"She has no weapons," Laurenna said. "And your *laran* is strong. How can she harm you? You jump at shadows."

It was spring. Word had spread of the change of lordship. To the east, the neighboring lords muttered. A new lord took time to gain the loyalty of his vassals. And in that time, an ambitious neighbor might gain. News trickled in of a raid here, a vassal seeking patronage from another lord there. Justin grew twitchier with every passing day. He said, now, "If I could harness her gift... Her father sought to make only servants and toys, but I could breed soldiers who would seek only to serve and to please their master."

"Then have Carsten teach her." Laurenna hesitated. "He... I would be there, of course, as chaperone. She likes him. And he is gentle with his students. Of course, it would be even better if you taught her yourself, but you are needed elsewhere. And," and she hesitated, "I fear she finds it hard to forget that her father died at your hand. Let Carsten soften her for you, and then... Her Gift will be at your disposal."

"It should be already," Justin grumbled.

"Perhaps," Laurenna said, "that is the danger you sense, her lack of training. Of course, I am happy to work with her, if you wish. But Carsten has the experience, and he's stronger than me." She rose. "Think it over. I know Carsten is willing. He was praising her potential only yesterday."

Two days later, Justin sent Mirella to the Tower, with Laurenna to help her and Valli to wait on her, and Janet, too, whom he pulled from her kitchen duties. "You will study and you will work, and you will do as I wish," he said, putting a hand to her jaw to make her look at him. "My enemies gather and I need more weapons. Do you understand?"

"I do, my lord." And so Mirella went to the Tower, and Justin had to do without her for a season. He took me back to his bed, and others, too, including Mikhela, who had a look of her. He seemed not to recall he had granted her to Lord Bruno. Men are careless of such things, I think, or at least lords are. They are born to rule, and those under them are there to serve. His mother *Domna* Kathia, who ran his household, did not mind about me, nor about Tessa, who worked in the stillroom and had been married to a guard who died of the sickness. He tried to take Patryce, and she clawed and bit him and then locked herself in his privy, and he had her flogged. *Domna* Kathia watched and afterwards scolded Patryce for her waywardness. She did not even mind when, drunk, he dragged *Domna* Elena to his bed. But she frowned over Mikhela.

Lord Bruno frowned, too. And when, in late spring, *Dom* Justin sent him as envoy to Lord Aillard of Aillard, who called himself King and was a distant cousin to *Dom* Ranald-Istvan, he did not come back.

Bandits, said *Dom* Justin, weeping for his *bredu*, and sent his swiftest messenger to complain to the King. "Assassins," said kitchen gossip, "and not the king's, neither." Assassins in the pay of a man who could not stand to be questioned or checked. *Dom* Justin drank more in those days, and grew ever more suspicious of those about him. "The drink clouds your *laran*," said Laurenna, but he sneered at her and sent her away.

When his sister Robina, who had gone through threshold sickness the year before and showed signs of the Rossell Gift, asked if she too might study with Carsten, he snarled at her that she sought to rival him, and locked her in her room for a week. And when *Domna* Kathia protested on his daughter's behalf, he struck her also.

I think that was when the women started talking. At least, that was when Laurenna took to coming to the sewing room. "I need a respite from my Tower work," she said. "And stitching is so restful." They met in twos and threes, over the mending and the cooking, in the schoolroom, where Elena sought to make Robina and Lilias attend to their lessons, in their bedchambers and in the halls. Elena and Patryce, Mikhela and Tessa, Janet and Chrysa, Moira and Laurenna. They smiled and laughed, exchanged compliments and embroidery stitches. There was nothing to see, except...

"They whisper," whispered Valli to me, late one night when she had sneaked away from the Tower and *Dom* Justin pleasured himself with Mikhela. "They use words I don't understand." She snuggled closer, under the blanket. "Lady Mirella is happy in the tower. Lord Carsten is nice to her. So is Lady Laurenna. Lady Laurenna says..." and she took my hand, "she says *Dom* Justin was wrong to burn me, because I'm a person, like her. She says he's a bad man and wants more wars. Lady Laurenna told him that Lady Mirella was learning well and was happy, and he hit her."

It was true about the wars. For a turn of the seasons, Justin was content with *Dom* Ranald-Istvan's holdings. But as fall came round again, his ambitions grew. "I'm as much an Aillard as any of them, through my mother," he told me one night. "I'm young and strong, and the king is aging. Why should I not be King?"

"I don't know, my lord," I said, and he laughed.

"How could you, you stupid creature? Would you like me to be King?"

"Oh, yes, my lord, if it pleased you."

"And Lady Mirella, do you think she would like it?"

"Why not, my lord, if you were happy?"

His smile died. "What makes you say that, thing? She would rather die than see me happy."

I dropped to my knees before him, "Then she is wrong, my lord. I think you would make a very fine King."

"So do I, yet I am troubled, troubled..."

The next day, he went to the tower, to command Carsten to increase the production of clingfire. He found his friend alone with Mirella, both bent over some book, and laughing.

We all heard the screaming.

When he came back, he was covered in blood. Mirella lay in his arms, unconscious and bleeding. And, in the tower, Carsten lay dead.

~oOo~

Mirella was once again confined to her bedchamber and no one was allowed to tend her, apart from Valli. "The rest of you are against me," he yelled, when first Laurenna, then Kathia, remonstrated with him.

"She needs a healer, *caryo*."

"She has *laran* of her own. Let her heal herself."

"At least let the *riyachiya* take her a pain-killing draught."

"She is my enemy! Don't you see that? She won't use her Gift to make my armies. She plotted with Carsten against me. And you are all in it, too, I sense it. You hate me! You all hate me."

"I am your mother, and I love you."

But Justin would not listen, retreating to his rooms. In the sewing room, the women gathered, me amongst them for once. "Well, if his high lordship is sulking, he's not watching," said Patryce. "I'm going to my lady, and no one will stop me."

"*Dom* Justin has the key to her chamber," Moira said.

"Then I'll break the lock."

"Wait," said Laurenna. She looked at me. "Immie, sweet, I have left my blue veil in my chamber. Could you fetch it for me, please? It should be in the small chest."

"Of course, *damisela*." *Dom* Justin had not summoned me, nor had he forbidden me to wait on Lady Laurenna.

"And when you find it, could you come back via the kitchens and ask Janet to bring up bread and hot wine?"

"*Z'par servu, vai leronis.*" I curtseyed and obeyed. It took me some time to find the veil, for it was not where Laurenna said, and then Janet was busy and did not want to hear me. When I returned, Laurenna smiled and thanked me, and sent me to bed.

If there had been whispering in the castle before, now it redoubled. Without Carsten the Tower—small enough already—was too small to make weapons efficiently, even if *Dom* Justin worked in it himself. The remaining guards—and they were few, in those last days—muttered amongst themselves, and one night a third of them slipped away. The servants were afraid. "The *Dom* is crazy," one said to me. "He's drunk half the time and he talks to himself. I've heard him. He'll kill us all in our beds, like poor Lord Carsten. And poor Lady Mirella!"

"They hate me," said *Dom* Justin. It seemed to amuse him. "They hate me and fear me. I can live with that." He spent his days in the Tower, from which he had banned everyone, including Laurenna, and his nights with me. "They all hate me but you, *chiya*. But you love me, don't you."

"Yes, my lord." It was my function to love.

It was three nights after that that Lady Laurenna gave me the wine, as I made my way to *Dom* Justin's chamber.

He drank deep, and held out his cup for more. I rose to fetch the bottle to refill it. Behind me, he began to choke. I reached for him, but my hands did not know how to heal. I had not been taught how to keep a man from death.

Outside the chamber, I could hear running feet and the cries of men.

~ooo~

"I sneaked down to the stables," Robina says, "and let the horses and chervines out, so the guardsmen couldn't send a message for help. And I helped Lady Laurenna weave her illusion, too. "

"You did," Laurenna said.

"Janet put sleeping stuff in the servants' food," says Lilias. "She let me stir it. And my mother stole *Domna* Kathia's keys. She and Chrysa locked the guard in their quarters and barricaded the door."

"The sergeant tried to get to *Dom* Justin, and Patryce killed him with her axe. Mikhela and Moira took drugged food to the sentries. And then we all ran away to Forest Lodge. We were heroines, like in the old stories."

"Immie killed the *Dom*. She was bravest of all." Lilias said.

"I didn't mean to," I say. My hand shakes, and I make a blot on my page. "I didn't know. It wasn't right. I didn't mean to do it. *Dom* Justin was my master."

Laurenna comes and puts a hand on my shoulder. "I know," she says. "That was why it had to be you. He'd have sensed the danger, from anyone else. But you... You were loyal."

Zandru's Gift
by Vera Nazarian

The Ages of Chaos were marked by incessant warfare, the creation of terrible *laran* weapons, and the development of Gifts to produce them. Marriages were arranged according to meticulously kept genetic records, but breeding for aptitude was not the only method used to enhance specific psychic talents although it may well have been among the more benign.

Vera Nazarian is a two-time Nebula Award Nominee, award-winning artist, and member of Science Fiction and Fantasy Writers of America. She describes herself as having, "a penchant for moral fables and stories of intense wonder, true love, and intricacy." She is the author of critically acclaimed novels *Dreams Of The Compass Rose* and *Lords Of Rainbow*, as well as the parodies *Mansfield Park And Mummies* and *Northanger Abbey And Angels And Dragons*, and most recently, *Pride And Platypus: Mr. Darcy's Dreadful Secret*. Her latest work is the epic fantasy *Cobweb Bride* Trilogy set in an alternate Renaissance. After many years in Los Angeles, Vera lives in a small town in Vermont, and uses her Armenian sense of humor and her Russian sense of suffering to bake conflicted pirozhki and make art. Her official author website is www.veranazarian.com.

There is a saying among the plain folk of Darkover that the Alton Gift was born of a woman's pain. Its power, in the most extreme form, is closest to madness, and it cuts you—sometimes cleanly, sometimes leaving ragged lacerations in the soul—but always, like a knife.

~ooo~

Rohan Alton wed Gabrielys Delleray in the winter of the year that the child Carolin was born, heir to the Hastur king. Rohan, people said, was either exquisitely mad, or a misanthrope, or possibly both. Spindly-limbed, gaunt, and devious, he was known to commit acts that some regarded as noble caprice, and others called simple cruelty.

His lady, Gabrielys, was a strong-willed, heavy, and sensual woman. She had great plans for the House and their line, and very quickly took the reins of control in her own able hands. With a background of Tower training and a considerable *laran* talent, she managed to will her husband, like an unbridled stallion, into submission and to curb his unspeakable oddity, a least outwardly.

The union of Alton and Delleray produced two children. Nellan, the oldest son, was introspective since birth, and, having shown *laran* talent, was being instructed at Hali Tower, as recommended by the breeding program. The younger daughter, Lissa, was at fifteen a beauty, rich and dark and earthy as autumn.

But there was yet one more child. Born of another woman, Rohan's first wife who had died in childbirth, Dyana was a thin girl-child, self-effacing and silent. She had skin so pale and colorless that it was almost albino, except for a fine sprinkling of freckles. Lashes and brows she had that were bleached out and translucent, and a sunburst of hair, so red-gold that it hurt one's eyes to look upon.

Her hair called attention upon her. And the quiet stepdaughter wordlessly hated herself and her hair, because they would always know her for it, would always notice her....

~oOo~

They gathered in the Music Room, ladies of the House, busy with embroidery and woman talk. Gabrielys, Lady Alton, sat with old Dame Yllira and three of her women, talking in loud voices before the ornate window. Outside, framed with stonework lace, was the world, rolling viridian hills and icy lavender, with the sun-torch burning mildly through the morning haze.

A little away from the older women sat the girls of the House, gathered around an embroidery table. They whispered in muted giggles, often glancing up from their needlework to see if the older women heard them. One of them, whose skin was blandest and hair brightest, was silent.

"What's with you, Dyana?" said Lissa at last, the one whose giggles rang bright like a mountain spring. But then, there was a hint of darkness in her autumn eyes. "Why so silent, sister Red-Hair? Dreaming of our cousin again, are you?"

"Dyana is always silent! Need there be a reason?" said one of the young girls.

"Oh, but there's always a reason with Dyana," said Lissa.

"Only—dream all you like for nothing, poor sweet sister Red-Hair. Caerall has eyes only for me...."

At that, the silent one looked up from her embroidery. Opaque eyes met Lissa's. Dyana's lips were thin, like a slender incision of color against the white of her face. And yet the voice that issued from them, when it did, was precise, controlled. "What dreams I have are my business, Lissa. But if you must know—for, I see you're dying to know—Caerall has no place in them."

She then lowered her gaze again and continued to move the needle.

"He has no place! Well! Because you're too feeble even to admit it. Besides, Caerall is kind to you because we are sisters. But then, he's equally kind to your dog!"

They burst out in wicked giggles.

"You know, I think Dyana is just a stupid, feeble-minded wench." Lissa suddenly declared, her beautiful face taking on a crafty look. "Just look at her. Her hair, uncombed, barely decent. Do I see drool on her face?"

"She's flat as a board besides, no shape to her at all," whispered another of the girls to a third, loudly and not bothering to conceal her words.

In the House, people often spoke in Dyana's presence as though she weren't there.

"And another thing," continued Lissa, her voice rising, "She's had that ugly mutt of hers for almost two winters now, and it still has no name! 'Dog' she calls it, just plain 'Dog!'"

Lissa turned to her silent older sister. "What if I called you 'wench,' instead of using your pretty name, Dyana? What would it sound like then?"

You call me that and other things, thought Dyana. Her eyes remained averted, but she had no need to look up, seeing the room and its occupants clearly in her mind's eye. For a long time now she had known that odd sense, akin to omniscience. And lately she knew everyone's nearly every thought before it was voiced.

She had also known that Caerall, tall and strong, with hair like summer flax, and eyes warm as the fireplace, was kind to her in a genuine way. Knowing that, she remained quiet.

"Would you say something, stupid girl! Look at her, dumb as a vat of butter!"

Their taunts, especially Lissa's, had grown so loud that the Lady Alton took note and, looking in their direction, said languidly, "Lissa, let your sister be." And then, turning her intense critical gaze on the thin stepdaughter, added, "And you, girl, stop being obstinately dim-witted. Don't let them push you around and then expect me to speak up for you all the time."

Dyana again glanced up. "Madam," she said, "I do not."

"Do not what?"

"I do not expect you to do anything of the sort."

"Good," said Gabrielys. "Then the next time I expect *you* to speak up for yourself." And she turned back to Dame Yllira. "A pathetic child she is, Yllira. Oh, how weary I am, weary of her personality. Aldones knows, she is good for nothing."

"Who is good for nothing, Aunt?" said a handsome young man, entering the room and kissing Gabrielys on the cheek.

"No one is, if you don't listen in on other people's conversations." The lady turned her cheek up to him, looking closely, with secret pride, at her brother's son. Her words bore only a semblance of sternness.

As always, Brandon Delleray was a fine sight, dark and slim, with brows like taut crescents, and confident midnight eyes. If he weren't so close of kin, Gabrielys would have gladly wed him to her own daughter.

"So you are all returned from the ride, my boy?" half-croaked old Dame Yllira. "And what of the others, where are they?"

Brandon inclined his head respectfully, the very picture of fine, manly decorum. "Lord Alton is at the stables still. Caerall is with him."

Then, abruptly remembering something, he turned to Gabrielys: "My lady aunt, there is a man here to see you. We met him on our way in. He is—he appears important, judging by his escort and trappings. Also, I believe he wears the robe of a Keeper—"

"Ah, of course, Mellior!" exclaimed Gabrielys with animation. Quickly she got up, and the rest of the women with her. "The Keeper of Hali, I was expecting him." And with that, she headed out the door.

Dame Yllira, an old kinswoman of the Altons, was supported on both sides as she hobbled out of the room with the others. The young people remained. Brandon grinned boldly and walked up to the seated girls.

"All of you *damiselas* make the prettiest things," he said, looking directly in each girl's eyes and pretending to examine their work.

The girls blushed. More than half of them had a crush on Brandon, who was only slightly older and definitely perfect in their eyes, despite the usual leering charm.

In that moment the door came slightly ajar, and a small bony dog silently padded into the room. He headed straight for Dyana and, wagging his tail, settled at her feet under the table.

"You left the door open, Brandon. Look what you've done!" whined Lissa. "That beast isn't supposed to be let in here. The foul thing will make us all dirty! Out, out, get it out of here!"

Dyana reached down almost unconsciously to protect the dog, to hold him to her. Putting down her embroidery, she then got up. "I'll take him outside."

Her voice had been soft, nearly a whisper. Brandon stared at her pale, vulnerable skin, her colorless lashes.

How ugly she is... She could read a fragment of his thought. There was more, but she did not quite catch the rest, because at that point the dog yelped in pain. Lissa had kicked him with her pretty foot.

Dyana held on to the dog and started to go, but Brandon barred her way.

He just stood there, saying nothing, looking into her eyes. A smile played on his fine lips.

Dyana decided it was not a good smile. "Let me by," she said, not meeting his gaze. "Please."

"Why, cousin?" he said. "Why should I?" He planted himself firmly at the door, while the girls began to giggle, knowing that a game of sorts was about to ensue.

It was a game they all knew well, one which now made Dyana's heart beat rapidly in anticipation of sickness, of something fearful and inevitable. Thoughtlessly she made a lunge for the door, ignoring the cries breaking out around her....

"Hold her, hold her!"

"Don't let her go!" they cried.

And then she felt the steel clasp of Brandon's fingers on her shoulder and wrist. He was strong and he was sadistically pinching her in his grip, slowly tightening his large hand over her pale, delicate skin.

"What's the matter, sister Red-Hair, can't get out now?" came Lissa's voice from behind, and her rapid breath hissed in Dyana's ear.

At Dyana's feet the dog began to yelp helplessly. It was then quickly kicked into silence and cowered a few steps away.

Someone else pulled her hair painfully. They were all around her, a mess of bodies, pinching, pulling, hurting her from all sides. Worst of all was Brandon. He continued to hold her, and now she found herself pressed against the length of him somehow, and his fingers strayed, unnoticed by all, to stroke and pinch her buttocks.

"You wouldn't tell anyone, cousin..." he whispered, "or you'll regret it. Remember what I told you I'd do to that dog...."

Silently, clenching her teeth, Dyana Alton nodded to him, to them all, and struggled no more.

~oOo~

Mellior, Keeper of Hali, sipped the aromatic tea. "Tell me, *domna*," he continued. "How is it all progressing?"

Gabrielys, Lady Alton, sighed and lowered her eyes. "Not well at all, I'm afraid," she said. "The girl is stubborn as Zandru and about as easy to provoke as a rock. No matter what is said or done to her, she bears it all, weirdly, inhumanly."

"And what of the other in our plan, her father?"

"Alton is imbalanced. What little I've tried, provoked enough of a response from him on the mental level to show me that his talent amounts to nothing. He can probe very deeply, it is true, and he can cast an illusion that makes one cringe and obey. But he cannot *bend the will*. Now, the girl, on the other hand—she is very promising."

"Tell me," said Mellior softly, with a calculating look in his eyes, "what exactly have you tried with her?"

Lady Alton tightened her expression. "Really, Mellior, what do you take me for? I've tried subtly, helped things along, shall we say. She is very easy to bully, you know. Everyone else does it perfectly, without my intervention."

Mellior got up and paced the chamber. After moments of thoughtful silence, he concluded, "Then, my lady, you must do your own part in this, no longer just rely on—chance."

"I see. For the sake of this vital thing, I must."

"Yes. Without an emotional outburst from her, the new talent can never sprout fully. It must be activated now, before it is too late. Rohan will—I can tell you safely—bear no more children. He is the last one to carry the genetic potential. His offspring by you, my lady, are not Gifted that way. And since you so greatly desire this *laran*, this *thing* upon your and your Lord's line—"

"Yes, because of this, I must do what I must," said Lady Alton, and her eyes, for one second only, held in them too the look of madness.

"Fine then, *Domna* Gabrielys," said the Keeper. "I now return to Hali, but will impatiently wait for any news from you."

~oOo~

Dom Rohan sat back in his chair before the fire and regarded the thin, flame-haired girl with silently terrified eyes who was his daughter.

"My lady wife tells me, child, that you've been un—unkind to her." he said, his voice like silk and poison, but breaking once into a stutter. "Come here, child. Come to your father, who must now *look into your eyes.*"

Dyana stood powerlessly before him. She knew what he was about to do, having experienced it once when barely nine, for having misbehaved. Back then, it had left her screaming and hysterical for several days after. It was an agony of—

An agony of inner vision.

She felt a link, a snap upon the outer barriers of her mind, as the eyes of Lord Alton came to pierce her with an acute, wrenching intensity. And then she was trapped....

In a chamber of darkness, she was alone. A pressure upon her temples, a crawling on her skin. Things moist and thick, pricklings on her spine. There came a human form then, cold and harsh to the touch. And all around, the smell of excrement.

Something began to pull at her, against which she struggled, but her resistance was weak. Heavy she was, dull and formless as water. She submitted with her mind even then, submitted as she had done always in reality. It was the only thing she knew to do that had ever stopped the pain....

Her soul's private parts were laid bare, and then she felt herself pierced by a fierce agony of intrusion, like white angry coals—an intrusion to a place so deep within her that she never even knew of it being there. She floated in the void of pounding black pain, relentless, thrown from a cliff deeper and deeper into the night....

When she emerged from the trance, her father's eyes calmly watched her, and a thin delicate smile shifted on his lips.

"Now, child," he said. "Tell me that you feel better now, that you will no longer be unkind to your stepmother."

As she continued to stare numbly at his fine, mad face, Lord Alton began to quake. Silently at first, he shook with mirth, and then his voice burst through, turning into shrieks of high-pitched banshee laughter, odd and unnatural.

Swift as a monkey, Rohan leaped up from his seat, planted a moist kiss on his daughter's brow and, still shrieking, left the room. For minutes afterward, the notes of his laughter resounded in echoes through the stone of the great House.

Dyana, encased in her private shell of numb silence, paid no heed to the sound. She stood with head lowered and considered with detached curiosity that this time, this second time, she did not break down, did not struggle or fight *him*. She had learned.

She had known his illness and even now loved her poor, gentle, mad, wicked father, continued to love him. Even if he did, for the second time, defile her soul.

~oOo~

Gabrielys, observed, fuming inwardly, a subtle transformation taking place, a calcification of sorts. Dyana, her silent stepdaughter, was turning to stone before her very eyes. With each passing day it seemed her expression grew duller, until it was effaced completely. Nothing, it seemed, evoked the least reaction from her—no emotional affect.

When reprimanded, Dyana would apologize in a wooden whisper and do what she was told. In fact, she rarely gave cause for any reprimands at all, obedient as she was. Even the girls stopped teasing her, at first bored with her lack of response to their taunts, and later somewhat frightened by it.

In House Alton, Dyana became a living ghost-shade, a self-effacing nothing. No movement ever passed her stone-white features, no tension could be observed around her glassy eyes.

The only thing of value to her seemed to be her pathetically thin dog. She never coddled it, never spoke to it words of endearment as people did to their pets. She only fed it whatever scraps she could, and hid the dog in her own cubicle of a chamber at the slightest hint of it coming to the attention of others.

It was only surprising that Gabrielys Alton hadn't noticed this earlier, hadn't noticed that, of all things, the dog mattered to this living-dead one.

"The girl is mad, too," Gabrielys would say to Dame Yllira in private. "In her own way, she has inherited even this tendency from her father. Only, it is a different, soft madness, and one which I plan to make use of...."

~oOo~

With the coming Feast Days there were many get-togethers between Alton, Delleray, and distant MacAran kin. During one of such, as the candles in the chandeliers burned themselves out, close to midnight, Lady Alton quickly drew young Caerall MacAran to her side and spoke to him in conspiratorial whispers. She pointed subtly to the group of unwed girls, at the fringe of which stood a solitary wallflower. Dyana Alton stood silent and withdrawn in the middle of the Festival.

Gabrielys told the young MacAran what she had in mind, what she expected him to do. Although betrothed to her own daughter, Lissa, Caerall was to attempt the seduction of cousin Red-Hair, explained Lady Alton. She had noticed, she told him, that Dyana's dimmed gaze came into sudden clear focus whenever it fell upon him—which might mean something, or nothing at all. And yet, if there was the barest chance of the girl's interest, he must try to awaken her, try....

"You must understand, it is for her own good, my boy..." whispered Gabrielys in her dark sensual voice (at that instant truly believing it herself), and the young man thought he heard the calling of crows in it, and saw even more darkness in her eyes.

Caerall—tall and fair as the candlelight, and nobler than any of them—took a step back in involuntary horror. He bowed his head then, bowed before the Lady Alton, and refused adamantly to be the instrument of her dark will.

But Brandon—originally directed here by jealous cousin Lissa to observe and listen in on her betrothed, and now lurking in the nearby shadows, for that was his way—heard the secret will of Lady Alton. With that, he knew what he must then do with the cousin Red-Hair, the one who was as ugly as Zandru's deepest hell, and yet who often came to haunt his soft, secret, perverse dreams.

~oOo~

In the velvet softness of the night, Dyana *sensed* with that other part of her mind, through layers of slumber, the dog's pitiful stifled whimper, its *distress*.

She came awake with a start and then felt the weight and warmth of *another* next to her.

"Sh-h-h..." came the hurried whisper. "Don't be afraid, sweet Dyana, it is I, Caerall.... I am here to be with you at last, knowing how much you have wanted me. I, too, had always desired you—"

Dyana gasped. "You—What lie is this! You are not Caerall! I can *see* you even now, clear as day, and you are not Caerall at all—*Cousin Brandon!*"

"Shut up!" he then snarled at her and forced a hand roughly against her mouth.

Dyana instantly eased her muscles and lay, a dead weight.

Do not resist....

"You'll not use my name, bitch!" he continued. "I'll tell you instead why I'm here. I want to see you scream, Dyana. After I'm done with you, you'll squirm and scream in bitch-pleasure and beg for more, and weep for my touch!"

"Why...must you do this?" was all she asked then, oddly at peace in that wildest of moments. There was a sensation of being half within and half outside her body, an observer looking *down*....

In answer, he groped her and came to lay on top of her, already hot and moaning in anticipation of her body. As an afterthought, he added, "By the way, sweet cousin Red-Hair, if you speak of this to anyone, I will take your dog and—"

But Dyana no longer heard. High above this place she floated, in her own shell of gentle mother-of-pearl. So far away she retreated that she never felt the actual violation of her body.

~oOo~

In the morning, when they found Dyana Alton bleeding in her bed, with dark bruises covering her body, there was a commotion in House Alton. Lady Gabrielys made an unprecedented appearance at the girl's chamber. She arrived with healers, with the women of the household, and, with a great show of raving grief, demanded that Dyana tell them who had done this to her, who had committed the outrage.

Sunken in the large bed, the girl lay as one who is dead, with eyes closed. Her pallor had reached an unspeakable level, standing in even more contrast with the bright orange wisps of hair scattered on the pillow like the sun's corona.

When addressed, she opened her bleak eyes to look at Lady Alton. But she said nothing.

"The girl will not speak," said an old *leronis* of the household. "Furthermore, great, impenetrable barriers have been raised in her mind...."

"Do you think that I, with my Tower training, don't know that?" exploded Gabrielys. Her expression darkened with insight. "Dyana." She turned again to the girl. "Tell me, child, who has hurt and violated you?" As she spoke thus, she attempted to pry her way into the mind of the girl, or at least pick up a stray thought. As expected, she met with a wall of soft yet unbreachable psychic silence.

In the corner, Lissa was sobbing in confused fear. "I am sorry..." she mumbled constantly, "I am so sorry...." No one bothered to inquire why she was sorry, or even to once look her way.

Then a truly dark course of action occurred to Gabrielys. Turning to a servant, she said, "Call here the young MacAran, Caerall. Bring him here this instant. Make haste!"

Gabrielys wasn't sure what had happened to her stepdaughter. In truth, she didn't care. What pumped energy into her mind now was the chance that she had at her fingertips.

She had wanted Caerall to seduce Dyana—not violate her, but sufficiently disturb her, thus inducing in her a breakdown. Whether he had done this or not, it didn't matter. Someone else had done the deed, done it in fact to a crueler extent than even Gabrielys planned. And yet, because Caerall had refused to do her bidding, she also saw an opportunity to punish the youth for standing firm against her will.

Lady Alton knew Caerall well enough to be sure he hadn't had a part in this.

Then who did? Zandru only knew. Whoever that one was, Gabrielys owed him a dark debt of convenience. What she herself was about to do—

There was a commotion in the hall, and unexpected to all, Lord Alton came into the room, humming a bawdy street tune. He stopped, looking around with very clear, blank eyes—as the mentally ill sometimes do. "What a gathering." he whispered. "All of you, in my lover's room!"

He had obviously gotten confused in his mind, and yet the embarrassing mistake was obvious to all.

"It is—nothing, my *husband*," said Gabrielys. "You should leave the room, for your daughter has the—women's illness." She purposefully lied, not wanting to bring him into this already too convoluted thing, this situation that was just on the verge of either realizing her long-sought goals or getting completely beyond her control.

"Women's illness?" echoed Rohan lightly. "Is that why there is blood on the sheets? But why is she bruised? Why—"

And then, like a stroke of lightning, a rage was upon him, together with the understanding of the truth—for he too could read minds.

"Who has done this, daughter of mine?" he cried, his voice no longer womanish but an eruption. It resounded through their heads—all of those with *laran*.

At that instant, Caerall MacAran, with a troubled face, strode into the chamber.

Without a moment of pause, Gabrielys pointed a bejeweled finger at the young man, and spoke one word only. "He."

On the bed, the eyes of Dyana Alton—pale and lucid and great as the sky—came wide open.

Rohan screamed. An agile beast, he threw himself upon the

throat of the newcomer and, struggling, they both fell to the floor. Everything happened so fast, in the span of a heartbeat, that Caerall did not even understand what hit him.

"Oh gods! No, Father!" sounded a parched voice. Dyana Alton had raised herself weakly into a seated position on the bed. Gabrielys—no, not just Gabrielys, but everyone—turned to look. Never had they seen Dyana, poor cousin Red-Hair, like *this*. When plaster is poured into a mold and then cooled, permanently taking on a shape, the only way for it to change shape is to crack asunder. It seemed now, that something had indeed crumbled away in the face of Dyana.

Sensing this, her father himself froze, releasing the MacAran. Straightening, they both regarded the girl.

Dyana's face was contorted like a wound. The bruises and swellings stood out harshly against her white skin. Her mouth shook, and liquid gathered in her eyes."Let Caerall go, Father," she whispered, putting all her strength into her voice to make it steady, just that once. "Caerall has never touched me. He has done nothing."

"Then are you accusing me of lying, you wretched girl?" flared up Gabrielys. "Ungrateful wretch! I have been like a mother to you! I, who even now am trying to have justice served against your misfortune—"

"You, a mother?" Dyana's eyes showed honest surprise. "Why, if such is a real mother, then I wish the whole world be orphaned! You, my lady, with your motherly love, have turned me numb as ice!"

Gabrielys slapped her resoundingly. "Why, you insolent hussy!"

At that moment there came a growling from under the bed, and the thin dog sprang out from underneath the bed coverings and, for the first time in its sorry life, bit someone—Gabrielys.

With a yell, Lady Alton kicked the animal away from her with all her strength. Fury was on her beautiful, awful face. Gathering composure, she turned around, saying to a servant, "Enough! Early tomorrow, have this beast killed as a lesson to her." Turning back to Dyana, she added, "Learn well your lesson of respectful womanly obedience, daughter of Alton."

And not saying another word, seemingly forgetting the reason for her and everyone else being here, she stormed out of the chamber, followed by her retinue.

Rohan Alton also did not seem to remember anything. Silently, aimlessly, never glancing back at MacAran, he wandered out of the room, in their wake.

Caerall alone stood like an obelisk, rooted to the spot. Having ceased her weeping, in shock, Lissa huddled in the far corner. Tottering on her feet, Dyana stood up, clutching her robes about her.

"What have they done to you, merciful Avarra, what has been done here...?" whispered Caerall, meeting her gaze with his empathetic, kind eyes.

Seeing the intimate expression of his eyes when he looked at Dyana, Lissa gave a sob.

Dyana stood, shaking, looking at both of them. "Leave me...be." And the tone of her voice made it so that the request could not be denied.

"Please..." said Caerall, the last one to leave the room. "Is there anything I can do for you?"

~oOo~

When they were all gone from her chamber, Dyana went to the door and locked and bolted it. She was a silent shadow. Being sure that she was completely alone at last, she knelt on the floor and whispered, searching desperately around the small room: "...Dog...my dog. Come, my dog...."

Soon the animal revealed itself from behind a drapery and tentatively approached her, still fearful from the hurt. It then began to wag its tail, raising its gentle brown eyes at her, and licked her outstretched hand. There was a trace of blood on its short drab fur.

As twilight began to creep into the chamber, she sat on the floor, her hands gently holding the creature to her. Closely she held it, and torrents ran down her cheeks, now contorted into a grimace of agony. Only occasionally would she mouth the words "...dog, oh, dog...." And then, because she knew it was their last night, she would say no more.

When true friends say goodbye, it is best done in silence.

~oOo~

At dawn, the red sun of Darkover lifted itself over the rim of the Kilghard Hills, and there came a loud knocking on the door of Dyana Alton. Servants and guards had come to do the bidding of Lady Alton.

But there was no answer from inside.

More servants were brought. Their knocking echoed down the corridors, growing louder and louder, to no avail. For that reason, Gabrielys herself was notified.

"The little red bitch has run away!" fumed Gabrielys, yelling indiscriminately at the servants of the household, "I should've expected something like that from her! A mad thing, quiet as a fox! I should've known! But then, she's weak, she won't get far...."

The servants were told to break down the door. Gabrielys herself marched down to observe, followed by the frightened women. A steward was brought, and with an axe he struck down the lock and bolt. When they entered the small room, *stillness* greeted their eyes. The form of Dyana Alton, motionless as a statue, sat in a chair next to the window. There was no sign of the dog anywhere.

Gabrielys stared intently, trying to grasp with her mind the psychic emptiness that filled the chamber. She knew that the girl was living, but she was now different, *changed*. Gabrielys, for once in her life, was afraid, genuinely at a loss of what to do. She was about to open her mouth, to call for other *leroni* to fetch here the Keeper of Hali—

But she never had a chance. Dyana slowly turned away from the window to face her. Something in her face made Gabrielys want to be small and invisible, and to dissolve into the very ground underneath her.

"You have wanted me to learn my lesson, Madam. And I have learned it."

"What?..." whispered Gabrielys, unconsciously afraid of raising her voice. And then recalled, "Where—where is the dog? Where are you hiding it? Where is it, speak immediately! Do not attempt to lie to me!"

"It is where you have no means of reaching it, not ever."

"What? How dare you?"

Her pale, red-haired stepdaughter said nothing, only regarded her blankly, like a dead thing.

Gabrielys fumed inside. She could read nothing with her *laran*, and so she had to resort to screaming for the servants, telling them to search the house for that dog, to turn it upside down if necessary.

Still the stepdaughter said nothing. Her eyes, like incandescent coals, burned.

"Hah! I know! You killed your own dog!" Lissa, who stood with the others, exclaimed. "How beastly cruel you are, sister Red-Hair!" Again breaking out into a fit of weeping—for she would never forget now how Caerall had *looked* at her own sister Red-Hair—Lissa cried out in a burst of wounded pride and fury, "I wish you were dead! Dead, dead, dead! I wish you would rot and shrivel away like that disgusting, filthy—"

Gabrielys had a new, even darker idea. She locked her barriers around her mind so that no thought of her deception would leak out, and then pretended to go to the door and speak with a servant outside.

When she came back within, a black smile was on her lips. She spoke craftily and in a newly calm, measured tone. "Well! The mystery is solved. The creature has been found and destroyed already, some time ago, I am told—just before dawn. Apparently Caerall was very useful in that regard. What? Did you honestly think he was going to hide that dog for you? But there, you needn't concern yourself about it any longer, willful child. What is done is done, and I am sorry for you that it had to be Caerall, of all people, who lied to you when he merely *pretended* to help—"

And as the words were spoken, one after the other, at first incomprehensible, and then sinking in with a cold like the wind of the Hellers, as the fabric of the world itself seemed to betray her and come crashing down...at that moment the mind of Dyana Alton, stretched to its limits, broke asunder.

Like lightning she struck out all about her, with a *scream* of a death deeper than bottomless hell, a *scream* that pierced the open sky, and was heard in the far away Tower—the Awakening of the Alton Gift.

The Alton Gift and Curse.

Not many clearly remembered that day. There were many deaths, they said, destruction and maiming of the minds and souls. The Lady and Lord Alton of the time were both struck down, together with their younger daughter and cousins. The bodies of Gabrielys and Lissa Alton were hardly recognizable—their faces no longer theirs. The demented Rohan was found running through the halls, holding hands to his temples, to his ears, contorted like an agile monkey, and letting no one near him. The *leroni* that later attempted to reach his mind found that the psychic *scream* still echoed in his head—at which point all attempts to reach him were stopped.

And in a distant room of the great House, they found Brandon Delleray, lying dead, his mind burned out by a lightning strike.

Only Caerall MacAran was left untouched where he sat in a small secret alcove in an older part of the house. For there was a living dog curled up at his feet—thin, poor, decidedly underfed, but warm and alive, and lovingly hidden away as promised—and even in the midst of her madness, Dyana could *feel* its dear presence—indeed, both their dear, warm presences together, like shining lights amid the despair of her storm. Both of them—honorable young man and loyal, loving dog—had thus remained by Dyana's side throughout her madness, and Caerall was later bound to her *di catenas*—her chosen one.

And the new Lady of Alton, after she had raged for several days thus, was restrained at last, with great difficulty, but not by reinforcements sent from Hali Tower and their Keeper, as much as by the love of two beings; love, as it cooled her hellfires into a slow burn of steady self-control and power.

She was one of the last "fine examples" of the breeding program.

She was the strongest of the Altons and was thus to rule the House—which she did, fairly and with clean, good justice, after regaining her reason.

The Gift was passed on through the Alton blood, together with pallor of skin, fire-red hair, and loyalty to kin and friends. A love of animals came always to be a part of the Alton spirit, expressed by the strong, fine horses that the Alton folk bred.

And yet, those same folk said, it had all come from simple loyalty, and the love of a woman for her only friend, a dog who, it was also said, soon enough grew healthy, round, and well-fed with a splendid coat of fur, and was ever at her side, well unto their golden years.

Late Rising Fire
by Leslie Fish

A number of stories in this anthology are related to *Stormqueen.* Some are "variations on a theme" and others arise more directly from the characters and situations described in the novel. One of the pleasures of short fiction is the opportunity to fill in the gaps and go "behind the scenes" as does the tale below. Here Leslie Fish brings together two elements of Darkover—the nonhuman *chieri* and their *emmasca* human descendants.

Leslie Fish learned to sing and to read at a very young age, playing guitar at sixteen, and writing the first of hundreds of songs shortly thereafter, including settings of Rudyard Kipling's poetry and the "all-time most notorious" Star Trek filksong ever written: "Banned From Argo." She's recorded a number of albums and composed songs, both alone and collaborative, on albums from every major filk label. She was elected to the Filk Hall Of Fame as one of the first inductees. In college, she majored in English and minoring in psychology, protest and politics, joined the Industrial Workers of the World, and did psychology counseling for veterans. Her other jobs included railroad yard clerk, go-go dancer, and social worker. She currently lives in Arizona with her husband Rasty and a variable number of cats which she breeds for intelligence.

Prince Felix Hastur had learned at an early age how to evade his bodyguards; he went into the castle garden at the edge of the woodlot, knelt down as if to study a flower, poked a finger into the little silk drawstring-bag at his throat to touch the blue stone therein, and pictured everyone's eyes skipping over him, looking away from him, distracted to anything but himself. After that it took but a quick dash into the woodlot, and he was gone.

Beyond the woodlot lay the king's hunting-forest proper, and Felix plunged into it. He ran uphill, toward the distant peaks, ran like a hunted stag, ran until fatigue made him slow and stop. No one from the castle was anywhere near; none could see him or report his weakness—more weakness, as expected, of the king's *emmasca* son.

Called 'son' only for courtesy, he admitted again to himself.

And now the king's only son, and heir to the throne—and obviously, being sexless and unable to breed heirs, unfit for it. The political nightmare didn't bear thinking about, though every other noble in the Domains could think of nothing else.

No one bothered to consider that Felix had lost his beloved older brother.

Did no one imagine I could grieve?

Felix dropped to his knees beside a huge ancient featherleaf tree and threw his arms around it for support, digging his six-fingered hands into the bark, as the memories rose and flooded him. *Laszlo...*

Laszlo: big and bluff and almost always laughing, generous and sunny of disposition, who never did worse to his little brother and sister than tease—and that not cruelly.

Laszlo: patiently teaching his fearful little brother how to ride a stag-pony, carefully extricating his wailing little sister Ellora from a thornbush, gently bandaging a nervous hound's injured leg, and singing lustily beside the fire to distract the castle servants from worrying about the raging blizzard outside.

Laszlo: brave to the edge of madness, whether fighting forest fires or marauding bandits, always assuming himself to be the shield between any danger and what he considered his people—which was almost everyone in the Domains.

Laszlo: who had been in particular the shield between his little brother and sister and the ruthless politics of the royal house.

Laszlo: whose courage and generosity had led him—no doubt shouting bravely to encourage the troops—to his death.

Laszlo: gone. A hole in the world where he once stood.

Felix clutched the tree and howled in hopeless pain. Birds took flight and small animals fled away, leaving Felix alone and unwitnessed, miserably free to pour out his sorrow to earth and sky. He dropped his mental shields and let it flow.

—Laszlo gone and I am no true man and a woman can't inherit the crown so my father has no heir, and the landed lords are already scrambling for the position or allying with those who have the best claim which right now means Uncle Stephen Hastur and after him his son Damon-Rafael, and the one is cruelly ambitious and the other worse, and the gods know what they would do to Ellora and to me—far too much to hope that I'd be

sent to a Tower and Ellora allowed to choose a husband she likes or allowed to wait until she's full-grown before breeding—no, more likely I'll be quietly killed and Ellora sold to some greedy lord at least twice her age who'll force her to breed endless streams of children until she dies of it... And I can do nothing—nothing!—to prevent it because I am no true male and Laszlo is gone!

Despair poured through him in waves for what felt like hours, and ebbed away slowly for no other cause than exhaustion. Felix clung to the tree in stunned silence, dumbly wishing that this moment of safety could last forever.

Why not simply walk away into the forest? an oddly warm and hopeful thought intruded. *Food is abundant if you know where to look, and shelter, and all the simple requirements of survival. You would be safe and free.*

Felix idly considered the thought before casting it away. *That would abandon my sister to utter loneliness, a wretched life and a miserable death. I can't walk away until I find some means to protect her.*

That warm and hopeful feeling shifted to thoughtful calculation, and then solidified to another thought, a question. *If you could become fully male, would that solve the problem?*

Well, of course! That was so obvious that he'd never thought to question it.

...So obvious that it couldn't have been his own thought.

Felix lifted his head, turned, and saw without surprise that he was no longer alone.

The creature standing some three meters behind him was human-shaped, tall, slender, pale, silver-haired, with six fingers visible on each hand. It looked remarkably like himself, except for being ethereally beautiful in its sexlessness rather than frail.

A chieri, Felix marveled. He'd heard of them, of course, like most people, but had never seen one. Hardly anyone in several lifetimes ever claimed to have seen one. He felt awed. *You're very beautiful,* was his first thought.

I thank you, the creature replied, likewise in thought.

Felix looked closer and was unsurprised to see a small blue stone pendant strung around the *chieri's* slender neck, nestled in the soft cloth of its long mist-gray tunic. He got the distinct impression that the creature's name was *Irtlandess*. Felix pulled himself to his feet and gave the *chieri* the formal greeting usually reserved for members of the royal family, ending with the standard phrase: "How may I serve you?"

Show me yourself, Irtlandess replied, a warm and gentle request.

Felix understood, and for once wasn't frightened or ashamed. He knew this would be as painless, accepting, and even comforting as being monitored by old Lorna, back at Arilinn Tower. He had known so little of tenderness since leaving Arilinn....

For an instant a spike of yearning stabbed him. *Oh, if only—*

With a whispered oath, Felix deliberately dropped his mental shield and stood as if physically naked, holding back nothing. There was a polite pause, and then he felt Irtlandess' awareness, feather-light, skimming over his desires, memories, body-sense, passions, all—condemning nothing, gentle as promised. *...Arilinn...*flickered to the surface as the mist-light awareness withdrew.

Felix waited patiently, studying the lovely, near-mythical creature before him, calmed as he hadn't been in days, his blazing grief and despair momentarily forgotten. For that respite he was profoundly grateful.

Irtlandess smiled, and spoke in words. "I can help you."

I have stepped into a legend, a child's cradle-tale, a dream, Felix thought. *And why should I not, when the waking world is so bleak and hopeless?* "How?" was all he asked.

The *chieri's* next words could have been taken from a myth-tale, too. "Take me to your father's house. Bring me within, as you would a maid you were secretly courting. Take me to your chamber, bring food and drink for both of us, and let me lie in your bed."

"I will," Felix promised, stretching forth a polite two fingers to lead his guest home.

~ooo~

All down the long walk back through the forest, through the barest touch of their fingertips, Felix could feel Irtlandess warmly calculating, planning—plotting, his father would have called it, except that there was no feeling of malice anywhere in it. The busy hum of the *chieri's* thoughts was hopeful, joyful, almost playful. He felt a sudden surge of *laran* in those velvety fingers, and turned to see that Irtlandess had neatly constructed a covering illusion, a *glamourie,* of a pretty, pale-haired maid in plain clothes such as a simple farmer's daughter might wear.

"Your secret *barragana,*" Irtlandess explained, almost gleefully. "A humble forester's girl, of far too low a rank to consider for marriage, but good enough for breeding healthy *nedestros*. The sort a young prince would sneak in through the back door for an evening's dalliance. You have some silver rings in your belt pouch, yes? Use one of them to bribe the silence of any guard who sees you."

"That will guarantee the story spreads through the whole castle by dinnertime," Felix noted.

"Precisely!" said the *chieri*, and giggled like the girl she seemed.

Felix caught the image—*the prince sneaking a girl into the house*—and giggled, too. It was, he realized, the first time he'd laughed in weeks.

Sure enough, guards were searching for him in the garden. Felix made an elaborate show of tip-toeing through the herbs and flowers, ducking down behind the bushes, tugging Irtlandess with him—and managed to keep a straight face while doing it. He knew old Cory had seen him and was waiting by the back door to the kitchen, but he managed to look surprised and guilty when the aged guardsman stepped into his path and demanded to know where he'd been.

"Just out walking," Felix mumbled, doing his best to produce the illusion of a blush. He knew that the old guard was secretly snickering inside at the sight of the pretty girl half-hiding behind Felix's cloak. "Ah, look, Cory..." Felix almost whispered, digging into his belt pouch, "It's nothing important, nothing to rouse the guards about. Just don't tell anyone you've seen us, right?" He looked about guiltily and stuffed a silver ring into the old man's hand.

"Ah," old Cory smiled knowingly as he stuffed the ring into his own pouch. "I understand perfectly. Get on with you, lad. ...And good luck."

Felix was blushing in truth, but with the effort not to laugh, as he hurried past Cory and though the kitchen door, pulling Irtlandess after him. Once inside, he was briefly dismayed to see a clutch of scullery maids puttering about at the sinks. They stopped to stare as Felix and Irtlandess hurried through.

Ask one for food service, Irtlandess nudged.

Felix duly paused by the last maid, pressed another ring into her hand, and whispered into her ear—with the *chieri* guiding his words. "Bring some bread and cheese and fruit—oh, and a jug of berry wine and two goblets—up to my chamber. And don't tell anyone!"

The maid snickered and nodded vigorously, and Felix and Irtlandess fled for the back stairs.

They made it as far as the door of Felix's chamber before

anyone else saw them, but the guard marching up the hallway caught sight of them and raised his eyebrows. Felix got the door open and hurried the two of them through before the guard could draw close enough to cost him another ring. With the door safely closed behind them, the two of them scampered to the bed and collapsed on it, smothering explosive laughter in the pillows.

Irtlandess recovered first. *Don't undress completely,* she warned, and somewhat disconcertingly altered her *glamourie* to show her wearing a simple shift, with an image of her outer dress on the floor. *Remember, the maid will come soon with the food.*

Felix caught the image of what the scullery maid was supposed to see, and quickly pulled off his cloak, boots and tunic. He reached for the *chieri's* hand again. *The tale will be all over the castle in an hour,* he thought. *How long can we maintain the illusion?*

Irtlandess's fingers tightened briefly on his. *It shall not be an illusion long,* she promised.

Behind that flickered the wordless image: himself, as a man. Felix trembled at the thought. At that moment a knocking sounded on the door. Felix hurried to the door, pulled it open just far enough for him to reach for the laden tray—saying quickly, "Thankyouthatwillbeall"—and to give the ogling maid a good view of the room. To complete the effect, he trotted the tray to his bedside table, turned back to the door, and frowned as he repeated, "Thankyouthatwillbe*all*," before closing the portal with a decisive slam. Finally he put up the bar, making certain that the sound of it settling in its brackets was audible outside.

Now that they were alone, Irtlandess dropped the *glamourie* and resumed her natural form. Felix sat down on the bed beside her. "Well played," he sighed. "Within the hour, the word will be all over the castle that Prince Felix is not so *emmasca* as everyone had thought."

Irtlandess pointed toward the tray. Felix took up the flask and one of the goblets. Irtlandess silently reached for her belt pouch and pulled out a small glass flask that contained a pale-gold liquid. *Among my own kindred,* she explained, as she unstoppered the flask, *I am somewhat famed as a healer.*

Wordlessly, Felix held up the goblet. Irtlandess poured perhaps a finger's width of the gold liquid into it. A scent wafted up from the liquid, subtle but piercing.

For an instant a hundred apprehensions galloped through his mind, the uppermost being that this might be a cleverly plotted poisoning, clearing his ambitious uncle's way to the throne....

Ridiculous! He had seen Irtlandess's mind, and knew better. Besides, if Uncle Stephen wanted him dead right now there were far simpler ways to do it than by suborning a *chieri*.

Felix raised the goblet in salute and slowly drained it. The flavor of the wine was unchanged, but a ghost of the scent still lingered. "How long?" he asked, carefully setting the goblet back on the tray.

"At least a day and a night," said Irtlandess, as she put the flask back in her belt pouch, "Possibly two. You should begin to feel the effects within a few moments."

By the time he'd pulled away his breechclout, Felix's fingers felt numb. He lay back on the pillows and turned to look at Irtlandess while he could still move his head. Naked, she was almost sexless, slender, but ethereally lovely. His own body felt as if it were turning to mist, though it still looked solid. ...*Tell me...* he implored, not quite clear about what he wanted to know.

Irtlandess rested a nearly weightless hand on his bare shoulder, defining the welcome limits of his skin. *Surely you encountered* kirian *during your training at Arilinn?* she asked.

Felix recalled a few drops being poured carefully into a spoon. *Only that, only once,* he managed to form the thought. *Lorna said I had* laran *enough without stimulation...* He remembered those few drops spreading his mind open to Lorna's probe, and almost passionlessly wondered what ten times that amount would do.

Irtlandess stroked his chest, making the skin feel as if it were thick velvet, and he could feel her awareness spreading out, searching the castle.

The scullery maids, the guards, are gossiping together, she reported. *The maids speculate that you have finally found a maid who stirs you, and they wonder if you were struck by true love. The guards rejoice that the King has an heir again. The eldest— Cory —sternly warns them all to keep silent until they know more. All of them are determined to keep you from being interrupted. Even the house* laranzu *knows nothing yet. We shall have at least our day and a night....*

Reassured, Felix let himself sink into soft brightness, bewildering sweet strangeness of touch, and the steady awareness of Irtlandess's presence. Wordlessly he asked to see this mystery explained.

Long ago, Irtlandess complied, stroking onward, *we made a great error. We toyed too much with living things. We...bred ourselves too much for power, too little for sturdiness.... We made our blood too thin and weakened our...breeding. We lived long, but our numbers dwindled. In desperation, we searched the overworld for any like us, any close enough in...flesh that we could breed with them. We sensed a...ship full of them, near enough that we could pull it to us, bring it to land... We used various...tricks to interbreed with the shipwrecked passengers. The children that we kept did indeed reinvigorate our bloodlines; there are enough of us now that we may well survive.*

Through the softly burning mist, Felix managed to form a thought, a question. *If increasing, why are* chieri *so rarely seen?*

Ah, but the answer to that was so obvious that it followed instantly. Any creature that could form an illusion could walk unseen and unheard through even a crowded marketplace, let alone forest and farmland. *Chieri* simply didn't wish to be noticed.

Irtlandess gave him another long, feather-light stroke that dissipated thought, and went on with the mind-touch tale.

The children that we left among the newcomers, and their descendants, had many of our...characteristics: six fingers, the mind-gifts, and...some difficulty becoming fertile. The degree of these varies with the...amount of chieri *blood. Though we try to avoid human attention, we prefer not to abandon those descendants of ours who are...most like us. That is why you are here, Felix—and why I am here also.*

Felix understood, inasmuch as he could think at all. His body turned to glowing mist, like the strange waters of the Lake of Hali, and only the steady flowing touch of Irtlandess's fingers gave him definition, sketching lines of soft blue fire that pulsed sweetly in long, hot trails. Time vanished, and awareness followed.

At one point Felix drifted close to consciousness, fierce with hunger. Hands—*Irtlandess*—held out food to him, and he took it and ate, scarcely aware of chewing and swallowing, until the hunger eased and he sank back into the burning mist. At another point he was roused to awareness of noise nearby and opened his eyes to see a pretty blonde girl in a plain shift—*Irtlandess*—standing at the chamber door exchanging an empty bowl and flask for full ones. Once more there came hunger and thirst, eating and drinking, and hot drifting again for measureless time.

Eventually the bright mist sank away, leaving Felix solid and aware of time and place. He opened his eyes to see candlelight, darkened windows, and Irtlandess lying beside him. She looked more distinctly female now, and very beautiful. A nameless feeling drew his body toward her, like iron filings to a lodestone, pulsing through him and centering... *Ah, there!*

Felix raised his head and looked down, and saw that—oh yes,

definitely—he was a complete male now: distinctly, and actively male. He stared for long moments, fascinated, connecting the undeniable sight to the insistent feeling.

Yes, Irtlandess spread the image before him. *Now make proper use of it.*

Felix rolled toward her. The shock of contact was enough to drown him in a different brightness, one that left him with feeling and awareness but obliterated all else.

~oOo~

When Felix came back to himself again, he wanted nothing but to lie quietly and marvel over this new knowledge. Irtlandess stroked his back idly, and he could tell that her awareness was elsewhere, scanning the castle and all the minds in it. *You're my guard, too,* he smiled, feeling a first flicker of soft heat rising. *How long has it been?*

A night and a day, and early into another night, she informed him. A wisp of grimness floated across the near surface of her mind. *Human politics proceed apace. You shall have to deal with them shortly.*

Not now, Felix groaned mentally.

I fear so. Irtlandess combed her fingers through his hair and spread a clear image before his mind: the scene below, the situation, and what he must do to change it.

"Zandru's hells!" Felix snapped aloud, appalled and quailing inwardly. *Gods, I can't do this I've always been such a coward I can't....*

Here is your one chance to save yourself, and your sister. Irtlandess showed him another image: Ellora hiding in her chamber, crouched in the furthest corner, weeping in hopeless terror.

Felix rolled over and sat up, briefly distracted by the unaccustomed weight of his manhood. *This once, I will be brave— and a man.*

He stood up, found that the cold of the stone floor burned his feet, and paused to pull on his fleece-lined boots. An instant's thought sent him to the clothes-hooks on the wall, from which he took down his light cloak. He wouldn't need anything else; he wouldn't be gone long. The rough cloth rubbed irritatingly on his swollen flesh.

I'll await you here, Irtlandess promised, not needing to add that she would monitor his progress.

Felix tossed her an unnecessary salute, and unbarred the door.

The sound of scampering feet told him what to expect; when he opened the door, the maids were partway down the hall, trying to look as if they had business there and trying not to be noticed staring at him. *Gossiping merrily,* he thought—and then realized that the thought wasn't entirely his own. Irtlandess was keeping mental contact with him, at the same time scanning his path ahead and feeding her knowledge back to him. Felix stood up straight, pulled back his shoulders and—like the warrior Laszlo had been— marched down the corridor.

The guard at the head of the stairs saw him coming, said no word, but raised his pike in salute. *Bravo, Prince,* the man was thinking, giving him a knowing smile. Felix returned it and marched on. At the bottom of the stairs the chief housekeeper was scolding one of the maids, and they both paused as they saw Felix coming down the steps. The housekeeper frowned, intending to confront Felix, trying to choose just what question to ask.

Felix felt a brief flash of irritation from Irtlandess and then her thought shaping the muscles of his face into an impatient scowl, then a dart of fear stabbing the housekeeper so that she drew back without a word and let him pass.

You forced her! You overshadowed me.... Felix didn't break stride, but he felt a shiver of horror at what Irtlandess had just done. There was a flash of embarrassment and apology, and the wordless explanation that this coming scene must be played perfectly, for all their sakes.

Felix marched across the main hall, into the side corridor, to the guard-flanked door of his father's office, wondering, *Do the* chieri *keep apart from men for their safety, or for ours?*

Both, came the wordless reply.

And then he came up to the office door, and there was no more time to speculate. The guards formally crossed their pikes before the door, the polite signal that the king wished not to be disturbed. Felix pulled up to his full height and pronounced, as firmly as his voice would allow, the words he already knew he would have to say. "I must see my father. The matter is urgent."

The guards raised their eyebrows, glanced quickly at each other, pulled away their pikes, and let Felix push open the door.

He took two steps into the chamber and almost halted, almost failed. It was bad enough knowing that his uncle Stephen and cousin Damon-Rafael were there, but actually seeing them— needing no *laran* to know their determined malice and his father's ill-hidden despair—was almost enough to break him. Almost. Felix kept marching, almost to the paper-littered table where the three of them sat, before he halted, swept them all with a stern glance, and then fixed upon the carefully expressionless face of his father and king.

"Father, forgive the intrusion, but I will be brief. Is it true that you have prayed to all the gods in the calendar—" *...since Laszlo died...* "—for some sign that I am, at last, fully your *son*?"

He let the stressed word hang in the air, in all its meaning, until his father simply whispered: "You know I have."

"Then behold it!"

Felix gripped the edges of his cloak and spread his arms wide, letting the cloth flap like wings, revealing his bare body from head to boot-tops, and thereby displaying his undeniable and rampant manhood.

And oh, the looks on their three faces—and the blazing emotions behind them, which Irtlandess gleefully reported: his father's amazed delight and renewed hope, Stephen's stunned dismay and scrambling amid shattered plans, Damon-Rafael's shock and... *Good gods, envy!* Felix could hear Irtlandess laughing like merry bells ringing in his skull.

To his own amazement, Felix recovered first of all of them. He lowered his arms and drew his cloak together, putting a decisive end to the show. With a calmness that surprised himself, Felix continued: "Therefore, you may now start seeking a suitable bride for me. Meanwhile, I ask your leave to withdraw..." He couldn't help adding, "...and return to my *barragana,* and hopefully begin begetting a long string of *nedestros.*"

For the first time in his life, Felix heard his father snicker.

"Oh yes, yes," snorted the Hastur King, giving an exaggerated dismissive wave. "By all means, depart on that errand." His eyes were no longer on his son, but raking over his brother and nephew.

As Felix bowed and backed toward the doorway, he heard his father say, "Well, that does put rather a different face on the situation, doesn't it?"

He also felt Damon-Rafael stab him with a look of miserable hatred.

Felix stood and turned to go—and then realized that the guards had left the door open. *Well, of course,* he thought inanely, *they had to make sure that my presence was welcome, or at least harmless....* And that meant that the guards, and the chief housekeeper, and the maid, and perhaps half-a-dozen other servants who seemed to have materialized from nowhere, had all witnessed that scene. *Far too many to silence,* Irtlandess smiled warmly in his mind. *Your new standing is assured.*

Felix struggled to keep his face stern and unblushing all the way back down the corridor, across the great hall, up the stairs, and through the upstairs hallway to his own room. There seemed to be a remarkable number of guards and servants saluting and bowing to him. He wondered how the news had spread so quickly.

Servants' quarters, Irtlandess giggled silently. *For folk lacking mind-powers, the lower castes have remarkably efficient communications....*

Felix pulled the door open, passed through, and barred it behind him. The exhilaration of victory was rising fiercely, and his almost painful desire with it. He hastened to the bed, casting off his cloak on the floor behind him, paused only to pull off his fleece-lined boots, and tugged the blankets down.

Irtlandess lay there waiting for him—if anything, more vividly female than before—her welcoming smile, bare arms, and delighted mind all open to him. *Victory, my prince! Come claim it.*

Felix fell into the welcoming flames with a shout of triumph.

~oOo~

This time Felix awakened with a feeling of simple hunger and honest physical fatigue. Irtlandess, sitting up against the carved headboard, only smiled distantly and pointed toward the bed-table. A refilled flask and bowl waited there. Felix addressed himself to both for several long minutes. As his hunger eased, another need asserted itself and he reached under the bed for the chamber-pot. He noted with amusement that he wasn't used to dealing with such functions in his changed body. Irtlandess chuckled and offered suggestions.

Afterward, Felix closed the pot, shoved it back under the bed, and studied his new form. "Will I keep it?" he asked softly, "Or will I...revert?"

Irtlandess thought awhile before answering. "You will keep this form until, and unless, you choose to change it—and that will require..."

"I have no intention of changing it," Felix cut in hastily, climbing back into the bed. "I've waited long enough to become truly male, and the political advantages..." He thought of Ellora.

Irtlandess caught the image, and frowned. "Human politics are not my art or skill," she murmured. "Our own are complex enough. I have given you what advantage I can; it is you who must make further use of it."

Felix noticed for the first time that she hadn't spoken mind-to-mind to him since he woke. "Surely you can scan the minds around me, give me warning..."

"I must leave very soon."

"Leave?!" Felix clutched her arm, appalled. *How will I live without you?!*

Ah, have you come to love me, so soon? she asked.

My first lover, how could I not? he answered. *Please don't leave me!*

"I must," she said in words, gently pulling out of his grasp. "Already questions are flying, about the simple country maid who wakened the prince's manhood. I believe the castle bard is creating a ballad, and the castle *laranzu* is arguing with the healer. I have drawn too much attention. Need I explain further?"

"The illusion..."

"I cannot maintain it constantly, and too much scrutiny would reveal the truth."

"You could slip away into the forest, and I could meet you there...." Felix realized that even this much separation would deprive him of Irtlandess's constant watching and guidance. He would have to fend with the kingdom's politics himself. *And I have no idea how to do it,* he admitted, shivering.

And did you learn nothing at Arilinn Tower?

With a jolt Felix realized that except for his little escape-illusions, he hadn't so much as touched his starstone since returning from Arilinn. He'd kept himself shielded, afraid to touch the minds around him, knowing what pain he'd meet with his father's disappointment, his sister's misery, the unloving thoughts and emotions of everyone else....

But all that was changed now.

"I have given you your chance," Irtlandess whispered.

I am a man now, Felix understood, *and there is more to manhood than just breeding-organs...*

"Yes. Be brave."

Felix sat up, opened the little bag of insulating cloth that hung at his neck, and tipped out his matrix into his naked palm. The polished stone, as big around as his thumb, twinkled vivid blue in the candlelight, warm and welcoming, igniting memories of Arilinn Tower—the one place in the world where he had been accepted, even welcomed. It took no effort to recall old Lorna's lessons and how eager he had been to learn. More vivid still were the memories of working in the circle, joining minds willingly, plying his skill among the glowing presences of his friends' minds, being honored for himself and not his bloodlines, of having useful work, being of *use*....

Oh, Arilinn! Arilinn Tower, that I shall never see again... The spike of his sorrow was as fierce as his grief for his lost brother.

Is that's your heart's wish? Irtlandess asked.

Oh gods, yes! Felix clutched his matrix until it seemed to burn like a blue coal in his hand. *I'd go there this very night, if I could.... But I must save Ellora and be my father's heir.*

Then use your stone, and see what you must do.

Felix quailed at the thought, then caught himself. While Laszlo was alive, his little brother and sister had sheltered under his wing, and never learned to be brave. But this was something that Laszlo could never have done. This was Felix's skill, and he must use it now.

Courage, Irtlandess whispered in his mind.

Felix took a deep breath, closed his eyes, and applied his training. First the deliberate calmness, then the opening, then the reaching...

It was surprisingly easy for a skill he'd carefully not practiced all these many long days, especially among these untrained and unshielded minds. He grew aware of the guard in the upstairs hall, peered closer, and saw the fellow automatically watching the corridor while chuckling to himself about how the prince's new status would improve life in the castle—and then deliberately backing up under a glass-cased torch to let fly an almost-silent fart. Felix laughed and moved on.

Father...

The Hastur King was in his massive bed, but not asleep. He sat propped up against a mound of pillows, jotting notes—names of eligible noblewomen and their connections. Felix sighed, knowing he had asked for exactly that.... Oh, but there was worse; his father was making a parallel list of eligible noble sons and their connections, and possible alliances among them. Felix shuddered at some of the names, knowing what Ellora thought of them. Not even his father would let Ellora wed where she chose, or live as she chose. Saddened, Felix moved on.

...To Ellora's room. The princess was not asleep, either. She was huddled in her bed, under the light of a single hooded lamp, whispering intensely with... Zandru's hells, was that one of the maids? Yes, it was one of the waiting maids, named Linella, close to Ellora's age and her secret confidant. They were discussing Felix's dramatic revelation, and how that would change royal politics.

"—been considering husbands for me," Ellora was saying, "And now he'll be doing it for Felix. The best I can hope for is to persuade Felix to complain about any suitors that I absolutely can't stand. Even so, I don't know if that will sway Father. You've seen how stubborn he is."

Felix grimaced in sympathy.

"Oh, please!" Linella burst into tears and flung her arms around Ellora's neck. "There must be another way! We'll run away together, and join the Sisterhood of the Sword."

"I've never used a sword in my life, and neither have you."

"The Ladies of Avarra, then. We'll become healers—"

"Father pulled Felix out of Arilinn Tower, where he was bidding fair to become a great Keeper. The king can command me out of even the House of Avarra."

"Then the Sisterhood it must be. We'll find a way—"

Sadly Felix pulled his mind away and moved on. He knew full well that his father would never let Ellora have her choice of husband, nor was he likely to allow her to keep her favorite maid when she was married off. The nearest outpost of the Sisterhood of the Sword was many long mountainous miles away, and Ellora's chance of reaching it was nearly nil. No, there would have to be another way....

If only I could take her to Arilinn with me...

Hopeless. If Father couldn't spare him from the burden of the crown—and the duty of breeding more heirs—he wouldn't spare Ellora, with her much weaker psychic gift. She was too useful a pawn in the game of kingship.

I'll have to do it.

With that thought in mind, Felix resolutely moved on toward the bedchanbers of his uncle and cousin.

Go ahead, grasp the blade. Felix gritted his teeth and focused on Damon-Rafael.

His target wasn't hard to find. Damon-Rafael was in bed, slaking his rage by rutting with one of the older chambermaids. The woman was smiling, cooing encouragement, gasping at what a splendid stallion Damon-Rafael was—and it was all lies. The castle staff all knew about Damon-Rafael and his tastes. After a brief, tense discussion, this particular maid had volunteered for the task, simply because—having been an army camp-follower and a whore in very truth—she could endure Damon-Rafael better than the younger maids. She had prepared herself beforehand with internal shields and ointments. Now she was cynically measuring the duration of his strokes, trying to guess when he'd finally finish, giving judicious squeezes and lunges of her own to hurry him along.

Damon-Rafael was stabbing angrily, his attention alternating between his own sensations and imagined images of himself as a spear, plunging into Felix—*that upstart! How dare he?!*—at various unspeakable target points. He hadn't given up his hopes of the kingship. It would only be more difficult and complicated now to get Felix out of the way. With each thrust he sorted through various assassination plans, the bloodier the better.

Felix withdrew, shaken. It was almost a relief to move on to the cold and calculating mind of his Uncle Stephen.

Stephen Hastur sat awake in bed making notes, like his brother, and including some of the same names in his jottings. His plans were many-layered, including assassination of Felix if a clear opportunity occurred, but that too was considered as coolly as a formula in mathematics. Far more likely was the possibility of marrying Ellora off to a staunch ally, subtly nudging his brother to marry Felix to some weakling girl, waiting until the King died and then eliminating Felix and any of his male children. That would be a long and subtle game, but Stephen could wait. The difficulty would be reining in his impatient son until the moment was right....

Felix withdrew, contemplating his still-bleak future. Aside from plotting murder himself—and after scanning Damon-Rafael, that was not too repugnant an idea—he could see no escape. Ellora's mad plan of running away looked more enticing by the moment.

This is another reason why we prefer to keep aloof from humans and their politics, Irtlandess chuckled close by. *Yet I know enough of them to see a pathway through this thicket.*

Felix looked up to meet the *chieri's* eyes, noting that she was fully dressed and shod for travelling. "Then in Aldones' name, Irtlandess, I beg you tell me!"

Irtlandess pulled her feet up under her. *What does everyone want? Your father wants the continuation of his bloodline and rule. You and Ellora—and her* breda—*want to escape, preferably to Arilinn. Stephen Hastur wants to rule, and his son after him. Look at this as a pattern, as a complex weaving of threads, and see the way for everyone to have what they...think they wish.*

Yes, he could see it—the weak point where the threads crossed, where the pattern could be changed. Oh yes, it included some deception, but there were worse sins. It would also involve a technical problem; if Stephen saw Felix holding his starstone, he'd close his mind and agree to nothing.

For that I will assist you, this last time, Irtlandess promised.

Leave your starstone in its pouch; I will walk beside you, unseen, and transmit my perceptions to you as I did before. With that, she gave off a surge of *laran* and disappeared before his eyes.

Brilliant illusion, Felix admitted, though he smiled as he noted the wrinkles in the bedcover as Irtlandess slipped to the floor. With a sigh, he reached for his clothes, including his belt and then his sword. *Will I ever see you again?*

Indeed you will, the silent voice answered out of the empty air. *Surely you will see me when you and your sister come to Arilinn.*

All the more reason for me to succeed.

~oOo~

Lord Stephen Hastur was studying his notes when he heard a peremptory rapping on the door. With the speed of long practice, he flipped his notes over and scribbled a harmless salutation to his estate manager on the blank side.. "Who is it, at this ungodly hour?"

"Felix," said the unexpected voice at the door.

Felix?! Stephen set his writing-tray aside, pushing the notes even further out of view, and cast a quick glance at where his sword hung nearby on the wall. Showing no sign of his bewilderment, he slid out of bed, padded to the door, unbarred and opened it a slight way. Yes, there stood Felix, fully dressed right down to his boots, cloak, belt—and scabbarded sword. The boy seemed taller than he had yesterday, or perhaps that was the effect of his standing up straight. "It's very late," Stephen temporized, torn between caution and curiosity.

"Nonetheless, I would speak to you—for our mutual satisfaction."

The boy sounded older, too. How had he matured so quickly?

"Come in, then." Stephen pulled the door wide and stepped back, giving the guard a clear view, not taking his own eyes off Felix. He backed carefully to the small writing-table, where the usual flask and goblets waited, and sat in the further chair.

Felix waited for a long moment in the open doorway before coming in, closing the door behind him but not barring it, and pacing to the nearer chair. He glanced at the flask, but didn't touch it. Stephen barely noticed a last puff of wind briefly flicking the lamp.

"It's late," said Felix, "so I'll not detain you with trivialities. Uncle, tell me flat out: do you truly want to be King?"

Stephen blinked, jarred by the blunt—and surprisingly refreshing—honesty. "Well, who would not?" he smiled.

"Me," Felix replied, his eyes boring into his uncle's. "*I* would not."

Stephen blinked again. "Might I ask why?" he asked.

"First..." Felix ticked off on his six spread fingers, "because I'm not fit for it. I was never trained in kingly craft, have never learned warcraft, and never commanded anything larger than a small hunting party. I would make a terribly incompetent ruler."

Stephen blinked several times, rapidly. "That is...a most remarkably mature evaluation," he murmured.

"Further," Felix went on, tapping another finger, "I learned at Arilinn that I would make a very good Tower technician, possibly even Keeper. That is, in fact, what I want to do with my life. I can serve the realm—and myself—far better as a good *laranzu* than a bad king."

"You prefer life in a Tower to life in a castle?" Stephen asked, on surer ground now.

"I do indeed." Felix leaned closer. "I also have no liking for the prospective brides my father is considering for me. Frankly, I prefer *barraganas* of my own choice."

Stephen gave a bark of laughter, understanding that perfectly.

"And so," Felix added slowly, "would my sister."

Stephen shut his mouth, seeing another possible advantage here.

"We all know what my father would prefer," said Felix, boring in closer, "but now I have some word in my own fate. I will persuade him to let me go back to Arilinn, and I will find some fault with every bride he proposes for me. With any luck..." For a moment he looked distracted, then somber. "I may play this game until my father's *natural* death shall overtake him. Upon gaining the throne, I will abdicate in your favor. Will that satisfy you, Uncle?"

Stephen sat frozen for long seconds, scarcely able to believe what he was hearing. This was so absolutely perfect, he couldn't trust it. There had to be a hidden barb in it somewhere. "Is that all you wish?" he asked slowly.

"There is one other thing."

Stephen tensed, ready for anything. "What is that?"

"Ellora shall come with me."

"What?" It was the last thing Stephen could have expected.

"This I insist on." Felix leaned closer. "You shall not—and you will help me make certain that Father shall not—marry her off to the first lordling who offers a shred of political advantage. My sister does in fact have a Gift for healing, which could be trained at

Arilinn." He leaned back again. "I am more concerned with breeding for the Gifts than breeding for crowns. Do you understand me, Uncle?"

"I do indeed." Stephen was sure he did. "And...the Tower *leroni* have a better understanding of breeding for Gifts than we mere politicians, eh?"

"Just so," Felix said shortly.

Stephen sat back, seeing how he could further this marvelous opportunity that had been dropped in his lap. "And no doubt, you want me to use my influence with my brother to nudge him, whenever possible, toward giving you your desire?"

"Just so," Felix said again. "In exchange for your assistance, I will hand you the crown the day it is on my head, if not sooner. Do we have an agreement?"

"We do!" Stephen pounced, then caught himself. "Ah, don't wait for your coronation. Renounce the crown the very hour you hear of the king's death."

"In a Tower, I may learn of it before you." Felix narrowed his eyes. "And in a Tower, be assured, I will know if my father's death is natural or not."

"So be it." Stephen smiled at Felix in genuine respect. "I will bend all my efforts to sending you to Arilinn...." He paused just long enough to hint at the physical distance to Arilinn, quite far enough to keep the Prince out of politics in the capital. "But, since we are being blunt, how do I know you will keep your word?"

"You will know," Felix retorted coolly, "by the way I avoid political marriages for myself and Ellora. I'll expect your assistance on that, too."

Stephen Hastur examined the bargain from every angle he could think of, and could find no fault in it. Felix was deliberately taking himself out of the succession, and his sister's children, too. There were ways Stephen hadn't mentioned to ensure such a bargain, but he felt oddly certain that they wouldn't be needed. Felix's argument rang with sincerity. Stephen stretched out his hand. "Agreed," he said. "Do you wish me to swear blood-oath before Aldones?"

"Your word is enough." Felix smiled and took his hand in the formal clasp. "And now, the hour being late as you said, I'll retire to plot my own persuasions with Father."

"By all means," said Stephen, releasing his hand. "And I'll plan mine, gladly."

Felix left without another word. He paused a brief moment by the open door, letting in a puff of wind, then went out.

Barely restraining a whoop of delight, Stephen seized up his notepapers and happily threw them into the fire.

~oOo~

Now to the kitchen, Irtlandess guided Felix invisibly down the stairs. *Then you need only open the back door, and I'll away.*

Must it be so soon? Felix mourned. *I couldn't have done that without you; my courage, and surely my knowledge, would have failed.*

For answer, Irtlandess gave him a graphic image of how to obtain a proper-sized setting and affix his starstone in such a fashion that the bare stone would touch his skin under his shirt. He would not have to hold it visibly to use it.

You have the courage now to do your own scanning, she told him. *Your own courage upheld you in settling with your uncle.*

Felix thought over that conversation as he made his way down the night-darkened hall. *Irtlandess, will my father truly live long?*

He will. His...flesh and blood are balanced and strong, and your house laranzu *and chief of guards are most adept at preventing external threats. Your uncle, on the other hand, has a weakness of the blood-vessels that guarantees him a shorter life. His reign will be competent, but not long.*

Felix considered his next question as they picked their way through the kitchen. *And will Damon-Rafael follow him? What manner of rule will that be?*

Irtlandess paused, with a distinct feel of calculation, before answering. *Having to wait long for power will not improve his impatient temper. His reign will be much less competent, and shorter. In brief, someone will kill him.*

Felix paused with his hand on the garden door. *Do you...remember the future, as humans remember the past?*

No, not like that, he felt Irtlandess chuckle. *It is more that we see patterns—in nature, and in human nature—which indicate which events will come, and what choices will be made. It is like knowing the cycles of the moons so as to predict conjunctions. This is a skill you can learn.*

Felix pulled back the bar as soundlessly as he could. *And Ellora?* he asked. *Does she truly have enough* laran *that the Tower will want her?*

Her empathic talent and minimal telekinesis can indeed be trained to a useful healer's talent. It will take time, and that will be your excuse to your father.

The night sky was remarkably clear, and the stars and moons

shone brilliantly. It was a lovely night for parting, for saying farewells.

"Oh, why must you go?" Felix wailed softly, knowing he was acting like a child.

"Because I must go back to my own people to prepare for the birth," whispered the soft voice in his ear. "We have both gained from this encounter, my prince. I am pregnant."

"What?!"

True, Irtlandess assured him, even as he felt the slight breeze of her passing. *No doubt you will see your child at Arilinn.*

With that, she was gone. Even the sense of presence in his mind faded quickly, leaving him truly alone. Without thinking, he reached for his starstone.

—*Not yet*— came a last sharp warning.

Felix sighed and pulled away his hand from the little drawstring bag. Yes, he must let the *chieri* escape with no one—even himself—knowing where she had gone or how to find her. There was a strange, delicate balance between humans and these ancient people, and he must do nothing to upset it.

For if upset, that balance might be in our favor, he realized with a sudden chill. The *chieri* had immense mental powers—*enough to pull a ship off course,* he remembered—enough to pass unseen or disguised through a crowd, enough to simultaneously scan and transmit and even force the thoughts of humans, enough to change the bodies of humans into something they could use....

Nothing but the good will of the chieri *keeps humans alive on Darkover! If they willed, they could kill us all—except the few they keep for breeding.... Instead they quietly bought the use of our blood and paid us with settlement on...*

Now that he thought of it, if the world were indeed a globe as the scholars claimed, then humans occupied less than a quarter of it: only one continent, from the Hellers to the Dry Towns. Most of it was forest, the rest desert and snow-peaks, with precious little farmland. Without the help of the Towers, there would be little if any mining for metals. Simple survival was a constant struggle, leaving no resources to spare for exploration. Humans had simply never looked—*or never thought to look!*—beyond the seas, or the Dry Towns.

For that matter, they had never expanded their knowledge, their skills, beyond the uses of *laran*. There were ancient books preserved at Arilinn which spoke of mysterious *technology* which humans had once possessed, and was now lost. Why had it never been regained? Why had humans, for the last several centuries, specialized in developing only *laran* sciences—the *chieri's* arts—and nothing else?

Are all our lands their game preserve? Felix wondered, staring up at the vast dark sky. *Are we their pets or livestock?*

The sky gave no answer, but he remembered the mental contact with Irtlandess. It had all been kindly, gentle...benign. Then he thought of the contrast with Damon-Rafael's mind, or even Uncle Stephen's.

How desperate must the chieri *have been, to blend their bloodlines with creatures as savage as we?*

And yet they had paid well, with a whole continent to live on. If the *chieri* had limited humans' learning in certain directions, they had let it run free in all others. They had left the seeds of their own powers among humans, let them develop, even encouraged them, as if hoping that eventually humans might grow to meet them as equals.

We could have worse keepers.

...Indeed, we have done worse for ourselves, all too many times.

Felix turned back through the kitchen door, closed and barred it, went out to the main hall and up the stairs to Ellora's room, thinking of how much he had to tell his sister.

He would have still more to tell to the circle at Arilinn.

Evanda's Mirror
by Diana L. Paxson

When *The Shattered Chain* was published in 1976, it resonated deeply with a generation of women wrestling with the nature of sexism and how to counteract life-long conditioning. Women-only groups held intense discussions about empowerment and identity. Over three decades later, our focus and understanding of gender roles and sexuality has evolved, forcing us to consider traditional definitions in a new light. Marion's approach was never one-sided or simplistic, and neither is this sensitive, insightful story from Diana L. Paxson.

Diana L. Paxson counts herself among the many writers who were inspired by Marion Zimmer Bradley. In addition to the Chronicles of Westria and historical fantasies such as *The White Raven* and the *Wodan's Children* trilogy, she continued Marion's Avalon series, most recently with *Sword of Avalon*. She is also the author of 86 short stories, including contributions to most of Marion's anthologies. This story takes place a generation after the events in "The Motherquest" and "A Season of Butterflies."

I had just straightened the garland of piñona above the door of the Guildhouse when a resonant clangor vibrated through walls and floor.

"Goddess! Why do new women always turn up the day after a festival?" My lover, Kiera, winced as she pushed back a lock of ginger hair from her brow.

Last night we had celebrated Midwinter, and the spice-beer had flowed freely. So many of our women had work that took them away from Thendara, this was the only time when everyone was at home, and there were always tales to tell and news to share. But Year's End also brought women who had finally decided they could bear their lot no longer to the door of Thendara House to demand admission to the Free Amazons. Flurries of snow were splattering the octagonal window panes. To seek our door on such a night, one must be truly desperate.

Kiera frowned. "Lassandra's on door-duty, isn't she? She's still pretty young. Cassi, you had better go and back her up while I fetch Mother Doria."

Even hurrying up a flight of stairs, Kiera moved with an unconscious, elegant grace. I never knew if it came from her early training or was one of those Comyn gifts. She had come to the Renunciates rather than marry when her *laran* proved too undependable for work in a Tower. I rarely thought about the gulf between us, but at moments like this I remembered that she was a daughter of the Comyn, while my father had made boots in a shop in Castle Square.

The bell clanged again. I paused to check my hair and saw my face in the ancient mirror, round and snub-nosed, framed by the carved wooden draperies of the goddess Evanda that twined around it like sheltering wings. Then I hurried to the front hall, where Lassandra, who was still in her training year, stood dithering.

"In the Lady's name, *open* it!" I exclaimed, hauling the heavy bar aside.

As the door swung wide, a blast of snow swirled into the hall and with it a figure swathed in a grey cloak as if she had precipitated from the storm. Lassandra wrestled the door closed with a thump that vibrated through the worn floorboards, and we saw a tall, slim girl in a sodden cloak that shed melting snow in a pool on the floor.

"It's all right—you're safe now. Let's get that wet cloak off—" I reached out, but she clutched the edges of the grey wool to her chest, gazing around her with crystal-pale eyes.

She recoiled again when Mother Doria came in with Kiera and what seemed like half the Guildhouse behind her. Then she got herself under control and stood still, with only a little quiver in the folds of wool to show that she was trembling.

No wonder she's afraid, I thought, stepping between her and this babbling wave of female energy, but perhaps she had only been shivering, for she was looking at them with hungry eyes. Women, short or tall, lithe and wiry or as round in breast and butt as me, stared back at her. The silver gaze flicked briefly to me, then back to Mother Doria, who had glared the others into silence. With the grace of tall grass in the wind, the girl bowed.

"*Vai domna*," she whispered, pulling back her hood to reveal hair black as my own, but silky and straight where mine curled.

"I am *Mestra* Doria, and you do not need to bow to me," said the Guild Mother soothingly. "Welcome to Thendara House. Don't be afraid—no woman in need will be turned away. What is your name?"

"I am Adriana...n'ha Ysabet..." The lilt of the Hellers made the words musical.

"Do you seek refuge only, or is it your will to take the oath of a Renunciate here?"

Everyone had fallen silent. We had a saying that every woman who came to the Order of Renunciates had her own story, and all of them were tragedies. What pain, I wondered, had brought this maiden, with her fine-cut features and haunted eyes, to our door?

"I seek...to take the oath..."

From the others came a kind of wordless sigh, and the crowd spread out to form a circle around her. Mother Doria held out the little scissors we kept by the door. Some of us grew our hair out later, but the first act of a new Renunciate was always to cut her hair to affirm her new identity.

"You must signify your willingness to join us by yourself cutting the first strand."

Adriana loosened a strand of hair from the silver butterfly clasp and snipped it off below her ear. Her cloak had fallen open, revealing an odd assortment of ragged garments. The layered woolen skirts were of several lengths, and the sleeves of the jacket did not quite cover her bony wrists. The outfit surprised me. That clasp did not belong to the sort of woman who got her clothes from the donations bin in the city square, but perhaps this was a disguise she had used to get away.

When she had finished she held out the scissors and the lock of hair, and Mother Doria motioned to her to give them to me.

"Cassilde will take charge of this, my dear, until it is time to cut the rest. Now I must ask you to open your jacket and bare your breasts. It is only a symbol—" she went on as the girl flushed red. "But in the early days, when we were fighting for the right to live separate, the men sometimes tried to send in spies, and so in honor of our foremothers' courage we keep this custom."

"I *am* a woman!" Adriana breathed. From red, she had turned deathly pale.

"Of course, my child. It may seem strange at first, but living together, we see each other's bodies every day, and all our external differences only affirm our identity. Every woman here will be as a mother or a sister—" She gestured around the circle. "There is no need for shame."

I remembered how surprised I had been, soaking in the hot

pool after a session with the armsmistress, to find that breasts came in so many configurations. This girl looked as if hers were barely grown.

Little Lassandra was nodding, and big Raelle smiled. She was our most notable cook, clearly longing to put some more flesh on Adriana's fine bones. A wave of love filled me as I looked at wiry, mountain-bred Yllana, who had been both my best comrade and my rival during our training year, at Janetta and Gwennis, still lovers after forty years, at Stelle, our healer, a strongly-built woman who had studied medicine with the Terrans long ago, and at Irmelin, so ancient now that the only work she could do was to tend the fire. Some I had loved, some would never really like me, but at that moment we were all aware of our bond.

"Come, girl—" Mother Doria's voice sharpened. "It will grow no easier with waiting—"

Trembling, Adriana undid the clasps of the jacket. I wondered if she had been mistreated and feared to show her scars. She would not be the only woman here whose back was a testament to male brutality. She fumbled with the drawstring of the knitted blouse. Beneath was an undertunic of pod-silk, much finer than anything else she had on. Her fingers touched the button and froze.

"Oh for goodness sake, this isn't a Vainwal strip-tease!" exclaimed Yllana. Before anyone could stop her, she stepped up, gripped the neck of the undertunic and tore.

Adrianna swayed, trying to cover herself, but we had all seen her bare chest—not breast—for she had no more bosom than a child.

"My poor girl!" cried Gwennis, "are you *emmasca*, then?" Some of our most notable sisters had been desperate enough to seek the illegal operation that destroyed their female organs. But they had been born women, suffered the fate of women, and their souls were still female, whatever they looked like on the outside.

"This is no *emmasca*!" spat Yllana. "The work could not have been done long enough ago for the skin to have tightened, and that chest was smooth!"

I felt the hairs rise on my arms, for the atmosphere of the room had changed. This was not the hot fury of a maddened crowd that I had felt during the last riots against the *Terranan*, but something deadlier, compounded of hate, and disgust, and fear.

"I *am*—inside, I *am*!" Adriana wailed, but Janetta already had grasped her arms. She writhed in the older woman's grip as Yllana wrenched the waistband of her skirt around.

"If you wish to join us, stand still!" Mother Doria said sternly.

"This is our law!"

A button popped and went rolling across the floor. Adriana's shriek split the air as Yllana pulled down skirts and underskirts and the knitted pantlets that we all wore against the cold, and we saw beneath the black hairs at the groin the seedsack and male member, undeveloped and small, but definitely there.

Yllana and Janetta let go, rubbing their hands as if the touch had fouled them, and she, no *he*, dropped to his knees, sobbing. Around me I heard the beginnings of a feral growl. I blinked, seeing a boy and a girl in quick confusion, and then only a human in despair.

"Will they never learn?" Mother Doria said bitterly. "Go whore for the *ombrédi, Adrian,* if they will have you. There is no place for you here."

"Throw him out!" Lassandra, whose brothers had beaten her near to death when she refused to marry the man they chose for her, recoiled, and the murmur around me became a roar.

Someone hauled open the door as others laid hands on the boy. Outside the snow swirled, but it was kinder than the storm within. As Janetta thrust Adrian through the door, Yllana snatched up the fallen cloak and threw it after him. The house shook as the door slammed shut, then he was gone.

The lock of black hair was still in my hand.

~ooo~

That night, Kiera and I prepared for sleep in silence.

"Are you cold?" she spoke at last as I slid in beside her. She tucked the quilts in more closely and put her arms around me. The air was too chilly to think of love-making, but it was a comfort to feel the warmth of that strong, supple body that I had come to know as well as my own.

I shook my head and Kiera shifted so that I could lay it on her shoulder. "I can't forget that poor boy we cast out into the snow."

"Should I be jealous?" Kiera murmured against my hair. "Never mind, love. There's nothing we can do for him now." But I could tell from her voice that the memory bothered her, too.

I sighed. What I was really feeling was guilt. I had thought myself brave to leave my father's house for the Free Amazons, but I had only exchanged one safe space for another. Adrian had nowhere to go. Presently the cocoon of warmth we had created lulled us both to sleep, but I dreamed that I was wandering in grey mists, in a body that was not my own.

~ooo~

The next morning Stelle asked for two women to escort her on a call of mercy, and Kiera and I volunteered.

"I'm sorry to bring you out on such a day," said the healer as we trudged down the street beneath a dull gray sky. "But my patient lives in a rather rough part of town."

I understood. Kiera was good with weapons and often worked as a bodyguard for rich women who were traveling with the caravans. Glove-making was my trade, but everyone had spent all their coin for Midwinter gifts and I had no commissions just now. Three Renunciates, even if Stelle and I had only the basic training in self-defense they gave us all, would discourage any villain who might be about—at least by day.

I wondered if we would encounter Adrian. I could not bring myself to throw his lock of hair away. It lay now in the matrix-locked casket where I kept my jewelry, and the memory was heavier on my heart than that silky strand had been in my hand.

The boy—girl—had been so desperate for us to believe him. I found it hard to comprehend why someone born into the privilege of a male in Darkovan society, and judging by the quality of his undergarments a high class male at that, would voluntarily give up that identity. At least Adrian had known to seek the only place in Thendara where the lot of a woman without protectors might be tolerable, though I could not imagine how he had expected to maintain the disguise.

As we passed Comyn Castle, Kiera shifted position to put me between her and those pale walls, as if she thought her high-born kin might suddenly appear and drag her back inside. Her own choice was easier to understand. As a *comynara* she had had everything but freedom.

The house we were seeking lay nearly in the Castle's shadow—in more senses than one, I thought, stepping wide to avoid a rotted board as I followed Stelle up the stairs. The scent of old urine hung in the air. This was indeed the shadow side of Comyn splendor, and I could not help but wonder why, if our leaders refused Terran technology, they did not use some of our own matrix powers to improve the lot of the people they ruled. Out in the countryside the old bargain between Comyn lords and their folk still held, but people in cities needed something more.

A half grown girl carrying a toddler on her hip met us at the door. An infant slept in a cradle, and two older children played by the stove. The room smelled of burnt porridge and diapers. Looking at their ragged clothing, I was suddenly acutely conscious of the thick, russet and gold plaid wool of my skirt and the fur-lined over-tunic I wore. Yllana said I thought too much about clothes, but if I looked like a drudge no one would buy the gloves I made. I made a silent vow that when I returned to the Guildhouse I would ransack my clothes-press for something I could spare.

"How many children has she had?" Kiera whispered, eyes wide.

"Twelve..." replied Stelle grimly as we undid clasps and toggles and hung our cloaks on hooks by the door. "*Ser* Marco drives a cart and is often away with the caravans. You'd think that less opportunity to sow the seed would diminish the yield, but it seems he's one of those men who has only to hang his breeches on the bedpost to get his wife with child."

"Don't these women know how to prevent it?" I asked.

"I warned Mirza it would be dangerous to have more. I gave her the herbs myself. But *Ser* Marco...apparently sees any form of prevention as an affront to his masculinity."

"Is she pregnant again already?" I glanced at the baby.

"Goddess, I hope not," Stelle answered as she picked up her basket and led us into the second room. "The message said only that she had been fevered for a week and was very ill."

The woman seemed very small in the big bed. Mirza flinched as the healer turned back the covers and began to palpate her belly and womb. She was very thin, but I thought there was some swelling there.

"Mirza, have you tried to abort a child?"

"Nay, how could I, with Marco on the road since before little Esteban was born? There is no child! *She* said there will never be another child, but it hurts, Mestra. I cannot keep food down, and it hurts!"

"Who said, Mirza?" Stelle's voice was very gentle, but I shivered, sensing anger as one can sometimes feel a distant storm.

"The woman with the starstone," came the faint reply.

Stelle frowned. "Kiera, you have Tower training. Can you look at this woman's channels and tell me what you see?"

I could sense Kiera's reluctance, but she sat down on the side of the bed and closed her eyes, matching her breathing to that of the woman on the bed. She pulled out the little silk bag she always wore suspended from a cord around her neck, and I saw the glint of blue as she took out the crystal it held. She stretched out her other hand above Mirza's womb.

"Her channels are blocked," she exclaimed suddenly. "Avarra help us, her vital energies are backing up. She's burning up inside!"

The woman turned restlessly. "She said I would feel no desire, feel nothing, but I did not care, if it meant he could not get me with child...."

"I was taught to monitor at Neskaya, but I never had to deal with anything that had gone this far." Kiera stroked the air above Mirza's womb and the woman twitched and moaned. "I think she hurts so much she is resisting any touch."

"Get snow," ordered Stelle. She rummaged in her basket and drew out a bottle. I was already on my way to the other room, calling to the older children to help me. Whatever else Darkover might lack, snow was abundant, especially at this time of year.

By the time we had dulled Mirza's senses enough for Kiera to work on her, the early winter darkness was falling. When Stelle pronounced her stabilized, it was late indeed.

As the door shut behind us Stelle gripped my arm. "That 'woman with the starstone' must be stopped. I've been hearing stories about someone who promises great cures—for a great price. Some of them work. Others...go wrong. This is the worst I've seen."

"Avarra only knows how much damage a renegade matrix technician could do." Kiera's face was pinched as I had never seen it, even when she came in from a hard day on the trail.

"I questioned the children," I replied. "The boy said he escorted his mother to the street of the ale houses, but they would not let him come inside."

"They'll let *me*!" said Stelle, her white coif a pale blur in the gloom. "I'll go tomorrow." Kiera and I nodded, knowing this was our fight, too.

~oOo~

The address the boy had given lay just at the edge of the Trade City—a borderland where a woman alone was equally in danger from drunken *Terranan* who had wandered out of their sector in search of excitement and the Darkovan low-lifes who preyed on them. I wondered once more at the courage—or desperation—it must have taken for the carter's wife to go there.

"*Mestra* Raimonda, Matrix Mechanic" said the sign above the door, with an image of a blue star. Her staircase was cleaner than Mirza's, but I found myself oddly reluctant to touch the rail.

The big man who opened the door tried to stare us down, but we were too well-trained to give him the female deference he was expecting. His mistress was another matter. Thin, dressed in a grey woolen skirt and tunic that managed to suggest Terran attire without challenging Darkovan modesty, she greeted us with a smile in which there was neither warmth nor welcome. From a chain around her neck hung a blue jewel the size of an egg. One glimpse of Kiera's starstone had made my head swim, but I realized that I could look at this one with no discomfort. Whatever matrix *Mestra* Raimonda was using to play her tricks was elsewhere, but no doubt a woman like Mirza would be impressed by this piece of glass.

"Free Amazons! It is not often I see your kind. What may I do for you?"

"Stop harming my patients!" Stelle said fiercely. "They see your sign and think you are a *leronis*. Play your tricks on the *Terranan*, if you must—they deserve no better—but leave our people alone!"

"Why, what a feisty little rabbit-horn it is!" *Mestra* Raimonda shook her head. "You yourself are allowed to practice only because no one cares what happens to the poor. Who will question *me*? The City Guard are too busy trying to keep peace between our folk and the Terrans. The Comyn are too busy fighting each other. The Telepath Council is still arguing about the proper use of power. Go home to your Guildhouse. If you trouble me again, you will find my protectors are more than a match for a few girls who think they are warriors because they carry knives!"

I felt my face flush as I released the pommel of my dagger. Kiera was still gripping the hilt of the blade, its length an inch shy of a man's sword, that hung at her side. For a moment I thought Stelle was going to explode. Then her eyes went cold.

"I am neither warrior nor *leronis*," she said softly. "But I warn you that the goddess I serve will give you the justice you deserve one day."

I shivered, but *Mestra* Raimonda had begun to laugh. We could still hear her as we made our way down the stairs. Still shaken, I bumped into someone who was coming up. Kiera and Stelle stumbled to a halt behind me, blocking the way.

"Your pardon, *mestras*. Please to be letting me pass—" the murmured apology had the accent of the Hellers. The shawl fell away and I glimpsed a silver clasp and a tangle of black hair.

"Adrian!" I exclaimed. "You can't go in there!"

"By what right would you be stopping me? You threw me out into the snow!"

"But that woman—" I heard the door above opening, and blocked the way. "Before you do anything drastic, at least hear what we have to say!" Despite his height, Adrian weighed less than I. As *Mestra* Raimonda's guard appeared, the three of us hustled the boy back down the stairs and out the door.

"There's a decent wine shop two streets down where we can talk," said Stelle. Kiera and I dragged Adrian after her.

~oOo~

The atmosphere of the tavern was heavy with the scent of wood smoke and spilled liquor, startling after the brisk air outside. We settled ourselves at a table near the fire and ordered a pitcher of hot spiced wine.

Stelle pushed back her white coif and stared at the boy until he met her eye. "Now, Adrian, what were you doing at *Mestra* Raimonda's?"

"What business would it be of yours?" he muttered. "And I'd ask that you will be calling me Adriana if you insist on talking to me!" He stared from one of us to another as if we were a mirror in which he could see himself as he wished to be, and as I looked back I saw in him the maiden once more.

"I am a healer—" Stelle said more gently. "It is my business to save lives and ease pain. *Mestra* Raimonda's meddling nearly killed one of my patients. What did you think she could do for you?"

"They said...she knows how to make a woman *emmasca*. I was hoping that she might be able to do the same for me."

The healer sat back, eyes wide. "I never heard of such a thing. Why would a man—"

"Were your family pressuring you to sire an heir?" asked Kiera. "Surely no one would care if you found a *bredu* and lived with him once you had done your duty to your kin."

Adriana straightened, pale eyes flashing. "I do not desire a man! I do not want to *be* a man! I do not belong in this body—the gods made some mistake when I was born. Of all women in the world, you Renunciates should be the ones to understand. Didn't each and every one among you have to break the chains of law and love for the right to choose your own way?"

For me it had been easy. My father would have married me off to someone in his guild, but he had four other daughters to dower. When I told him I was a lover of women, he gave in and even escorted me to the Guildhouse door. But I still had to learn how to be free.

"*Mestra* Raimonda has not even the skill to block a woman's fertility, whatever she may say. Death is the only transformation you would find if you put yourself in her hands," Stelle said flatly. I had to look away from the suffering I saw in Adriana's eyes.

"Do you think I care?"

"Perhaps not. But there are those who do," responded the healer. "This woman is preying on our people. If you care so little for your life, help us stop her."

Adriana stared. Mired in his own pain, it had never occurred to him to notice the suffering of others. And why should it? I, with far less excuse, had been the same.

"You are Comyn, aren't you?" Kiera said suddenly.

"How did you know?" His pale eyes widened. I blinked, seeing suddenly the stamp of their caste in those fine-boned faces, and further, inexcusable for a glove-maker to have missed before, the fact that the boy had six fingers on each hand.

"My father was Edric Ridenow," Kiera said wryly. "We are brought up to recognize our kin. You are from the Hellers, by your speech. I would guess Storn, or perhaps Ardais?"

"They say that my father's grandfather was a son of *Dom* Gabriel Ardais. *Nedestro*, to be sure, for two generations back."

Kiera nodded. "The Ardais blood has grown thin. No wonder if they were scouring the hills for lost heirs."

"What they found was *me*..." Adriana said bitterly. "They were wanting to put me in the City Guard. But I couldn't bear it!" He shuddered fastidiously. "So I ran away."

"How old are you?"

"Last autumn I turned nineteen."

"Were you tested for *laran*?"

Adriana's gaze dropped. "There was nothing worth training," he replied. He looked younger, but I supposed that if he had any of the Comyn gifts, they would have shown themselves by now.

Stelle raised an eyebrow. "How have you been living, child?"

"As I can—" The thin shoulders hunched. "I had a brother who did the outside work, until he died. Since I would not act the part of a boy, my mother taught me the skills of a girl. Even in the city, there are floors to be swept, clothes to be washed, animals to be fed. I work for a place to sleep and a little bread. So you see," Adriana went on, "even if I would, I could be no help to you."

Stelle frowned, then signaled to the tavern keeper to bring some of the stew that was simmering over the fire, along with another pitcher of wine.

"There is neither wisdom nor courage in an empty belly," she said as the steaming bowls were set down. "Eat, my children, and perhaps we will find some better counsel."

The floor of the wine shop was none too clean, but their stew was excellent. The morning's excitement had given all of us an appetite, and Adriana ate like a starved banshee. It gave me an odd pleasure to see some color in those thin cheeks, and once more I could see him as a girl.

"I would go to the Terrans, but everyone I knew in their Medical Section was transferred long ago. In any case, it is the duty of this new Telepath Council that *Dom* Regis has put together to prevent misuse of their powers," Stelle said thoughtfully as the bowls were cleared away. "But *Mestra* Raimonda was right when she said they only listen to their own." Kiera flinched as the healer turned to her. "Can't you try to contact them, dear?"

"If my half-brother Donal had not been sent off-world to study, there might be a way. But now that my father is dead, my oldest brother, Lorenz, rules. It was his best friend that I refused to marry. When I joined the Free Amazons he declared me dead. He will not speak to me."

I reached out to squeeze her hand. I knew she was still wounded by the breach with her kin. Adriana was watching us with haunted eyes, and my heart ached, knowing there was no Guild to replace the family he had lost. I wanted to hug him, but there was something defensive in the set of those thin shoulders that said he would push me away.

"That leaves *you*—" Stelle turned to Adriana, who shook his head with a bitter laugh. "I will make you an offer," she went on. "We will find you a room and give you enough to live on. In return, we ask you to put on men's clothing once more and go to *Dom* Danilo. He is the head of your family, and he has *Dom* Regis's ear. Tell him what is going on."

How could she ask this, I wondered, after what he had told us? But I suppose that as a healer, she often had to cause pain in order to cure.

"We cannot bring you into the Guildhouse, but we will honor you as a sister," I added quickly. I was rewarded by a look of wonder. Then a flash of bitter humor lit those clear eyes.

"Very well..." he fingered the shorn end of the lock he had severed in the Guildhouse. "For you, I will cut off the rest of my hair and pretend to be a man."

~oOo~

"I know that many of you find our Training Sessions a burden," Mother Doria leaned forward, her hawk-fierce gaze moving from one woman to another until everyone was still. "But what happened a few days ago proves they are needful."

I shivered, the image of Adriana standing half-naked in the entry hall overlaid by a memory of how he had looked in the male clothing we had found for him. He had not seemed a girl, but he was not quite like a boy, either. Something that was neither or perhaps both, I thought, but however strange his guise, he had been beautiful.

Kiera put her arm around me. I relaxed against her, acutely aware of the whipcord strength hidden in those limbs. Knowing Adriana had made me more aware of bodies—his, Kiera's, my own.

"We need to understand not only what our rules are, but why they were made. Lassandra, remind us why we require that every woman who seeks refuge here strip naked before us all."

Lassandra colored up to her hairline. As the only Renunciate now in her house-bound year, she got more than her share of such questions. She cleared her throat self-consciously, then closed her eyes, as if the better to remember what she had read in our *Book of Years*.

"They say that in the time of Varzil the Good, when the Sisterhood of the Sword and the priestesses of Avarra had just joined together and were seeking a charter for the *Comhi-Letzii*, a spy was sent by the men who feared and hated the idea that women might live free. He was a *gre'zalis*, and had been an entertainer of the kind who mimic to the point of parody everything they think is female. But his heart was given entirely to his male lover, and he told him all our secrets, and opened the doors of the Guildhouse to our enemies."

Mother Doria sighed. "Some of our own sisters love men—does that mean they are traitors, too? Mhari—what do you say?"

This time it was Mhari, who was heavy with the child she had conceived at Midsummer, who flushed angrily.

"I can hardly deny that I like lying with men." She patted her belly. "The very difference between us makes me more aware of being a woman, not less."

I did not know whether or not to envy her. Once or twice I had let a man paw me at the Midsummer festival. It had not been unpleasant, but I had felt no spark of desire.

"I wish men and women could live together as equals," she went on, "but the world goes as it will, not as I would have it. I have given my oath to my sisters, and I will not betray them."

Janetta shook her grey head. "Mhari, I know I must not call you a traitor, but I have never understood how you can bear the touch of a man. I feel most completely what it is to be a woman when I look into my *breda's* eyes."

I noted the glance she exchanged with Gwennis, and sighed. Their devotion was one of the great love stories of Thendara

House, like that of Kiera's oath-mother Caitrin and Stelle. I felt Kiera's hand on mine and leaned against her, wondering whether the girls would tell such tales about us when we were that old.

"The spy betrayed us because he loved men, but what if he had loved women?" Mother Doria asked then. "If he cut off his male parts, would he qualify?"

"The minute we all got into the hot pool for a soak the difference would be clear...." someone laughed.

"Even if he went to the Terrans? I am told they can change a man's face or make an ugly girl into a beauty. Why not alter his sexual parts as well?"

"It wouldn't matter!" Janetta shook her head violently. "He wasn't *born* a woman."

"He could never feel the changes our bodies put us through!" added Mhari.

"The sacred mystery of blood—" said little Cora, who had just had her womanhood ceremony.

"He didn't face the scorn we see in men's eyes when we claim the right to be equal human beings in this world!" Yllana cried.

"What makes the difference is what is inside," added Gwennis. "No one who has not grown up as a woman can ever really understand."

And yet in these sessions we were learning to change the way we had been taught to think in the days before our breasts were grown. Couldn't the same training change someone raised as a male? The image of Adrian as I had last seen him came to mind, his willowy grace blurred by the male clothes.

I was still wrestling with the question when the woman who had been left on door duty came in with a message for Stelle. I saw her face darken, then she whispered to Mother Doria and motioned to Kiera and me.

"Another one of your pregnant mothers?" Kiera grinned as we crept out of the meeting. "Why do babies always choose the middle of the night to arrive?"

Stelle shook her head. "Adrian was attacked on his way back from the Castle. I don't know how badly he was beaten, but I delivered his landlady's last child, and she had the wit to send to me."

As I bundled up in my warmest clothes, I felt sick with guilt. If we had not persuaded Adriana to carry our message, he would not have been in the streets. I knew all about the risks to lone women; it had never occurred to me that a young man out at night might be in danger as well.

The lodging we had found for Adriana was a cabin behind a family's home. As Kiera and Stelle carried the battered body to the bed, I built up the fire.

"Cuts and bruises..." muttered the healer as she pulled the torn clothes away. At least, I thought grimly, he would never have to wear those hated garments again. "A cracked rib, here—" she said as he moaned. "Cassi, fill a kettle and set it to boiling."

"*Dom* Danilo—says they will send someone..." came a whisper from the puffy lips. He whimpered as the healer teased apart the blood-clotted locks and began to probe his skull.

"What did this? A club?"

"The man from *Mestra* Raimonda. Waiting he was, outside the Castle gate.... He said...we might accuse, but we'll not live...to testify. But a *leronis*...will question *Mestra* Raimonda. She'll know...." His lips twisted in a painful grin.

"He wanted you to carry the message, then—" the healer said wryly. "I wondered why he left you alive."

"The bitch must have a spy in Comyn Castle," Stelle peered out the small window. "If I mention your name, I might get in to warn *Dom* Danilo."

"No!" Adriana struggled upright, sobbing. "If they know who you are they'll be after you, too!"

"Hush, child!" Kiera sounded oddly protective. "You may not know how to fight, but if that bully tackles *us*, he will be in for a surprise."

Stelle finished binding the cracked ribs and cleaning the boy's wounds. Adriana grew calmer, and drank down a potion that the healer said would help with the pain. "And it will help you sleep. Rest is what you need now."

"Mustn't sleep—" He tried to sit up again. One eye was swollen shut, but the other fixed me desperately. I cast a quick glance at Kiera and saw her nod.

"We'll stay with you, Adriana." I clasped that thin, six-fingered hand. "Tell them at the Guildhouse, Stelle. We'll call you if there is need."

~ooo~

The next few days brought a blizzard that blocked streets and turned the steep roofs of the houses to a range of snowy peaks. The world lay locked in Avarra's cold embrace. In such weather, it was impossible to imagine that Evanda would ever return, bearing the warmth of spring. Kiera and I scarcely noticed what was going on outside, for by morning Adriana was burning with fever. Scraps of speech told us of a father who beat this useless child who could have made the family's fortune if he would only be a proper son, a mother who tried to shelter the only one of her children who had survived, boys who had teased and tormented and girls who had welcomed, until their menfolk taught them to scorn. But if the words were fragmentary, the images blossomed in my mind with brutal clarity, until I wilted beneath those insults and cringed from those blows.

We took turns cradling Adriana's slight form, and in the cold dark hours just before dawn huddled together beneath the quilts. On the third day, I woke just at daybreak to feel an icy breath of air on my face. Kiera lay snoring lightly at my side, but the door was open and Adriana was gone. I scrambled from the bed, jammed my feet into my low boots, and snatched up a shawl as I hurried to the door.

It had stopped snowing. The red sun rose in a sky whose purple was lightening swiftly into lavender. Violet-shadowed footprints led to Adriana, who stood clad only in a shift, barefoot in the snow. In the rosy light, the pale features beneath the shock of dark hair seemed to glow.

"My dear, what are you doing out there?" My breath puffed as I called.

"Going away..." came the reply. "It is so pure...so still... Already my feet are gone. Soon I will feel nothing at all...."

"Come back, silly child. You'll freeze—" I spoke softly, as if I feared to startle some wild thing.

"Yes...I will.... Go back to bed, Cassilde, and let me be. You have been very kind, but I have no place in this world. It is better this way."

"*Kind!*" My shriek brought Kiera stumbling from the bed, knife in hand. "You idiot, do you think we have nursed you for three days from *kindness*?" I leaped down into the snow and floundered toward him.

Adriana had stood still too long to run. By the time we had chafed life back into cold feet, our patient had fallen so deeply asleep we feared we had lost the battle, but perhaps that hour in the snow had been what was needed to rout the fever, for the next day Adriana woke with eyes clear and a cool brow.

Throughout the long hours when we watched, I had replayed that moment when I ran out into the snow. If not from kindness, why had I cared for Adriana so devotedly? In the Guildhouse, my love for Kiera was accepted and admired. What could I call the fascination Adriana stirred in me? What place could it have in the world?

From that day on, the cold began to ease. Deep hollows formed in the snow. If I found it hard to meet Adriana's clear gaze, I smiled often to see vigor coming back into the long limbs. Stelle brought more clothes—the bulky quilted pants and fur-lined Free Amazon tunics that even my vanity found practical at this time of year. I knew it was time for us to leave, but Kiera said nothing, and I did not ask her why for fear she would put the same question to me.

~ooo~

A tenday had passed when *Mestra* Raimonda's men came. Stelle had sent word that the Telepath Council was arresting the unlicensed matrix mechanics. Our testimony was hardly needed when the Council had people who could read their very souls, so I suppose that the bullies were out for revenge.

At the first knock, Adriana snatched up the big carving knife from the cutting board. For a moment, Kiera and I simply stared. Then we were on our feet, hearts pumping with the same alarm, drawing knife and dagger from the sheaths that hung from our chairs.

"Come out, you bitches, and pay the price for your meddling ways!" Another knock shook the timbers of the door.

"Stand back, *bre'suin!*" Kiera cried gaily. "If you're tired of diddling yourself, get away from the door and we'll come play with you!"

I had scarcely a moment to wonder if I would remember my training before she had thrust the door open, and the three of us came out in perfect step, forming a fighting wedge as neatly as if we had rehearsed it.

There were five of them, armed with clubs and swords. We came in fast, under their guard. The first man was down before the others could react, blood spraying crimson across the snow. That taught caution to the others, but Kiera's attacks were deadly, and as we guarded her flanks, Adriana mirrored my every move.

By the time men in the green uniforms of the City Guard pushed through the crowd, only one of our attackers was standing, crimson-faced as he listened to their jeers.

"By Aldones, you Amazons fight well!" the fair-haired commander exclaimed.

Kiera grinned and hugged me, and I reached out to Adriana.

"Congratulations! You've certainly proved yourself a hero!"

Adriana went deathly pale. "A *hero*? Not a heroine? He thought

I was one of you! Cannot you even now bring yourself to think of me as a girl?"

He—no—*she*—fixed me with an icy glare. I stared back. *If I speak to you as a woman,* I thought then, *I will have to admit that what I feel for you is love.* I had not said those words aloud, but somehow, Adriana knew. Her face grew radiant. I cast a quick glance at Kiera and saw her smile.

Breda—did I hear her with my ears or my mind? *Don't you know that I have come to love Adriana, too?*

"I'll buy you a drink if you'll honor me with your company!" Oblivious to the turmoil of emotions around him, the young commander gestured toward the wine shop down the road.

He wants to boast to his mates about how he drank with the three fierce Amazons! Was that thought Kiera's, or my own? Though we were already drunk on the exhilaration of having survived and hardly needed wine, arm in arm, Kiera, Adriana, and I followed him.

~oOo~

It was very late when we reeled back to the cabin. I shed my cloak and the woolen tunic and stood shivering in my shirt, waiting for the fire to warm the room.

Kiera put her arms around me from behind. She had started to strip down, too. I leaned into the warmth of her breast and belly with a sigh, then gasped as she brought her hands up to cup my breasts and I felt the first pulse of response. My laughter died as I caught sight of Adriana's stricken gaze.

How could we make love when she was here? I started to push Kiera away, but my beautiful, generous lover was already reaching out, catching Adriana's arm and pulling her into my embrace. My arms closed reflexively around the slim form. During her illness I had not allowed myself to know how much I wanted to touch that long, delicate body, to run my fingers through the shining black hair.

A shock ran through me; I could feel its reflection in Kiera's stronger frame. Adriana's crystal eyes were alight. I drew her head down, and it was a woman's kiss. Kiera nuzzled my neck, and I felt Adriana quiver in reply.

The world was whirling around us. Another step brought us all to the bed in a tangle of limbs. Lip met lip, hands caressed. Breast nestled against breast like nesting doves, and legs twined in a melting sweetness until I did not know where my own body ended and those of the others began. Images flickered through my awareness—the long smooth line of Kiera's back and thigh—but that could not be my vision, because I was kissing her lips. Through the eyes of the others I saw my round arms, the sweet curve of my thigh, and realized that I was beautiful.

This is what it is to be a woman...and this.... Which of us had spoken? I did not know, but firelight glimmered on Kiera's pointed breasts, on my own generous bosom, and on Adriana's glowing body, a swelling softness, barely budded, but manifestly there.

And this... The male member that had caused so much trouble had become a mere nub. All that had been pendant was retreating into smooth folds, that which was outer becoming inner, Adriana's entire body transforming beneath my reverent hands. Kiera's hands traced glowing lines above Adriana's body, and I knew without being taught that they were those of a woman, the energies flowing free and clear. Ancient tales of the *chieri* who lay sometimes with mortals and left their beauty as a legacy teased at my memory.

Beautiful One, you lend us grace... Was this thought mine? *I see the Goddess in you.*

I gaze at you, came her thought as she looked from me to Kiera, *and you become my mirror.*

Seeking the heart of desire, we merged, confirming, affirming identity once more in a single cry.

~oOo~

We awoke, still entwined. A rosy light filtered through the melting frost-flowers on the window, kissing Kiera's high brow and elegant cheekbones with color. Adriana's translucent skin seemed lit from within. The brief thaw that we called the Breath of Evanda must have come. We often had a few such days at this time of year. It would not last, but it was a promise that someday spring would return to the world.

"Anyone hungry?" my lover asked.

"I have feasted," I answered, and we both laughed as a blush intensified Adriana's glow. She was staring around her as if she had awakened to a new world, and it was true.

Kiera scrambled out of bed, pulled on a shirt, and went to wake up the fire. I gave Adriana a kiss and followed, scarcely feeling the chill in the air.

"You're Ardais..." Kiera said to Adriana as we sat down to a steaming porridge of nuts and grain. "That's why we were picking up each other's thoughts. Your family's Gift awakens telepathy in others. When your true nature was suppressed, you must have blocked your *laran*. You've certainly strengthened mine, and discovered untapped depths in Cassi as well—" she grinned and I blushed, remembering how her touch had penetrated my soul. "That's why we fought so well."

"That's why we loved so well—" Adriana replied with a shy smile.

"Will you come with us to the Guildhouse?" I asked. "You would pass even Janetta's inspection now."

Adriana shook her head, the light dying out of those clear eyes. "I know that you must go back, but I cannot. I have a woman's body now, but in their minds there will always be that image of how I was before."

"You can't live here alone," I objected. Boy or girl, it was clear Adriana did not have the skills to live on her own. "I'll stay with you." I cast a quick look at my *breda*, willing her to understand.

"But you are *Kiera's* lover—" Tears glistened as Adriana looked from her to me.

"So I will stay, too." Kiera shrugged. "Is there a law that says we can love only one? When I was at Neskaya, we were all open to each other. My great-uncle Damon was a Keeper, though he was male, the first since the time of Varzil the Good. They called his circle the Forbidden Tower, and they say he loved all the others, male and female, life-long."

"You would leave the Guildhouse?"

"Those who marry as freemates often do," I said thoughtfully. "Our oath does not require Renunciates to live together. It is easier, that is all." I stifled a pang as I realized how much I would miss even the things about my sisters that had exasperated me the most. Would they feel we had rejected them? Would Kiera's oath-mother understand when she returned from visiting her son Donal off-world? I could not allow fear of their reaction to rule me. Adriana was my sister now.

"And if someone came to you, someone like me but without the *chieri* blood to make her body a match for her soul?" Adriana's face was grave. The clarity of communication we had shared was fading, but the intensity of her emotion throbbed in the air. I looked at Kiera, and felt her agree.

"We would look into her soul, and find the woman hidden there..."

"We could call ourselves the Forbidden Guildhouse." My lover grinned. "Renunciates have always challenged the boundaries. We're pushing them a little farther, that's all."

I reached out and saw, refracting from mind to mind, the image of the Goddess reflected in my lovers' eyes.

At the Crossroads
by Barb Caffrey

Not all Renunciates lived apart from the larger world, after a period of re-education and training. The enduring gifts of ruthless self-examination include integrity and the development of critical thinking. For those Renunciates with the interest and aptitude, the justice system offers a way of putting those qualities to use for the betterment of all Darkovans. So it's not surprising to find a Renunciate judge untangling a mystery or two in the early years of recontact with the Terran Federation.

Barb Caffrey is a writer, editor and musician from the Midwest. Though "At the Crossroads" is her first-ever Darkover story, she has written a humorous fantasy novel, AN ELFY ON THE LOOSE, that will be published in 2014 by Twilight Times Books. Previous stories and poems have appeared in *Bedlam's Edge* (with late husband Michael B. Caffrey), *How Beer Saved The World*, the *Bearing North* anthology, the Written Word online magazine, Joyful Online, the Midwest Literary Magazine, and at e-Quill Publishing. Find her at Elfyverse (AKA "Barb Caffrey's Blog") for discussions of all and sundry, or at Shiny Book Review.

Moving now into the years of adjustment and conflict between Darkover and the Terrans, she offers another tale of challenging boundaries and the Renunciates.

"The trouble in the Hellers started over a chervine." Fiona n'ha Gorsali stood before the Courts of Arbitration in her best judicial robe with her short brownish-gray hair tidy as always, and hoped she looked calmer than she felt. She was here to answer for her actions, but by Zandru's ninth Hell, she'd not bow to anyone. "It rapidly grew in both time, effort, and scope. My report should've given you some idea as to why I involved the *Terranan*, especially because of the crops and the bees—"

"Your report was somewhat sketchy. We need to know why you made these particular choices." Chief Justice Coryn di Asturien's gray eyes gave Fiona no clue as to how this hearing would go, and none of the other seven justices on the Courts of Arbitration gave her so much as a hint, either. The Chief Justice sat in the center behind a long, high wooden table with the other justices seated to either side of him, three by three. A chair at the end of the right-hand side was vacant, the chair Fiona had one day hoped might be hers—but after she'd had to make the difficult judgment she was now about to answer for, it was most unlikely she'd ever manage to claim that chair for herself.

"I'm the Circuit Court judge for the Caer Donn region," Fiona said. "We had unexpected trouble in the Hellers—"

"Isn't there always?" mocked Andres MacAnndra, the youngest justice on the court. Still auburn-haired, he was an even-tempered and fair-minded justice. Fiona had met him many times at judicial conferences, and he usually had a smile on his face rather than the scowl he wore today.

"Silence!" the Chief Justice thundered. "Continue, *mestra* Fiona."

"When the litigants came to me, I did not know the scope of the problem," she started. "In my court were two angry people, fighting over an unexpected chervine foal. Here's how it started...."

~oOo~

"That foal should be mine by right," Donal the harnessmaker said as he stood before Fiona. A thin, balding, and unassuming man from Nevarsin entering his fourth decade, most women wouldn't give him a second glance. "Just because my old chervine Dusty didn't show signs of pregnancy before I sold her, that doesn't mean anything!"

"It takes nearly twelve months for a chervine to foal," Fiona pointed out. It might be spring, but she wore her warmest homespun robe. Being so thin, the cold affected her. "Yet most chervines do show signs of pregnancy by the second month, do they not?"

"They do," Donal admitted. "But there have been many miscarriages in the Hellers lately, ever since the *Terranan* came—and the crops are dying, too!"

"Stick to the issue at hand," Fiona instructed. "Dusty had a foal and died giving birth. But by this time, Dusty belonged to the plaintiff, Jessamyn n'ha Doria?"

"Yes, Dusty did," Donal agreed. "I sent Dusty away, mostly because I thought she should live out her remaining years in a climate that might be easier on her than Nevarsin. Jessamyn told me she lived in Temora—"

Well, Temora was far to the south and was certainly warmer than the Hellers. Fiona followed Donal's logic, but she still had to ask, "Is that true?"

"Yes, *mestra*," Jessamyn, a youthful, stocky brunette, agreed. "I was born and raised in Temora, and I hope to return there soon." Jessamyn's clear hazel eyes showed she was far from intimidated by these proceedings.

Which is just as well, Fiona thought. She hated people coming into her court who were obviously overwhelmed, as it was hard to get accurate testimony.

"There were no signs of Dusty being in foal at the time you bought her?" she asked Jessamyn.

"No, *mestra*, there were none," Jessamyn said. "And I didn't think to have any of the Guildwomen who are specialists in veterinary medicine check her over, either, as Dusty was twenty-two years old and had never previously foaled."

"Understood," Fiona said. Why would a chervine that had never foaled suddenly give birth at near to twenty-three years of age—ancient for a chervine—only after she was sent down from the Hellers? Fiona needed to consider this in more depth.

"Had you attempted to breed Dusty in the past?" Fiona asked Donal.

"I had, yes, mostly because she was steady, sure-footed, and intelligent—a model chervine in every respect," Donal said. "But the pregnancies never took. Anibal told me there must be something in the water causing the miscarriages."

"Anibal the veterinarian? From here in Caer Donn?"

Donal nodded. "He's well respected. I valued Dusty very much."

"So you did," Fiona murmured. Anibal was the best veterinarian in the Hellers. "Please continue."

"I never would've sold her, had I known she was in foal," Donal said. "I think she lost her life because the plaintiff insisted on riding Dusty all the way to Temora."

"That had nothing—" Jessamyn started hotly.

Fiona banged her wooden gavel. "Most chervines can handle being ridden up until their eighth or ninth month of pregnancy. They are working animals. So there's no cruelty involved, as I see it. Besides, Jessamyn n'ha Doria didn't know Dusty was pregnant."

"Absolutely, *mestra*," Jessamyn agreed. "Once I knew Dusty was in foal, we were on our way back to the Caer Donn Guildhouse. So I consulted with Anibal."

Fiona said, "He told you Dusty was pregnant and about how far along she was, correct?"

"Yes, *mestra*."

"What did you do next?"

"I put her in Darrell's barn," Jessamyn reported. "It's the safest, warmest barn around. It has its own water supply that's reputed to have never been befouled, not by the *Terranan* or anyone. And I made sure to feed her what Anibal recommended for pregnant chervines; I did everything he asked."

Out of the corner of her eye, Fiona saw her court clerk, Miralys n'ha Rakhaila, gesture for her judge's attention. "The court will now take a recess for one hour," Fiona decided. She watched the litigants file out of the courtroom—actually a converted space near Darrell's barn—while she waited for Miralys. The dark-haired, dark-eyed bailiff, Randal, closed the door behind the litigants with a thump. "What did you want me to know before I rule?" Fiona asked.

To her surprise, it wasn't Miralys who spoke; it was Randal. "*Mestra* Fiona, there have been many problems with chervines aborting foals in the Hellers. Donal is telling the truth."

"This seems like a simple case," Fiona said. "You don't think so?"

Randal said, "No, I don't. But all I can offer is my own evidence, if you're willing to hear it."

"I'm always willing to hear from my court officers," Fiona said. "What do you know about spontaneous miscarriages in chervines?"

"My favorite chervine, Star, has been in foal four times in the past five years," Randal stated. "Every time, I've done what the veterinarians tell me—Anibal or one of his assistants—and every time, Star has lost the foal. My well abuts the *Terranan* base.... Anibal thinks the well water is causing the miscarriages."

"Has he said why it must be the water?" Fiona asked.

"No, he hasn't," Randal said. "But he said this didn't happen anywhere near as often before the *Terranan* came. And for whatever it's worth, my well was clean then."

Fiona sighed. Involving the *Terranan* was risky, especially since neither the Courts of Arbitration nor Lorill Hastur wanted them to know much about Darkover. But if they were somehow harming chervines, water, or anything else in the Hellers, they needed to know so they'd stop doing it. That much was clearly under her jurisdiction.

She must ask Anibal about this without delay. "Do either of you know where Anibal is likely to be at this hour?"

"At the Starmaker's Tavern," Miralys said promptly. "He likes their tripe stew, preferably with dark ale."

"We need Anibal to testify and confirm—or deny—Randal's report," Fiona started. "Please bring him to me."

"Certainly." Miralys hurried out.

Fiona turned to Randal. "Donal said crops were dying and insisted it's the fault of the *Terranan*. Is this superstitious blather, or does Donal have any facts supporting his allegations?"

~oOo~

"You asked the question exactly like that?" Chief Justice di Asturien asked.

"Yes, *vai dom*, I did," Fiona confirmed. "I've had many of the lower-ranked *Terranan* in my court. They're like anyone else; they get drunk and disorderly, have disputes over property, and other than a few female spacemen—who are no rowdier than many who've slept off a night's drunken carouse in a Renunciate Guildhouse—there's nothing at all to remark upon them."

"That's why you wondered if the *Terranan* had really done something wrong, or if it were all just reputation?" asked Justice MacAnndra.

"Yes, *vai dom*, it was." Fiona sighed. "While I'm sure the *Terranan* can be just as venal and corrupt as anyone else, and aren't opposed to making a quick profit, either, I saw no reason for them to deliberately pollute our water. They keep saying they want to be our friends, that we're descended from them—which seems very odd, but then again, they look almost exactly like us and act like us, so maybe they're right."

"Careful," the Chief Justice warned. "Lorill Hastur wouldn't like you saying that."

"Is he here?" Fiona asked. "Even if he were, my goodness, *vai dom*! We search for truth wherever it leads us, even if it's unpleasant or upsets the current social order. Jurists *must* stay impartial in order to mediate clashes of clan or creed. That's one of the earliest laws on the books, as it comes down from the Ages of Chaos, and it's one of the holiest laws I know."

"You are, of course, quite right." Di Asturien nodded his gray-haired head. "So you were questioning your bailiff—"

"Randal, yes," Fiona said. "And he said…"

~oOo~

"Donal is correct, at least in part," Randal said. "But I also think the *Terranan* may be getting blamed for more than their due. I haven't been up to Nevarsin in years, but I have heard the Aldarans imported pesticides for their crops about three years ago."

"I've heard the same," Fiona allowed. A *nedestro* brat of the Aldarans she'd met in a local tavern had bragged about them. The chemicals supposedly did everything but cure the wasting sickness, the way he described it. That is, until someone pointed out she was a judge...then he clammed up. "I heard from my investigator Aleki, though, that to use pesticides correctly, you must follow all of the instructions precisely. Many Aldaran retainers gave up because crops didn't seem to increase after a year. Only a few continue to use the pesticides."

"Not to impugn Aleki," Randal said, "but I've heard it's more than that. While pesticides are hard to use, crop yield improved markedly in the second year. Some smallholders decided to use pesticides last year but didn't use them the way they were supposed to. This could be part of the problem."

"Then I'm going to have to send Aleki back out again, and hope he can get better information," Fiona said as dread curled in her stomach. She knew the *Terranan* pesticides could be poisonous if used incorrectly. "So we may have polluted water, which may or may not have pesticide residue in it? And this residue may trigger miscarriages in chervines?"

Randal nodded.

"But what about the dying crops? I don't understand...pesticides should not cause crops to die even when misused."

"It's not those crops that are dying," Randal said. "For example, if someone's growing corn and using a pesticide, it might be their wheat that dies. Or if someone's growing rye, their sweet potato crop might suffer. It seems completely random, and if I were you, *mestra*, I'd get an agronomist to study the problem." Randal didn't stumble over the *Terranan* word.

"You mean, go directly to the *Terranan* and ask them to look into this?" Fiona felt uneasy, even though she'd already figured out she might have to do just that. If she went to the *Terranan* and was wrong about their involvement, the Courts of Arbitration would surely rake her over the embers for overstepping her authority. That would not be pleasant. Yet if she didn't and there were widespread crop failures in the Hellers because of the *Terranan* pesticides, people would die when she might've been able to prevent it. She definitely couldn't live with that. "Why should they help us?"

"If it's their fault, they have to fix it," Randal said.

Miralys brought Anibal in, and they conferred briefly with Fiona. Then Randal ushered the litigants back into the courtroom.

After the litigants had settled themselves again, Fiona said, "I've asked Anibal to give evidence regarding the water issue." As Fiona questioned him, Anibal confirmed everything Donal and Randal had said, finishing with, "In the past fifteen years since the *Terranan* came, I've seen the percentage of spontaneous miscarriages go from perhaps twenty percent up to seventy percent. It's a miracle any chervine carries to term, and horses—the few we get up here—are no better. As far as I'm concerned, that's evidence enough the *Terranan* have damaged our land and should leave."

"I've heard they're building a spaceport at Thendara and probably will remove there in the next five to six years," Fiona said. "Won't that be far enough away?"

"It should be," Anibal said. "I'm not a specialist in water, but since the problem didn't happen overnight, it's probably not going to be cured overnight, either."

"Understood," Fiona said quietly. "I appreciate your testimony in this matter, Anibal. You are dismissed but may be needed later, so hold yourself ready to return."

He nodded, bowed formally from the waist, and walked out.

Before either litigant could speak, Fiona said, "This case presents unexpected difficulties. I need to check Anibal's data from an independent source—" she hoped her investigator Aleki would be up for a challenge "—and I also intend to contact the *Terranan* before I rule."

"Why?" Jessamyn asked.

"If their chemicals have damaged the water and are triggering miscarriages in chervines, including Dusty's previous miscarriages, they must fix it." *And if crops truly are dying—one of the things I also intend to check, though it seems to have little bearing on this case—it is their responsibility to help us find out why.*

"Let me assure you, Donal and Jessamyn, that I will get to the bottom of this matter as soon as I may." She banged her gavel and said, "I'll contact you with my decision once all the information has been gathered."

Jessamyn nodded, but Donal scowled. "Who's to raise the foal, then?" he asked. "And who's to pay for its care in the meantime?"

"Both of you will pay for its care. But Darrell, who owns the barn, will supervise the raising of the foal, as he has for how many days now?"

"Ten, *mestra*," Jessamyn supplied.

"You may both check with Darrell once a day until this matter is resolved, but you must abide by his decisions, or Anibal's decisions if he's consulted in the interim. Is that acceptable to you both?"

They agreed, then Randal ushered them out.

"A difficult case," Miralys said. "There's much to consider here."

"That's why I'll have to get Aleki involved."

"If anyone can get to the bottom of this, he can," Miralys agreed.

"We don't have time to survey the entirety of the Hellers," Fiona said, thinking rapidly. "But Aleki has sources we don't and should be able to help. Then, if we can get confirmation from the *Terranan*..."

~oOo~

"But you didn't do things in that order," the Chief Justice pointed out. "Why?"

"*Vai dom*, after court adjourned, two smallholders came to me privately as I dined in the tavern. Both said their crops were failing. They had used pesticides. But they didn't think their crops had been properly pollinated, and they noticed far fewer bees about than normal."

"Why was that significant?" Justice MacAnndra asked.

"Without bees, crops cannot be pollinated very easily," Fiona stated. "It is possible to pollinate some crops by hand. There are some crops that can even be pollinated by a beetle that lives near the Dry Towns. But the easiest way is for bees to pollinate crops."

"These smallholders—freeholders, I suppose?" MacAnndra asked.

"Yes, *vai dom*," Fiona said. "They told me even on the great estates, such as Ardais, nothing was growing the way it should. That's why I had to go to the *Terranan* before Aleki returned with his report."

The Chief Justice looked at her somberly. "And you did this...why?"

"*Vai dom*, I've seen starvation once." Fiona swallowed hard. "I never wish to see it again."

"Commendable," the Chief Justice said, "though it would've been better had you waited for this Court's judgment."

This was tricky. "*Vai dom*, I was worried that a message would not reach this court in time to alleviate unnecessary suffering, even if the weather stayed clement. No *leronis* was available of sufficient strength to send a more urgent message, and I was unable to get the *Terranan* to send a message, so I sent a written message via chervine—"

"We received it, six weeks after the fact," the Chief Justice interrupted. "That's when we sent a message, via the Lady of Arilinn, empowering you to act on your own best judgment."

Fiona, even now, felt warmed by this. "Thank you, *vai dom*. I appreciate the Court's trust."

She regathered her thoughts. "As to why I knew it was likely I would have to approach the *Terranan*? Now I knew there was something wrong with the crops—possibly due to pesticides—and the bees. This was beyond my knowledge."

"Quite sensible," Justice MacAnndra said.

"Also, as I'm the justice who has had the most dealings with the *Terranan*, it seemed logical for me to be the one to discuss these problems with them. At least I was able to get the *Terranan* to send you someone who could explain what was going on, once we knew—"

"She called herself a scientist," MacAnndra said.

"I thought it was an 'agronomist'?" the Chief Justice asked, stumbling over the unfamiliar *Terranan* word. "Someone who studies farming in detail?"

Fiona nodded.

"What did she find?"

"I can't sum it up quickly, I'm afraid," she apologized.

"Just do your best, *mestra*," the Chief Justice advised.

"It began this way...."

~ooo~

The scientist in question was named Vida Allgood, according to the nameplate on the door. As Fiona and Randal were ushered into the spartan white meeting room and sat down at a rather low table made of something called 'plastic,' Fiona pondered the letters after Allgood's name—MS, DAgro, and so forth. The *Terranan* must put much faith in Allgood's abilities.

"You're the judge?" a tall, buxom brunette asked in passable *cahuenga*, giving her a sidelong look that could've meant anything.

"Yes, I am so honored," Fiona said. "I need your help—rather, my people do."

"What does a judge—especially a Darkovan judge—want with our science?"

"The case in question deals with a dead chervine—" Fiona

began. "Do you know what a chervine is?"

"Horse analogue," Vida remarked. "You ride it and it carries burdens, just like a horse."

"Yes." Fiona gathered her thoughts. How could she explain any of this, especially across the language barrier? "According to our best veterinarians, chervines have been miscarrying at a rate of seventy percent in the Hellers."

Vida whistled. "That's high."

Fiona nodded. "It's only been since the *Terranan* arrived, which points to some change in our farming. I've heard from several reliable sources that many crops have been lost, untimely, for no reason we're able to discern."

Allgood asked a number of rapid-fire questions, while Fiona did her best to answer calmly. Then Fiona said, "Crops are withering in the fields, and all we know so far is the water may be polluted from your pesticides and the bees may not be pollinating the crops, either."

"Still, why are *you* here, rather than one of the farmers? You're a judge. What about your aristocrats?"

"The *Hali'imyn*—the 'aristocrats,'" Fiona stumbled over the *Terranan* word, "—are often more concerned with themselves than with the common people. While I've asked for guidance from Lorill Hastur himself, it will take months for my request to reach him. Many people will die between now and then if I do not act." She decided she would not even attempt to explain the Courts of Arbitration, much less how she'd have to answer to them.

"Yet you're not what I expected." Vida exhaled, long and gustily, before she went on. "Darkover is male-dominated, and supposedly has only two women of any authority in what passes for its government."

"I'm a special case," Fiona said. She wished she could tell Vida about the Order of Renunciates, but the law was clear: Fiona could not give out any information unless Vida asked directly for it. And then, Fiona could tell of only the restrictions the Renunciates must deal with, rather than the benefits.

"Why?"

"My father, Dominic, was a judge. He had no apprentices, except me. My mother realized early that I had a gift for the law, and had no objections to me studying it." This was all the truth Fiona was allowed to give.

"Well, if there's one woman like you, maybe there might be more in the future." Allgood nodded firmly. "All right. I'll help you. What do you need?"

"Can you get one of your flying machines to look at several places?"

~oOo~

"The scientist then did what, *mestra*?" Justice MacAnndra asked.

"She looked at the maps, then commissioned a *Terranan* flying machine to overfly the blight. She told me afterward it was a horror; she even made *infrared photographs—*" Fiona made sure to pronounce the *Terranan* words very carefully "—which I have right here if you would like to see them, that showed the extent of the damage."

The Chief Justice waved this off. "Not right now, thank you."

"But why did this all happen, *mestra*?" asked the learned, balding, bespectacled Justice Doevid, a *nedestro* son of the Syrtis clan.

"As Randal and I feared, the pesticides had been used incorrectly, *vai dom*," Fiona said. "Our people, even the Aldarans who were closest to the *Terranan* from the beginning of their arrival here, didn't truly understand what they were supposed to do."

"I'd like to hear more about the bees," Chief Justice di Asturien said. "Why did they die off?"

"I'll explain, *vai dom*, as best I can—" Fiona started.

~oOo~

"You have no doubts?" Fiona asked her longtime friend and investigator quietly across mugs of ale in a secluded corner of the Starmaker's Tavern.

Aleki's blue eyes were grave. "Everything I saw confirms what the *Terranan* scientist told you, *mestra* Fiona. The crops wither in the fields. Our rye crop, in particular, will be badly stunted, and people will starve; worse yet, there won't be enough seed from that crop to use in planting next year, especially if farmers didn't lay more than the usual amount of seed aside."

"They probably didn't," Fiona said thoughtfully. "Because why would they do such a thing?"

"If they had any of the Aldaran *laran*, they might have foreseen this," Aleki muttered. "They're the ones who can see through time." Like most without *laran*, the entire subject had always made him nervous.

Fiona searched his familiar face. "There's something else, isn't there?"

"Yes, *mestra*. There is."

"What, then?" Fiona stifled her impatience. People would die, and quickly, if she did not act. "What must I know?"

"The bees, *mestra*." Aleki suddenly looked as if he'd swallowed something nasty. "They're dying. They're all dying, higher in the Hellers where many pesticides have been used. And that's one reason why the crops aren't flourishing—"

"Because they're not getting pollinated in the first place." Fiona finished. Fiona's mother had been a beekeeper, so she knew how important bees were.

Now it was all starting to make sense. "Can you give me hard evidence that the bees are dying?" she asked. "I might be able to get the *Terranan* scientist to confirm—and if she can, maybe she can somehow help reverse this."

Aleki snorted. "I've never known the *Terranan* to be good for anything, except causing trouble."

"Even so." She smiled, even though she'd rather kick him. She needed this information and his good will. Otherwise, she'd have to find a *leronis* and confirm it that way, which meant money and other resources not immediately to hand. "They say they will help, so I'm taking them at their word."

Aleki pulled out two documents and laid them before her. "Old MacAran gave me his story. He's lost most of his hives. Few bees survived, only a couple of queens, including one that is not laying eggs. Also, here's what I saw on his farm, in detail."

"He gave you this willingly?"

"I told him we were suspicious of the pesticides," Aleki reported in a matter-of-fact tone. "He's hoping to pry money from someone to replace his hives. They are desperate to have good hives wintering over."

"If the *Terranan* can help, I'll find a way to get the Lowlander *Hali'imyn* to share some of their hives, if it comes to that." *Presuming they haven't been damaged yet, of course,* she thought.

~ooo~

"He found the proof," Justice MacAnndra said. "The bees were dying. The crops that were still good weren't getting pollinated, which is why they were withering in the fields?"

"Partly, *vai dom*," Fiona said, striving for accuracy. "Vida Allgood said the *Terranan* knew all about this phenomenon; they call it '*colony collapse disorder*,' and it happens when pesticides are overused and the water gets fouled."

"We've discussed this with Master Herbalist Rodolfo Lindir," Justice Doevid put in. "He confirmed that this problem with bees has happened before, but only rarely, and only near the Dry Towns. Usually it's happened when the water has been befouled with some sort of refuse that doesn't break down properly."

"The water near the *Terranan* base was also befouled?" asked Chief Justice di Asturien.

"Unfortunately, yes it was, *vai dom*," Fiona said. *Mestra* Allgood had taken a reading on one of her *Terranan* machines and swore viciously in a tongue Fiona didn't recognize. "The *Terranan* seem to believe the water overall has been damaged by pesticides, even in Caer Donn itself. Since they're willing to help fix the problem, I didn't argue."

"Let's get back to the start of this case," said the Chief Justice. "What did you do about the chervine? And how did you manage to get all of the nobles to agree that the *Terranan* had to come in and fix whatever they could?"

"The second question is easier to explain, *vai dom*," Fiona said. "I went to each of them, starting with the Aldarans, of course, and explained what had happened." Fiona remembered *Domna* Rohana Ardais's reaction, all right; she'd first been startled, but then gave Fiona a satisfied look that Fiona hadn't been able to understand. "I told them their smallfolk would be desperate for food in the winter if the *Hali'imyn* did not allow the *Terranan* to come in and assess the damage, then mitigate whatever part of it they could. The *Hali'imyn*, of course, would not have to pay for this service."

"That's probably why—" Justice MacAnndra started.

The Chief Justice waved him off. "Continue, *mestra*."

"What surprised me were the short growth cycle grains the *Terranan* had, including some that worked well in our rather snowy climate in the Hellers. Between those grains and the irrigation that was quickly instituted, especially in the Ardais Domain, many crops were either able to be replanted or salvaged, once new colonies of bees were brought in—quickly, and thankfully, from Lorill Hastur's own estates." She bowed from the waist. "Thank you for your intercession."

"It was no trouble," Chief Justice di Asturien said, speaking for the entirety of the Court. "Now, as for the chervine—what happened, good *mestra*?"

~ooo~

Fiona looked at the litigants, again gathered before her in the makeshift courtroom near Darrell's barn. Anibal, Aleki, the *Terranan* scientist Vida Allgood, and a number of workers from both Darrell's barn and the Starmaker's Tavern were also present. "I've gone over all the information," she stated. "Donal, you were right about the water; it had been poisoned, all unwittingly, by the *Terranan*. That poison has now been cleansed, and *chervines* should not miscarry at such an alarming rate any longer."

She shuffled the papers before her, then looked at Jessamyn. "You bought Donal's *chervine* Dusty, not knowing she was gravid. The bill of sale is in order, so your ownership of Dusty herself is also in order."

Jessamyn looked triumphant until Fiona raised her hand. "I have not finished," Fiona murmured. "The damage to the crops, which Donal pointed out during our prior hearing, has also been rectified. Because Donal is the one who let this court know about this particular problem, the *Terranan* have agreed to give Donal a rather large sum of money. I have the money right here." She jingled a large, leather purse in her hand full of *Terranan* bits that would convert easily into Darkovan currency.

"What does this have to do with Dusty's foal?" Donal asked.

"I'm getting to that," Fiona said. "The bill of sale said nothing about Dusty's foal. So the foal itself is currently not owned outright by either one of you." Fiona knew this was a nifty bit of legal hairsplitting, but there it was: the foal had no owner. "My thought on the matter is this: Jessamyn, if you are willing to take half the money Donal was given by the *Terranan*, you would give up all rights to the foal. Donal, by paying Jessamyn to give up her rights to the foal, would buy full ownership of the foal. That allows Jessamyn to buy another mount, or six, so Jessamyn should not be discommoded. Is this agreement acceptable to you both?"

"I accept," Donal said. "If Dusty's good qualities bred true, her foal will be a truly fine animal."

Randal passed him the legal contract and Donal signed, making an X as he was not literate.

"I also accept," Jessamyn said. "I don't know anything about raising a foal. I don't want to stay here indefinitely, as my life, and Guildhouse, is down in Temora. But I have one condition before I sign my name."

"Name it," Fiona said.

"I wish to take only enough of the money to buy a good, reliable chervine and trail supplies; then I want to give the rest of the money to the Caer Donn Guildhouse."

"You are free to do whatever you wish with your half of the

money," Fiona said. "But I believe that's a wise decision."

Randal brought Jessamyn the contract; Fiona watched as Jessamyn signed her name.

"Unless there's any further business, court now stands adjourned."

~oOo~

"So Donal gained the foal and the good will of the *Terranan*, not to mention some money as well, while Jessamyn gained the good will of Donal, the good will of the *Terranan*, and also some money?" the Chief Justice summarized.

"Yes, *vai dom*," Fiona murmured respectfully.

Chief Justice di Asturien took a deep breath, and looked at his fellow justices. Each nodded in turn, MacAnndra being the last, before di Asturien turned again to Fiona. "*Mestra*, we justices stand at the crossroads of a truly interesting time. We need someone with your wisdom—not to mention your experiences with the *Terranan*—on this court."

As hope rose within her, she heard the Chief Justice say with great relish, "We, the justices of the Courts of Arbitration, wish it formally known that we invite you, Fiona *nikhya mic* Gorsali, to become a member of this Court. Anyone who can get the nobles, the smallfolk, and the *Terranan* all to agree to something is worthy of becoming one of us.

"So, will you accept?" the Chief Justice asked. "Or would you rather stay in your current position in the Hellers?"

"I am honored, *vai dom'yn*, to join the Courts of Arbitration," Fiona heard herself say. *Of course I want it—I've wanted it all my life,* she wanted to say, but had the wit to keep back.

The justices all rattled their walking sticks in approval.

Then, to her surprise, Miralys and Randal walked into the room. Miralys carried a cake, while Randal rolled in a cask of ale. As they started to sing the ancient songs of celebration, she wondered why they had named her to the Courts of Arbitration now. She was the same justice she had always been, and she'd been told in no uncertain terms three years ago by the Chief Justice himself that she'd never be promoted, all because she was a *woman*. Moreover, she was a *Renunciate*.

So why had they changed their minds?

Randal came up with two glasses of ale. She took one, feeling dazed. "I really didn't expect this," she murmured.

"My friend, the *Hali'imyn* wanted you here," Randal said.

"What?" She could hardly believe her ears, but she was sure

Randal was telling her the truth.

"The *Terranan* wanted you, too. Even the smallfolk—Zandru's Hells, Fiona, they don't care that you're a woman, or a Renunciate, either. They care that you're an excellent judge. And you did what none of them, not one, would've thought of. They are lucky to have you."

Surprised by his vehemence, she blinked. Her actions had been the only logical course of action. "Do you truly think so?"

Randal laughed. "They will be talking about it in the streets of Thendara for months...maybe years. But when the Lowlanders forget why you're here, the highlanders will remember. They know you're one of their own. They've wanted a highlander judge on the Court for years now."

"But—but Doevid studied at Nevarsin, and—"

"And he's one of the Syrtis clan, even if his father hasn't legitimized him." Randal snorted. "While he knows some of the Hellers very well, Doevid is a scholar, Fiona. He's really good at what he does. But he doesn't understand people—not the way you do."

Fiona felt both surprised and gratified. "I didn't think anyone had noticed," she admitted.

"The highlands know your worth," Randal growled. "Never doubt it."

Miralys abruptly came up and hugged her. "The Justices confirmed I'm to be the next Circuit Court Justice for the Hellers, and Caer Donn in particular," she said happily. "I was so surprised!"

"Well, our apprentice Piet surely isn't ready," Fiona said dryly. "And you'll do an excellent job, Miralys. Just...trust yourself, will you?"

"I promise you, I will."

"So when will I have to take up my new duties?" she wondered aloud.

"Next week, *domna*," the Chief Justice said. He'd materialized, seemingly out of nowhere, at her elbow. As she turned to him in surprise, he continued with, "I insist on the title. You've earned it." Then, in a much lower tone of voice, he said, "You saved many of my cousins from certain starvation this winter, not to mention MacAnndra's mother and stepfather and Doevid's *cristoforos*. We are forever in your debt."

Then, resuming his normal tone of voice, he said, "Now go and enjoy yourself. Please."

Fiona resolved to do just that.

Second Contact
by Rosemary Edghill & Rebecca Fox

Many of Marion Zimmer Bradley's early Darkover novels examined the clash of cultures between the technological Terrans and the "primitive" Darkovans with the inevitable misunderstandings. Federation officials negotiated with the Comyn Council, most notably the Hasturs, for access to a spaceport as well as trade and cultural exchange. All too often, the space-faring Terrans viewed Darkovans as ignorant and unsophisticated, sometimes with disastrous results. There are two sides to every story, however, as Rosemary Edghill and Rebecca Fox point out.

Rosemary Edghill (aka eluki bes shahar) has published stories in *Marion Zimmer Bradley's Fantasy Magazine* as well as Marion Zimmer Bradley's long-running *Sword & Sorceress* anthology series. This led to her ghost-writing the urban fantasy series *Ghostlight*, *Witchlight*, *Gravelight*, and *Heartlight* under Bradley's name. A woman of many talents, she's also an anthologist and editorial mentor. Her most recent books include the *Shadow Grail* series.

Rebecca ("Becky") Fox started writing stories when she was seven years old, and hasn't stopped since. Becky lives in Lexington, Kentucky with three parrots, a chestnut mare, and a Jack Russell terrier who is not-so-secretly an evil canine genius. In her other life, she's a professional biologist with an interest in bird behavior.

"Cottman Four is no name for a world," Armsmaster Zhenyar snarled. "Do the *Terranan* have so many worlds that they must number them like storehouses?" Zhenyar was not a stupid man (and he was also a man entirely used to disasters); he rather suspected the wretched *Terranan* did.

For once, Antonno held his tongue. The *teniente* fell into step behind his master as the two of them walked from the barracks wing of Castle Aldaran. Zhenyar was grateful for the silence. Antonno was a good man, but he had a habit of speaking when it was unnecessary.

Zhenyar had been Master of Arms at Aldaran Castle these last fifteen years and more, and until that day the thrice-damned *Terranan* had come, those years had been peaceful. And then the *Terranan* came down out of the sky with a great groaning of metal, and settled at Caer Donn. Of course—in addition to building a place for even more of their ships to come—the arrogant strangers insisted on renaming the place. *Shigashik* or somesuch. It sounded like Trailmen chatter, which Zhenyar supposed was fitting; the *Terranan* reminded him of Trailmen, and he wanted just about as much to do with them.

He could smell a fire even before he reached the Great Hall, even though it was barely even autumn. Undoubtedly, this waste of fuel had been committed in deference to their thin-skinned guest. It gave Zhenyar no small amount of satisfaction to contemplate how much the *Terranan* would enjoy their first Darkovan winter.

"You might at least consider being polite," Antonno said in a voice meant for Zhenyar's ears alone.

Whatever Zhenyar might have said in retort died in his throat when he saw it was not only *Coridom* Rumail with the stranger in the Great Hall, but *Dom* Barak and *Domna* Istvana as well. They stood together in front of one of the great fireplaces. Behind them—practically in the fire itself—stood a slight youth in the clothing of the Terrans. Zhenyar approached. "*Vai dom*," he said, bowing his head.

"We will speak Trade," Lord Aldaran said, "out of courtesy to our guest."

Zhenyar nodded. He straightened his shoulders and tried to keep from grimacing. It would be dishonorable to show such discourtesy before his lord.

Domna Istvana smiled faintly, as if she knew Zhenyar's thoughts. "Armsmaster Zhenyar," she said, "allow me to present Jenny Lauren of Port Chicago. She is the Terran Cultural Reconciliation Specialist."

The youth was no youth, but a woman. Wearing trousers and short-cropped hair like one of the *Comhi-Letzii*! She stepped forward and offered her hand—a *Terranan* gesture. Zhenyar sighed and took it; he could tell from the expression on Rumail's face it was expected. *Coridom* Rumail lectured him regularly on courtesy, though it seemed to Zhenyar that fine manners hardly fell within the purview of an armsmaster's duties.

"It's a pleasure to make your acquaintance, Armsmaster Zhenyar," she said. "I only wish it was under better circumstances. Lord Aldaran asked me here to discuss a matter that concerns both my people and yours."

Zhenyar could not imagine what matter could possibly require his own involvement, but then *Dom* Barak held out an object. It was made of a silvery not-quite-metal; a tube a couple of handspans long attached to a grip that was clearly meant to fit a man's hand. When he took it, he found it was surprisingly heavy. Whatever it was, it was an ugly thing—soulless, with no hint of craftsmanship about it. Zhenyar regarded it with mild puzzlement.

"A servant discovered this in the castle today, and destroyed one of the windows with it before it was removed from his possession," *Dom* Barak said, the frown lines in his face deepening.

"I offer my apologies on behalf of the Terran Imperial Federation, Lord Aldaran," *Mestra* Jenny said regretfully. "I am aware that you made it quite clear to Commander Stone that things like this are taboo in your culture."

"They violate the Compact, to which all have sworn," Lord Aldaran said mildly, ignoring the insult.

This is a thing that could kill at a distance with no risk to its wielder. Carefully, Zhenyar set the gun down on the table beside him.

"And so of course," *Mestra* Jenny continued (apparently she liked to talk even more than Antonno did), "we've been careful to keep all of our weapons in Port Chicago as you requested—" *Dom* Barak regarded her with a brooding look that Zhenyar recognized but *Mestra* Jenny clearly did not, because it looked very much as though she meant to keep speaking.

"But clearly this one came here to Castle Aldaran," *Dom* Barak said. "And I should very much like to know how."

"I'm afraid I don't know what to tell you, Lord Aldaran," *Mestra* Jenny said, holding out her hands in a gesture of apology. "The first thing we'd have to do is go back to Port Chicago and take inventory. Of course we keep records of everything removed from our Armory—"

Lord Aldaran smiled thinly, but there was no amusement whatsoever in his eyes. "Of course," he said. "As a gesture of my goodwill, I will send Armsmaster Zhenyar and his *teniente* Antonno to assist you, since this will undoubtedly be a significant undertaking."

For a moment, Zhenyar was almost certain he had misheard. But then *Dom* Barak said that certainly Korin could look after Zhenyar's duties for the few days that Zhenyar and Antonno would be gone, and *Domna* Istvana wished them good hunting, and he knew he hadn't misheard at all. He looked at the *Terranan* woman who was dressed like a boy and sighed softly.

~oOo~

Mestra Jenny wished to return to Port Chicago at once. Antonno smiled at her—too friendly as always—and said he would gather his things. Zhenyar squared his shoulders, told *Mestra* Jenny to await them in the forecourt in an hour's time, and went to do the same. When he descended the stone steps into the cobbled forecourt wearing his autumn cloak and carrying his traveling pack, *Mestra* Jenny regarded him with a look of naked horror. He stopped on the last step and studied her, one eyebrow raised.

After a moment of silence, she finally said, "Your sword, Armsmaster," and pointed at it as if she did not expect him to understand what she was talking about. "Certainly you will have no need for such a—an *object*—in Port Chicago!"

Did she truly expect Zhenyar to go unarmed as if he were a woman? Perhaps the *Terranan* were even madder than he believed.

Just then, Antonno arrived, armed in much the same manner as Zhenyar was. *Mestra* Jenny's eyes lit on his sword, and she frowned.

"Darkovan custom," Zhenyar said gruffly, and her frown deepened, but she at least did not say anything more on the matter.

"I will be glad to offer you the use of one of the castle mounts," Zhenyar said as they neared the stables by the outer gate. "As surely your horse is tired from your long journey."

To his immense surprise, she merely laughed delightedly and smiled at him as if she were imparting a great secret. "My 'horse' never gets tired, Armsmaster. Come, I'll show you."

She led them down into the village surrounding Castle Aldaran, chattering all the while about trade, as if Zhenyar were some merchant she hoped to flatter. He wondered whether all *Terranan* babbled like this. "And of course," she said, "the Imperial Federation has a very great deal to offer you—technology, especially. 'Horses' that never get tired. Machines the size of a book that can hold entire libraries—"

Antonno kept smiling at her. (Antonno never learned.)

"And what," Zhenyar asked, perhaps a bit more irritably than courtesy permitted, "does Darkover have to offer your Imperial Federation, as we are so backward?"

Mestra Jenny simply beamed. "Cottman IV was one of the first planets settled in the Age of Exploration, Armsmaster. I'm sure your records are fascinating."

Zhenyar merely shook his head. He couldn't help it.

They were on the far side of the village before she stopped to take a breath. Of course, before Zhenyar could so much at sigh with relief at finally having peace in which to string two thoughts together, *Mestra* Jenny gestured portentously.

"And here you see my 'horse,' Armsmaster Zhenyar, Antonno," she said, smiling. "You can see why he didn't find the journey from Port Chicago at all exhausting."

While the design of the thing was clearly foreign, Zhenyar recognized a flier when he saw one. "It's a wonder you're not dead," he said, studying her with a mixture of awe and horror.

"Oh, I assure you, Armsmaster, flying is perfectly safe!" she exclaimed with a little chuckle. "And much faster than riding a horse."

"Not this time of year, it's not," he said with a frown. "Even for an experienced pilot, which I beg leave to doubt you are. The autumn winds in the Hellers are fierce. So before you get me and Antonno here killed, explain to me about your weapons."

It was her turn to stare at him. He rather relished it.

Finally she regained her equilibrium, and said, "Our guns are based on very straightforward technology. You'll have to tell me how much you know about physics, Armsmaster, because I'm not really sure where to start—"

He cut her off with a sharp gesture. "I don't care how they work," he said. "Who has them? How many do you have? Who guards your armory?"

"I'm sorry, Armsmaster, but you'll have to come and see for yourself. You simply don't have the cultural referents to understand what I'd tell you."

"I understand one thing already," he said between gritted teeth. "If there was a *Terranan* weapon at Castle Aldaran, someone brought it here."

~oOo~

He was right about Jenny Lauren not being an experienced pilot, but neither was the woman entirely stupid. She avoided the worst of the winds by flying so low she terrorized everything on four legs between Aldaran Castle and Caer Donn. Zhenyar sighed, thinking of the demands for compensation that would shortly be arriving at the castle from the farmers and herdsfolk. And there would be no decent hunting to be had for a fortnight or more.

At least they arrived in one piece.

By the time he'd been in the city of the *Terranan* three hours, Zhenyar was positive that he never wanted to set foot in Port *Shigashik* again. The entire place was a sea of squat little gray square buildings, all alike. ("Prefab architecture," *Mestra* Jenny said breezily. "Not the prettiest, but it keeps the rain off.") Every interior was lit to a glaring white brightness and heated until it was hotter than Zandru's Forge.

"I'm sorry, Armsmaster," *Mestra* Jenny said. "Our climate control just can't keep up with your weather. This is as warm as it gets."

Zhenyar cast a look at Antonno, who was trying to unobtrusively wipe the sweat from his brow. "Oh no, *Mestra* Jenny," Antonno said genially. "It's plenty warm enough for us."

If this was what the *Terranan* considered home, Zhenyar wanted nothing further to do with it.

Or them.

Or their damned guns.

To make matters worse, this warren of bake-ovens in which the *Terranan* lived was full to bursting with people, none of whom had any manners at all. They all spoke to him as if to an equal, though he was Lord Aldaran's man, and their speech was a tangle of meaningless phrases and chatter about the weather. He was grateful to find he could not easily tell the men from the women, for they all went about half-naked, their necks exposed, as if this were some vast brothel. Since he dared not look any of them in the eye for fear of what he might see, he kept his eyes upon their feet. He noticed Antonno did the same.

"And this way, gentlemen, is the gymnasium and spa facilities, which—"

Zhenyar stopped. "*Mestra*. I am here to see where you keep your weapons."

"But I just wanted to—"

"I do not care," Zhenyar said. "The armory. At once. Of your courtesy."

She studied him for a long moment, as if she were a huntsman and his face the land across which she must track her quarry. At last she sighed.

"Of course, Armsman Zhenyar. It is this way."

~oOo~

The moment they walked into the Armory, Zhenyar knew they had a problem.

It was the largest chamber he had seen so far. The dead stink the *Terranan* seemed oblivious to was gaggingly strong here. Everything was as gray as old ice, and between that and the ever-present white glare, it took a moment for his eyes to adjust. When they did, he wished they hadn't.

The walls were covered with racks, and the racks were filled with devices. He gestured wordlessly.

"Those are rifles," *Mestra* Jenny explained. "They're like the handguns you've seen, but of course, more powerful and capable of shooting over a greater distance."

"And you *use* these?" Antonno blurted in horror.

"Of course we hope we don't have to," she answered obliquely. "Come on. I'll show you the rest."

Every child on Darkover grew up learning of the Ages of Chaos, the time before the Compact when the Hundred Kingdoms made war with terrifying weapons. Cities hundreds of miles distant burned to ash. Forests turned to wastelands where nothing grew. People slaughtered by enemies too far away to see.

Zhenyar felt as though he had somehow fallen through a door into that time. There were hand weapons in several sizes, both those that discharged a small pellet with lethal force, and those that fired an equally deadly beam of light. There were items *Mestra* Jenny called "heavy weapons"—guns even larger than the rifles—and grenades, things that could be hurled through the air and explode on impact. She said, as if it were nothing at all, that they had disarmed their fliers, but that many of these weapons were meant to be mounted on those vehicles. The room contained, by a rough count, perhaps a thousand items. Enough to arm each of the *Terranan* of Port Chicago twice or three times over.

"*Mestra*, who do you think is going to attack you?" Antonno said helplessly. "Lord Aldaran has given his promise of your safety."

"If you need protection, ask for armsmen," Zhenyar said bluntly.

"Of course we don't doubt his word, Armsmaster Zhenyar," *Mestra* Jenny said, studying his face. "This is all standard equipment. It's only a precaution. A gun is a lot more use than a sword if you have to defend yourself. No need to get so close to your enemy!"

"Armsmaster Zhenyar likes his sword fine," Antonno said, recovering his equilibrium. "It has been a good companion to him these many years."

Zhenyar just rolled his eyes. Antonno made him sound like an old soldier in his dotage. And *Mestra* Jenny—charmed by the good Antonno, just as all women seemed to be—was smiling.

"I'd think you'd all be glad to finally get out of the Middle Ages," she said.

"I have no idea what these 'middle ages' of yours are, but I like my way of life just fine," Zhenyar growled. They were supposed to be counting guns, but all she seemed to be doing was talking.

"But your way of life is so inefficient!" she cried.

When he felt he had a handle on his temper, Zhenyar said, "We tried your 'efficiency' once."

"And?" she asked curiously.

"We decided we'd rather be alive." Clearly *Mestra* Jenny had not read a single one of those records she was sure were so fascinating.

"Well, now you've seen the Armory, and—"

"And now we will count your weapons," Zhenyar said. "And check them against your tally board."

He'd hoped that at last they could begin to accomplish what he had been sent to do, but his mention of a tally board led the infernal woman to show off more of her *"Terranan* wonders." This one was a glass-fronted box that displayed unfamiliar symbols in brightly-glowing letters.

"So you see," she said brightly, "there's no need to check anything. All of our weapons are numbered." She tapped some keys, and the picture on the glass changed. "The one found at Castle Aldaran was reported missing yesterday. All the rest are accounted for." She began to explain what the glass box was, and what it did.

"Does your...thing...say how many of each kind should be here?" Zhenyar interrupted.

"Why...yes. Of course." More tapping. More pictures. "Adjusted for loss and damage, there are two hundred seventy-nine energy rifles, thirty-five pellet-rifles, four hundred type one hand weapons, three—"

He waved a hand irritably, silencing her. "Can you put that list on a tally sheet?" he asked.

She sighed, and tapped a few more buttons. Thin sharp-edged pieces of paper began rising up out of a slot on the desk. He took one. It wasn't quite paper, and had an odd unpleasant feel to it. "That's everything," she said. "Now what?"

Zhenyar smiled. "Now, *mestra*, we count them."

~oOo~

"All the rifles are here," Antonno called out.

Mestra Jenny had sent for a clip-board and a stylus. Zhenyar scrawled notes and numbers beside the indecipherable Terran script. Since counting the rifles meant touching them, he had left that part of the task to Antonno. Antonno was eternally willing to throw himself in front of the avalanche, particularly to save a *chiy'lla* in distress.

It took them several tedious hours to determine that the remainder of the *Terranan* weapons were all accounted for. All were here, save for the handguns currently signed out to the *Terranan* armsmen. Two guardsmen stood outside the door at all times. (Zhenyar had seen them as he came in, but he could not imagine what use armsmen without armor could be.) At the end of each shift, the armsmen of Port Chicago returned their weapons to this place as the next shift picked theirs up. The two shifts overlapped, as weapons were checked out to relieve a shift before that shift checked their own weapons back in. *Mestra* Jenny said the "computer" did a "continuous inventory."

The weapon discovered at the castle today had been reported as missing. There were no other missing weapons.

"Well, I am sure Lord Aldaran will commend you for your...thoroughness," *Mestra* Jenny said as they emerged from the armory into the fading autumn sunlight. At least outside, the temperature was comfortable and the light no longer hurt his eyes (*Mestra* Jenny closed the fastenings on her heavy coat and pulled the hood up around her face). "I'm sure this was an isolated incident, but I'll warn Commander Stone to keep an eye out for anything suspicious. In the meantime, I'm glad to have had this chance to get to know you. I hope we can be friends." She offered her hand once more, in that curiously rude *Terranan* gesture.

With a sigh, Zhenyar took her hand and shook it. And probably, he should say something meaningless and thank her on behalf of Lord Aldaran, but there had been enough meaningless noise today.

"I'll be happy to fly you back to Castle Aldaran," she said cheerfully. "You'll be home in time for supper."

Zhenyar squinted at the sky and decided he preferred not to risk getting his brains smashed out against the rocks of the Hellers twice in one day.

"I thank you," he said carefully, "but Antonno and I will stay in Caer Donn tonight. There is a livery here. We will ride back in the morning."

"There's no need to trouble yourself, *mestra*, truly," Antonno added quickly.

Zhenyar saw *Mestra* Jenny gathering herself to protest that it would be no trouble at all, and walked off, deliberately making his strides long.

"You might have been a little kinder," Antonno said in mild reproof when he caught up. Alone, Zhenyar was relieved to note.

"Why?" Zhenyar asked. "I don't like her. She is entirely unwomanly. And she talks too much."

Antonno drew breath to speak, and then seemed to think better of it. They reached the gate separating Port Chicago from Caer Donn. There were two guards there, but the gate stood open and the guards did nothing to stop them. Beyond the gate, the stone path led to the walls of Caer Donn, where the gates were properly barred, and the armsmen upon the wall challenged them before they permitted them to enter.

Zhenyar breathed a sigh of relief when the gates shut behind him. He was back in a world he understood. Now to the stables to bespeak horses, then an inn, and a tankard of mulled ale by the honest light of lanterns.

Antonno permitted the silence to last until they were within sight of the stables, but it could not endure forever. "Master? There's one thing I don't understand about all of this."

"And what thing would that be, Antonno?" Zhenyar asked wearily.

"How did that lost gun get from here...all the way to the castle? And inside?"

Zhenyar merely growled.

~oOo~

A month after her encounter with Armsmaster Zhenyar, Cultural Reconciliation Specialist Jenny Lauren still wasn't quite sure what to make of him. Darkover was her fourth posting. She was good at what she did. And her job was a necessary one.

It had been over a thousand years since Terra had sent her children forth to find new homes for the human race. Desperation as much as exploration had fueled that early effort, for Earth itself had been dying, wracked by plagues and ecological disasters. A war with the colony worlds of the Solar System had brought a new

Dark Age to Earth, leaving its isolated survivors to reclaim their world and rebuild their civilization. When they had at last succeeded, they'd thought the Age of Exploration was a myth. Then they discovered the first of the lost colonies, and suddenly the Terran Imperial Federation had a new mission.

Rediscovery.

Some of the colonies had suffered no interregnum. Others, through isolation, mischance, and even war, had devolved into primitive superstition and barbarism. It was the task of the Cultural Reconciliation Department to discover the best way to educate those people, and bring them into full equality with their galactic siblings.

Darkover was a problem.

Darkover was snow, sorcery, superstition...and seven ruling families called the Comyn. The natives here held the red-haired ruling caste in superstitious awe, attributing to them miracles and mystical powers—a notion that undoubtedly served their Comyn overlords very well indeed. The ITF was just lucky to have arrived in a part of Darkover where the local divine warlord was a reasonable man. But reasonable or not, Lord Aldaran was firmly opposed to accepting Terran ways, Terran ideas, or Terran technology.

Jenny sighed. A cultural reconciliation specialist's job was much easier when the members of *both* cultures wanted to be reconciled. She supposed Armsmaster Zhenyar was a typical specimen of the sort of mindset her department would need to overcome to make any real headway here. She'd much preferred the company of the affable Antonno. She wondered if she might arrange to see him again. Her department was conducting interviews with all the natives it could manage to corral, trying to build a picture of Darkovan society that would let them send in undercover anthropologists to do the real work, but she knew they weren't getting a reliable picture of what was clearly a very stratified feudal society. The chance to learn more about Antonno would fill in a few gaps.

Assuming they didn't all freeze to death first. The survey teams who had braved the endless snow to finish mapping Cottman IV's single continent had suggested perhaps Thendara would make a better place for a spaceport. It lay south of here, so it might be warmer during the winter, and more to the point, Thendara was not only already a major trade city, but the seat of what passed for a ruling body: the Comyn Council. And certainly Lord Hastur was open to letting the Terrans settle on his lands. The only real hitch was going to be moving to their new home. By the time all of the ritual forms had been satisfied and Lord Aldaran was once again reassured that the Terrans were not merely a bunch of ignorant savages, it would be winter again. Next winter. If they were lucky.

Nothing on this planet moved quickly.

She was preparing to (once again) petition to expand the range of goods offered in the Trading Post when there was a racket in the outer office. A moment later, her door flew open to reveal Armsmaster Zhenyar, looking thunderous, with four security officers and her assistant, Palmer, in hot pursuit.

"Sir! You can't just go in there! Sir—" Palmer shouted.

Zhenyar ignored him and strode into the room.

"Armsmaster Zhenyar, I wasn't expecting you," she said, standing up. "What can we do for you?"

Scowling ferociously, he upended the sack he was carrying over her desk. Its contents tumbled out with dull, damning thuds. Two standard issue security sidearms. An energy pistol. A game console. A radio. None of which, according to the agreement the Imperial Federation had reached with Lord Aldaran, should be in Darkovan hands—Zhenyar's or anyone else's. She looked from the pile of illicit technology to Zhenyar and back again. Palmer was still stammering about how you couldn't just barge in on the Cultural Reconciliation Specialist without an appointment. Jenny held up a hand to silence him.

"Where did these come from?" she asked.

Zhenyar told her, scowling furiously. The three weapons from Castle Aldaran (she groaned inwardly), the game console from a small village a short journey from the castle, and the radio from St.-Valentine-of-the-Snows.

"The monks had no idea what it was," he said. "They found it in the offering box."

"No one from Port Chicago has been anywhere near Nevarasin. Anyone planning to travel off-base has to go through me. If they'd been there, I'd know."

"Get me a map," Armsmaster Zhenyar said. Out of the corner of her eye, she could see Palmer bristling at his peremptory tone, but Jenny nodded at him, adding: "Hardcopy, please." Reluctantly, he went.

A few minutes later, Palmer came back with the map. They spread it out on the big table under her window. Zhenyar glared at it for awhile, rubbing his chin with what Jenny suspected was irritation rather than thoughtfulness. It was very detailed; he should be able to recognize the landmarks even if he couldn't read the Terran.

Finally he stabbed a blunt forefinger at the map. (Jenny thought the surveying teams would be glad to know they'd proven themselves useful.)

"Here," Zhenyar said. "Aldaran Castle. And here," the finger stabbed down on the mark that indicated Port Chicago. "Caer Donn." His finger slammed down accusingly on a point almost halfway between—a logical waypoint if you were on horseback or taking a leisurely journey from Port Chicago to the castle. "This is the village where we found the game console."

"My people would not give your people items that violate our agreement with Lord Aldaran!" she said indignantly.

"My people," said, his finger still resting on the map, "would not steal them. And if you think Lord Hastur is going to give the *Terranan* a better deal in Thendara than you received from my Lord Aldaran, you're deluding yourself."

She stared at him, dumbfounded. How on earth would someone like Zhenyar have any idea the Terrans were quietly negotiating with Lord Hastur to build a port in the Trade City?

Zhenyar shrugged. "Do you think Lord Hastur didn't ask my lord about your folk?"

"How?" she demanded. It was a long journey between Castle Aldaran and Thendara, one already difficult, if not impossible, on horseback.

He gave another of his one-shouldered shrugs. "I don't meddle in Comyn affairs," he said in a warning tone. "And neither will you, if you're wise."

Jenny gritted her teeth in irritation. One of the first things she meant to do was strike off the chains of superstition that kept Darkover mired in its damnable regressive past. Fortunately, before she could say anything of the sort, her commlink buzzed. On the other end was the quartermaster's most junior assistant; he was calling from the gatehouse.

"Beg pardon, Specialist Lauren," the assistant said, "but Sergeant Jeffries sent me to tell you that there's a bunch of stuff missing from the trading post and you'd better come and see."

"I'll be there at once," she answered. "You might as well come," she said to Armsmaster Zhenyar.

"Good," he said. "I'm not finished with you yet."

~oOo~

The trading post was a stone building within the walls of Caer Donn. They'd tried setting it up inside Port Chicago, but the natives wouldn't come. This was a compromise, reached at the cost of disassembling and reassembling a portion of the village wall to enclose the space. The building itself was the same sort of prefab structure as the Armory was, but its exterior had been coated in plaster and its plasteel roof given a thatchwork coating. As disguises went, it wasn't a very good one. Jenny supposed that was part of the attraction.

The trading post was crowded with Darkovans, but despite the press of bodies, it was cold. There were a few battery-powered lamps lighting the room, but the room was dim. *If I had to live here without power, I'd go blind,* she thought randomly.

She averted her eyes from the pile of animal skins on the counter. She'd done her best to become used to this sort of thing, though Terra had outlawed animal slavery and animal exploitation centuries ago. It didn't make it any prettier when she encountered it.

She tried to head to the back room, but there were too many people in the way. When he realized their destination, Zhenyar gave the nearest man a shove. At the sight of his livery, all conversation died, and the traders opened a clear pathway. Jenny wasn't sure whether to be impressed at the efficiency, or sickened at the privilege it represented.

Quartermaster Sergeant Jeffries glared at Zhenyar when he stepped through the door behind Jenny. "Out—" she began.

"Rachel, this is Armsmaster Zhenyar," Jenny said quickly. "He's investigating the weapons disappearances on behalf of Lord Aldaran. Armsmaster Zhenyar, this is Rachel Jeffries, our quartermaster. She keeps track of all the property in Port Chicago."

Jeffries gave a minute shrug and turned to gesture at about six vacant spots on the shelves. The only thing left in any of them was the outlines of whatever had been there, clearly demarcated in a sea of undisturbed frost. It was as if whatever had been there had simply vanished where it sat.

"It's all little stuff," Jeffries said with a grimace. "Dried food, some toys, cups, tinware, some glass. Nothing contraband—we don't let it off the port, and we certainly don't offer it for sale. I figured it was just kids, but someone would've had to've seen them leaving with this much stuff."

Zhenyar studied one of the empty places carefully and looked thoughtful, but whatever he was thinking, he apparently didn't feel like sharing. "When did you lose these objects?" he asked.

Jeffries shrugged, a twist of the shoulders. "Sometime last night after the trading post closed," she said. "Gordon found the stuff gone when he opened this morning. He radioed me, and I came down to see for myself."

Zhenyar's frown got even deeper, if that was possible. "And the other items?" he asked. "The ones that vanished from the port? When did they go missing?"

Jeffries glanced from him to Jenny, and Jenny nodded fractionally.

"At night," Jeffries said. "All the thefts were reported at the start of First Shift."

"I'm going to spend the night here," Zhenyar said, looking as if he meant to put down roots.

"Of course," Jenny said, startled. "I'll arrange a room for you, unless you—"

"No," Zhenyar said, speaking slowly and clearly, as if to a small child. "Here." He gestured at the shelves.

~oOo~

It was either very late or very early when Jenny was startled out of sleep by a loud pounding on her apartment door. She stumbled into a warm robe and a pair of sheepskin slippers. The pounding resumed before she was halfway to the door, more urgently this time.

"I'm coming!" she shouted. "Just hold on." *Normal people*, she thought, *would call first*. She hauled the door open, shivering in the cold. Somehow she was totally unsurprised to find Zhenyar standing there, his arms folded. She couldn't fathom why he wasn't shivering so hard his teeth chattered, given that his outerwear consisted of a knitted cap and a quilted jacket.

As usual, he was staring in the direction of her feet. "You were asleep," he said accusingly.

"It's the middle of the night!"

"It's dawn," he answered, and shrugged, dismissing the matter. "I know how your missing objects are being removed from your custody. What I don't know is why."

"You caught the thieves?" she asked. She stepped back, gesturing for him to enter. She wondered if she'd be able to intercede for them, or if he'd already murdered them.

Zhenyar was now staring fixedly at the wall to her left. "No," he said shortly. "I still have no idea who's doing this."

"Then how?" she asked, belting the robe more tightly around herself.

"*Laran*," he said.

She sighed and tried not to rub her temples. "You're saying the armory and the trading post were robbed by magic?" It would be nice when Cottman IV decided to join the rest of the Imperial Federation in the present day.

"Not magic," Zhenyar said, sounding as if he was trying to be very patient. "*Laran*. Starstones."

"Magic rocks, then," she said wearily.

Zhenyar was opening his mouth to say something more when there was another knock at the door. Schooling her expression into what she hoped was something polite, she opened it.

Antonno was standing there (dressed no more warmly than Zhenyar, but at least he had an escort), looking apologetic. She wondered if he'd come all this way in the middle of the night (oh no, of course he hadn't, she thought sarcastically; Zhenyar had said it was *dawn*). "I'm sorry for the intrusion, *mestra*," he said.

She shrugged and stood aside to let him in. "I'm already up," she said with a faint smile. "Can I get you a cup of tea?" Antonno made it much easier to be polite to him than his master did.

"Thank you, no," he said, still standing on the threshold. Rather than freeze, she gestured him inside, and waved his escort away. "I came to find Armsmaster Zhenyar. My news cannot wait."

"You found something?" Zhenyar demanded. He was actually willing to look at Antonno, Jenny noted.

"I've spent the last fortnight staring at records," Antonno said, stretching as if he had only just now stood up from a desk in some dusty library. "With *Coridom* Rumail's help, I've traced every member of the Aldaran line back ten generations."

This is a hell of a time for a genealogical side trip.

"And?" Zhenyar asked impatiently, folding his arms.

"Anjali Aldaran—cousin to Lord Aldaran's great-grandmother—is the only one who had it strong enough to train. She'd be very old by now, if she's even still—"

Zhenyar cut him off. "Where in Zandru's nine hells *is* she?" he demanded.

Clearly Antonno did not wish to answer. "*Vai dom*," he said softly, "she went to Tramontana thirty years ago and never came out."

Jenny frowned in confusion. None of the conversation made any sense. "Tramontana?" she asked, looking at Antonno. Just like Zhenyar, Antonno looked away from her. She wondered if she were violating some obscure Darkovan taboo.

"Tramontana Tower," Antonno said. "It's not far from here. But the last time there were enough people for a circle there was fifty years ago."

Jenny recognized the term. Towers were where Darkovan sorcerers—*leroni*, wielders of *laran*—had supposedly roosted, once upon a time. Apparently both Zhenyar and Antonno believed *magic* was at the root of these thefts.

Zhenyar actually shuddered. "Then it is a matter for the Comyn now," he said. He turned to Jenny, nodding curtly in the direction of her knees. "My investigation is finished," he announced. "My *teniente* and I will trouble you no further."

"You've been looking for the person who's been smuggling illegal technology out of Port Chicago for months," Jenny said incredulously. "You've tracked the thieves to this *Tower* and now you want to let them go?"

"This is a Comyn matter now," Zhenyar repeated between gritted teeth. "And I will take it to Lord Aldaran as soon as may be. You," he said, stabbing a blunt finger at Jenny, "would be wise to remain in Port *Shigashik* where it is safe."

Jenny scoffed. She knew it was rude, but she couldn't help it. "You're afraid of wizards and ghost stories?" she asked incredulously. "If this Anjali person is the one behind the thefts, we should go and get her!"

"That really wouldn't be a good idea, *mestra*," Antonno said diplomatically. "You see—"

"We are finished here," Zhenyar announced. "Come, Antonno."

He motioned to Antonno, and left without a further word.

And good riddance, Master Zhenyar, Jenny thought acidly. *Superstitious primitives.*

~ooo~

The sky outside the windows of *Dom* Barak's private sitting room was a dark solid gray with the first storm of winter. Zhenyar gratefully accepted a mug of warm spiced wine from a servant. He and Antonno had arrived home just in time. He'd not have wanted to be caught on the road in this misery.

Dom Barak's face had remained impassive throughout Zhenyar's report, but now he ran a weary hand through his graying hair and sighed. "It is as you said. This is a Comyn matter now, and when the storm has broken, I...shall go and see Tramontana for myself. The thefts will stop."

"As my lord says," Zhenyar answered. He wanted nothing more right now than to return to the barracks. No doubt he would lead the escort when *Dom* Barak went to Tramontana, but that would not be for some days yet. And he would not have to go inside.

"But come, Zhenyar, I have news that will lighten your spirits," *Dom* Barak continued. "You are no longer to be afflicted with the *Terranan*. Lord Hastur is pleased to welcome them to Thendara. They will be gone by summer."

"If it is news which pleases you, my lord, then it pleases me also," Zhenyar said formally. In fact, it would please him if they all vanished into the Ninth Hell at once, but those were words best reserved for Antonno's ears alone. He wished the Hasturs much delight in the little *Terranan* woman and her Trailman chatter.

Dom Barak dismissed him, but he had barely put his hand on the door when it was flung open in his face. It was Timas, one of the guardsmen.

"My Lord!" he said. "Armsmaster, a *Terranan* craft has crashed inside the outer courtyard. Antonno has taken men and gone to fetch the passengers—assuming they survived that landing," he added under his breath.

"What sort of madman flies in this weather?" *Dom* Barak demanded, getting to his feet.

"*Terranan* madmen," Zhenyar said darkly. "I think they believe themselves to be immortal."

"Zhenyar, bring the passengers to the Great Hall if they are not too badly injured," *Dom* Barak said, setting his cup on his desk with a thud. "I will join them momentarily."

~oOo~

There was only one person in the flyer, a dark-skinned *Terranan* who had been a frequent guest at the castle. There was no one with him, so Zhenyar assumed the idiot must have piloted his own craft. He was standing beside the wreckage, looking properly shaken, when Zhenyar arrived.

"Come inside, man!" Zhenyar said. "It's snowing."

"My name is Carroll Stone," the visitor said in barely-understandable Trade. "I must see Barak Aldaran at once."

"I will take you to him," Zhenyar said.

"Commander Legate," *Dom* Barak said, when they arrived in the Great Hall. "This is unfortunate weather for flying." He gestured for his guest to sit.

The *Terranan* winced as he lowered himself into a chair near the fire. "My apologies for this unexpected visit, Lord Aldaran," he said in his slow Trade.

"Certainly nothing but an emergency could have moved you to fly in this weather," *Dom* Barak said. "How may we be of assistance? This is Armsmaster Zhenyar. You may speak freely in his presence, for he holds my trust."

The Commander Legate nodded formally, and (much to Zhenyar's relief), did not offer his hand. "Perhaps Armsmaster Zhenyar can help me," he said, sounding relieved. "He knows Jenny Lauren."

Zhenyar waited impassively, not having been given leave to speak, but his thoughts were whirling.

"First I must ask: did she perhaps return with your people today?"

Dom Barak looked at him. "She did not," Zhenyar said.

"I'd hoped to find her here," the Commander Legate said, looking unhappy. "She apparently told her assistant she knew who was behind the thefts from our stores. Then she vanished."

"She's gone to Tramontana," Zhenyar said heavily. He did not know who deserved the greater blame: Antonno, for speaking of where *leronis* Anjuli might be found, or himself for permitting it. *He is your man. The blame is yours.*

"When the storm abates, we will of course send out search parties," *Dom* Barak said firmly. "Please, Commander Legate, accept my hospitality until it passes." He lifted his hand. "Zhenyar, please tell Rumail to attend me."

Zhenyar bowed, and took his leave.

~ooo~

He would as soon abandon a helpless child to the tender mercies of the weather as a *Terranan*, no matter how rude and foolish she was, but by the time Zhenyar finally reached the outskirts of the land surrounding Tramontana Tower, he thoroughly regretted his noble impulse. Even under layers of fur and wool and oiled leather, he was chilled to the core.

He wasn't sure if he was disgusted or pleased that the chervines seemed utterly unperturbed by the blowing white snow. He would have preferred horses, but if one was foolish enough to travel in a blizzard, the sure-footed little stag-ponies were the only reliable mounts. He gritted his teeth and ducked his head against the snow-thick wind. He fervently hoped *Mestra* Jenny was still alive; he wanted to strangle her himself. And in comfort, which was why he'd brought a second beast, saddled in the hopes that the idiot *Terranan* woman had actually survived her ill-considered journey.

He could see the Tower silhouetted against the sky when he came upon the flyer in a clearing. It was half buried in snow. He hoped she'd had the sense to stay with it.

But the flier was empty.

The snow had covered any tracks. He frowned, trying to imagine what she had done. He and Antonno had left Port Chicago a little after dawn. It was a four hour ride to Castle Aldaran from there, but the morning had been clear; the storm clouds had only begun to boil over the Hellers around midday. Tramontana was two hours north of Caer Donn, but in a flyer, only a few minutes. *Mestra* Jenny had remained in the Terran City long enough to speak to her servants—some hours perhaps—before coming here. The weather would still have been clear; she would have landed, and gone ahead on foot. Zhenyar sighed and clucked to the chervines. He hated the thought of going into the Tower, but there was nowhere else to search: if *Mestra* Jenny wasn't at Tremontaya, she was dead.

~oOo~

The tower was a dark looming presence against the grey brightness of the storm. Zhenyar shivered, and not from the cold; when he was a child, his grandmother had told him stories of the days when the *leroni* worked at Tramontana, of how the tower's stones would glow with an eldritch blue radiance that could be seen for miles.

He dismounted to ring the bell beside the gate leading in to the inner courtyard, for it did not matter how deserted the place seemed, it was a thing which belonged to the *leroni*, and only a madman would offend them.

Nothing happened.

He pushed the gate open cautiously and led the chervines inside. At least the walls around the courtyard would keep off the worst of the wind. He left the chervines looking for whatever might be hidden under the snow, and once again rang the bell, this time at the door of the Tower itself. Again, there was no answer, and he hoped to all the gods he could name that the Tower was no longer warded, for if it was, he risked death or worse with his next step.

Again, nothing happened.

It wasn't any warmer inside than it was outside, but at least the thick walls muted the howling of the wind.

Pale witchlight rose from the stone as he shut the door behind him. This, at least, was something he'd seen before: it was matrix-work, but a thing that could be set and forgotten. Many of the interior rooms at Castle Aldaran had such light. He stamped his feet to shake the snow off his boots, and brushed off the sleeves of his outer coat. And then he looked around himself.

The entirety of the chamber floor was covered with a jumble of

Terranan...junk. Dozens of handled cups stood in precarious towers. There were many bright objects of the material named *duraplast*; it was as if anything small enough to fetch had been swept up and dumped here. Weapons, too: a greater number than *Mestra* Jenny had admitted were missing. *Or she did not know. Their quartermaster is clearly an incompetent fool.* Drifts of that substance that was paper-but-not-paper had gathered against the walls.

Armsman Zhenyar had never in his life been so unhappy to be proven right.

The ground floor was deserted. It had never been meant for any purpose other than receiving visitors and storing supplies, and had clearly been unused for a very long time. If *Mestra* Jenny was in the Tower, she was on an upper level. After a long, suspicious look at the stone staircase, he set one a hand on the banister and the other on the hilt of the sword he dared not draw under any circumstances, and proceeded cautiously upstairs.

He found nothing on the first three floors. He searched every room, but they were empty of everything save witchlight, echoes...and dead *kyrri*. There were a dozen of the nonhuman servants and protectors of the *leroni*, all dead. Possibly from age, for their fur was white as frost, but the fact there were so many bodies, all lying where they had fallen, was troubling. He was starting to make, in his head, the story of this place, and it was not a happy one.

Finally he reached the top of the Tower, and the last possible place *Mestra* Jenny could possibly be. The old Working Room. It was a place no one like Zhenyar had ever been meant to see, and he did not want to see it now, but he had no choice. Swallowing hard, he reached to touch wood of the door.

It was as warm as living flesh.

And it swung open on its own.

The chamber beyond was as bright as any in the Terran city. Fighting the instinct to turn and run, Zhenyar stepped inside, squinting against the light.

The room was thirty feet across, round, and windowed. The walls were layered with fine tapestries and the floor was heaped with rugs. There was no furniture here, if there ever had been, save a single throne-like chair that faced the door. Sitting in it was the oldest woman Zhenyar had ever seen, her face deeply lined, her skin translucent, her long white hair nothing more than a drift of cobwebs across her arms. She wore what must have once been a fine gown, heavy and ornate. A starstone blazed at her throat. Both her hands were heavy with gold and copper rings, and they cradled the thing she held in her lap: an enormous gun of dull gray plasteel, one of the kind that could spit a gout of fire across a great distance. Zhenyar wondered, a bit wildly, if the old woman could even lift the weapon.

Kneeling beside her throne was *Mestra* Jenny, her eyes wide and utterly empty. Bespelled.

"I would have thought Aldaran himself would have had the honor to come to me," the old woman said in a clear thin voice, meeting his gaze.

"He will come as soon as the storm passes, *vai leronis*," Zhenyar said soothingly, taking a cautious step forward.

"It was to have been him," the old woman said in the same cool, dispassionate voice. "I thought surely my riddles would have brought him by now. The Comyn must understand the danger I have Seen. The *Terranan* will plunge us into a new Age of Chaos. All my life I waited, Armsmaster, but when their ship came, I was too old, too weak to rip it from the sky. I am so sorry. I could not save you. And so you must save yourselves. Drive them from our home with fire and the sword!"

The old woman could be no one other than Anjali Aldaran, who had come to Tramontana half a century ago and never left. The other *leroni* had left, one by one, until she had only *kyrri* to tend her, but she had waited steadfastly. Watching for the danger she had Seen. Terror and reverence and love filled his mind, too muddled together to separate.

Then she lifted the enormous gun and held it out.

"It should have been Barak," Anjali said, "My precious little cousin. But you will have to do, Armsmaster."

Mestra Jenny, her face as still as a mask, took the weapon.

Horror replaced all other emotions as Zhenyar saw *Mestra* Jenny's finger tighten on the trigger. He tried to move, and found he could not.

The beam went wide, as any first shot from an unfamiliar weapon might. It struck the hangings on the wall with an electric sizzle. They burst into flame.

Mestra Jenny dropped the gun in shock, and Zhenyar found his limbs were his own once more. The fire was spreading hungrily; here, where the *kyrri* had brought all the Tower's furnishings, there was much for it to feed on.

"*Domna!*" he shouted. "Quench the flames!" *Fire is the first spell. The simplest spell. She can do this. She must.*

Her head lolled now against the back of the chair; the starstone at her throat flickered as she gasped for air in the weakness of age. "Darkover is burning. Darkover will burn. I have Seen...." And the flames glowed brighter, and began to race over the walls with unnatural speed.

He lunged forward, grabbed *Mestra* Jenny by the wrist, and ran.

Down, down, down, with the inferno licking at their heels, roaring hungrily as it fed. Did *Leronis* Anjali still sit in the Working Room crowned in Sharra's own flame, smiling as if at some secret joke?

When he reached the courtyard he had let go of her wrist to catch the chervines. The falling snow melted in the air, and the courtyard was nothing but mud and water now. Even in the middle of this, *Mestra* Jenny was trying to talk to him. It was surely Cassilda's mercy she did not run back inside to try to find someone else to talk to when he ignored her. He lifted her onto one of the chervines and led both to the outer gate. It opened easily, and they galloped through the gate and out into the snow.

~oOo~

It was immediately clear that *Mestra* Jenny had no idea what to do with a riding beast, but the little stag-pony would follow its herdmate. The whole of the sky was orange with fire. There was no difficulty now in seeing the trail.

He let out a long slow sigh of relief when they reached the trail hut. "You're just lucky this place is already stocked," he said. The least likely to be used were provisioned last, and there was nothing up this way but Tramontana.

He shoved the door open and dragged *Mestra* Jenny inside. The two chervines followed immediately, glad to be out of the storm. He settled the beasts and found fodder for them, glancing at *Mestra* Jenny as he did. All she did was huddle in a corner and shiver. He supposed he wasn't surprised. Away from their 'efficiency,' the *Terranan* really didn't seem to be good for much.

Once a fire was burning brightly, he handed *Mestra* Jenny a trail bar from his pack and asked her what in Zandru's nine hells she'd been thinking.

"I had no idea a storm was on its way," she said numbly, turning the food bar over in her hands. Zhenyar held his tongue as she explained that she'd decided to go up to the Tower and root out the nest of bandits he was clearly too superstitious to clear out himself. "And then the fire started," she said, rubbing her temples and wincing against the headache she undoubtedly had. "One of the band of outlaws living there must have drugged me."

Zhenyar rolled his eyes, and took the trail bar away from her to unwrap it. "Eat," he said, handing it back. The *Terranan* had their own superstitions, and he was far too smart to argue.

"But we were the only ones who got out of there," *Mestra* Jenny said. "So I guess the problem is solved now, isn't it?"

"Oh yes," Zhenyar said with some relish. "*Our* problem is over. The Hastur has ruled. You're to go to Thendara in the spring."

You'll be someone else's problem then.

But Zhenyar could not help but wonder, studying the *Terranan* woman as she sat there as haughtily as any *leronis* in her heavy parka, had *Leronis* Anjali been mad?

Or had she been right?

A Few Words for My Successor
by Debra Doyle & James D. Macdonald

Humans, both Terran and Darkovan, are endlessly resourceful and just as endlessly befuddled by the gap between their own expectations and reality. Sometimes this results in disaster and other times in hilarity, as Debra Doyle and James D. Macdonald's departing diplomat so aptly puts it: *"Just... don't ask."*

Debra Doyle was born in Florida and educated in Florida, Texas, Arkansas, and Pennsylvania—the last at the University of Pennsylvania, where she earned her doctorate in English literature, concentrating on Old English poetry. While living and studying in Philadelphia, she met and married her collaborator, James D. Macdonald, and subsequently traveled with him to Virginia, California, and the Republic of Panamá. Various children, cats, and computers joined the household along the way.

James Douglas Macdonald was born in White Plains, New York, the second of three children of W. Douglas Macdonald, a Chemical Engineer, and Margaret E. Macdonald, a professional artist. After leaving the University of Rochester, where he majored in Medieval Studies, he served in the U. S. Navy.

1.0. Welcome, Future Replacement!

You're probably wondering what you did to deserve this job.

So did I, when I first got here, and I'll tell you what my old mentor told me: A tour on Darkover's been the making of a lot of careers—but it's broken a whole lot more. Somebody wants to push you out.

Or maybe somebody wants to put you under pressure and see if it makes you shine.

1.1. Just in Case I'm Not Here to Give You the "Welcome Aboard!" Talk, I'm Leaving This File Behind for You.

Because sometimes people leave this job in a hurry. They piss off a Comyn Lord (I'll get to them later) and have to be smuggled off-planet in the freezer hold of a long-haul freighter; or they show up on post one day with all of their Terran clothing packed in a big box, ship it home to their next-of-kin, and tell everybody they're leaving the Service to go up-country and live in a monastery in Nevarsin.

I'm not planning to do either of those things, but on this planet you never know.

2.0. When They Say It Gets Cold on Darkover, They Really Mean It.

High summer in the temperate zones is like a brisk autumn day in a temperate zone on almost any other planet where Terrans have decided to settle.

(The key word here is "decided." This world was settled by accident... which explains so very, very much.)

2.1. Winter in the Temperate Zones Is like the Bottom Floor of Dante's Hell.

If you haven't already bought one of every piece of cold-weather gear in the post exchange, go do it right now before all the other newbies figure out they have to.

This includes wool socks. *Thick* wool socks. Multiple pairs. You'll thank me later.

Also long underwear. The synthetics they sell at the exchange all suck. You want to hit the off-planet mail-order houses and get the genuine silk. Pay extra for fast delivery. By the time your slow mail gets here you may have already moved on to your next tour of duty. And spent a cold, miserable tour of hypothermia in the meantime.

2.2. Winter in the Polar Regions Is Officially Too Cold to Allow Human Life.

Even the locals don't go up there. We *definitely* don't go up there.

Every so often, off-planet investors want to send out prospecting teams to look for whatever they think is hiding under the ice.

Official policy is to discourage this. The locals don't like it—there's some bad history here; the sealed reports are above my pay grade and probably above yours—not that the top brass likes it, either. Something about having to mount one too many rescue missions for damned fools and idiots.

3.0. Sex Pollen!

Telepathy-inducing pollen, actually. The sex is just a

common side-effect.
3.1. This Is Why You Have to Make Sure All Off-world Tour Groups Sign That Waiver.

Otherwise, some crew of well-meaning ethnomusicologists is going to come back from a song-collecting field trip in the Kilghard Hills with one of their party gone googly-eyed crazy and another one swearing she got knocked up by an elf when the Ghost Wind blew, and their university is going to sue our collective ass into bankruptcy.

3.2. Yes, This Really Happened Once.

No, it didn't happen on my watch, and it's not going to if I can help it. And it better not happen on yours, either, unless you want to end up looking for a new job on a different planet, with no references.

4.0. Yes, The Locals Really Do Wear Swords.

Also knives. And other things with edges and points. They seem to like them.

4.1. They Don't Just Carry Them for Fashion Accessories.

They know how to use them; they train in using them; and they *will* use them if they think they have to. Try not to make any of them think they have to.

4.2. Don't Even Think about Trying to Outgun Them.

Not even if you think it's going to make you safer. Because it won't. And don't think that they don't know what you're thinking, either. See section 3.0 above.

Our weapons aren't legal here; getting caught with one is a good way to get a chilly berth on that slow freighter heading off-planet. A piece of paper signed by somebody in an office on Terra may keep you out of trouble back home, but you're going to have to get home first for it to do you any good.

And remember—you can't always count on a slow freighter being in port when you need one.

4.3. They Don't Just Do It to Save Face about Being a Culturally-Devolved Lost Colony.

(Honestly. I heard a visiting scholar say that once. But not where anyone local could hear him.)

They call it a Compact, which means it's something they agreed on. And they agreed on doing it before we even showed up here.

As my old mentor said to the visiting scholar, you aren't going to have an agreement about not using certain weapons if you don't already have the weapons you're agreeing not to use.

4.4. Try Not to Think Too Hard about What Kind of Weapons Could Scare an Entire Planet into Going Back to Machetes and Steak Knives.

I'm pretty sure that sort of speculation is *way* above our pay grade.

Also, probably not healthy.

5.0. Which Brings Us to All Those Pretty Blue Crystals.

Don't let appearances fool you. Those gemstones are matrix crystals, and they're serious stuff.

5.1. They're Actually an Important Part of the Local Technology.

Which is psi-based (no, I am not kidding) and doesn't export. This is not good for us, because we could use something like that. Also, because it means we haven't got much to sell that the locals would want to buy.

Be glad you're not the Commercial Attaché. Balance of trade is his problem, and we haven't had anybody solve it yet.

5.2. The Matrix Crystals Are Not Controlled by the Comyn.

The Comyn say so, and they wouldn't lie.

Yeah, right. Almost all the people on this rock have at least a smidgen of telepathic ability, but the Comyn have it coming out of their ears. They're not just at the top of the heap in local politics, they're a caste of high-powered superspecialized telepaths.

Everyone says that they don't breed for it—anymore. Which is oh-so-reassuring, if you do even a little reading in the open history files. My old mentor's theory was that they took the eugenics program as far as they dared, then closed it down and went back to ordinary upper-crust intermarriage.

So they're all cousins, and they're all a little bit crazy. Especially about those crystals.

5.3. Which Means, Don't Touch the Pretty Rocks.

Literally. It's been known to give people seizures.

Likewise, metaphorically. Serious cultural gaffe/bad political move/danger!danger!danger! Careers have crashed and burned over this. Also, people have died. Don't be one of them.

Unless you're really a spy and this is your job. In which case—well, try not to die, and don't do anything stupid. (For the record—I think messing around with the pretty blue crystals *is* stupid. But nobody's asking my opinion about that.)

6.0. I Suppose Now I Have to Talk about the Comyn.

Or, as the Commercial Attaché calls them, "those redheaded bastards."

6.1. The Commercial Attaché is Somebody's Nephew.

Which, again, explains so very, very much. You won't have to worry about him, though... he'll be gone before you get here. Probably smuggled out on a slow freighter.

6.2. The Commercial Attaché Should Have Kept His Mouth Shut.

But he had a point.

6.2.1. The Comyn Do Mostly Have Red Hair.

And it's not your typical aristocratic inbreeding, either. (Or not *only* that, anyhow. They do tend to marry each other a lot.) Their DNA—at least the handful of samples our forensic people have managed to pick up in the course of one investigation or another—is just plain weird.

6.2.2. Some of Them Can in Fact Be Bastards.

My old mentor used to classify the Comyn families into Occasionally Helpful (usually just the Hasturs, but they're pretty much "first among equals" in that crowd so the situation isn't as bad as it sounds), Not Really Our Problem (most of the rest of them, really), and the Aldarans.

The Aldarans are serious bad news; they've almost always got a political agenda (or two or three) and they've got the juice to back it up. See, *pretty blue crystals*. Also, *Sharra*.

There's more bad history here, buried deep—you can tell by the holes it leaves in peoples' conversations when they start reminiscing about things that happened three or four decades ago. Again, way above my pay grade. And yours, unless you're an intelligence agent slipped into this job as a cover, which I hope you aren't, because the job needs somebody who's giving it their full attention, not just what they can spare from poking into other peoples' business.

7.0. I Was Going to Finish Up with Talking about Sharra, but Then I Had a Better Idea.

I'll just tell you what my old mentor told me, when *I* got curious.

7.1. Don't ask.
7.2. Just... don't.
   Unless you really are a spy, sent in under cover.
   Which would explain... so very, very much.

Darkover® Anthologies

THE KEEPER'S PRICE, 1980
SWORD OF CHAOS, 1982
FREE AMAZONS OF DARKOVER, 1985
OTHER SIDE OF THE MIRROR, 1987
RED SUN OF DARKOVER, 1987
FOUR MOONS OF DARKOVER, 1988
DOMAINS OF DARKOVER, 1990
RENUNCIATES OF DARKOVER, 1991
LERONI OF DARKOVER, 1991
TOWERS OF DARKOVER, 1993
MARION ZIMMER BRADLEY'S DARKOVER, 1993
SNOWS OF DARKOVER, 1994
MUSIC OF DARKOVER, 2013
STARS OF DARKOVER, 2014
GIFTS OF DARKOVER, 2015

www.mzbworks.com

About the Editors

Deborah J. Ross writes and edits fantasy and science fiction. After her first short story in 1983 in Marion Zimmer Bradley's first volume of *Sword & Sorceress*, her short fiction has appeared in *F&SF*, *Asimov's*, *Star Wars: Tales From Jabba's Palace*, *Realms of Fantasy*, *MZB's Fantasy Magazine*, and many other anthologies and magazines. Two of her short stories ("Mother Africa" in *Asimov's* 1997 and "The Price of Silence" in *F&SF* 2009) were awarded Honorable Mention in *Year's Best SF*. She made her editorial debut in 2008 with *Lace and Blade*. Her most recent books include the Darkover novel *The Children of Kings* (with Marion Zimmer Bradley); *Collaborators*, an occupation-and-resistance story with a gender-fluid alien race (as Deborah Wheeler); and *The Seven-Petaled Shield*, an epic fantasy trilogy from DAW. She's part of the secret cabal of former SFWA Secretaries and a member of the online writer's cooperative Book View Café.

Elisabeth Waters spent two decades working for Marion Zimmer Bradley and still works for the Marion Zimmer Bradley Literary Works Trust. She sold her first short story to Marion in 1980 for *The Keeper's Price*, the first Darkover anthology. She then went on to sell short stories to a variety of anthologies. Her first novel, a fantasy called *Changing Fate*, was awarded the 1989 Gryphon Award. She is now working on a sequel to it, in addition to her short story writing and anthology editing. She also shares Marion's love of opera and has worked as a supernumerary with the San Francisco Opera, where she appeared in *La Gioconda*, *Manon Lescaut*, *Madama Butterfly*, *Khovanschina*, *Das Rheingold*, *Werther*, and *Idomeneo*.

Made in the USA
Lexington, KY
08 March 2015